VERLAG

About the Book

It didn't surprise me that I was still by Danny's side. I would never leave this man voluntarily, not in this lifetime. And I was absolutely certain he would never leave me of his own free will, either. Where that knowledge came from, I couldn't say. It was just there. I knew it the way I knew people needed air to breathe and the sun provided warmth. Although I was aware it might not be long before his past caught up to us, I also knew that, without that past, we'd never have found one another.

A story of deep love.
A story of trust, courage, pain, despair, and the strength to let go.
A true story.

About the Author

Jessica Koch was born in Ludwigsburg, Germany, and began writing short stories when she was still in high school - but never submitted her work to publishers. Shortly after finishing school, she met Danny, a German-American dual citizen. Her experiences with him eventually formed the basis for *So Near the Horizon*, though it was nearly thirteen years before she felt ready to bring the manuscript to the public.

The author describes a life lived somewhere between hope and fear, between optimism and despair. She reflects on events from her own past with raw honesty, confronting more than one difficult subject along the way.

Jessica Koch lives near the city of Stuttgart with her husband, their son, and two dogs.

The second and third books in the trilogy, *So Near the Abyss* and *So Near the Ocean*, are already best-sellers in Germany as well.

This book is dedicated to my son,
and also to my husband,
whom I would like to thank here
for his infinite understanding
when my thoughts were
beyond the horizon again,
hour after hour, day after day.

For Danny
Door 2, Danny! It will always be Door 2!
THANK YOU!!!

Love you, too.

For more information on the author, visit
www.facebook.com/SoNearTheHorizon or www.so-near-the-horizon.com

Be sure to subscribe to our newsletter, so that you can be the first to hear about our **new releases**, **author news,** and exclusive **giveaways**:
www.so-near-the-horizon.com

Original German edition published in March 2016
© 2017 FeuerWerke Verlag, all rights reserved
Maracuja GmbH, Laerheider Weg 13, 47669 Wachtendonk, Germany
Cover design: ebooklaunch.com

Translation: Jaime McGill
Editing and proofreading: Annie Cosby
ISBN: 978-1974201792

Based on a true story. All names have been changed for reasons of privacy protection. Any similarities to other actual persons are purely coincidental.

So Near the Horizon

Book 1 of The Danny Trilogy

Jessica Koch

Translated from the German

by Jaime McGill

Contents

Prologue

Summer 1996

Danny jolted awake at the sound of the telephone. Instinctively, he glanced first toward the closed bedroom door, and then to the open window. It was still dark out, though the sky was already hinting at dawn.

The radio alarm clock showed that it was just after five. No big deal for an early riser like him. But it was Sunday. Who the hell was calling him so early?

The ringing continued, but he decided to just ignore it.

Tina, he realized suddenly. She was probably in some kind of trouble again, maybe having an emotional breakdown or looking for a place to crash. She usually called his cell phone, though.

Whoever it was, the caller was apparently hell-bent on getting him out of bed. He rose reluctantly and padded into the hall in his T-shirt and boxers, to the phone hanging on the wall.

"What happened?" he asked sleepily into the receiver.

"It's me. Your father."

Danny recognized the voice after the first syllable, and he was immediately wide awake. The hair on the back of his neck stood up. Every nerve ending in his body vibrated. "What do you want?"

"I'm your dad. Can't I call my son?"

"No."

"I need to see you. Can you come visit me?"

"You think I want to see you?"

Danny could sense his father's growing impatience. He always lost patience far too quickly.

"Danny," he said, "this is important. I'm dying!"

"Well, finally some good news for a change."

"I'm serious."

"Yeah, me too."

"Please." His father was speaking softly now, almost tenderly. "I need to talk to you before I die. There's something I have to tell you."

Danny knew that tone. The beseeching note in his father's voice sent an icy shiver down Danny's spine.

"Just go ahead and die," he said. "Whatever it is, I'm not interested."

He was about to hang up when his father suddenly shouted, "This is your fault, you little piece of shit. It should have been you! Not Liam! It should have been you! Then everything would have been different!"

"Save your breath. You can't hurt me anymore." Although he said it with complete conviction, it wasn't the truth. His father's words were like knives to his heart. They always had been.

"You're an arrogant, condescending prick, Danny."

"Hm, wonder who I got that from…"

"Fine. You asked for it!" His father's tone shifted abruptly once again, this time growing dangerously quiet. "Listen carefully, because I'm only going to say this once."

Danny listened. His hand cramped painfully around the receiver; sweat beaded on his brow. For a moment, he thought the ground was quaking beneath his feet, but it was only his knees threatening to give out. He nearly laughed out loud at the sheer absurdity of his father's words. Unbelievable. Ridiculous.

But deep down, he knew they were true.

Chapter One

October 1999

"The north wind," I announced in a dramatic voice, pointing toward the horizon. "Never a good omen!"

"You don't even know which way north is," Vanessa retorted, laughing.

Our Ferris wheel car had stopped at the very top. I leaned out, theatrically stretching my arms toward the sky. It almost felt like I was brushing the clouds with my fingertips. The view out into the distance was amazing. "It was as though the heavens had silently kissed the earth…"

"Hey!" Vanessa waved a hand in front of my face. "What's up with you? Since when are you such a poet?"

"I'm not," I said, switching back into my normal voice. "That just popped into my head."

The Ferris wheel started turning again, and I settled back into my seat, impatiently drumming my fingers on the railing as we descended for what seemed like forever. We had big plans for tonight, and I couldn't wait to get started.

Back on the ground, the feeling of weightlessness stayed with me as we climbed out of the car. Pleased, I followed Vanessa across the fairgrounds, which were still relatively empty this early in the evening. Vanessa was wearing skin-tight jeans and a short sweater that showed a strip of bare skin every time she moved. With the right shoes, she could have made the most of her long legs, but she hated heels and was in ordinary sneakers as usual.

I couldn't afford the same luxury—the platform heels on my black, knee-high boots were my only hope of at least halfway keeping up with her in terms of height and leg length. My own top was a green-and-white pullover that, in my humble opinion, looked great with my long, auburn hair. It was an unusually warm October evening; only the wind gave any indication that winter was around the corner. And I could have sworn it was coming from the North.

"Let's get something to eat, okay?" Vanessa steered me toward one of the tables scattered around the fairgrounds.

Vanessa and I were on our annual pilgrimage to Stuttgart, the city nearest our hometown, for the *Cannstatter Wasen* festival. This was our first time going alone—in previous years, our parents had always insisted that my older brother, Thorsten, chaperone us. Vanessa and I had both started our very first jobs that summer. I'd found an entry-level position that would let me train as an architectural drafter before taking exams for certification in a few years. But Vanessa had struggled to find anything, and the position she'd finally landed was in Munich, nearly two hundred miles away from our hometown, while I lived at home. We were both planning on getting driver's licenses soon, but until then, we would just have to survive without each other. Except for special occasions like this one.

Vanessa sat down across from me, and we were just tucking into our French fries when she suddenly kicked me under the table. "Look over there," she said, nodding to her left. "They've been checking us out for a while now."

"Hm?" I glanced in the direction she'd indicated. Three guys were standing maybe ten feet away from our table, very obviously talking about us. "Oh, God," I groaned, indignant at the very thought of anyone stealing my precious time with my best friend. "I hope they don't come over here."

"Why? They're cute."

I looked them over skeptically. They were all at least twenty, probably even older. She was right, though: they really were pretty easy on the eyes. One was strikingly tall, with broad shoulders, pitch-black hair, and olive skin. Southern European, I guessed. Maybe Spanish. The other two were blond. The shorter one had close-cropped hair and glasses, and I could see his freckles even at this distance. He was average-looking at best, nothing remarkable, while the other two looked like they'd stepped straight out of a *Seventeen* magazine poster.

When they saw that we'd spotted them, they elbowed each other and pointed at us, then started in our direction.

"Great," I muttered, staring down at the Coke I was gripping in both hands. I'd been looking forward to this weekend with Vanessa for months.

"Evening," the boys said when they reached our table. Apparently, they'd discussed seating arrangements in advance, because they chose seats without hesitation: the Spaniard and Average Joe sat on either side of Vanessa, and the third guy straddled the bench I was sitting on. His hair was a hot mess, sticking out in every direction, but other than that, he looked put together—unnervingly attractive, even. Not like he'd just rolled out of bed.

Two for Nessa, one for you, my inner voice taunted me. We were always competing like that.

12

At least there's one for me, I retorted. I'd probably have continued my internal monologue if the cute blond hadn't stuck a hand out in my direction.

"Danijel," he said. He pronounced it like "Daniel," with an American accent. Was he American?

I shook his hand, purely out of manners, and looked up at him.

His eyes are way too blue. Why is he wearing colored contacts? Who does that? The intense blue confused me; I forgot to look away.

"My friends call me Danny," he added, in flawless, native German. Not American then.

"What about your enemies?"

It threw him off for a fraction of a second, but he recovered quickly.

"I don't have enemies. Everyone likes me." The crooked smile he gave me was so gorgeous, all I could do was stare. He gave me a moment—apparently, he was used to such reactions—before asking, "Do you have a name?"

The other two guys introduced themselves as Ricky and Simon, but I barely registered the information. It took me a second before I managed my own response. "Jessica."

Normally, I could talk to just about anyone. So why did this guy leave me so tongue-tied?

"Jessica," he repeated softly, nodding. Then he asked a question I didn't catch, because I was still too busy staring at him: his high cheekbones, narrow chin, symmetrical features. His permanent grin revealed a row of even, snow-white teeth. The sleeves of his gray hoodie were pushed up over his elbows, and his arms were sinewy, muscular. He had a generally slim build, but he obviously worked out.

Athlete, my uncharacteristically slow brain reported.

Had I been alone, I would have given myself a sarcastic slow clap for noting the obvious rather than formulating a reply.

Suddenly, Danijel snapped his fingers right in front of my face, jolting me out of my trance. "Still here?" He looked downright amused.

"Yeah," I said, frantically wracking my brain for a clever reply.

"Am I annoying you?" he inquired good-humoredly.

"Um… It's just that I'd rather be alone with my friend."

"Aha," he said, casting a meaningful glance at Vanessa, who was now deep in conversation with Ricky. The tables around us were mostly full now, and I couldn't make out their conversation over all the noise, but it was fairly clear that *she* didn't want to be alone with *me*.

Simon glanced around at the rest of the table, clutching his beer and looking a bit lost.

"If that's the case..." Danijel said, swinging his leg around to the other side of the bench so he could lean back against the table. He fell silent, watching the people around us with interest. My brain made a series of futile attempts to gather up what was left of my intellect and rummaged around frantically in search of my missing speech skills.

Just then, I noticed a thin, jagged scar on Danijel's face. It was only visible upon close inspection, though it ran all the way across his left cheek.

"What'd you do there?" I asked, pointing to his cheek. Immediately, I felt like smacking myself for failing to come up with anything better than that overly personal question.

Fortunately, he took it in stride.

"You mean this?" He ran his finger along the scar. "That was my dad. Hit me in the face with a bottle."

"He *what*?" Was this guy serious?

Danijel smiled to take the edge out of his words. "He didn't mean to. It was an accident."

"But still awful." I couldn't imagine any scenario where something like that could happen completely by accident. But there was no relying on my mind at the moment, anyway. There was still a giant "Out of Order" sign hanging in front of it.

Danijel shrugged.

"Not too bad," he said. "I'm still plenty hot."

Cocky little snot, I thought. He was right, though.

I couldn't think of an appropriate response, so I didn't say anything at all, and I could tell Danijel was starting to get bored. He turned his attention to two extremely attractive blonde girls in high heels and excessively short skirts. He watched them intently for a long moment, and I threw an irritated *Help me!* look at

Vanessa. She only beamed at me for a moment before turning back to Ricky. I rolled my eyes.

Simon had noticed the blonde girls as well. "Not a chance!" he called to Danijel.

"Wanna bet?"

"Three to one!" Simon said, stretching a hand out across the table.

Ricky broke off his conversation with Vanessa to look at the girls as well. "I'll take that bet, too. Four to one," he told Danijel, extending his own hand.

"Twenty minutes." Danijel stood up, shook his friends' hands, and walked over to the girls. I gave Simon and Ricky a questioning look, but they were too busy grinning stupidly to notice. I briefly considered starting a conversation with Simon—I'd be able to come up with a million things to say to *him*—but I didn't feel like it. Instead, my eyes again sought out Danijel, who was now standing between the two girls, chatting to them. Even from here, I could see them blushing and giggling nervously. Danijel put one arm around each of them and led them away, out of my field of view. I could only shake my head.

What kind of sick game are they playing?

After what felt like a million years, he returned and smacked a scrap of notebook paper down on the table in triumph. "Both!" he announced proudly.

Ricky raised his hands above his head and clapped three times. Simon whistled admiringly and pushed some money toward Danijel. Ricky reached into his own pocket and laid a bill on the table as well. Danijel stuck the cash and the card into his pocket, then sat down beside me again.

"Where were we?" he asked, giving me a friendly smile.

"What the hell was that about?"

"It's a game," Danijel explained. "It's called Number Hunt. We play every weekend."

I made a face. "How mature." Suddenly, I felt sorry for Simon, who most likely went home as the big loser weekend after weekend. On a whim, I decided to give Simon my number without him asking.

But Danijel foiled my plans by declaring, "I'm bored."

"Go home, then," I suggested, secretly praying he wouldn't.

"I have a better idea. Come with me!" He jumped up, grabbed my wrist, and pulled me up from the bench. The others blinked at us in surprise.

"Where are you going?" I practically had to run to keep up with him.

He stopped in front of the drop tower. "*We* are going on *that*," he announced. "And afterwards, you're giving me your number."

"No on both counts!" I said defiantly, putting my hands on my hips.

He gave me a tender look. "You're not like the others," he said. "I like that."

Oh, does Mr. I Get Everything I Want need to get shot down for a change? Well, he's come to the right place.

"I'm just getting warmed up," I deadpanned.

Laughing softly, he placed an arm around my shoulders and drew me closer. His eyes found mine. I felt like they were boring straight into my soul.

"You. Are. Going. On. That. Ride. With. Me. Now." He smelled like shower gel and aftershave. My knees felt weak.

"Okay."

What the hell? How does he do that?

Less than two minutes later, I was strapped into that nightmarish contraption, clutching the safety harness in terror. It was dark by then, and the view of the colorful festival lights as we rose was breathtaking. The car stopped at the top for a moment, giving us one last brief reprieve.

"Are you scared?" Danijel asked.

"Hell, yes!" But I was determined to keep from screaming on the way down.

I failed miserably.

When I finally stumbled off the ride, more or less in one piece, I felt like kissing the ground.

"That bad?" Danijel's voice was sympathetic.

"I will hate you forever for that." It almost sounded believable.

We made our way back to the others, who were looking around for us. "We're gonna go on the roller coaster," Vanessa said. "You guys coming?"

"Sure," Danijel responded for the both of us. I rolled my eyes.

Vanessa sat beside me on the roller coaster, and I took the opportunity to whisper, "Let's get out of here!"

"Why?" She looked alarmed.

"Bathroom! After!" That was our code for *We need to talk, stat!*

After we got off the ride, Vanessa followed me into the women's restroom, looking annoyed. I breathed a sigh of relief when we were finally free to talk.

"What's your deal?" she hissed at me. "I finally meet a cool guy, and you want to go home?"

"Hello! They're just playing us! Didn't you see what they do? They just flirt with girl after girl. I think they're keeping score!"

"So what?" Vanessa shrugged. "I didn't say I wanted to marry him, I just want to have a little fun."

"You're ridiculous."

"And you're a prude. Come on. You've got Dennis or whatever his name is. He's gorgeous."

"He's rude and full of himself, and I can't stand him."

"Please, just one more hour," Vanessa begged. "Then we'll have to leave anyway if we want to catch the last train."

I sighed in resignation. "Fine. One hour. Then when I give you the sign, we're taking off."

Desperate, I coughed for the third time and added an exaggerated throat-clearing sound. But Vanessa, though standing well within hearing range, was practicing selective deafness.

"Frog in your throat?" asked Danijel, who'd been clinging to me like a tick the whole time. It wasn't like he was getting on my nerves or anything. I just didn't feel completely in control of my senses in his presence. I did things I didn't actually want to do.

Without responding to his question, I strode past Vanessa into the crowd. Finally catching on, she followed, albeit reluctantly. I hastily turned a few corners, deliberately pushing my way into the densest crush of people. The festival was packed now, meaning it was easy to lose sight of someone…or shake someone off. Resolutely, I grabbed Vanessa's hand and dragged her along behind me.

"What are you *doing*?" she exclaimed. I kept right on marching triumphantly until we reached the exit.

"Did we lose them?" I wheezed.

"Yeah. Great job." Vanessa scowled. "I *like* him. What am I supposed to say when he asks why we just disappeared?"

I smiled blissfully. "You're not supposed to say anything. Because you'll never see him again."

"He promised he'd call me. Get this: he comes to Munich sometimes for work, and he said he'd visit me the next time he was there. He's a telecommunications engineer, so he travels a lot."

I smacked my forehead with my palms. "You gave that jackass your phone number? Enjoy your disappointment. Just don't call me crying your head off."

"I won't," she snapped.

We turned the corner, onto a wide, pedestrian-only street, and headed toward the train station. Suddenly, we were the only souls around. Everybody was back at the festival.

"Seriously, Jessica," Vanessa grumbled. "You need to chill out. I just want to have a little fun with him."

I knew all about Vanessa's ways of having fun with men. I picked up the pace, leaving her a little ways behind me.

I didn't see the car approaching. It seemed to appear out of nowhere, hurtling toward me at an excessive speed. Before I could react, the huge, black BMW spun ninety degrees, tires screeching, and stopped in the middle of the walk, blocking my path. I stopped dead in my tracks, gasping for air, frozen in absolute terror. The driver's-side window rolled down, and Danijel leaned out.

"Didn't you forget something?" he asked, batting his strikingly long lashes at me.

Gathering my wits, I shook my head, completely perplexed.

With a smug grin, he stretched his hand out, palm upward. "Telephone number, please!"

"Jesus Christ," I snapped, looking around self-consciously. "You have serious issues!"

"True," he remarked dryly. "But that's neither here nor there. Your number?"

"Why? Just so you can win your stupid bet?"

"Exactly." He grinned, confident of victory.

"Forget it." I veered to the left, around the front of the car. He jumped out, ran around the back, and planted himself in my way. A few of the other festivalgoers on their way to the station were loud and vocal in their dissatisfaction with the car's ridiculous—and illegal—parking spot.

Danijel ignored them. "We can do this all night," he said to me quietly. "I'm not letting up. Sooner or later, you'll give me your number."

Wordlessly, I tried to push my way past him, but he held me fast by the shoulder. He placed the thumb and index finger of his free hand under my chin, forcing me to look at him. Again, he gazed at me with the full force of his ocean-blue eyes. My heart leapt into my throat, and stomach muscles that I'd never even known I had tensed up.

Danijel tilted his head and leaned in, his scent wafting toward me.

Don't hold your breath, Jessica. Breathe.

I parted my lips expectantly and closed my eyes, leaning toward him. He laughed softly to himself and leaned away.

My stomach plummeted. Wow, did I feel like an idiot.

"First, your number," he breathed into my ear, pulling his phone out of his pocket.

I whispered it to him, mainly to get away from this humiliating situation. He keyed it into his phone triumphantly.

"Thank you very much," he said with exaggerated politeness, before giving me a quick kiss on the forehead. Then he got back into his car, leaving me standing there in the middle of the street.

The motor roared to life, and the taillights lit red as Danijel backed up a few feet, only to stop beside me once more. He held a white business card out the window. "Just to be fair," he said.

Obediently, I took the card. "What's this for? You're not going to call me anyway. And I'm sure as hell not calling you!"

He was already rolling up the window. "I'll call you," he said gently. "Promise."

His tires squealed as he reversed down the nearly deserted pedestrian road far too quickly.

I don't know how long I'd been standing there, totally lost, staring after his headlights, when I heard a quiet *ahem* behind me.

Vanessa was tapping her foot on the asphalt, her hands on her hips.

How long had she been standing there?

"So," she said, looking smug. "I'm an idiot because I gave some arrogant jackass my phone number, hm?"

I shrugged helplessly. "I couldn't help it, I swear. I think he hypnotized me!"

Chapter Two

November 1999

During the day, my phone became my greatest enemy. At night, I dreamt of blue eyes following me, penetrating me with their intensity. I'd tucked the business card neatly away in my purse and hadn't even looked at it since. Hell would freeze over before I called him. Why would I? I didn't even like him. And he obviously wasn't interested in me, either—otherwise he would have gotten in touch. And he hadn't. Secretly, I knew it was naive of me to hope he'd call, but I couldn't get his promise out of my head.

My inner voice laughed itself sick at the situation. *If you actually believe he was the least bit interested in you, you're a complete idiot!*

After two weeks, I started agreeing with the voice and prepared to forget Danijel.

I hadn't heard anything from Vanessa since the festival, either, so I decided to call her. I caught her on her cell. "Hi," I said, "long time no talk. Stressed out with work?"

"Jessica, hi!" she cried. She was anxious—I could hear it in her voice. "Sorry, I don't have a lot of time. I've gotta get ready. Ricky will be here any minute!"

"Huh? Aren't you in Munich?"

"Yeah. He's coming to spend the weekend with me."

Jealousy rose up within me like boiling lava. "Well, then. Have fun."

She noticed the hollow note in my voice. "What's wrong?"

"Nothing. Everything's great," I nearly growled. "Enjoy your arrogant jackass."

"Oh, crap!" She sighed empathetically. "It's Dennis, isn't it? He didn't call, did he?"

"His name is Danny," I said, annoyed. At her *and* myself. Why did I just call him by the nickname reserved for his friends? "And no, he didn't call. Which was to be expected."

"Sorry. Hey, I'll ask Ricky what the deal is later."

"Ugh, don't. Don't bother. I couldn't stand him anyway."

Despite the great distance between us, I could sense her smile through the phone.

"Right," she said. "Well, I gotta go. I'll call you soon as I get a few minutes. Love you, talk soon!"

Furiously, I punched the red "end call" button. Somehow I couldn't help resenting Vanessa's new fling, though I knew it was unfair of me. After all, I'd been in a long-term relationship up until just two months ago, while she'd been living the single life for years.

And, God, breaking up with Alexander had been difficult and stressful. I knew he was still holding out hope, because he called almost daily, embarking on campaign after campaign to win me back. The fact that I hadn't heard from him in two days was almost a miracle. I shook my head. One guy called too often, the other not at all. It wasn't the worst problem in the world to have, but still.

It was early on a Friday afternoon, and I didn't know what to do with myself. Not that evening, or for the rest of the weekend. Vanessa wasn't in town, and I sure as hell wasn't about to go to Alexander's. Sighing, I fetched my purse and pulled out the small, white business card. I studied it for a moment. *Danijel Alaric Taylor* was printed on it in thick, black letters. *Odd way of spelling his first name,* I noted.

His address was printed beneath the name. Besigheim—maybe half an hour away by car, but an epic journey by bus.

The bottom left-hand corner read:

Certified Personal Trainer

His work address would be equally impossible for me to reach without a car. And then, in the lower right corner, it said:

Martial Arts Center – South

Youth Coach

Martial arts. He spent his weekends kicking people in the face. Well, wonderful. Just getting better and better.

I took out my phone and dialed the number listed beneath his address.

He picked up on the second ring. "Hello?"

I swallowed hard—and didn't say anything.

He hung up without another word. I stared at my phone, using every ounce of self-control I had to keep myself from calling back.

Finally, I threw my phone on the bed in exasperation and decided to take my dog, Leika, for a walk.

***

My phone rang unusually early for a Saturday. My heart leapt for joy. Pulse racing, electrified with anticipation, I retrieved my phone from the desk with trembling fingers—and discovered, to my disappointment, that it was Vanessa. My heart rate slowed back down to normal as I answered.

"Yeah?"

"Jess?" Vanessa was on Cloud Nine. I could tell immediately. "He's amazing! Next weekend I'll give you all the details."

"Do it now," I said.

"I can't," she whispered. "He's in the bathroom!"

"Oh." He was in the *bathroom*. Glittering jealousy came over me again.

"Good news," she went on. "We're going to the Mouse Trap next Saturday." That was our usual dance club here at home. "Ricky's picking me up and bringing me from Munich. You wanna come?" After a brief pause for dramatic effect, she added, "Danny and Simon are coming, too."

My pulse sped right up again, and it wasn't at the mention of Simon's name.

"No way!" I snapped.

"Oh, come on. We're meeting outside the Mouse Trap at ten. I thought maybe your brother could drop you, and then Ricky and I could drive you home."

"I dunno," I said. Mentally, I was already going through my closet, trying to decide what to wear.

***

As Thorsten pulled up in front of the club, he offered to come pick me up as well.

"No need," I told him, opening the passenger-side door. "Tell Mom and Dad I'm staying at Alexander's and might not be home until tomorrow."

My brother nodded. He knew Alexander and I had broken up, and that I was just using our relationship as an excuse to stay out late without my parents worrying. But he covered for me without asking any questions.

I shuffled toward the Mouse Trap uncertainly.

Simon and Danijel were already standing at the entrance. I'd spotted them almost immediately, but I kept out of sight until Vanessa and Ricky came around the corner, hand in hand. Then I made a beeline for them.

"Nessa!" I cried, and she threw her arms around my neck. She was wearing skin-tight jeans again, and a different crop top underneath her short jacket. She looked fantastic. I shook Ricky's hand and nodded to Simon. Danijel, I ignored.

"Don't you disappear on us again tonight!" Ricky said, winking at me.

Ah. Vanessa had tattled on me. Put all the blame for our quick exit on me. *Thanks a lot, friend.*

The club was still fairly empty, and we found a quiet corner where we'd all be able to chat for at least another half hour or so. Assuming I managed to form words this time.

Vanessa and I sat down while the guys got drinks for us.

"Here!" Danijel pushed my Bacardi and Coke toward me with that pretentious grin of his. "Maybe that'll make you a little chattier."

That one sentence was enough—I made the mistake of looking at him. Even in the dim light, I noticed that his eyes were even bluer than I'd remembered. He traced his chin with his thumb and index finger, throwing me completely off guard all over again.

"You're mad because I didn't call," he said plainly.

Ricky and Vanessa couldn't get enough of each other. They were still holding hands and kissing constantly—not paying any attention to us. And Simon just drank his beer and smoked a cigarette.

I turned back to Danijel. "A promise is a promise," I admonished him.

"You need to listen more closely," he replied easily. I could feel his eyes on me. "I said I would call. I didn't say *when* I would call."

I gulped down nearly all of my drink at once. "When were you planning on calling, then?"

"I always keep my promises. I really had a lot to do. In all seriousness, I would have called."

I almost wanted to believe him.

"And, speaking of that... The next time you plan on calling someone and not saying anything, it would be advisable to block your number." He took a sip of his drink. "Comes across as rude otherwise."

23

My cheeks reddened. I hoped it was dark enough that Danijel couldn't see.

"What were you so busy with, then?" I demanded. It came out much angrier than I'd intended.

"I had an important competition that first weekend. The weekend after that, I had to work. Side job."

"You mean you do martial arts competitions yourself, too?" I'd thought he was just a coach. The whole conversation thing was starting to work. Darkness and Bacardi were my friends.

"Yeah," he responded curtly.

"Do you win?" I polished off my drink.

"Usually." He pointed to my glass. "You want another? Seems to help."

I nodded, and he fetched me another Bacardi and Coke. I threw most of it back immediately. The alcohol was already going to my head. I offered him the glass and what little was left. "You want some?"

He shook his head. "I don't drink."

"Why not?" I asked, shocked.

"Personal reasons."

I shrugged and drained the glass.

"So what do you like to do?"

"Horseback riding," I said. "Tournaments. Mainly dressage, through Class L. I win now and again, too. And amateur radio. I've just got a dinky little thing, though—only gets forty channels, which sucks because you get so much noise. Someday I'll be able to afford one that gets eighty channels."

"Ah."

The club was starting to fill up, and it was getting progressively more difficult to talk.

Vanessa and Ricky indicated that they were going to go dance, and Simon followed them.

"You want to dance, too?" Danijel called to me.

"Do you even know how?" I shot back, suddenly cocky. Alcohol was a beautiful thing.

He nodded. "Just enough to get by." With practiced smoothness, he grasped my wrist and drew me off to the dance floor like a puppy on a leash.

24

Just then, I felt my phone vibrating in my pocket. I stopped, pulled it out, and held it up. "Sorry, I have to take this."

I extracted myself from Danijel's grip and headed toward the bathrooms in hopes of finding a quiet spot. He followed me, probably afraid I would make another escape.

"Hello?" I shouted into the phone. It was Alexander. Just who I needed to talk to right now. I told him that no, I wasn't at home, and yes, I was at the club, and no, not with 'some guy,' as he put it.

"No, I'm not coming over," I said at the end. "Ever. Take care. Bye." I stuck my phone back into my pocket, resolving not to answer it again.

Danijel raised a questioning eyebrow. "Your boyfriend?"

"Ex."

"Hm." He didn't seem particularly convinced. "Is he aware of that?"

"We're working on it. He is finding it a little hard to grasp." I'd lost interest in dancing for the moment. "I need to find Nessa real quick," I said and headed off. Danijel followed. Out of the corner of my eye, I could see his white T-shirt glowing under the black lights.

It took forever to find Vanessa. She and Ricky were off in the corner, completely entangled. A few feet away, Simon was dancing with a slightly pudgy redhead.

"Alexander called!" I shouted into Vanessa's ear. "I think he's going to show up here!"

I knew she was rolling her eyes, even if I couldn't actually see it. "Why do you always tell him where you are?" she asked.

"This is where we always go dancing. He's not stupid. Nessa, if he shows up here, I want to go home. Can you guys drive me?"

She didn't exactly seem enthusiastic about the prospect of having to cut the evening so short—it was barely after midnight. "Just don't answer your phone again. He'll never find you in this crowd!"

Now I needed another drink. Somehow, I'd lost Danijel in the chaos, this time completely unintentionally. I decided to start by getting myself a Jack and Coke, take the opportunity to use the bathroom, and then look for him afterwards. If he hadn't already found me by then, anyway. The guy seemed to stick to me like gum in my hair.

As I was drying my hands, my phone rang again. Angry, I grabbed my drink from the sink and chugged it. And that was too much for me. All at once, everything began to spin. I'd only taken my phone out so that I could shut it off, but I accidentally answered the call instead.

"I'm here," Alexander said.

"You're where?" I asked, slow to catch on.

"In the Mouse Trap parking lot. I know you're in there."

"What do you want?" I shrieked into the receiver.

"I just want to talk," he assured me. "I came all the way out here. Just come out and talk for a minute, and then I'll leave."

A little fresh air would probably do me good. The restroom was now swaying ominously. I retrieved my jacket from the coat check and left the club.

Alexander's enormous Jeep Grand Cherokee was hard to miss. It was parked across two spaces, with music blaring from the stereo and all four front lights on. Alexander himself was leaning against the chrome grill.

When he saw me, he started walking toward me. His blond hair was neatly gelled, and he was wearing the thin beige sweater I'd given him.

Suddenly, he narrowed his eyes and pointed behind me, glowering. "Who's this douchebag?"

I turned around, confused. I hadn't noticed that Danijel had followed me. He'd come out into the cool night air without a jacket and was standing a small distance behind me, his bare arms folded across his chest.

"That's Danny," I said, belatedly realizing I'd used his nickname yet again. It was probably too late to stop now. "We're here together."

"Good evening," Danny said politely, but he made no move to uncross his arms and extend a hand.

"Right. Vanessa." Alexander's voice was full of contempt. "What's he doing here with you?"

"I'm watching out for her," Danny replied on my behalf, giving me an admonishing look. "She's had a little too much to drink." As if on cue, I tripped over my own feet and nearly fell.

"I'll take over from here." Alexander opened the passenger-side door. "Get in. We're going home."

I nearly obeyed the command on autopilot, but Danny stepped in front of me. "Maybe you should ask her if she wants to come with you," he chided Alexander.

"She's coming. End of story!"

Danny didn't move. He fixed his eyes on Alexander, letting him feel the full effects of his penetrating, intimidating gaze. "Ask her if she wants to," he snarled. His tone was so vicious I wasn't even surprised when Alexander did as he was told.

"Would you like to come with me?" he asked with an exaggerated bow.

Tentatively, I shook my head. "Actually, no, I wouldn't."

Danny slammed the passenger door shut again. "Well, that settles that." He slipped an arm around me. "Let's get back inside. Why did you get so drunk, anyway?"

So that I can actually speak to you...

The intimate gesture must have set Alexander off, though, because he planted a rough hand on Danny's shoulder. After halting our progress, he grabbed my wrist and pulled me back to his car.

I couldn't suppress a laugh. Why did everyone like yanking on my arms so much?

Danny released me from Alexander's grip, staring him down. Without warning, Alexander wound up and punched at Danny, who ducked away effortlessly.

"Now this is getting truly ridiculous," Danny said calmly. "I suggest we end this little scene. Get back in your tricked-out toy and leave. Maintain what little dignity you have left."

Without hesitation, Alexander grabbed Danny by the collar. In one quick motion, Danny spun free and twisted Alexander's hands behind his back, holding them fast as he pushed Alexander toward the Jeep. He opened the driver's-side door, shoved Alexander in, and slammed the door. "Drive safe," he said, smacking the roof with his palm.

My ex was seething, but he didn't dare get out again. He turned the radio all the way up and revved the engine loudly. For a moment, I was afraid he was going to run us both over, but he just swerved and sped out of the parking lot far too quickly. The scene seemed so familiar to me that I had to laugh again.

Danny watched the Jeep go. "Nice guy, that Alexander is."

"Well, he doesn't bet on getting girls' phone numbers, so he's got that going for him." I let myself drop to the ground. It was pitching and rolling, which made me giggle even more.

Danny eyed me critically. "You should be in bed," he declared as he gripped me beneath the arms and hefted me to my feet. "We'll just go in for a second so I can get my stuff and let everyone else know, and then I'll take you home. My car's over there."

"I'm doing great!" I protested.

Back inside the packed club, he dropped me off at the bar. "Don't move. I'll be back in two minutes."

For the first time ever, I saw that there were plush mice hanging from the ceiling of the club, and the discovery made me burst out into gales of laughter.

Without my even noticing, Danny had returned. He gave me a concerned once-over. "Ricky's gonna take Simon home later. I told them I'd take you. Can you walk?"

"Of course," I slurred as I stood up from the barstool and then promptly went sprawling onto the floor.

Sighing, Danny helped me up, drawing one of my arms across his shoulders so he could guide me out to the parking lot. He unlocked his car from a distance and opened one of the back doors for me.

You have to go in the back like a dog, my inner voice piped up as I sank down onto the pale leather. The floor mats, the radio display, and even the inside lights were blue. *Blue!* He'd decorated his car to match his eyes. I dissolved into another fit of giggles.

"What's so funny?" Danny asked as he got in.

"You!" I cackled.

"I'm glad I amuse you." He turned on the GPS. "Tell me your address."

I immediately sobered up a tick. "W-what?" I stammered. "I can't go home like this. My parents would kill me!"

"Well, I guess you should have thought of that earlier. Address?"

"Just take me to the cemetery," I moaned theatrically. "I'm sure there's a grave free somewhere. Just throw me right in."

I heard him sigh in resignation. Then I passed out.

The next thing I was aware of was Danny dragging me out of the car. Cold night air hit my face.

"Where are we?" I asked as he pushed me along in front of him.

"My place. It's warmer here than the cemetery."

I shrugged. Anything was okay with me, as long as I'd be able to sleep in peace.

We stopped in front of a small duplex, and Danny helped me inside the first-floor apartment. I heard quiet voices as soon as we stepped into the hallway.

"Wait here a second." Danny gestured to make sure I'd understood the instructions, then walked down the hall into the living room. I followed him anyway, of course. To the right, there was a huge couch that also served as a room divider. To the left, there was a TV mounted on the wall—some sitcom was on. Danny picked the remote control up from the table and turned the TV off. There was a girl asleep on the couch. Jet-black hair concealed most of her face and hung all the way down to the floor. I guessed she was probably a year or two older than I was. Danny reached for the cotton blanket at the foot of the couch and covered her up.

"Who's that? Your girlfriend?" That was a question I probably wouldn't have had the guts to ask if I hadn't been so drunk.

"Something like that," he replied, pushing me back into the hallway. Carefully, he closed the door behind us. "That's Christina. She's sort of a fixture around here. You're lucky she's on the couch—it means you can sleep in my bed."

For some stupid reason, that actually did make me happy. By the time we got to the bedroom, all I could think about was lying down. I threw my boots and jeans in a corner and wondered vaguely why I heard him sigh again.

As I began to remove my sweater, Danny took a T-shirt out of his dresser and threw it at me. "Here, you can sleep in that," he said, turning his back to me so I could change. I wouldn't have cared if he hadn't.

I flopped down onto the double bed in my underwear and his T-shirt. Everything was spinning. I was dimly aware of him covering me up to the hips and then moving away.

Impulsively, I grabbed his hand and pulled it to my cheek. "Stay," I pleaded. "I'm sick. I don't want to be alone. I think I'm dying."

"People don't die that easily," he said gently. There was an undertone in his voice I couldn't quite place. But I was too tired to think any more about it.

"Stay here," I murmured again, still clutching his hand.

"I'm staying," he said, slowly getting into bed behind me. He slid his arm underneath my head, so that I was lying in the crook of his arm. Cautiously, he brushed a few strands of hair from my forehead and stroked my head a few times. Though I was half-asleep, I noticed what a soft touch he had. His sheets smelled like him, and I immediately felt safe and secure. Within seconds, I was out cold.

The sun hammered down on my eyelids. Sluggishly, I blinked into the hideously bright light. My head was killing me. The whole bed smelled so much like Danny that I immediately remembered where I was. The other side of the bed was empty, of course, and it didn't look like anyone had slept there. I sat up carefully. If I moved slowly enough, the throbbing pain in my head stayed within manageable limits.

I looked around with interest. The bedroom was white, with pale beechwood furniture: a huge wardrobe, two night tables, and a dresser. The sheets I was tangled in were blue-striped cotton, and it didn't surprise me that the curtains and bedside rug were blue as well.

The room was extremely clean and tidy, except for one pile of clothes in the corner. It took me a moment to remember who they belonged to. I felt a hot blush spread across my face.

One last time, I buried my nose in the pillow, drawing in the scent of shampoo, shower gel, and conditioner. I wished I could stay in his bed forever, but suddenly I was also incredibly embarrassed that I'd been lying around here half-naked. A painful realization dawned on me: even then, he still hadn't tried anything. How much more evidence did I need that this guy wasn't interested in me? Maybe he was gay...

Far too vividly, I recalled how he'd flirted with those two attractive girls at the festival and discarded the gay theory immediately.

Reluctantly, I climbed out of the bed to look for the bathroom. Clutching my pile of clothes to my chest, I snuck into the next room. It wasn't a bathroom—it was a combination office and workout room. There was a desk beneath the window in one corner, and a punching bag in another. A gym mat was lying on the ground, and there was a chin-up bar or something like it attached to the ceiling. The wall was plastered with certificates, and a small collection of trophies was arranged inside a glass display case. Curious, I took a closer look.

Kickboxing, I discovered. Why couldn't he play soccer or tennis like everyone else?

Another certificate was hanging to my left.

Oh my God!

He'd won the World Amateur Kickboxing Championships last year. Full contact, middleweight.

What the hell am I even doing here?

Suddenly I recalled that I was standing around in an unfamiliar apartment wearing only a T-shirt and panties, and that shook me out of my state of shock. I headed back into the hallway and tried the next door.

Bingo. I promptly got into the shower, found some women's shower gel, and soaped up with it. The fact that a girl named Christina apparently lived here didn't suit my plans at all.

Who the hell was she?

I took a towel out of the closet and dried off, then put on my jeans. My sweater stank terribly of cigarette smoke, so I decided to wear Danny's T-shirt again. I toyed with the idea of using his toothbrush, but I couldn't be sure if the blue one was really his, so I made do with gurgling a lot of mouthwash. Then I combed my hair out thoroughly and even used some of Christina's deodorant. When I was finished, I felt like a new woman.

I emerged from the bathroom a good deal more self-confident. Hearing dishes clattering at the other end of the hallway, I followed the sound. The kitchen was small and cozy, with pale wood cabinets and a small, round table with two chairs.

"I set the table here in the dining room," a friendly female voice called from the next room. "Come on in."

Dining room? How big was this place? Why would one guy need this much space all to himself?

He's not by himself, Jessica.

Resolutely, I went through the open door. The girl I'd seen on the couch the night before beamed at me. Christina. She was thin and delicate, with a remarkably pretty face.

"Good morning, Jessica," she trilled.

At any other time, in any other situation, I would have liked her immediately, but I'd already decided to hate her with a burning passion for all eternity. Her outfit only increased my fury: even though it was autumn, she was wearing hot pants and a tank top with spaghetti straps and a plunging neckline. Her voluptuous breasts, clearly visible underneath the thin material, swayed with every step she took, leading me to conclude that she considered bras unnecessary. She studied me with emerald-green eyes nearly as piercing as Danny's. If they'd been blue, I'd have assumed the two of them were siblings, just based on the intensity of the color. Apart from that, though, they didn't look a thing alike.

"Sit down," Christina said politely, pulling up a chair.

"Thank you," I said and did as I was told.

"Danny's out running," she explained. "He should be back soon. He didn't expect you to be on your feet this early. Would you like some coffee?"

"Yes, please."

Christina bent across the table to fill my cup. Automatically, I stared at her cleavage—everything there was to see, I saw. Jealousy bubbled up within me like bile as I wondered whether she poured Danny's morning coffee the same way.

She passed me milk and sugar, and I stirred both into my cup. There were fresh biscuits on the table, along with butter and several kinds of jam.

"Who are you, anyway?" I drank my coffee quickly, even though it was still much too hot.

"Christina," she said. "But everyone calls me Tina."

"Yeah, I know that. Are you guys roommates?"

She shook her head defensively. "No, this is Danny's place. I'm just here temporarily." She shrugged sheepishly. "Trouble at home, you know?"

"And he was kind enough to offer you his couch?" A fresh wave of jealousy washed over me.

"Actually, I have my own room. I just fell asleep on the couch last night."

She was staying here temporarily, but she had her own room? Just how long was "temporarily"?

"Be glad I slept on the couch," Christina went on. "Otherwise you would never have gotten into Danny's bed." She paused dramatically before adding, "Unfortunately, I must confess he spent the night in my bed, since you were in his."

Was she trying to provoke me? Well, it worked. I took the bait. "You slept in the same bed? How nice."

She smiled affectionately. "No, not yesterday, we didn't. I was on the couch, remember? But I do sleep in his bed sometimes. Mostly when I can't sleep, or I'm lonely."

"How touching!" I said through gritted teeth.

Just then, Danny joined us in the dining room. My heart skipped a beat.

"Morning," he said. He was still in his workout clothes, sweaty from running, his hair sticking out every which way. "You survived," he said, beaming at me. "It's a miracle!" He came up to the table and laid a hand on my shoulder for a moment. It felt like sparks flew out under his touch. I stared at him as though suffering from electric shock, but he kept walking toward Christina.

"I'm gonna take a quick shower," he said, bending and kissing her on the temple like it was the most natural thing in the world. "Thanks for making breakfast, Tina."

She gave him a friendly nod, and I gaped at him as he walked out again.

Seemingly sensing my distress, Christina sat down beside me and said, "Don't worry. Danny's not my boyfriend. Never has been."

"Sure looks that way, though." As I grumpily chewed a biscuit, I decided maybe I should at least try to like her.

When Danny joined us again, I acted like I didn't notice.

"You all right?" he asked.

"Hmph."

"Hey, how about I show you around," Christina suggested. Although I'd have rather stayed with Danny, I followed her into the open-plan living room with large glass doors. The furniture was black wood, and for some reason, I found it comforting that none of it was blue. Christina opened the back door and slipped outside, wearing far too little for as chilly as it was. A tall hedge separated the small yard from the neighbors', and there was covered patio furniture on the deck. It was all pretty idyllic.

Shivering, we went back inside, and she led me through Danny's bedroom into the room beside it.

"This is his office and workout room," she told me. "He usually works out in here at night, before he goes to bed." I kept quiet about having been in there already, but I couldn't help wondering what gave her the right to stroll around like she owned the place. To top it off, on the way back through his bedroom, she shook out the covers and neatly made the bed.

Then she showed me the room just to the right of the front door. "This is my room," she declared proudly.

Size-wise, it was the same as the other one, minus the connected office. It had a bed, a couch, and a small desk with a clunky old laptop on it. Her clothes were strewn across the floor, along with untold quantities of high heels. I stared at the pencil-thin heels, trying to convince myself that I wouldn't have broken my legs just trying to stand upright in them.

That's when Danny came into her room. "I'll take you home now," he said, and I didn't argue, though I would have liked to stay a while longer.

"It was nice to meet you," Christina said, holding out a hand. She had an astonishingly firm handshake for such a skinny little thing. "See you around sometime."

I couldn't tell from her tone whether she wanted that to happen or hoped it wouldn't. "Yeah, for sure," I replied weakly. "Thanks so much for breakfast."

She waved, and I gathered up the rest of my things and followed Danny to the car. He opened the passenger door.

"Oh, today I get to sit up front?" I asked sarcastically.

"Just for today," he replied playfully. "Don't get used to it." He started up the GPS, and I told him my address. Pumping music I didn't recognize thundered out of the CD player for a moment before he turned the volume down. All at once, I felt like I needed to thank him. After all, not everyone would have let someone they didn't actually know just spend the night in their house.

"Thanks," I said quietly. "For looking out for me and all that."

"No problem. In the future, though, you should probably only drink as much as you can handle... So, ideally, just stick to water, I guess."

He followed the GPS's instructions—driving much too fast. But something about him made me feel entirely safe, so I decided not to say anything. Idly I checked my phone and discovered two texts from Nessa.

Did you get home okay?

Jess? Let me know!

I typed a reply:

Hi, Nessa, everything's fine. I stayed at Danny's; he's taking me home right now. I'll call you later.

Grinning, I put the phone away. "I think Vanessa's pretty crazy about your friend Ricky," I told Danny. "I hope he isn't using her."

"They're both old enough to know what they're doing," he said.

"So, Christina," I said. "Who is she?" I couldn't help it. I had to know.

"My best friend. She's staying with me for a while."

Right. And I probably wasn't going to get any new information with this tactic. I decided to drop it for now.

The drive didn't take long. Danny maneuvered his BMW into the guest parking space beside my parents' building and then pulled the parking brake. He left his hand there and looked at me expectantly. "You're home," he said.

Hesitantly, I reached for his hand, wanting to take it as I said goodbye, maybe even give it a quick kiss.

"Don't," he snarled, jerking his hand away, looking at me like I'd tried to bite him.

I could only gape at him.

He crossed his arms.

"Um. I... I was just...um... I mean, I thought... I thought..."

"I couldn't care less what you thought, Jessica. Goodbye."

I remembered the way he'd tenderly run his fingers through my hair just a few hours before—in his bed. What the hell was going on here? This guy was a walking contradiction.

"Are you throwing me out or something?" I asked, hurt.

"Not yet, but I'll have to if you don't get out soon."

"Why are you treating me like this all of a sudden?" At the very least, he owed me an explanation.

He pursed his lips and took a deep breath, as though he was having a hard time controlling himself. "Listen," he said, a shade more gently, "I'm sorry if you got the wrong idea somehow, but I'm really not interested in a relationship and all that crap. My life is complicated enough. There's no place for you in it. So I'd really appreciate it if you'd just get going."

I felt a painful twinge in the pit of my stomach. Then the disappointment gave way to rage. "You're pathetic! A pathetic, fake asshole!"

"So," he said in a dangerously calm voice. He got out of the car, strode quickly around the front, and opened the passenger door. "*This* is when I throw you out."

I scoffed indignantly. "Go to hell!"

"I can't until you get out of my car!"

Without another word, I sprang from my seat and batted his hand away from the door before slamming it shut. Then I pushed past him with my chin held high, clutching my purse against my chest. I just wanted to get inside so I could lick my wounds. Tears of disappointment sprang to my eyes before I reached the front door. I wept silently, grieving the loss of something I had never even had.

That night, I tossed and turned for a long time before finally falling into a fitful sleep.

I'm running down a narrow alley, drenched in sweat. My heart is hammering wildly, and the ground is melting away underneath my feet. I turn around, terrified. The road behind me is blurring as well, sinking into an ocean of icy blue. The walls on either side of me are closing in slowly, transforming into thick, blue fog.

The color blue is everywhere, enveloping me, choking the air out of my lungs.

Chapter Three

December 1999

Jörg Pfisterer read the file through once more before closing it for the last time. It wasn't like he didn't know it backwards and forwards already—it just seemed like it might make saying goodbye a little easier. But really, the only thing that made it easier was knowing that it didn't necessarily have to be goodbye forever. This was mostly just a formality.

He'd worked with the boy for five years. The kid had been at the children's home the first year, and then he'd gone to the teen group home. Finally, in the summer of 1996, Jörg had helped him move into his own apartment. That had been just after the verdict.

The trial had lasted more than a year. Going through the whole story all over again in court had been hard on Danny, but he'd stuck it out bravely. Together, they'd fought their way through his father's string of appeals, and, ultimately, they'd won the case. Justifiably, of course, and to be expected. But the whole thing should have gone a lot faster. There'd been no doubt of his father's guilt. His mother had proven to be an obstacle, though. She'd defended her husband and contradicted herself constantly.

They'd barely finished that ordeal when the next blow hit. Even harder than the one before it. Jörg knew Danny hadn't come to terms with this madness and probably never would, not in all his life. It would be too much for anyone to handle. Too cruel, too unbearable, too final.

Danny had gotten excellent grades in school, despite everything, but he'd given up on his plan of going to college and getting a degree in something sports-related. Inescapable as his fate had seemed to him, he didn't see the point of staying in school. The whole thing hurt Jörg's soul. The boy had become like a son to him. He loved Danny, and if necessary, he'd have adopted him immediately, without hesitation.

Ever the optimist, Danny had decided to become a personal trainer instead and had gotten a job at a gym. Soon, Danny had started training young athletes as well, and his own list of athletic achievements had become truly impressive. College really wouldn't have benefited him all that much, Jörg supposed.

He wrapped a rubber band around the file and put it away. Preparations for Danny's birthday party were in full swing downstairs. Danny was celebrating at the children's home this year. He still had friends here, felt at home among them.

37

Christina, Ricky, and Simon would be by soon. Jörg's gift for Danny was already meticulously wrapped and waiting downstairs with the others. He'd invited Danny's mother as well, but he didn't really expect her to show up. She'd never come once in all these years.

There was a short knock at the door, and Danny walked in. "Hey," he said. "You coming down to join us?"

Jörg stood up and embraced him. "Happy birthday, kiddo," he said, looking Danny over. He knew the kid well enough to see that something was on his mind. "What's wrong?"

Danny shrugged.

"Sit down," Jörg commanded him, dropping back down into his desk chair. Danny obeyed but didn't say anything. "Tell me!"

Danny nibbled on the skin around his fingernail. "I met a girl."

"Hey, that's wonderful."

Danny gave him an accusatory look. Even after all this time, Jörg still sometimes flinched at the sheer intensity of the kid's gaze. "It's not wonderful, and you know it."

Jörg was torn. He wished more than anything that Danny could enjoy a functioning relationship, but the kid's previous experiences had just been so painful. Danny'd had his first girlfriend when he was sixteen, just after his father had gone to jail. She was a delicate, dark-haired girl, shy and inexperienced enough that Danny had felt like it was a relationship he could handle. But they'd still only lasted a couple of months. The girl just hadn't been able to handle Danny's withdrawn nature... And she'd never understood why he could touch her, but she could never touch him. Finally, she'd broken up with him.

The fateful call from Danny's father had come soon after the relationship ended. After that, Danny had sworn off women entirely. But two or three years later, he'd tried to make things work with another girl. This one was completely different from the first—self-confident, outgoing—but the problems had been the same. With the third girl, Danny had left feelings out of it entirely, resulting in what was more or less a functioning affair. Until his conscience had finally forced him to come clean to his partner, and she'd disappeared forever.

Jörg wanted so badly for the kid to find someone. But what could he tell him? To keep his secret to himself? Wasn't it his duty as Danny's guardian to emphasize the importance of honesty and fairness?

Then he remembered that he wasn't Danny's legal guardian anymore, and his mood brightened. Now he could give him advice as a *friend*.

"It *is* wonderful, Danny. You just can't make the same mistake. Don't tell her."

Danny stared at him, aghast. "You can't be serious."

"I am. Nobody can force you to do that. You've got to think of yourself every once in a while. And you're not an idiot; you know when to exercise caution. As long as you don't put her in danger, keeping it to yourself is a totally legitimate option."

"I don't know." Danny's expression darkened, and he began chewing on his fingernail again. "I'm not very comfortable with that."

Jörg took a deep breath. "I've been giving you advice for five years. And for five years you've been ignoring my advice and doing whatever your stubborn head tells you to do. You could at least listen to me this one time."

"I'll think about it." Danny sank down further into his chair and tilted his head back to stare at the ceiling. "Though it's probably a moot point anyway," he added thoughtfully. "I was pretty rude to her a couple weeks ago, told her in no uncertain terms that I didn't want a relationship."

Jörg shook his head. "You need to work on yourself, Danny. You're too impulsive."

"It wasn't impulsive. I did it on purpose. Out of fear of the future."

"You think way too much. At your age, relationships come and go. Most of them end after a short time, anyway. Don't think about the future at all." Jörg smiled almost euphorically. "Call her. Apologize. Smooth things over!"

"How am I supposed to do that? How can I apologize? I can't explain myself to her without actually saying anything about…you know."

"True." Jörg pondered for a moment. "Well, think of something. Tell her you just got out of a failed relationship. Tell her you needed time."

Danny shook his head in amazement. "You can't be suggesting I start a relationship based on a lie!"

Jörg shrugged. "If necessary, that's exactly what I'm suggesting. There has to be a way. Don't just throw in the towel."

"I'll think about it," Danny repeated.

"Tell me about her. What do you like about her?"

"Her name is Jessica." Danny's unusually blue eyes seemed to light up. "She's a couple of years younger than I am. Slender, with long hair. She's kind of bitchy, but she's sweet, too." Danny squinted one eye in thought. "But most importantly, she stands up for herself. I can't just wrap her around my little finger like I can most girls. She gives as good as she gets...and she seems like she's interested in me as a person. She doesn't just like me for my looks, the way everyone else does." He smiled crookedly. "I think I need that. I need someone who will look beneath the surface sometimes, not just tune out the things they don't want to hear... Yeah, I want someone who will really get to know me. It'll have to be a girl who doesn't scare too easily. You need pretty damn thick skin to put up with me."

Chapter Four

January 2000

"Light pink or bright blue?"

"Neither," I said. "I don't like nail polish."

Especially not blue!

Vanessa sighed. "Fine. But at least let me do a clear coat. Otherwise it's not a proper beauty weekend."

"Come on. I've already had a hair treatment, a facial mask, ad a manicure. Presumably I'm the most beautiful person on the planet."

I know someone more beautiful!

Good God, didn't that hateful little voice ever shut up?

I gave in and held my hands out to Vanessa.

"Jessica." My mother knocked and then opened the bedroom door. "Package came for you."

I stared at the small box in confusion. "I didn't order anything."

"Maybe a follow-up delivery?" My mother held the package out to me.

I blew on my now-clear-coated fingernails. "Just set it here. I'll open it in a minute."

"Dinner will be ready in half an hour," my mother said as she went out.

"Who could that be from?" I murmured. "Open it, will you, Nessa?"

Vanessa labored away at the tape with a nail file until it finally broke. She pulled out a smaller box wrapped in paper. "It's a CB radio," she said. "Oh my God, a Midland Alan 80-channel!" Her eyes widened in wonder. "Crazy. How can you afford that?"

"I can't!" I said, thinking of the cheap contraption Nessa and I had been using. "They must have sent this to the wrong address."

"There's a note in here."

"Let me see." I plucked the letter from her hand. A suspicion was already beginning to come over me as I unfolded the sheet of lined notebook paper. "It's from Danny."

"What's he say? You mean he's sending you this as a gift? I thought you guys got in a fight!" She rocked back and forth impatiently. "Jess! Answer me!"

"It's an apology," I said and read the letter a second time. My heart was pounding wildly. "And a poem I don't really get."

"What's it say?"

I read the note aloud:

Jessica,

I wanted to apologize for how I acted that Sunday morning. It was wrong of me. Sorry.

You just read too much into the night before, way too much.

I'm sorry about that, and I wanted to give you something—by way of apology, or maybe just because I like you.

We still have to go our separate ways, though. It would never work between us. You see something in me that I'm not.

Sorry,

Danny

Pain is a feeling

Cold moment at the pond

No one is watching

The flight of a knife

The death of a snake

I know the sea of lies

When the dogs bark

No one is listening

I am the bird of death

The death-bringing bird of the night

"He apologized for his behavior. That's good." Vanessa nodded thoughtfully.

Weeks later, after I'd already come to terms with the idea of never seeing him again. Wonderful. "What's he trying to say with this poem?"

Vanessa shrugged. "Let me see," she said, reaching out for the letter.

While she read, I inspected the radio, marveling. This would really increase my range. Eighty channels! Finally, enough options that I'd be able to get around signal problems. It had noise-suppression controls, a port for an amplifier, and even an automatic channel search.

"It's a warning," Nessa said.

I was only half-listening. "You think? What's he warning me about?"

"About him, I think."

"Huh?" Most of my attention was on disconnecting the old CB unit and hooking up the new one.

"Jess, you've gotta send that back to him, preferably along with that T-shirt of his you still have, and then tell him to go jump in a lake!"

"Are you nuts?" I exclaimed. "He's not getting the Midland back!" *I'm keeping the shirt too*, I added in my head.

"Dude's a few ants short of a picnic, that much is obvious."

I suppressed a grin. "So what? He looks good, and he's generous. Let him be a little crazy."

Vanessa stared at me, aghast, before taking away my new toy and pressing the note back into my hand. "Jessica, seriously! This guy isn't playing with a full deck. He takes you home with him and then throws you out of the car…and then sends you presents weeks later?"

That was the problem with having a best friend: she always knew everything. I read the poem a fourth time, trying to read between the lines.

Vanessa stood up and put her hands on her hips. "I think he sounds like a serial killer. He probably makes shoes out of women's skin."

"He doesn't look like a serial killer," I said.

"Oh?" She scoffed. "What would you say they look like?"

"Muscular, lots of tattoos, balding. And they chain-smoke and have 70s mustaches and crazy eyes, of course. Everyone knows that."

She knitted her brow in disapproval. "Can you please be serious about this?"

I was beginning to understand some of what Danny had written. Or at least I liked to think so. "He sounds pretty hopeless in this note," I remarked.

"Could be. He's probably a hopeless case."

All of a sudden, I didn't even care. Vanessa could say what she wanted. It didn't make a difference what the letter said. He could have told me he was Freddy Krueger himself and liked to eat small children, and it wouldn't have been enough to scare me off.

"I'm going to write him back," I said resolutely.

"Oh, for God's sake, now you've lost your mind, too." Vanessa threw up her hands.

My mother called us for dinner, but I told her I'd eat later and sat down to write a reply.

Dear Mr. Taylor,

Thank you very much for your letter. Regretfully, however, I must inform you that you are corresponding with an junior architectural drafter and not a scholar. Poetry and philosophy are above my pay grade.

And, to be honest, that's all right with me. I'm perfectly fine without them!

But I did manage to figure out that you were trying to warn me. Thank you for that, as well, though I have to add that it was an unnecessary effort on your part— I have survived perfectly well for nearly eighteen years now without your help.

In other words, I can take care of myself.

Let's get to the point, shall we? I like you, but I'm not in the market for a cryptic pen pal, so here are three response options for you. Mark your choice below:

A) Let's go to a movie. I'll pick you up on Saturday evening.

B) I'll go jump in a lake.

C) I will continue to send completely indecipherable letters in the knowledge that they will go unanswered.

Sincerely,

Jessica

PS: Thank you SO MUCH for the radio. It's really great!!

After dinner, I took the bus to Ludwigsburg and bought two tickets for *The Blair Witch Project*, Saturday, at 8 p.m. When I got home again, I stuck the tickets into an envelope with trembling fingers, added my letter, and quickly sealed it. That same evening, I took Leika for a walk to the mailbox and sent the letter on its way before I could change my mind.

The alley is so narrow. Fortunately, the blue light isn't as harsh anymore. It's diffuse now, like it's coming from weak bulbs. I'm out of breath, running much too fast. I want to stop, but I can't.

I have to get away. But am I even running in the right direction? Which way is 'away'? Am I running away, or am I running toward the very thing I'm trying to escape?

***

I heard my phone beep while I was in the shower and reached for it with wet hands.

The message said only:

Response A

My heart leapt for joy. I was instantly wide awake, adrenaline shooting through my veins. I wanted to write back immediately and tell him how happy I was, but I forced myself to keep my message as short as his. Nothing good came to me, so I just sent a smiley.

His next message arrived less than a minute later:

Dinner before the movie?

I'll pick you up at 5 PM, in the parking lot where I threw you out last time.

I slapped my thighs and let out a shriek of joy.

Even my inner voice was cheering and applauding thunderously.

There was a knock at the bathroom door. "Jessica? Can you hurry up? Other people want to shower, too!"

"Be right out!" I called to my dad. Two more days until Saturday! I just had to make it through two more days.

***

I scrutinized my reflection in the mirror. The results were worth seeing. I was wearing tight jeans, a short, carmine pullover with batwing sleeves, and black, knee-high stiletto boots. My long, wavy hair fell down around my shoulders. My makeup was very subtle, but I'd taken forever getting it right.

My mother regarded me curiously. "Are you going over to Alexander's tonight?" she asked hopefully.

"No, I'm going to a movie with Nessa," I lied. By that point, my parents had found out I'd broken up with Alexander, but Mom still held out unfounded hope that we might get back together. She liked him, and more than anything, she liked his mom. Alexander and I had been together for nearly three years, and our mothers had become best friends—which had meant plenty of freedom for me. Alexander's parents had let us do basically whatever we wanted. Even when we'd stayed out at the club until the wee hours of the morning, nobody had ever asked any questions.

My mother looked disappointed.

"Maybe I'll go to Alexander's afterward," I said to placate her.

"I'd be so happy if you two got back together," she said for what felt like the hundredth time.

I shrugged. "We'll see. I gotta go, Mom, see you!" My stomach fluttered nervously as I grabbed my purse and coat and left the house. The fifty-foot walk to the parking lot felt like miles. What if he didn't show?

As soon as I turned the corner, I saw him. In jeans and a royal-blue hoodie, he was leaning casually against a gleaming, black, thirty-foot limousine—a Lincoln Town Car—his arms folded. As always, his hair was sticking out in every direction. When he saw me, his face broke out into a radiant smile. A man dressed in black was standing at the front of the car, eyes downcast.

Chauffeur and everything? This is crazy...

My knees were threatening to give out, and my brain switched into offline mode again.

As I walked toward Danny, gaping in astonishment, he straightened and held out his hands. I took them, and his fingers closed briefly around mine. Once again, it was like he'd hit me with an electric shock.

"W-wow," I stammered. "What's all this for?"

"Because I'm falling in love," he said quietly.

For a moment, the world stood still.

In love?

I was too stunned to react.

The chauffeur opened the car door, revealing an interior bathed in dim violet light. Still reeling a little, I settled onto the cream-colored leather upholstery that stretched across the entire length of the limousine, and Danny climbed in after me. The long marble-topped table in the center held a chilled bottle of champagne and two flutes already filled.

Danny handed me one of them, and we clinked our glasses together.

"I thought you didn't drink," I said shyly.

"Exceptions prove the rule," Danny replied and took the first sip as the vehicle began rolling slowly out of the parking lot.

"How can you afford this kind of thing as a personal trainer?" I had no idea what it actually cost, but it surely wasn't cheap.

He suppressed a grin. "I earn good money in my side job."

"I knew it! You steal cars and sell them in other countries."

"Um, no." He looked genuinely perplexed.

"So you do the grandson scam? Knock on confused old ladies' doors and make big eyes at them, and cry about how the Mafia is after you, and beg for money?"

He stared at me in surprise. Apparently, he hadn't pegged me as someone with that much imagination. "It's a lot less spectacular than that. Pretty boring by comparison, really. I just pose."

I raised an eyebrow.

"For photos," he clarified. "For a fashion label."

"You *model*?" I shrieked at him. So he didn't just *look* like a glossy-magazine model, he actually *was* one.

What the hell did this guy want with *me*?

In love, he said...

"Yeah," he replied easily. "It's nothing to scream about. They're just photos. Ads, clothes, the usual. The pay's good."

"So that's why you didn't go to college?"

His expression turned grim. "No. That was for other reasons. Personal reasons."

There it was again, that darkness in his eyes.

"Aren't you afraid the modeling work will dry up someday when you're old and ugly?" My curiosity knew no bounds.

"No, I'm not worried about that." Then why did his voice sound so melancholy?

My champagne glass was empty by that point, but I felt awkward about refilling it, since Danny hadn't taken his eyes off me. "There's something I really don't understand," I began, emboldened by the champagne. "Why did you try to warn me away from you? Do you chop little girls up into pieces and bury them in the forest?"

The violet light gleamed in his hair as he tilted his head and regarded me. "I make drugs in my basement," he said. "I have to be careful. Can't let anyone find out."

I regarded him skeptically. The problem with Danny's dry humor was that you never knew whether he was joking.

He laughed quietly to himself when he realized I was trying to decide whether to believe him.

"Sarcasm is the sword of the intellectual," he finally said. But then, all at once, his relaxed demeanor shifted again. "Seriously," he said, "the fact is my life is one giant catastrophe. I don't want anyone else to get sucked into it."

Half relieved drugs weren't involved, I shook my head. "Hey, I've never met a catastrophe I couldn't handle!"

"I'm not joking," he insisted. "If you have an ounce of sense in your head, you'll walk away and never look back."

"Sense was never my strong suit. I'm told teenagers aren't sensible people."

He sighed deeply. "Okay," he said theatrically. "I'll give you three choices, since you were kind enough to do so for me. All right?"

I nodded, a smile creeping onto my face.

"Then come on down, you're the next contestant!" he said in his best TV-announcer voice. "Here are your options! One: A happy, worry-free life as a single woman. Two: Me. Three: You find a guy who's right for you and live happily ever after. Pick a door, any door!"

"Door number two, please," I announced, playing along.

"I'm serious!" Danny protested.

"So am I!" But I couldn't help giggling. "It's just hard not to laugh. You're really funny!"

He raised a questioning eyebrow. "Funny ha-ha or funny strange?"

"Both."

"Is it at least an equal mix?"

"No. One more so than the other." I turned to look out the window, at the pedestrians watching with interest as our limo pulled into the movie theater parking lot.

The driver stopped at the entrance of the restaurant beside the movie theater and then hastened out of the vehicle to open the door for us with a demonstrative bow. Danny got out and extended a hand to me. Everyone in the area was looking at us, and suddenly I felt completely out of place. He could easily pass for a film star, but me?

The feeling of inferiority lingered as we stepped into the classy restaurant. We followed a black-tuxedoed host to an elaborately decorated table, complete with lit candles. After inviting us to sit with an elegant gesture, he handed us our menus, and we spent a moment looking them over.

"I think I'll have the pork medallions with mushrooms and vegetables," I proclaimed. "You?"

Danny quirked an accusing eyebrow. "I don't eat dead animals." Instead, he picked a vegetarian Asian dish and placed both of our orders with our waiter, who also sported a fine black tuxedo.

"So why'd you leave home so young?" I asked spontaneously.

"Young?" His eyes darkened again. "I'm twenty."

"That's young!" I insisted.

"My parents died in a car accident when I was fifteen. After that, I was in a home for a while, and then I got my own place," he explained rather curtly.

"Oh, I'm sorry." I could certainly understand that he wouldn't want to talk about that.

"It was a long time ago. I wasn't in the car when they had the accident." His eyes roamed the room, and it was clear he didn't want to talk about it any longer.

The waiter brought us our drinks, and I searched for a less tumultuous topic.

"Where are you from originally?" I asked. "Your name doesn't sound German…"

"I was born and raised near Atlanta," he said.

"Really?" For some reason, that surprised me, even though I'd considered the possibility of him being American. "You can't tell from your German. How come you don't have an accent?"

"I'm only half American—my mother was German. I grew up bilingual. So, technically, German is my mother tongue." His gaze shifted into the distance. "When I was in elementary school, we had a little wooden house out in the countryside. Georgia's a gorgeous place. And we had a pool in the backyard, and the weather was always nice. And I had a sheepdog."

I smiled. "I have a dog, too. A black-and-white hound mix named Leika." I took a sip of my Coke. "So why did you move to Germany?"

Our appetizers arrived, and just as I was starting to think my question would go unanswered, Danny said, "My mother had a miscarriage when I was ten. It really hit her hard. She, uh, just needed to come back home. To be with her family."

"And you didn't like it here." It was meant to be a question, but it didn't come out that way because his tone said it all.

"No, not really."

"But your grandparents live here? Don't you get along with them?"

"I do," Danny said without looking up. "But my dad fought with them constantly. Just, all the time. Until we finally lost all contact."

After finishing my appetizer in silence, I put my silverware down on my unused napkin and sat there for a moment, trying to screw up enough courage to ask my next question: "Why didn't you like it here? Because of the fighting? Or was it later, when you were in the children's home?"

"There have been worse periods in my life," he murmured. But he was closing up before my eyes. I could practically feel the walls he was erecting to hide his feelings from me. I wouldn't be getting any more information out of him.

"Enough about me," he said, as if on cue. "What about you? Do you have any siblings?"

A young waitress with a blond ponytail and a very short skirt brought our entrees. I saw Danny regarding her curiously. She blushed. When she set Danny's plate in front of him, her fingers lingered at the table a moment longer than necessary. Her eyes sought his.

Where was the waiter we had before?

"I have an older brother," I said, eyeing the waitress critically. "He's an office clerk."

"So you ride dressage, you're studying to become an architectural drafter, and you get along great with your parents," he said. "And you enjoy a lot of freedom." Apparently, it was his turn to make assumptions.

Not that this one was wrong.

"Yeah," I said. "My parents trust me completely. But reliability is also my middle name."

He smiled. "You really have the picture-perfect family, don't you?"

I never would have thought to call my family "picture-perfect." We had our share of problems, too. But my parents were still alive, which was a lot more than he had.

"The food here's really good," I remarked, and for a while our conversation veered into banal territory, like wondering what was in the salad dressing, even though I didn't know the first thing about cooking.

At last, we pushed our plates aside, and Danny signaled for the check.

"We should get over to the theater," he said. "The movie's starting soon."

To my relief, it was the tuxedoed waiter who returned with the bill. Danny paid it and then took my hand, and we strolled next door. We stopped to get popcorn and drinks, and Danny didn't let go of my hand until it became unavoidable as we squeezed down a narrow row of seats.

Once we were seated, I noticed several female members of the audience turned to look at him. One nudged her friend and pointed at him, and they both giggled and turned red. If Danny was aware of the commotion he was causing, he didn't let on. My face grew hot, and I shifted in my chair. Only when the lights finally went down did I breathe a sigh of relief and settle back into my seat.

Danny looked at me attentively. "Everything all right?" he asked.

"Everything's great."

He took a sip of his drink and then held the cup out to me as though it were the most natural thing in the world. My heart did another somersault. I was going to have to be careful before I ended up with a heart murmur or something. Hastily, I accepted the cup and took a drink, even though I had one of my own. I liked the thought of sharing with him.

"Hey, how are we getting home afterwards?" I asked quietly.

"Same way we got here, of course."

"Do you pick girls up in limousines a lot?"

"No, you're the first." He winked at me.

The theater fell silent as the movie started.

I let my head sink onto Danny's shoulder. I barely paid attention to the movie—I was too intoxicated by his presence. His sweater smelled like fresh fabric softener, and he himself smelled like shower gel and aftershave, with maybe a hint of musk. Beneath my cheek, I felt his quiet, even breathing.

I snuck a glance at him. He had a perfectly straight nose and soft features. His blue eyes were framed by the longest lashes I had ever seen. His slender hand rested on his knee. I don't know how long I stared at it, tracing his long fingers with my eyes, before I finally worked up the courage to put my hand on his.

He flinched at the unexpected contact and jerked his hand away reflexively.

"Sorry," I whispered, concerned. My gut told me his violent reaction had nothing to do with me—or the horror movie.

"No worries," he murmured and held out his hand, palm up.

As soon as the credits began to roll, Danny pulled me out of my seat. "Come on, let's get going and beat the rush." He dragged me down the row, ignoring the protests of the other moviegoers. Just before we reached the exit, I stumbled over someone's foot and nearly fell down. Laughing stupidly, I used Danny's hand to pull myself up again and nudged him onward. The woman cursed at us and waved an umbrella threateningly in our direction.

"Run," I told Danny, pushing him forward.

He actually started running, dragging me along behind him. For reasons likely evident to us alone, we ran like maniacs until we got outside, where we stopped, gasping for breath and laughing giddily. Danny's laugh was so infectious that I couldn't stop.

"Come on!" He grabbed my hand again and took off running through the parking lot.

"Why are we in such a hurry?" I wheezed.

"We aren't!" he said, but he didn't slow down until we were nearly to the limousine. When the driver saw us, he got out to open the door, probably assuming we were drunk.

Of course, we weren't. Yet. Two full champagne glasses were waiting for us inside.

"To you," Danny said, raising his glass.

"To both of us!" I cried. Running through the movie theater like that had made me boisterous, almost euphoric.

"We could really give this a shot," Danny said quietly, looking into my eyes. Then he drained his glass.

My heart tried its damnedest to get back into a normal rhythm. "What about the whole catastrophe thing?"

If you don't shut up, you'll ruin everything! My inner voice was frantically waving its hands, trying to get me to zip it. But it was too late.

I bit my lip. The words were already out there. But I had to know. I was too afraid he might act friendly and approachable for a while and then just coldly brush me off again.

He raised his eyes and gave me a penetrating look. "I'm hoping you're sick of me before the catastrophe starts."

"You're *hoping* for that?" I repeated. He shrugged apologetically. I polished off my champagne.

This stuff is really good, I thought. I wasn't used to champagne, and it was going to my head. "I'll never be sick of you," I promised.

"We'll see," he said. "I'll make every effort to prove otherwise."

I stared into my empty glass, shaking my head. "What kind of catastrophe could we be talking about here?" I was speaking more to myself than to Danny.

Gently, he lifted my chin with his index finger so he could look into my eyes. I saw blue, dark blue, like water, and even then I knew I was in danger of drowning in it.

His sigh made me uneasy—he definitely had a flair for drama. "If I could explain the problem to you that easily, I wouldn't have tried to keep you away from me. If you're still with me when things have the potential to get dangerous, I'll let you know well in advance."

Danny squared his shoulders and set his chin resolutely. It nearly hypnotized me all over again. "Do you trust me?" he asked.

Don't forget to breathe, Jessica!

I nodded. "Yeah, I trust you." It came out as no more than a whisper.

"Thank you. I promise I'll watch out for you."

How much had he had to drink? Three glasses? Was he just drunk?

My chin was still in his hand, and his eyes still held me fast. I had to focus on taking deep breaths from my abdomen to keep myself halfway calm. He tilted his head and parted his lips slightly. The tip of his tongue touched his sharp canine tooth for a moment, and I could not and would not hold back any longer. I leaned toward him. He hesitated briefly before leaning in to me and pressing his lips to mine.

His scent enveloped me, and his fingers found mine. His breathing accelerated, and my heart leapt into my throat as my tongue brushed against his…

Abruptly, he pulled away.

"Jessica," he whispered. His chest was rising and falling heavily.

"Yeah?"

But he only closed his eyes for a moment, leaving the sentence unfinished. Whatever he'd been about to say, I would never know. He cursed under his breath, poured himself another glass of champagne, and drained it.

The limousine stopped in the guest parking lot in front of my parents' building, and the driver opened the door. We didn't move, so he retreated discreetly.

"What have I done?" Danny gave me a look of despair.

Fear suddenly welled up within me.

Not again, no, please, not again!

I leaned in and touched his cheek. "Everything's okay, Danny. Door number two. With all the consequences. It's my decision and mine alone. I don't care what the other options are. It will always be door number two!"

He nodded.

"See you next weekend?"

He nodded again, and I let out a sigh of relief.

"Thank you," I said, meaning both for this evening and for the fact that he wanted to see me again.

"See you next weekend. I'll be in touch." His voice sounded less self-assured than usual.

We both got out of the limousine and stood there for a moment, looking at each other in silence.

"Everything's okay, Danny," I assured him as I turned to go. "Everything's okay," I whispered, not knowing that I was repeating what would one day be our code word.

A code word that symbolized our trust in one another, one that would nip all uncertainty in the bud.

Chapter Five

February 2000

This time, Danny didn't keep me waiting long. It wasn't even five in the morning when my cell phone beeped. Half-asleep, I reached for it and read the text:

> *Good morning! Want to come with me to the old mill around the corner from my place on Saturday morning?*
>
> *I'd like to introduce you to a lady that has played a very important role in my life.*

I briefly considered waiting a while to answer, so as not to seem desperate, but my impatience won out.

> *I'd love to! I'm deeply honored to have an opportunity to meet a member of your royal court. Though it does seem a bit unusual that this fair maiden lives in a mill...*
>
> *Should I get myself a ballgown and practice my curtsies?*

Danny apparently had less difficulty with patience. His response didn't come until nearly two hours later, as I was walking up the stairs to the Civil Engineering Office.

> *I recommend jeans and sneakers. This is less about blue blood, more about hay and horsehair. Bring your dog, she'll like it there.*
>
> *I'll pick you up at 10 AM.*

The week dragged on forever. When Saturday finally rolled around and I rushed down to the parking lot with Leika, Danny was already there, waiting, leaning against his gleaming BMW, arms folded like always. Though it was still early in the year, the weather was warm and the sun shining brightly.

Danny stepped forward and kissed me on the lips. It was just a quick kiss, but the air around us still seemed to vibrate. Yet again, I had to remind myself to breathe.

A growl at my side stole my attention. In Leika's eyes, this stranger had definitely crossed a line. She pawed the ground, ready to protect me if necessary.

Danny smiled. "Well, that's a wonderful greeting."

"Sorry," I said. "She has some problems. Before I got her, she'd been living on the street, and she went through a lot. Some people really abused her—beat her, even shot her with a shotgun. Give her time. She'll warm up to you eventually."

Danny regarded her thoughtfully, his eyes gentle, almost tender. "No problem," he said. "We'll get there. I understand what abuse is like. She and I will be best friends someday." He opened the back door of the BMW. "You better be the one to invite her in for now. I brought her something, too, but we'll do that later. I don't want her to feel like I'm hassling her."

Leaving my dog alone was definitely the best way to win her trust. Most people immediately tried to pet her, to appease their own need for physical closeness, and that ruined everything from the beginning.

"You want her to just get in?" I asked. "Without a blanket?"

"Of course." He looked a little confused. Seeing my hesitant expression, he added, "I don't know what things were like with that Alexander guy of yours, but to me, cars are functional objects, not temples of worship. They get people—and dogs—from Point A to Point B. So get her in there."

"What if she runs around at the mill, in mud or grass or something, and then gets your car all dirty on the way back?"

He shrugged. "Doesn't matter." He grinned then, a cocky grin. "If it's ever too dirty for me, I'll buy a new one."

Suppressing my own grin, I took off Leika's leash and gave her the sign to jump in. Some people probably found Danny pretentious, but I liked that about him. He managed to walk the fine line between arrogance and charm.

When we turned onto the highway, there was a surprising amount of traffic, like everyone in our rural area was going out to run errands at the same time.

"We don't actually have the whole day today," Danny said. "I have a fight this evening."

"A fight? Kickboxing?"

"Yeah. Nothing big. Just a little competition in Feuerbach."

Somehow, I just couldn't reconcile the idea of Danny and martial arts. He seemed way too kind and friendly for something like that.

"Can I come?" I asked.

He looked surprised. "Sure, if you want."

I nodded happily.

"Let's do it, then… And, actually, you could come over next Saturday, too, if you're free. I won't be able to pick you up until evening, though. I'll be out during the day."

"Oh? Big plans?"

"I always go running in the morning, and I have a photo shoot in the afternoon. That shouldn't take long, though."

"I could go running with you," I suggested.

He laughed. "I don't think that will work."

"Excuse me? I can run, too," I snapped, offended.

"Okay, if you insist… Then I'll pick you up at eight on Saturday morning, and we'll go running together. And you can wait for me at my place afterward. Tina will be there, so you won't get bored."

In my head, I was jumping for joy. I'd managed to get my way again. But then something else occurred to me. "How does that even work? Doing martial arts *and* modeling?"

"What do you mean?"

"Well, you know. Black eyes, knocked-out teeth…"

He laughed again, making me realize just how much I loved the sound of his laughter. I couldn't imagine a more beautiful sound. "Makeup and the right lighting can work wonders. Anyway, these fights aren't about life and death, they're about technique. I rarely do full-contact fights anymore."

"Why?" I was sure the world championship certificate I'd seen at his place had said "full contact."

"Personal reasons. Full-contact fights can get really bloody. But light contact is about points, not about knocking the other person out. There's also semi-contact, but to me, that's not even martial arts. You might as well just join an arts-and-crafts club."

"So, I don't need to prepare myself for spurting blood? Life-threatening injuries?"

He shrugged and turned onto a dirt road. "Blood—not necessarily. Injuries—sure, but you can get those in training, too."

"You've never been seriously injured doing it?"

"Sure, I have. I've had stitches a bunch of times. Broken arm, broken collarbone, broken rib, tendon injuries… I've even broken the same bone three times. But that was my fault. If you're too dumb to master a certain kick, you should definitely not try it a million times."

"Good Lord. Riding sounds like kid stuff in comparison."

"Well, I started when I was eleven, and I've been doing it three to four hours every day since then. So, considering how long it's been, I haven't gotten *that* many injuries."

We drove past an old mill with a large, worn water wheel. A few pitiful patches of snow remained on the surrounding meadow, stubbornly resisting the sun. Danny parked the car horizontally across the grass, in front of a paddock.

"What made you decide to do martial arts in the first place?" I asked.

Danny pulled the hand brake and gave me a look I couldn't quite identify. Was there a challenge in his eyes? Daring me to dig deeper? "I suddenly had the feeling that I needed to defend myself," he said simply.

"Why?" I asked, holding his stare.

"We're here," he said, tearing his eyes away and rummaging around in his bag.

"So, if a gang attacked you today, do you think you could take them?"

"How many?" he asked, distracted.

"Hm… Let's say five."

"Yeah, I could handle five. Unless they had assault rifles." He pulled a plastic baggie out of his bag. It held pieces of cheese. After climbing out of the car, he opened one of the back doors. "I'll just say hello to your girl first, and then I'll introduce you to Maya."

I got out as well and watched him with my dog. He was squatting, his back to Leika, with his hand stretched toward her, the cheese sitting in his palm.

I was thrilled to see how well he knew his way around difficult dogs. He was doing exactly the right thing: making himself small in order to seem non-threatening and avoiding all eye contact, which the dog could easily mistake for a challenge. Leika ducked down, snuck up to him, but then jumped back and whined softly. Then, in one swift movement, she dashed forward and grabbed the cheese. Danny didn't move, didn't make the mistake many people made at that point, which was to try and touch her. Instead, he waited until Leika had retreated again, and then he slowly straightened.

"So," he said, "from now on, we'll do that every time we see each other. Come on, I'll introduce you to Maya."

I took the hand he offered me, and we walked to the nearby paddock.

Where Maya lived.

Because Maya was a pony.

A fat little pony, about four feet eight or nine, with a scraggly gray coat flecked with white. Her thick, black mane fell to either side of her stout neck. When Danny called her, she trotted over to us and blew her warm breath into my face. I didn't think I'd ever seen such a friendly pony. There were two other animals in the paddock as well, both probably at least part Shetland. As for Maya, I had no idea what breed she might be. Maybe a Norwegian fjord horse? But she wasn't the right color. Probably just a total mix.

Danny pointed to the other ponies. "That's Pablo, and the bigger one there is Josto. They belong to the children's home I was in. Maya's mine. The girls in the home take care of her and ride her. She's not the kind of horse you'd ride—she's old and partly lame, and she doesn't know a thing about dressage. But she's perfect for little kids to trot around on."

At some point in that explanation, he'd switched from German into English. I actually did know English, but Danny spoke too quickly and his American accent was too strong for me to catch every word. I tapped him timidly on the arm. "Um, wrong language," I said in German.

"Oh, sorry," he murmured, switching back. "Even though I've lived here for years, I still do that sometimes when I get nervous."

He's nervous? Why? Because of me?

"I mostly think in English," he said, tapping his forehead. "That's probably why."

Despite having lived in Germany for nearly ten years, he still seemed more American than German.

"Which language do you dream in?"

"A mix of both. I usually don't notice when it switches from one to the other."

His mind was fascinating. "You were saying something about Maya," I reminded him, eager to know everything I could about him.

"Oh, yeah," he said and repeated what he'd said before, except in German this time.

"In your text, you said she was really important to you. Have you had her long?"

"I bought her two years ago," Danny said. "All signs pointed to her not having long to live, but she made it through some rough patches and she's still trucking."

"Why in the world would anyone buy a sick old pony?"

"I dunno." He shrugged. "I couldn't help it. She was part of this circus that I drove past every day. She was injured and bedraggled, and no one was looking after her, so I asked if I could take her. It was a pity purchase. She was just as lost and lonely as I was."

My jaw dropped. *Lost and lonely?* Those were the last words I'd have ever used to describe him.

Suddenly, I wanted to touch him. I reached for his arm and pulled him closer— so close that I could smell him, could feel his breath on my neck. The air began to crackle with electricity. I sought his eyes and lost myself in them, the way I always did. I stretched my chin up toward him. He tilted his head and kissed me carefully, almost tentatively. I held back, let him take the lead. He parted my lips with his tongue. We kissed more deeply, almost urgently, and I met his tongue with my own...

I took a quick gulp of air and felt him breathing faster as well. I gripped his hair with both hands, then let my fingers glide down his neck and shoulders, toward his chest. He stiffened immediately and broke off the kiss, stepping away from me again.

He took a deep breath and gripped my wrist to stop my hand. "Come on," he said. "Let's go get Maya and take a walk."

Running away, I thought. *That's what he's doing right now, running away.*

But from what? And why?

When we reached the stall, he took a bridle off a hook on the wall and buckled it in place on Maya's head, along with the bit. I called Leika over, and we headed away from the paddock.

We walked side by side for a while in silence. Danny held the pony's reins in his right hand and held out his left to me. I took it, and our fingers intertwined. Two of his fingers, two of mine, one of his, one of mine...

A weird way of holding hands.

"When are you going to pick me up for the fight tonight?" I asked.

"You can just come straight there with me. We can get a bite to eat and then drive over together. Saves time."

I grinned. "But then I'll smell like pony."

He raised an eyebrow. "It's a martial arts arena, not a fashion show. Nobody will care."

"What about Leika?"

"Leave her at my place, and we'll pick her up afterward. Unless you think she'll get scared?"

"Aren't you afraid she'll break your stuff?" I thought of Alexander, who was constantly worried about Leika knocking things over or chewing his stuff up or peeing everywhere. Which she never did, of course.

He stared at me, genuinely baffled. "Why are you always so worried about her ruining my stuff? It's just stuff. It can be replaced."

"She won't break anything," I told him. "And being alone in unfamiliar apartments doesn't frighten her. We just have to spread out a blanket for her and give her a bowl of water."

Danny nodded. "No problem." He was wonderfully easy-going when it came to these kinds of things. "Let's go back." He nodded at Maya. "Want to get on?"

"You know how to ride?" I asked, shocked.

He shook his head. "Nope. Not at all."

I laughed. "Let me guess: just enough to get by?" I asked, thinking back to his dance skills at the Mouse Trap.

He smiled. "Exactly. Besides, she'll pretty much go home on her own."

"Can she carry us both?"

"Hm... I'm about one seventy-five. You?"

"One twenty."

"She can handle it this once," he decided. "It's not going to be all day or anything." He placed his hands on the pony's back, pushed up, and swung himself onto her. Then he scooted backward a little and patted the space in front of him.

"In front of you?" I asked, confused.

"Of course," he said with a crooked grin. "I have to keep an eye on you."

"Um..." I looked down in embarrassment. "I'll never make it up there without a saddle."

"No?" He gasped in mock horror.

I smirked. "I'm afraid not."

Danny rolled his eyes toward the sky and sighed theatrically, then swung his leg back over the pony's neck and slid to the ground. I bent one knee and gripped Maya's thick mane, and Danny hefted me up onto her back. Then he got on again, behind me. Reaching past my hips to take the reins, he clicked his tongue, and Maya set into motion immediately. She trotted along obediently, with no need for him to drive her on or slow her down, and even without a saddle, she was as comfortable to sit on as a stuffed rocking horse. She had to be a real blessing for the girls at the children's home.

After a while, Danny apparently got uncomfortable holding the reins, because he pressed them into my hand. They could just as well have been hanging between Maya's ears, though—it wouldn't have made a difference. The pony never strayed from her path to the paddock.

Without warning, Danny wrapped his arms around my hips. My pulse sped up as he placidly laid his chin on my shoulder and made himself comfortable.

It occurred to me then that, from where he sat behind me, his hands were completely free to roam wherever he chose. Not that they had so far. But the possibility completely distracted me. Maya sensed my change in mood immediately, turning her ears back like she was picking up radar, and she increased the pace.

At that exact moment, a tractor came barreling around the corner, moving much too fast. Instead of stopping, the driver honked at us. Frightened, Maya reared back. I was used to that kind of thing, and it wouldn't have thrown me off balance if someone hadn't been holding on to me. Danny and I slid back a bit before desperately leaning forward, trying to shift our weight. Maya set her front hooves down again, only to catapult her rear legs upward. Neither of us had expected that, and we flew over the pony's head in a high arc.

Of course, we landed on the gravel path instead of the soft grass to either side of us. Out of habit, I gripped the reins tightly, and Maya came to an immediate stop. The tractor drove onward. Leika bounded toward me, whining, and licked my face.

"Fuck." Danny sat up and shook himself. "Are you hurt?"

I struggled into a half-sitting position, laughing. "No, I'm fine. Man, Maya's really got energy. You wouldn't think it from looking at her. How about you— everything okay?"

"Never better." He grinned but still eyed me critically. "You're bleeding."

I looked down, and sure enough, my hands were scraped, and blood was dripping from a long, thin wound on my left wrist. I wiped it away with my right hand. The wound wasn't deep.

"You're bleeding too," I remarked, pointing to his knee. Danny's jeans were completely torn up at the knees. And his injury looked more serious than mine—a thin rivulet of blood was running down his leg.

"No, no, no, goddammit." He seemed panicked, which I couldn't understand. He was a kickboxer, so surely he wasn't afraid of a little blood.

He's clearly a nutjob!

Good to see my inner voice had survived the fall as well.

"Let me see," I said, reaching for his leg.

"Get away!" he shrieked, smacking my hand.

I stared at him, speechless. I'd just wanted to help!

"Sorry," he said quickly. "Sorry, I'm sorry, I didn't want to hurt you, sorry, sorry!" He was switching back and forth between German and English. According to his earlier revelation, that meant he was nervous.

His excessive apology confused me even more.

Lunatic! my inner voice howled at me. *He's not just weird about blue, he's weird about blood, too!*

"I just wanted to look at it and help you," I said defensively.

"No need, everything's fine!" He stood up, but made no move to help me up. Instead, he carefully wiped his hands on his pants. When he was finished, he seemed to have himself under control again. "Shall we continue?"

I nodded and stood up.

"Come here, I'll help you back onto the horse." He gripped my shin and lifted me back onto the pony's back, then began trotting along beside us, with Leika hovering close by.

"Aren't you getting on, too?"

"No."

"Why not? You scared?"

Danny laughed derisively. "Oh, for sure! I've never been so scared in my entire life." Then he fell silent, wordlessly regarding the blood smears on his hands. I could tell he was putting his walls back up. His whole mood had completely changed.

"Is it because of tonight?" I suddenly realized. "Are you not allowed to fight now?"

He glanced up at me, and I detected the faintest hint of a smile at the corners of his mouth. "Because of a skinned knee?" He raised an eyebrow and gave me a *have you lost your mind* look.

"What is it, then?" I asked quietly, but he'd shut down again, and he didn't say another word until we got back to his place.

***

Danny entered the apartment first. Christina met us in the hallway.

"Tina," Danny said to her quietly, and whatever he was communicating to her with just that one word, she understood it immediately. She nodded, then took my elbow and led me to one bathroom, while Danny disappeared into the other. As I washed my hands, Tina fetched disinfectant and a large Band-Aid.

"Hold still, Jessica," she said and rinsed the wound. I watched her. She had a beautiful face. She reminded me of an angel, though the hair color wasn't quite right. Although she was a little taller than me, she probably weighed a few pounds less. Carefully, she applied the bandage to the meticulously cleaned wound.

"Thanks," I murmured.

She beamed at me. "Sure. Happy to help."

"Why's he like that?" I asked, tipping my head toward the hall.

"Like what?" Christina blinked a tiny bit too innocently. Somehow, I got the feeling that she knew exactly what I meant.

"So dramatic. He made this tiny little incident into a huge thing. We fell off of Maya, and he's acting like it was the end of the world."

She shrugged. "You fell off his horse. He's probably really embarrassed. Putting all the blame on himself."

That sounded plausible. Why did I overthink everything all the time? I decided what I needed was a little distraction. "I'm going to his competition tonight. Are you?"

She shook her head with an apologetic smile.

"Okay. Well, Leika's going to stay here." I gestured to the panting dog, who had settled in a safe distance away from the girl she didn't know. "I'd like to leave her in Danny's room. It'd be best if you could give her a little space. She's not very good with strangers."

"No problem. I won't go in there." Christina touched my arm. "Come to the kitchen! I made dinner. Fettuccine with rutabaga sauce—I'm sure there's enough for all of us."

As we headed to the kitchen, Danny emerged from the other bathroom and fell in step behind us.

I was starting to really like it here, in this apartment that I'd only been to twice. Christina and Danny both made me feel right at home. Nobody minded my panting dog with her dirty paws, and there were no questions, no rigid expectations.

Suddenly, I wished I could be part of it, too.

***

There really was plenty of food for all of us, even though Danny ate enough for three people.

"I need energy," he said apologetically, as I stared at him in amazement, wondering where he could possibly put all that food.

Together, we set up a blanket and water bowl for Leika, and then he packed his gym bag.

"You'll meet Jörg there, too," he said as he stuffed a pair of jogging pants into the bag.

"Who's Jörg?"

"He's from the children's home. He looked after me. He's been my legal guardian ever since my parents...died." I saw him and Christina exchange a quick glance.

"You like him? Is he nice?" I asked.

"He's the best thing that could have happened to me. I love him." He picked up his bag and his car keys and went over to Christina. "Might not be back until late," he said. "Will you be okay?"

She nodded but bit her lower lip. For a moment, I was afraid she'd throw her arms around his neck and beg him to stay.

"See you later," he said tenderly, kissing her on the forehead.

Just when I was starting to think I could like Christina…

Snorting loudly, I followed Danny out to the hall.

"What's wrong?"

I rolled my eyes, shaking my head, and walked right past him to the car.

He raised his arms, looking baffled. "Did I do something wrong?"

Yes! I screamed at him in my head. *You're a moody freak with the audacity to kiss another girl in front of me—one who lives with you, no less!*

I crossed my arms and nearly chewed the inside of my lip bloody.

Danny regarded me for a moment. "You're jealous," he concluded at last.

I wanted to yell at him, *Ding, ding, ding! We have a winner!* Instead, I stared morosely at the ground.

"How do I explain this to you…" He hesitated. "Christina is like a sister to me. We're very close, but in a different way than you think. There's nothing sexual between us. I wouldn't sleep with her if she was the last woman on Earth."

Seems like he feels the same way about you! my inner voice pointed out disdainfully.

Sighing softly, Danny stepped closer and lifted my chin, the way he always did when he had something truly important to say to me. "You're going to have to trust me," he whispered. "One day you'll understand, and then you'll look back at your jealousy and laugh. Believe me!"

He kissed me on the lips and then got into the car.

"He's not concentrating at all," Jörg muttered, giving me an accusatory look, as though it was all my fault. I suppose it probably was.

I'd liked Jörg from the moment I met him. In his mid-forties, with two grown daughters, he was the typical friendly-dad type. His gentle, light-brown eyes had immediately made me feel like I could trust him unconditionally. Though, now that he'd realized I was affecting Danny's performance, those eyes weren't quite so gentle.

Danny's opponent was a young Russian who was half a head taller than him—and definitely stronger. But what Danny lacked in strength, he made up for in stamina and speed. Still, his trainer—a muscular Turkish-German who ran the gym Danny worked at—seemed dissatisfied with his performance. In the break between rounds, he stomped into the arena, snorting with anger, and pulled Danny aside.

"Uh-oh, Dogan's really mad," Jörg said. "Danny's about to get an earful."

We went down to the mats as well, to where Danny was leaning against the wall, breathing heavily. He was wearing his gym's colors, along with red bandages on his hands and feet.

Dogan was pacing back and forth in front of him. He reminded me of the red bull from *The Last Unicorn*.

"DAN, WHAT ARE YOU DOING?" Dogan bellowed. "What do you think this is, girls' ballet?"

Danny rolled his eyes, but his trainer ignored him as he began analyzing the fight. "This guy's stronger than you. Miles ahead of you—"

"Whoa, wait, really?" Danny gasped theatrically. "I know this will come as a shock to you, but…I've already noticed!"

"Well, I'm genuinely surprised, since you're lolling around out there like you're half-asleep," Dogan snapped. "If you know he's stronger than you, why are you trying to box him the whole time? You *can't* box, so cut it out already!"

Danny nodded in understanding.

"And all the stupid hopping around, what's that about? You trying to bore him until he falls asleep?"

"That'd be something!" Danny remarked jovially.

Dogan cuffed him on the shoulder. "Quit grinning. Pull yourself together and start using your damn legs. Kick, don't punch!"

"Yeah, I got it."

"Then *do* it, for God's sake. You had three perfect opportunities for a side kick! Three! How many of them did you see, hm?"

"None."

"Exactly, that's the problem. Why not?"

Danny shrugged. "Forgot."

"If you forget again, I'll forget that I'm not supposed to throw anything at your damn head." Dogan shook his head in exasperation. "You completely jacked up that flying kick earlier, too. Who were you trying to impress with that? My ten-year-old daughter can do better. What's the most important thing about a flying kick?"

"Kick at the highest point of the jump," Danny parroted obediently.

"So why the hell did you kick just before you landed?"

The referee stepped into the middle of the mats again, and Dogan gave Danny a rough jab in the ribs. "Get yourself together, kid. Feint low to the right, high kick left to the temple."

"Yeah, yeah, keep your shirt on," Danny muttered. "There's still another round left."

The referee shooed the trainers away from the mats, and we went back to our seats, Dogan following behind us. He gave me a friendly smile as we sat again. "Hey, I'm Dogan. Don't worry, Danny and I actually get along just fine."

Yeah, I got that. It was like a military barracks around here.

"Jessica." I extended a hand. "Have you been training him long?"

"Five years," Dogan said. "Since he moved here. So, long enough to know he sometimes needs a kick in the ass to get going."

Dogan seemed a tick too pushy to me. Maybe that was how trainers had to be, though. Maybe that was the whole reason Danny was so successful.

"Push kick, Dan!" Dogan shouted excitedly, clapping his hands. I decided then that I did like him. Suddenly, he jumped up and whistled. "Yesss! Now he's got it!"

Danny had hit his opponent in the shoulder with a crazy-looking kick. The Russian briefly struggled to keep his balance before returning to home position. At that moment, Danny faked a kick to the Russian's shin with his right foot, and when the other man moved to block, Danny smashed him in the face with the back of his left foot. But the Russian reacted with unexpected agility, catching Danny's foot and attempting to throw him backward.

"Why's he so lame today?" Dogan grouched.

Danny took the opportunity for a roundhouse kick, using the leg caught in his opponent's hand as support and then twisting around quickly to ram his right shin into the guy's ribs. The Russian stumbled several times, and Danny got in a few more kicks, adding to his score.

Slowly, he was catching up. He had changed his entire strategy in one moment. He'd stopped punching, stopped jumping away from his opponent—what Dogan had described as "stupid hopping around." It meant he took a couple more punches, but he got in quite a few kicks in return.

Danny took another hit that sent him stumbling backward, but he used it as a chance to rebound and get a running start. He jumped six feet through the air and hit his opponent's chest with both feet at once—the flying kick Dogan had requested. The Russian went sprawling to the mat, where he lay motionless for several seconds.

The kick looked great to me, but Dogan buried his face in his hands and shook his head. "He screwed it up again." Danny still got three points for it, though, which put him in the lead.

And he ended up winning, though not by much.

Dogan looked more or less satisfied with the results, and to my relief, no blood had been shed.

I followed Jörg down to the mats and threw my arms around Danny's neck. His T-shirt was so wet it would have created a puddle had I wrung it out, but I didn't mind—I was just glad he'd made it through the fight.

His kiss was salty, and his hair was sticking out in two clumps like antennae. Apart from a tiny, nearly bloodless mark on his cheek, he was unhurt. And I'd decided that I needed to start coming to his fights and practices whenever possible, so I could enjoy the sight of him. For I'd learned that I especially liked the way he looked in athletic gear. Just the way his jogging pants hung at his hips was enough to make me want to whisk him off to my bedroom. Even though he was sweaty and disheveled—or maybe precisely because of that.

After he'd showered and changed, we picked up Leika and he took me home. I nearly fell asleep in the car after the day we'd had.

Why the hell didn't Danny ever seem to get tired?

Chapter Six

February 2000

I was shivering in the foggy semidarkness, staring at my shoes and fully regretting having insisted on going jogging with Danny. The BMW turned into the parking lot, its headlights illuminating me and Leika. Along with the normal low-beam headlights, he'd also turned on his fog lights. They were blue.

Danny parked the car, got out, and gave me a fleeting kiss. "Morning," he said, wide-awake and in high spirits, as usual. "Before we go, it's Leika time." He had cheese with him again, and he repeated the same procedure as last week. It went quicker this time. Leika snagged the treat with less hesitation and even sniffed Danny's hand thoroughly. He still made no move to pet her.

"Leika's cool," he said. "She wants to make friends. It just takes her a little longer."

"A lot of people don't understand that," I said.

"That's the problem." Danny looked up at me with an almost pained expression. "Most people have all the time in the world. They'll live to be eighty or older. But they don't use the time they have. They waste it on the couch, in front of the TV, or at the computer. They don't have time for the things that make life really worth living: other people, their friends and family, the friendship of a dog, the beauty of nature… They've lost all mindfulness."

Here he was, philosophizing about time and human nature, and all I could think about was how cold my feet were.

"So much pain and suffering could be prevented if the people in this miserable country would open their eyes and see what's happening around them," he went on. "But they're just caught up in their own insignificant little problems, focused on their own pathetic existence. They could care less about the living beings around them."

"You really hate it here in Germany," I remarked. Even then, I knew I was misinterpreting his words, but I didn't have the mental power to think any deeper than that.

He laughed softly to himself and shook his head. "It's no better in America. People are the same all over the world."

Was I like that too? Someone who only cared about herself and her own life? Did I use my time well?

I resolved to pay more attention to that kind of thing in the future.

Danny opened the door for Leika, and she hopped up into the back seat without a moment's hesitation. We drove to Danny's place, where he parked his car so we could walk out to the fields. After a few minutes, we started running, and I immediately knew I'd never be able to keep up with his pace.

"Slow down!" I ordered. Obediently, he fell back and started running directly behind me.

"Stop crowding me," I grouched.

"Quit your whining," Danny chided, "you wanted to come." He ran close on my heels to make it clear that he'd much rather be going faster.

"You said we were going *jogging*," I said, still whining. "Nobody said anything about running around like maniacs."

"You need to listen better, Jessica." He grinned wolfishly. "I said we were going *running*. I didn't say anything about jogging, and I certainly didn't say anything about waddling around like ducks."

"Are you saying I *waddle*?"

His grin broadened. "Yep. Like a very waddly duck, in fact. Fortunately, there aren't any ducks around here, so I don't have to worry about mixing you up with—"

"That's it!" I whirled around and boxed him in the ribs. He laughed, and I knew he was picturing me with a little yellow duck face. I hit him harder.

"You're crazy," he said. "You're gonna leave bruises!"

"That's. The. Goal." One word per punch. That was effective. My outrage was beginning to subside.

Danny grabbed my wrists and held them in place behind my back. "You know what, Ducky?" He snickered. "Let's go back to my place and get my mountain bike. Then you'll have half a chance of keeping up with me."

"What did you just call me?" I tried to hit him again, but he didn't release my wrists.

"What? 'Ducky' is cute," he said defensively. "It's like 'honey' or 'dear.'"

"No, it's like what a toddler calls their rubber duck!" I complained. "Which is not a term of endearment!"

"Yeah, you're right," he admitted, his face still screwed up in laughter. In fact, he looked like he was about a second away from losing his balance, he was cracking up so hard.

"Let me go, and fight like a man!" I snarled, trying to kick him.

He dodged my foot effortlessly. "Surely you're not *growling* at me?" He feigned outrage. "Doesn't your dog do enough of that for everyone?"

"I won't growl at you if you don't call me a duck!"

"Speaking of your dog…" He looked over at Leika, who was standing beside us, wagging her tail as she glanced back and forth between us. "Can she keep up with a bike?"

"Of course she can. She's a hunting dog. I take her with me when I go out riding, too. She's in good shape!"

"Unlike you, you mean?"

"That's enough out of you for one day, you little—"

He bent down and kissed me for so long that I forgot what I was going to say.

Things went a lot better with the bike. The seat was a little high for me, but I managed. Danny ran alongside it easily, and after a couple of miles, I had to admit to myself that he might even pass me. Leika was loping along easily, almost in power-saving mode, her long tongue flopping out of her mouth.

After about four miles, as measured by the tachometer on the bike, Danny turned around and started for home. "Before you fall into a coma," he said with a wink. I tried to casually extend my foot and kick him, but I only succeeded in making the bike wobble all over the place.

He gave me a pitying shake of his head. "It would seem you survived without me for almost eighteen years, but when I watch you, I genuinely wonder how you managed."

I stuck my tongue out at him. Pedaling along beside him gave me time to watch him run. He was wearing a blue cap pushed far back from his forehead, a blue hoodie, and blue jogging pants with white stripes and white drawstrings at the waist. He seemed to have an infinite supply of sports gear. In my mind, I had already taken it off him a hundred and fifty times…

There was no point denying it any longer. I'd completely fallen for him. I wanted him more than anything in the world. I wanted him to belong to me, skin and hair and all. Someday he'd be mine.

Mine, my inner voice agreed. *All mine!*

I took a quick shower, changed into the clothes I'd brought, and joined Christina in the kitchen. We made breakfast together while Danny got cleaned up, and then the three of us ate together in the dining room.

After breakfast, Danny rose from his chair and said, "I'll be back by this evening." Christina and I both walked him to the front door. He pulled me close and gave me a tender kiss on the lips, then stepped over to Christina and kissed her on the cheek.

Suddenly, he seemed to find the whole situation a little strange, because as he was walking out the door, he stopped and glanced distrustfully between the two of us. "I can leave the two of you here alone, can't I?"

"Of course," we said in unison.

He nodded but didn't look convinced. "Be nice, Tina!" He gave her a look of warning that would have made me curl up into a ball, but Christina didn't even bat an eyelash. She held his gaze, staring back at him in defiance. I secretly admired her for it.

"Make yourself at home," she told me once the door had closed behind him. "What's ours is yours."

Nothing here is yours anyway, I sniped at her in my head, and then wondered why I was so hostile toward her. I recalled Danny's philosophizing from earlier, the things he'd said about people and their problems, and immediately felt like a jerk. She probably really was just trying to be friendly, and I was so hell-bent on not liking her that I couldn't even see it.

I'd actually been planning on retreating to Danny's bedroom until that evening, maybe poking around in his stuff, taking a nap in his bed, and dreaming of things that he apparently wasn't interested in. Instead, I followed Christina into the living room and dropped down onto the couch beside her. Leika followed me in and sniffed Christina's bare leg cautiously. Christina held very still for a moment, then lowered her hand with almost imperceptible slowness, so that Leika could sniff it as well. Suddenly, Leika laid her nose on Christina's knee.

I couldn't believe it. This could not possibly be my dog! Leika wagged her tail happily as Christina spoke to her in a quiet voice, telling her what a pretty girl she was. Like Danny, Christina hadn't tried to pet her. After a while, Leika rolled underneath the coffee table, looking perfectly content.

Christina took a nail file out of her purse and began filing her pink fingernails.

"What do you think of him?" she suddenly asked me.

What did I think of him?

He's fascinating. Breathtaking. Sexy. Amazing.

"He's really nice," I said out loud. "He doesn't really open up very much, but he's cool."

Cool? I wanted to collapse to the floor laughing and beating my fists against the carpet. That was the understatement of the century!

Christina glanced up for a moment, scrutinizing me with her green, cat-like eyes. Once again, I came to the nearly painful realization of just how similar she and Danny were.

"He doesn't have much experience with serious relationships," she said at last. "Just be a little patient with him. It'll be okay."

I laughed. "Yeah, sure. Christina, I wasn't born yesterday. Guys like Danny just have to snap their fingers and half a dozen women will come running from every direction."

"Maybe so…" She seemed to stretch the words out deliberately. "But he doesn't snap his fingers."

"I see. And why not?"

"You'll have to find that out for yourself."

My mood took a turn for the worse. I wished I'd gone straight to the bedroom.

But I remembered Danny's words about people once again, and as long as we were stuck here together, maybe I could try to befriend her—and get a little information along the way. "How long have you been living here?" I asked innocently.

"About two years. But not the whole time. I was gone for almost eight months last year, and then I came back. I drift around like a leaf in the wind."

"Why did you come back? Because it's cheaper to split the rent?"

She laughed out loud, looking genuinely surprised. "Jessica, I don't pay rent here. Danny does that. Electricity, water, food, insurance—he pays everything. He even buys me my clothes."

Was she trying to provoke me again?

"Isn't that totally unfair?" was all I could manage to get out with any semblance of calm.

Now she was really taken aback. "Everything about life is unfair," she told me. "He doesn't mind. He earns a lot, and I don't. So he foots the bills, and I take care of the house—clean, wash dishes, iron, things like that. It's fair in a way."

She's unbelievable! She just mooches her way through life!

I didn't get it. People didn't do things that way where I came from. They didn't just *give* things to each other—certainly not months of free room and board in an 1100-square-foot apartment with a huge backyard. No, the people I knew were penny-pinchers to the bone, dividing up every expense with pedantic meticulousness.

"How do you guys know each other, anyway?" I resolved to focus my interrogation on the most important facts.

Christina set the nail file aside and studied her nails intently. "We met a few years ago, in a therapy group for children who'd suffered severe trauma."

I blinked. Had his parents' deaths affected him that terribly?

"What exactly was he doing there?" I asked carefully.

She gave me a challenging look. "Why don't you ask him yourself?"

Right. I'll just bring it up casually this evening...

That would never work. And Tina knew that perfectly, if she knew him half as well as she claimed she did.

I couldn't come up with a response, so I returned to our previous subject instead. "To be totally honest, I think that's wrong of you," I found myself saying. "You live in his apartment, completely at his expense. I mean, I totally understand if you don't have the money to pay rent. But couldn't you look for a job?"

Her eyes widened, darkening with anger, and when she spoke again, her voice was dangerously quiet. "I used to earn a lot of money, but Danny didn't think it was such a great job. He wanted me to stop doing what I was doing and go back to school."

"Why would he care how you earn a living?"

She stared at me. "I sold my body. And then bought drugs with the money I got. Mainly heroin."

"Very funny," I said. I was about to get up and leave—there was no point talking to her.

"It's true," she whispered, showing me the underside of her bony arm. Her wrist was crisscrossed with thin white lines—razor blade scars—and the crook of her elbow had several heavily scarred puncture wounds. Long since healed, but there was no doubt they were needle marks.

The blood drained out of my face. For a moment, I felt nauseated, and I scooted away from her reflexively, before I even realized I was doing it. "I'm telling Danny." As soon as the words were out of my mouth, I realized how ridiculous they sounded.

Christina seemed to agree, judging by her laughter. "Wake up, Sleeping Beauty," she said bitterly. "He's known for a long time now. I just told you he wasn't okay with it."

"Never..." My voice was steely, like I was trying to convince myself. "He would never... I mean, y-you..."

"You mean he would never let a drug-addicted prostitute live with him?" Christina broke in sardonically.

I felt the blood rush to my cheeks, not wanting to admit that I'd been thinking exactly that.

"Wake up," she repeated. "Danny's not the prince on a white stallion you apparently think he is. Stop expecting him to be something he's not!"

"How dare you!" I shrieked. She'd gone too far now. "Unlike you, I'm not expecting anything of him! He can be whatever he wants!"

"Oh, yeah?" Her green eyes glittered furiously. "Then why did it shock you that he'd let a heroin-addicted hooker live with him? Why were you so sure he'd never do such a thing?"

I had no answer to that, so instead I said, "You sure are overly interested in him, considering he's not your boyfriend!"

Christina leaned forward and fixed me with a penetrating gaze that I already knew all too well from someone else. "Danny's more than my boyfriend," she said. "He's my family. I love him more than anything. I would die for him without hesitation if I had the chance."

She meant every word of it, there was no doubt about that. Was this conversation actually happening?

"Jessica, I don't know what you're after here, but if you're looking for a little slice of paradise where unicorns gallop beneath a rainbow, and laughing children sit in a meadow eating cotton candy...you've come to the wrong place. Things here aren't all sunshine and roses, so if that's what you're going for..." She gestured to the window. "Keep looking."

Now she'd finally succeeded in making me nervous. "If he's so unbelievably important to you, why are you trying to destroy his relationship and frighten his girlfriend away?"

"To protect him," she said icily. "From people like you."

"From people like me?" I was shrieking again. "*You* guys are the weird ones here! *I'm* normal!"

"That's exactly what I mean. People who think like that, I'd rather not have around Danny!"

"That's not your decision to make."

"Listen to me very, very carefully, Sleeping Beauty." She put her long, perfectly manicured fingernails against my chest. "Danny's been to hell and back. The last thing he needs is a person who's going to hurt him even more than he's already been hurt." Her eyes blazed dangerously. "So if you hurt him? I'll kill you."

I had no doubt of it.

"Christina." I held up my hands, trying to placate her. "I don't want to hurt him." After a hesitation, I added, "I love him."

She removed her fingers from my chest, and her expression grew soft. "Good, good," she murmured in a tone that was suddenly completely friendly as she extended a hand to me. "Then there's nothing standing in the way of us being friends. Want some coffee?"

We sat at the little table in the corner of the kitchen, drinking coffee as though nothing had happened. After that, Christina disappeared into the bathroom to take a long bubble bath. I decided to take Leika out for another little walk.

She was stretched out in the hallway and apparently didn't even have enough energy to lift her head. The early-morning athletics had clearly been too much for her after all. When I called, she sluggishly got to her feet and let me put her leash on.

Just as I was about to leave the apartment, I saw that the door to Christina's room was open. She'd said I should make myself at home…

So I stepped inside and started rummaging around. I didn't really know what I was looking for, but I was entirely convinced I would stumble upon some huge cache of needles or plastic baggies of drugs.

Of course, I found nothing of the sort. No heroin, no syringes, and nothing that even suggested she'd ever been a prostitute. Actually, there wasn't even any dust. Apart from a few pairs of high heels lying around, it was the cleanest room I'd ever seen. Not the way I'd picture an ex-hooker's room.

As I started to leave, my gaze fell on an old notebook sitting beside her bed. Tentatively, I picked it up and stood there thumbing quickly through it. It was full of poetry—something else she and Danny had in common. I turned to a page at random and skimmed it.

His scent on my body,
no one there to free me.
Please let him be finished.
I just want to die.

Shaking, I went to set the notebook down, to quit snooping before my shock became unbearable, but another poem caught my eye:

Mama, Stay Home!
I am alone, Mama cannot protect me.
All of my strength will do me no good.
I just lie there, still and helpless,
Wanting to scream that I don't want this.

But he creeps closer and comes inside.
"Come, child, you have to be Mama now!"
Pain and fear wash over me.

I raised my eyes from the notebook—and saw Christina standing in the doorway, hair wrapped up in a towel, arms folded, watching me. She even had the same *posture* as Danny. She was practically a mirror image of him.

"Sorry," I said, not really sure whether I was apologizing for snooping through her things or for her past.

Her lower lip trembled. "It was a long time ago," she said, as though that somehow made things better. "I was seven."

I nodded almost imperceptibly as I handed her the notebook. She didn't really seem angry that I'd been looking through her stuff.

"I'm sorry," I said again, this time definitely meaning her past.

"You don't have anything to be sorry for. It's not your fault."

Still stunned, I walked into the hall and left the apartment, with Leika in tow.

"Danny, too?" I'd wanted to ask Christina, but it seemed unfair to ask about him in that situation. Besides, I thought I knew the answer. She'd dropped plenty of hints, and suddenly so many things made sense:

"That was my dad. Hit me in the face with a bottle."

"There have been worse periods in my life."

"You really have a picture-perfect family."

"I understand what abuse is like."

"I suddenly had the feeling that I needed to defend myself."

They were both damaged goods, in one way or another. All at once, I realized how much I actually liked Christina. It was impossible not to like her. She was so like Danny—in fact, they were eerily similar. Like peas in a pod, yin and yang. Same body language, same dark sense of humor, same hot temper. Same cautious, almost mistrustful approach, while still managing to be friendly and helpful to anyone they met. They judged people based on what they were like on the inside, not on how well they measured up to society's standards on the outside. And they tried to protect each other from people full of prejudice and rigid expectations. People like me.

They shared the same fate, connected at an emotional level I would never understand, let alone achieve.

Chapter Seven

March 2000

Spring came, and Danny and I started spending a lot of time outside—whenever he wasn't holed up in the gym, anyway. He spent several hours training at a time, at least four nights a week. On weekends, he often rode his bike up to the stables where I was riding. It didn't bother him that it was fifteen miles each way.

"I don't think it's strenuous, I think it's relaxing," he said once. 'Recreational activity,' he called it. When he arrived at the stables, he'd throw his bike down in the grass and hop up onto the fence surrounding the riding grounds, seemingly content to sit there eating apples and watching me ride. I'd usually finish by riding out into the fields for a while, and he'd bike alongside me before helping me unsaddle the horse and bring it back to its stall.

Danny's presence exponentially reduced my popularity with the other girls. Suddenly, I was the one with the hot boyfriend who apparently nobody thought I deserved. No other place in the world is such a hotbed of female cattiness as a riding stable. The other girls were always hanging around us, or rather, around Danny, in order to check him out. He never complained, but I could tell how uncomfortable it made him.

At first, he was friendly and helpful, as was his nature, but then it got out of hand. They were constantly asking him to come over and help them out with something. Could he just come get the saddle down from the top pole, or could he throw this hay bale over the wall, or could he hold this horse steady so they could get on or off? Eventually, we just started trying to keep our distance, which obviously made the others like me even less.

My brother, Thorsten, often drove me over to Danny's, as well. I'd bring my inline skates to accompany him on bike rides. I couldn't keep up, of course, because my skates were old and worn out—at least, that was the reason I chose to believe.

Finally, one of Danny's friends from the gym soldered a bracket onto his bike's cargo rack, and we attached a rope to it, with a grip handle on the end. That way, when he went out on longer bike trips, I could just hang on to the rope and let him pull me along. And I did. I did it on uphill stretches to conserve my strength, and on downhill stretches so that I could brake more easily. And I didn't let go on level roads, either—having him pull me along was just too much fun.

That spring, Danny had exams coming up for a certification he was doing in sports and fitness management, so he did something highly unusual for him: he sat down and studied. He was determined to do well on the exams, even though he'd already decided to quit working in fitness clubs and go into business for himself as a karate and kickboxing coach. I didn't like the idea of him giving up the job security he had being employed by someone else. No doubt he earned plenty as a model—far more than he'd ever earn as a personal trainer—but modeling didn't seem like a very future-safe plan. Then again, personal training probably wasn't something he could keep doing until retirement, either.

At any rate, there was no talking him out of it. And when he finally took the leap, it started well: he quickly had so many students that he was working four to six hours every day.

At the end of April, he decided to stop competing himself. He wanted to start leaving the actual fighting to his students. I'd gone to one of his fights just a week before, a full-contact fight. It had been a knockout fight, and I'd nearly died of fright watching it. Danny had won, but he hadn't come away unscathed: a black eye, bloody nose, sprained knuckle, and a scrape above his eye. After seeing that, I'd been wishing he'd stop fighting, or at least stick to light-contact fighting for points.

Yet, for some reason, when he actually decided he wanted to quit altogether, it didn't sit well with me.

When I mentioned it, all he said was, "I've won everything I can win. I won't make it to the pro world championships in this lifetime, not anymore. So why keep beating people up for no reason?"

Once he'd made his mind up about something, arguing about it was like arguing with a wall. "You're throwing away so much potential," I told him.

"I don't care," he said. That was what he always said when he considered a discussion closed.

Chapter Eight

May 2000

When Danny aced his certification exams, Jörg, Christina, Ricky, Simon, Danny, and I all went out to celebrate. Vanessa didn't join us, though. She and Ricky had just broken up, and although they'd parted as friends, she didn't want to see him just yet.

After bar-hopping for a while, we all sat around Danny's backyard late into the night. Finally, Christina cleared away the empty bottles, and Danny drove us home.

"You won't have to drive me around much longer," I said as he drove up to my building and shut off the engine. "Four more weeks, and then I can drive myself home!"

"I don't mind driving you, Ducky," he said. "I'm happy to do it."

"I mind, though. I'd like to be able to come out to see you without my brother."

Danny nodded. "Okay, I can understand that. But then you'll need a car. What kind of car would you want?"

"I've never told you this, but I already have a car," I told him. "I've had one for almost a year now."

He blinked. "Why would you own a car before you have a license?"

"Back when I was still with Alexander... Well, he works for Mercedes, and buying old, rare Mercedes models and restoring them is a hobby of his. I bought one off him. A 190. AMG, DTM edition." I was proud of that car. It was one-of-a-kind, lovingly cobbled together. I wouldn't have wanted any other one.

But Danny wrinkled his nose. I didn't know if it was because the car was from Alexander, or because he wanted to give me one himself. Maybe both. I suspected he'd been planning on doing just that for my eighteenth birthday. "Is it halfway decent, at least? Is it safe?"

"Of course!" I was indignant. "It's a Mercedes. Cars don't get any safer."

He nodded, obviously trying not to let his irritation show. "Maybe you should just start sleeping over at my place on weekends."

My heart began to race. I'd been wanting to do that for a long time, but I'd never had the guts to bring it up. "Sure, if you want," I said, trying to sound nonchalant.

"Why not, right? I mean, you stayed over once before."

That felt like a hundred years ago.

"You'll be eighteen soon. Then nobody else can have a say in it."

"Nobody would have a problem with it now, either," I said. "My parents like you a lot." It was true, they really did. We'd all gone out to eat together a few weeks before, so that they could meet him, and they'd liked him immediately.

How could anyone *not* like Danny?

"As soon as I'm back, you can stay over every weekend," he said, interrupting my train of thought. "During the week, too, if commuting all that way isn't too much trouble for you."

Back?

I eyed him distrustfully. "As soon as you're back from what?"

He hesitated. "Promise me you won't completely freak out."

My pulse sped up immediately, and I grew warm. "Where are you going?" I studied his face.

"Tina has to go back to a drug rehab clinic. Follow-up care, so to speak." He gave me a meaningful look. "She told me about your conversation." Of course she had. I'd thought she might, but then, all this time, Danny had been acting like everything was normal. "She's clean already. She spent thirty weeks there last year. Involuntary inpatient. She's doing well. I spent a long time trying to get her off the stuff, but it was tough. She kept relapsing. So, it's important for her to go back again this year to reinforce the progress she's made. If everything goes well, she can start working part-time this summer. I think I can get her a job at the gym, working at the juice bar..."

When he talked this much, it was usually because he was trying to avoid discussing something specific.

"Well, I'm very happy for her," I said, and I genuinely meant it. "I'll keep my fingers crossed that everything works out. But what exactly does Christina's rehab clinic have to do with you?"

Danny took a deep breath, as if bracing himself. "I'm going with her. I'm going to *stay* with her. We're leaving next week."

"What? Why? Why didn't anyone say anything to me about it?"

His gaze held mine fast. "She needs me. She can't do it alone. Someone needs to be there to support her, and I'm all she has. I'll be back, I promise!"

"How long will you be gone?" I made no effort to hide my displeasure.

"Depends. The plan for now is eight weeks. Six, if everything goes well... Ten, if it doesn't."

"Ten *weeks*?" I shrieked at him. My stomach cramped up in knots, and my blood began pulsing hotly in my veins. "And you're telling me *now*? A few days before you leave? We couldn't have discussed this sooner?"

"There's nothing to discuss." His voice remained steely. "I don't have a choice. This is about her life!"

Determined not to lose all composure, I clenched my purse tightly, as if I were trying to crumple it into a ball. "You're not responsible for her." I sounded like a sullen child.

"That's not how I see it, Jessica. Like I said, I'm all she has!"

I sighed deeply. "Right." Peas in a pod. Yin and yang. "Where is this place, then? I'll come visit you."

He closed his eyes, drumming his fingers on the steering wheel. "Too far for you to drive by yourself. But Jörg and Ricky are each planning to come at least once. They agreed to bring you with them, if you want. So that's two visits right there."

Wonderful. Thanks a lot, Christina! "As soon as I have my driver's license, I'll drive myself," I told him, still trying to process all this information.

"It's a pretty long trip, and you're a new driver," he pointed out with a skeptical raise of his brow.

"You're not worried, are you?"

"Of course I am! I've seen the way you ride a bike." He took my hand and looked deep into my eyes. "I still need you."

I stroked the back of his hand with my thumb. "Have you ever thought maybe it wouldn't be such a bad thing if you spent some time away from Christina?" I asked gently, rushing on before he could answer. "How are you going to explain the fact that you're there together, anyway? Will they let you stay with her if you're not family? Are you going to tell them you're her boyfriend or something?" The thought alone made me grit my teeth.

"No, of course not. She'll be there voluntarily this time, so she's allowed to bring someone along to support her. And besides..." Taking another deep breath, he let go of my hand and crossed his arms over his chest. "It's also a therapy center for people working through childhood trauma, so I belong there, too."

"Danny... Why do you belong there too?" I tried to meet his eyes, but he shut them, avoiding my gaze. His fingernails dug into the skin on his bare arms, and he pursed his lips grimly.

Slowly, I scooted toward him. "Talk to me, Danny, please," I said, trying to pry one of his arms loose. But the more I tugged, the more rigidly he kept them crossed against his body as he shrank away from me as far as he could inside the cramped car. For a moment, I was afraid he would simply get out and walk away.

Too close, a voice whispered inside me. *You're much too close to him!*

I let go of his arm so I could slide back into my seat, and he relaxed almost instantly. He took several deep, slow breaths before opening his eyes and blinking at me through his long lashes.

"You know why," he whispered. "And someday I'll tell you myself. I promise. Be patient with me."

I swallowed. "Okay."

He took my hand again and drew it in to give me a kiss on the finger. "Thank you."

"So, Tina will be working through her own trauma there, too?"

"Yeah."

Now I was the one bracing myself for a difficult conversation. This was a good opportunity to bring up something that had been bothering me for a long time. "She told me...she gets in bed with you when she can't sleep."

"That's true." He shifted uncertainly. "She does."

"Which means she'll probably do that at the rehab clinic, too, right? Where she'll be facing all of that again? She'll sneak into your room at night to sleep with you?"

Danny began chewing on his thumbnail. "Maybe, yeah. Is that a problem?"

"It is for me." I twirled a lock of hair around my finger awkwardly.

Just tell him already!

"I don't like it because I want you all to myself." There. Now it was out, and there was no taking it back.

Danny's expression remained earnest. "She just wants to feel protected, to be close to someone else. It's not about intimacy, it's about safety."

"Don't you think it's weird that a girl traumatized by rape would climb into bed with some other guy to feel safe?"

Danny snorted and looked at the ceiling. "Not at all. I mean, it's not just some guy she's crawling into bed with. It's *me*." He shook his head, looking thoughtful. "Seriously, Ducky, you must have noticed by now. I'm not like that. All the flirting, the phone number hunting, that's just for show. It's a facade. It's not me." Still gazing at me, he added dryly, "You could tie Christina to my stomach naked and nothing would happen between us."

I didn't have the slightest doubt that he was telling the truth. "Yeah," I said. "I know that."

He turned his body toward me and laid his hand on my cheek. Even in the darkness of the car, I could see the gleaming blue of his eyes. "I love you, Jessica," he whispered. "I've never loved anyone else the way I love you."

All I could do was stare at him.

Danny laughed softly and held out a key ring with a single key. "In case you get bored or you feel like practicing your driving, you can come by and water the plants or feed the cat."

They didn't have a cat to feed, and I'd never seen a plant there, either, but I understood the gesture: his home was open to me at any time now. I could come and go as I liked.

***

They left on a Wednesday morning, and his first text arrived later that afternoon.

> *Ducky,*
>
> *We arrived safely. It's a beautiful house on a hill. The people here are super nice, and even the food is good.*
>
> *Tina's room is right beside mine, which she's obviously very happy about (she hates having to travel far!)*
>
> *But the best part are the girls here: all blonde, 36-24-36, with legs that go on forever!*
>
> *So I won't be missing you!*
>
> *Danny*

I had to laugh. I wrote my response while I was out walking Leika:

I'm glad you made it okay. Say hi to Tina for me, and tell her to give you a hug from me as long as she's crawling around in your bed at night anyway.

Glad you're keeping yourself amused. I'll be sure and live it up here, too.

As soon as I get my license, I'm driving to your place and throwing the goddamn cat out the window!

PS: My legs are long enough to reach the ground—that's good enough for me!

His reply came immediately.

I'll pass the message on to Tina :-)

And in case you haven't noticed yet, I live on the first floor, so the goddamn cat will survive the fall.

I really think this place is going to be good for both of us.

I miss you already. Hope you can visit soon.

PS: I don't even like blondes!

Chapter Nine

June 2000

"Jesus, why do you all drive so damn fast?" I grouched, peering at the speedometer.

"This is the perfect speed for the highway." Ricky smiled sheepishly. "But what does 'you all' mean?"

"Danny drives like a lunatic, too!"

"Well, we want to get where we're going." Reluctantly, he eased his foot off the gas to slow the Honda. "Better?" He gave me his most radiant toothpaste-commercial smile.

I nodded, though I knew him well enough by then to know he'd start speeding up again as soon as he thought I wasn't paying attention anymore.

I really liked Ricky. Besides being Danny's best friend, and a super nice guy, he was totally reliable, despite being a textbook bro. Then again, I'd thought Danny was a textbook bro at first, too.

Ricky loved all women, especially tall blondes with supermodel measurements and huge breasts. Vanessa wasn't blonde and didn't exactly fit his ideals, but he'd never been seriously interested in a relationship with her, either. They'd both known that from the beginning. They'd had their fun and then gone their separate ways once they'd had enough of each other.

"How did you and Danny meet?" I asked, watching the speedometer creep up again.

"I've known him since he moved to Germany," he said. "We went to the same high school in Rottweil."

"He lived in Rottweil?"

"Yeah, didn't he tell you that? He didn't move here until he went to the home."

"I didn't know... He doesn't like to talk about himself."

Ricky scoffed. "Who does?" But he seemed a bit too nonchalant to me.

We drove on in silence for a while, until, lost in thought, I remarked, "That must have really sucked for him, getting put in a home so far away. First, he loses both parents, and then he has to move away from his best friend."

Ricky stared at me for a second longer than was strictly necessary. Confusion bubbled up between us.

"He came out here voluntarily," Ricky said at last. "And it wasn't a problem. We never lost touch, not in all that time. I already had a car and a driver's license by then, and it was only about an hour's drive. Well, the way we drive, anyway." As if on cue, the speedometer inched up again, putting us back at Ricky's usual speed.

"I know Danny had a lot of problems with his dad," I began hesitantly, carefully watching Ricky's reaction—he bit his lip. "But it still must have been hard for him to lose both parents at once in that car accident."

"Car accident?" Ricky blurted out.

Yeah, something fishy was going on.

"Um, yeah," Ricky recovered, trying to smooth over his slip-up, "of course, that was really tough on him."

"I can imagine," I said emphatically, hoping I wasn't over-acting this.

"He handled it really well." Ricky seemed oblivious to my suspicion. But he was still eager to change the subject. "So when is your driving test?"

"Next week," I said, my thoughts still on Danny. I wasn't going to get any more out of Ricky, so I'd have to go straight to the source and ask Danny why he'd lied to me about his parents.

"I'll keep my fingers crossed for you, of course. You feel ready?"

"Yeah, I'll be okay," I murmured.

"There they are." Ricky pointed, and I squinted through the window into the distance.

I could just barely see Danny and Christina standing in front of a big building. Someone else was standing beside them—probably some kind of supervisor. The building was in the middle of the woods, with nothing but meadows and fields surrounding it.

As we got out of the car, before I even had a chance to greet Danny, Christina came running up and threw her arms around my neck. "Jessica!" she crowed. "I'm soooooo glad you're here. I missed you!"

Ricky contented himself with giving Danny a friendly jab in the ribs and shaking Christina's hand. She looked good—I noticed right away. Her cheeks were rosy, and she'd put on a few pounds. I felt bad about practically shoving her away from me, but I couldn't wait any longer to be in Danny's arms. He drew me in and kissed me passionately. His familiar scent enveloped me as I wrapped my arms around his middle, pressing him against me. Immediately, I felt him stiffen, so I let go again.

"How are you guys?" I asked brightly. "How is it here?"

"Tough," Danny said.

Christina's eyes lit up. "I haven't felt this good in a long time. Once I get out of here, I'm going to start living a normal life!" She was visibly proud of herself. "I'm going to do it, Jessica! This summer, Danny's going to get me part-time work at the gym, and then in a few months I'll start applying for full-time jobs! Man, I have so much to tell you…"

"Can I talk to you for a second?" I heard Ricky say behind me. Out of the corner of my eye, I saw him lay a hand on Danny's shoulder and take him aside.

Chapter Ten

June 2000

I finally had my license.

It was the day after my birthday, and I was excited to pick up my car, which was still at Alexander's workshop. But it was going to be awkward. We hadn't seen or spoken to one another since that night at the club.

When I arrived, he was tinkering with an exhaust system.

"Hello," I said, a little stiffly. "How are you?"

He greeted me with a curt nod. "Happy belated birthday, Jessica." He made an inviting gesture toward the car—*my* car—which was parked near the front. "Want to take it out for a spin together? I'll show you the features one more time."

"Okay." My brother Thorsten, who had driven me over, got into the back of the Mercedes—and buckled up, which he almost never did. I gave him a black look, and he shrugged apologetically.

"Just not sure what to expect," he said.

The car was heaven to drive. Thanks to the sport suspension, it hugged the road perfectly. With a little help from Alexander, I even managed to maneuver it into a parallel parking spot. Maybe someday we would actually find a way to be friends.

I arrived home that evening to discover a package waiting for me on my bed. Inside was a birthday card from Danny and Christina and a pair of inline skates— really good ones, with soft rollers and spring-loaded ball bearings. The card said:

Happy birthday!

(Now you don't have an excuse anymore!)

They were the most expensive-looking inline skates I'd ever seen.

***

Danny whistled admiringly through his teeth when he saw my car. Unable to resist showing it off, I'd done the long drive by myself the very next weekend. Of course, it had mostly been because I couldn't wait to see Danny again.

"Nice car," he said. "I'm amazed you got it up here in one piece."

I didn't take the bait. "Where's Tina?"

"She can't come out for another hour, when the monitors come outside. And she'll have to be back in by the afternoon. They always try to limit people's contact to the outside world for the first six weeks here, just to be on the safe side."

It didn't seem all that safe, really. "What if I'd just brought you some drugs to give her?"

"You'd never be able to smuggle anything in there." He looked up at the huge, half-timbered house with old-fashioned green shutters, nestled among the tall pines. "They strip-search you before you go in."

"You're kidding." I stared at him. "They search you every time you come in from outside?"

"Yep."

"Oh." Now I felt bad. I knew what a problem he had with being touched, and thanks to me and my visit, he had to let those complete strangers paw at him again. I decided this would be the last time I visited.

"They search our rooms regularly, too…so I'm plenty well supervised." He laughed and extended a hand. "Give me the keys. I want to take your Mercedes for a drive. If I'm allowed."

I was actually kind of glad Christina wouldn't be joining us until later. It gave me a chance to spend at least a little time alone with Danny. As it turned out, though, he was so fascinated by my car that he seemed to forget all about spending quality time together.

Danny pushed my poor car's tachometer all the way into the red. He just couldn't resist testing its top speed. While I cowered in the passenger seat in terror. "This thing's much too fast for you," he concluded as we climbed out of the car back at the center. "Way too much horsepower. I don't like it."

"I don't care," I said, putting my hands on my hips. "Unlike you, I'm a safe and careful driver."

He grumbled under his breath.

"Is Tina going to be okay?" I asked suddenly. Looking up at the center again, my thoughts were back with her.

"I think so," Danny said. "The biggest risk is always relapse, no matter how long she's been clean. I'll have to keep an eye on her. She doesn't want to stay here, at their sober-living facility, so I'll bring her home with me. Then we'll see what happens."

I nodded. "She's making great progress. She'll be fine."

Chapter Eleven

July 2000

One Friday afternoon, I stood in Danny's living room next to my suitcase, watching Danny and Christina return at last. I'd been starting to think I couldn't take their absence any longer, especially Danny's. It was so good to have them around again. I was determined not to leave the apartment before Sunday evening at the very earliest.

Danny cleared out part of his closet to make room for my stuff, and they gave me my own shelf in the bathroom. I'd brought along a little dog bed and set it up in Danny's room. They gave me complete freedom as far as settling in went—if I'd brought along three zebras, five emus, and two starving Namibian children, they'd probably have been okay with it.

Christina looked amazing, as I was forced to acknowledge to my great envy. She was slender now, not skinny. Her hair gleamed, and her eyes sparkled. She really was exceptionally pretty—she and Danny would have made a gorgeous couple.

"It worked! I feel great!" She beamed at me. "And I'm going to start working at the fitness center three times a week, at the juice bar."

"That's great, Tina. Really!"

"Danny will have to drop me off and pick me up, since there's no bus out that way. But it's just temporary, until I can find something full-time. I've sent out a million applications over the last few weeks. I'm sure one of them will work out."

"Tina," Danny said. "If you want to take driving lessons, I'll pay for them. And then we can share my car, or I'll get you one."

"No way! No to both. I want to save up for them myself!"

Danny sighed. "That's ridiculous. It's not a problem for me."

I watched with interest. So *that* was how it worked. Christina didn't mooch off Danny and beg him to buy her stuff—he practically forced it on her. I made a mental note so that I could give it some more thought later.

We ordered an extra-large pizza and spent the evening on the couch. Like Danny, Christina didn't eat meat, so we got a vegetarian pizza. I decided I would try and convert as well.

We really were a strange little group. Danny sat stretched out on the couch, while I lay beside him, against his strong arm, and Christina lay with her head on his stomach. We stuffed ourselves with pizza like it was going out of style, washing it down with countless soft drinks. Normally, Danny was very nutrition-conscious, but every once in a while, he really ran wild. We watched two comedies in a row and nearly fell off the couch laughing multiple times.

Around midnight, we decided it was time for bed, and all three of us went into the bathroom together. By that point, it didn't even surprise me to see Christina change clothes in front of Danny. As she brushed her teeth in a T-shirt and panties, the circular motions of her arm made her breasts swing cheerfully from side to side. Danny stood at the second sink, wearing boxers and a gray-and-white Armani tee.

Our eyes met in the mirror. Blue, green, and brown. I watched Danny as I picked up my own toothbrush. If he ever looked at Christina's chest, he did it so stealthily that I never caught him.

When I was finished brushing my teeth, I went into Danny's room to change. I had my limits.

The bedsheets were reversible satin: blue on one side, gray on the other. The material was pleasantly cool to the touch, and the sheets smelled freshly washed.

Danny came into the room and shut the door behind him. Leika was already curled up peacefully in her tiny bed. She'd been so happy to see Danny and Christina again that she'd actually rolled over so they could rub her belly.

"Mind if I leave the window open?" Danny asked. "I always sleep with it open."

"Sure. As long as you close it in the winter."

He smiled apologetically. "Only when it's below zero out."

Well, great. Christina and Danny were both pretty claustrophobic—in all the time I'd known them, neither one had closed the blinds on a single window or ridden in even one elevator. So this was going to get interesting.

"Which side is yours?" I asked.

"Doesn't matter. No rules on that."

"Well, which side does Christina sleep on when she sneaks in here at night?" I asked, trying to provoke him.

He gave me a challenging look. "She sleeps wherever I am."

Spontaneously, I chose the right side, leaving Danny the side closest to the door. He switched the overhead light off and climbed into bed, propping his head on his hand. The dim lamp on the nightstand was still on, giving me enough light to see him. His eyes were as unnaturally blue as ever.

"Now I finally know for sure," I said with satisfaction. "No contacts." He would have taken them out to sleep, right?

"Huh?" He looked confused.

"Your eyes," I explained. "They're so unusual. I thought maybe you wore colored contacts."

"No, they're really like that." He chuckled. "You mean you've been wondering whether this is my natural eye color since last year?"

"Yeah," I admitted, a little sheepishly.

"Ducky." He gave me an admonishing look. "You could have just asked."

I felt myself turn red and mumbled something about being "too embarrassed."

"Anything you want to know, ask. You can ask me anything."

I nodded, and he rolled over to switch off the lamp, but then stopped and turned back to face me. "You probably ought to know that this"—he pointed back and forth between us—"is new territory for me."

"What?" I asked. "You've never been in bed with a girl before?" He couldn't be serious!

"Sure, I have. Just not to sleep."

"You always kicked them out right afterward or something?"

He gave me a bashful grin. "Something like that, yeah."

I rolled my eyes. That sounded exactly like something he would do. "You're impossible."

"I usually didn't have to throw them out of bed, because we never made it that far—I mean, they were just casual hookups, and…" He broke off. "All I meant to say was, I don't know if I'll sleep tonight. I've never slept next to anyone but Christina."

We don't necessarily have to sleep, my inner voice piped up.

Well, Danny *had* just said that if there was anything I wanted to know, I should just ask…

"What am I doing wrong that all the others did right?"

"What? Why would you be doing anything wrong?" Danny was taken aback—apparently, he genuinely didn't understand the question.

"I mean…" I struggled for words, blushing again. "Apparently you…let all those others…be *with* you."

97

Now he understood, and he smiled. "'All those others,' as you put it, are a total of three people. And no, I didn't let them 'be with' me. Not even a little bit. They let me be with them. There's a big difference."

"But, Danny…" I tried to think of a better way of putting it but then decided it didn't matter. "I would let you be with me, too."

He snorted. Whether in amusement or in annoyance, I didn't know. After a while, he said, "Let me put it like this… What happened between me and the others was… How do I explain it? Emotionless. No, worse than that. Brusque, almost. Totally cold. It had nothing to do with real intimacy and romance."

Brusque and emotionless is better than not at all, I thought sullenly, but didn't say it aloud. "So you didn't love them?" I asked instead.

He was quiet for a moment. "I cared for the first two. A little. Not the way I love you. But neither relationship lasted long. Maybe a couple of months each."

I wanted to ask him why they hadn't worked out, but he beat me with his own question. "And you? What about you?"

"Just Alexander," I said. "I think I loved him. Or at least I thought so at the time."

Danny nodded briefly and then lapsed into a thoughtful silence. "I really do love you, Ducky," he said after a few moments.

"I love you too."

He turned away again to switch off the light.

"Danny?" I asked, before he could.

"Hm?"

"Why did you lie to me about your parents?"

He sighed and his shoulders drooped. He was still a moment before turning to look at me. "I'm sorry. The lie was so much easier than the truth."

"So there was no car accident?"

"No. They're both still alive."

I sat up as well and touched the scar on his left cheek. He'd told me his father had hit him with a bottle. "Was this a lie, too?"

"No. That really happened. It wasn't an accident, though. My father hit me in the face with that bottle on purpose. The 'accident' was just the version we told the hospital when I went in and got twelve stitches."

My heart twisted. "Why did he do that?"

"We got into a huge fight that evening. He was totally hammered, and I knew I ought to shut my mouth, but I couldn't help myself. Eventually, he got worked up into such a rage that he threw the bottle he was drinking out of right at me."

An icy shudder ran down my back as I imagined what his childhood home must have been like. How much would you have to hate someone else to hit them in the face with a glass bottle? Let alone your own child…

"How old were you?" I asked gently.

"Thirteen."

"And even now you're using the version you told the hospital," I said, shocked. "For outsiders. Like I was, back then."

Danny smiled humorlessly. "Always gotta keep up appearances. Very important. I learned that very early on in life."

"Is there anything else I should know?" It was obvious he kept some things secret from me. To protect himself, Christina had said. But I was starting to realize he mainly did it to protect *me*.

"Yeah," he said slowly. "There is something else. And I'll tell you, but not today."

"Why not?"

"I need to figure out how to put it," he explained. "I can't just blurt it out without thinking. Anyway, I've really dumped plenty on you for one night."

"Just tell me," I insisted.

He switched off the light and stretched out, tucking the covers up over his shoulders. "Good night, Ducky."

"Good night," I mumbled, but I let a few minutes go by before I lay down again—and scooted in close to Danny. I'd been completely throwing myself at him this whole night, so a little more probably didn't matter. Stealthily, with almost imperceptible slowness, I slid my hand underneath his side of the blanket.

It was like he'd been waiting for me to do just that. He immediately grabbed my hand, lacing his fingers with mine, and firmly pulled our hands down onto the mattress. I could tell he wasn't going to let go until morning.

***

My mother's and grandpa's birthdays were that weekend, and Danny and I spent the whole Saturday with my family at my grandparents' house. I'd been afraid that all the unfamiliar faces and commotion would be too much for him, but as it turned out, I'd misjudged him yet again.

Not only did they *not* bother him, he actually seemed to enjoy it. My relatives all liked him, and he spent hours listening to the old folks' stories, making me wonder again and again how he managed to be so patient. I could tell how much he loved the kids, and the appreciation was clearly mutual. They were constantly bringing their toys over to him, dragging him out into the yard, and climbing all over him. Suddenly, I could imagine him making a great dad.

When we finally returned to his place that evening, my head was buzzing and I was more than ready for some peace and quiet, but Danny was in a great mood—he'd probably have gone back every weekend if I'd asked him to. And that's when I made the painful realization.

That's how badly he wished he had a good, close family. I didn't know what the story was with his mom, since she was apparently still living, but they didn't appear to be in contact. And he'd never mentioned any siblings. I couldn't wrap my head around the idea that he was all alone here in Germany. The next chance I got, I decided, I would ask him about his mother and insist that he introduce me to her.

It wasn't long before we found a bedtime ritual that seemed to agree with Danny. When we went to bed , we usually chatted for a little while, and then I would turn onto my side, and he'd cuddle close to me, the big spoon to my little spoon. Then he'd curl his arm around my hip, lacing his fingers with mine. That way, he had total control and didn't have to worry about me touching him anywhere I wasn't supposed to.

I don't know if he slept at all during those first few weekends I slept over. If so, it couldn't have been very deeply, because I always woke up in exactly the same position I'd fallen asleep in.

And he never let me go for even a moment.

Chapter Twelve

August 2000

One hot Saturday, we took it easy. I'd driven out to the stables with Leika early that morning, while Danny had gone running and then spent some time training at the gym.

At noon, I brought Leika to my parents' house and then drove back to Danny's alone. Leika was so exhausted from the heat that I didn't want to make her go out into it again.

When Danny got home, we went for a walk with Maya, but not far, because it was already much too hot. Then we spent the rest of the afternoon underneath the huge linden tree beside the ponies' paddock. We thought about going swimming in the nearby river but decided we were too lazy. Instead, we dangled our feet in the water, eating ice cream we bought at a gas station, and listened to music.

Danny's taste in music took some getting used to. He either blasted dark, epic music that could never be loud enough for him, or he listened to soulful ballads with profound lyrics in English. I didn't understand a lot of them, because of the language barrier—or because I was just too superficial to understand poetry like that. So he'd always explain them to me and then try to speculate about their meanings.

We ate dinner at a little pub and then spent the rest of the evening on the couch. Christina was at a friend's house all weekend. She claimed she wanted to spend more time with Natasha, but I suspected she just wanted to give me and Danny time to ourselves.

We watched *The Matrix*, but Danny was lying on his back, and I kept catching myself sneaking glances at him instead of following the confusing movie. At one point, Danny laughed quietly to himself. I didn't really get the joke, but I couldn't help laughing along with him anyway. As always. He had me completely under his spell.

I scooted over to him on my knees and gently touched the blond hair on his tanned arm. He raised his eyes to meet mine and gazed at me intently.

My heart skipped a beat, and my stomach tensed up almost painfully. Danny extended his arm invitingly and patted his chest. Obediently, I crawled over to lie on him and laid my head on his shoulder. He curled an arm around me, pressing his lips to my forehead as he tenderly brushed a few strands of hair out of my face. His touch gave me goosebumps, and a delicious shiver ran down my back. I tilted my head expectantly and found his lips with my own, and he returned the kiss deeply.

Tonight would be perfect, I thought. *Tina's away—we're totally alone.*

Little by little, I slid further on top of him as we continued kissing passionately. My fingers found his T-shirt, and I tried to pull it off him. But he pulled away with a smile. "We should stop."

Why? I wanted to yell.

Determined, I pushed my hand underneath his shirt, but he caught it and pressed it against my thigh.

"No," he said in a friendly but firm tone.

Now I was really starting to lose my patience. "Why can't I touch you?" I asked petulantly.

"Because I don't want you to."

"Great," I growled. "What exactly would you say if I didn't want you to touch me?"

He raised both hands. "No problem. Then I won't do it anymore."

Sighing, I laid a hand on his shoulder. "Danny, you know that's not what I want. I was just trying to say that we should talk about this one of these days."

He didn't react, except to cross his arms and turn away from me, as he did so often.

"It's because of what your dad did to you?" Though it had come out like a question, I already suspected the answer.

He looked at me, his eyes wide. Then he sprang to his feet and left the living room at a sharp clip. I shook my head, shoulders sagging in frustration, and followed him to his room. He was sitting on his bed, staring out the window.

"Danny, I think I already know. He abused—"

"Abused?" he interrupted, his voice cold and derisive.

Dammit, I shouldn't have said anything!

Maybe if I just gave him a minute…

Danny leaped up again and began pacing across the room. "Abused," he sneered again, as though the word was nowhere near powerful enough for what had been done to him. "He raped me!"

I felt like I was falling from an unspeakable height. Suspecting something and hearing it directly were two very different things.

"Do you understand that?" He was nearly screaming. "He raped me! Over and over again! For two whole years. And my mom did nothing to stop it. Nothing!"

My breath was coming quickly. "Maybe... Maybe she didn't know it was happening."

"She did! Oh, yes, she did. She knew exactly what he was doing. He was in my room for hours, sometimes even the whole night. He'd scream at me, and I'd cry, I'd shout for her, beg her to do something. She ignored it. She ignored *me*. She created her own reality." He was pacing incessantly, like a caged tiger, and kept running both hands through his hair. He cursed under his breath in English. "But why am I even telling you this?" he suddenly snarled at me. "You say you already knew."

"Maybe because it does you good to talk about it," I said hopefully. "And because that's the only way we can figure out how to handle it."

He snorted. "I've talked about it enough. In court. On a continuous loop. To total strangers. Do you have any idea how that feels? Having to tell a room of strangers about that shit? I sat there in that courtroom feeling *guilty* while my father just grinned like an idiot, like it was his God-given right to do what he'd done to me."

Without warning, he kicked the dresser. I flinched. Although he was only wearing socks, the wood splintered immediately. But it wasn't enough for him. He kept kicking it, again and again, until the whole thing collapsed.

I sat on the bed and stared helplessly at my hands while he got it all out of his system. Suddenly, I was glad I'd left Leika at my parents' house—Danny's unusually aggressive behavior would have frightened her.

"I think I need a new dresser," he said at last. He sounded completely composed again. I looked up. "Will you come with me on Monday to buy one?"

"Of course."

Sighing, Danny sat cross-legged at the foot of the bed, his gaze locked on an imaginary point on the wall. For a few moments, he sat in silence, taking deep breaths. "For the first ten years of my life, everything was totally normal," he said. "Then I made a mistake, and my mother had a miscarriage—"

"Hold on," I broke in. "You made a mistake, and that's why your mother had a miscarriage? How is that possible?" What ridiculous stories had they been feeding him?

"Don't interrupt," he said. "Just listen to me, okay? You can ask questions later."

"Okay." I chewed my lip and kept silent.

"After she lost the baby, we moved to Germany, and my dad started drinking. Losing his son was more than he could handle, and then on top of it all, he hated having to be in Germany. And he blamed me for both of those things.

"He grew more and more dissatisfied and drowned all his problems in alcohol. Then, he started going out and picking up rent boys. Young guys, practically kids, selling their bodies on the cheap. My mother knew about it, and they argued about it a lot, but he kept bringing people home with him. More and more often, younger and younger. They'd have sex in my parents' bedroom. My mother tried to sugarcoat that, too. She told herself they were just friends."

He fell silent for a moment and shut his eyes. I wanted to take him in my arms, but I didn't dare.

When he spoke again, his fingers were trembling. "I wasn't quite eleven years old when he came to my bed for the first time. To 'snuggle,' as he called it. I had to let him touch me all over. He said I had to, or else he'd bring more boys back to the house, and my mother wouldn't like that, so she'd divorce him, and then I'd get put in a home—things like that."

As he spoke, all I could do was shake my head in horror, mouth hanging open.

"It escalated over time," he went on. "He made me touch him, too, and then later he started raping me. He told me that if I didn't do what he said, he would do it to my mom instead, and surely I didn't want to be responsible for him hurting my mom."

I shook my head. "What cheap, disgusting manipulation."

"It was. But back then, I thought I had to protect my mother, so I went along with it. I didn't really have a choice, anyway. Except for running away from home. I tried that a lot. I begged my mother to come with me, but she wouldn't. And then my dad would find me and bring me back home—again and again—and everything would continue as before." He looked at me uncertainly. "Do you even want to know all this? Maybe I should stop there."

Jesus, you mean there's more?

"I want to know," I whispered and closed my eyes, bracing myself.

"He'd come into my room and undress me," Danny said. "Sometimes he'd tie my hands behind my head with rope. Then he'd touch me everywhere. Not just with his hands—with his mouth, his tongue, his…" He shuddered, unable to finish the sentence.

I found myself wondering just how much damage his father had done to him, and whether at least part of it could be repaired. Images shot through my mind—thoughts I never wanted to have, that I would never be able to shake as long as I lived.

"My bed had two bedposts at the head," he went on. "I was supposed to lie on my back and hold onto them without moving while he did whatever he wanted. But I couldn't do it. The urge to pull in my arms, to shield myself from him, was just too great. And every time I let go, he'd hit me, and then we'd start again from the beginning. Of course, he could have just tied me up, but it was more fun for him this way. And when he finally left the room, I was supposed to stay in that position. So I did, sometimes for hours, because once in a while he'd stand in front of the door and listen. If he heard me turn over, he'd come in and beat me. With a stick or a length of rope…"

Was this where his automatic habit of crossing his arms at every opportunity came from?

"It was really awful, Jessica. Whenever he came back from the bar on Friday evening, I knew he'd come to my room. I'd sit there in bed like a trapped animal, wanting more than anything to get away. But where would I have gone? My room was upstairs, so there was no place to run. I'd hear the stairs creaking, and I'd know he was on his way up.

"At first, I'd hide in the closet out of desperation, but he'd just drag me out and shout at me to stop screwing around, that of course he knew I was in there. The older I got, the angrier he got. And the angrier he got, the harder he hit me…"

He hesitated for a moment before letting out a sigh of resignation. Then he stood up and jerked his T-shirt over his head roughly, as though forcing himself to do it before he changed his mind. He sat down beside me on the bed. "Look." His voice was toneless.

"Oh my God!" was all I could manage to get out.

His back was covered in fine, white scars. They probably weren't visible from far away, but they were definitely there, like an intricate spiderweb made flesh.

Without thinking, I ran a finger along the smooth, white lines.

"Don't," he whispered, putting his T-shirt back on before jumping up to pace around the room some more.

"He didn't care about anything," he murmured, shaking his head. Then, louder, "He wouldn't stop until he got what he wanted. Then he'd sit down on my bed and smoke a cigarette and want to chat. Eventually, he'd leave me crying in my room. It would stink of cigarettes and alcohol for days afterward." Danny stopped in his tracks, crossed his arms, and glanced at me with an absent, distraught expression in his eyes. "Now you can ask your questions."

I shook my head and buried my face in my hands. Unshed tears burned hot in my eyes. I couldn't ask anything, couldn't say anything. I didn't have the words. "Come here." I patted the bed.

He sat down beside me. He looked...*confused*. "The worst part is my mom. She never helped me. Just the opposite—she practically handed me to him on a silver platter. I hate them both. I should have killed my father when I had the chance."

"What?" I whispered.

"There was this one huge fight. I was fifteen and already getting pretty successful in martial arts. He'd been drinking again and wanted to take his rage out on me, beat me for his own amusement, but suddenly, just this once, my mother stood in his way. It was the only time. She told him to leave me alone.

"My dad ordered her to move out of the way, but she stayed right where she was. So he hit her and knocked her to the ground. And I just blew a fuse. I got between them and started kicking my dad, again and again and again. I should have beaten him to death. But instead I left him bleeding on the ground, and went and reported him to the police. I never went back. They got Child Protective Services involved, and I ended up in the children's home, and he ended up in prison."

"You did the right thing," I assured him. "There would have been no use ruining your own life over someone like him." *More than it already is*, I added in my head. It was clear his childhood had ruined plenty for him without the added consequences of killing someone.

Danny snorted again. "I still wonder, all the time, why she never helped me. My mother. I'm never going to have children, but if I did, I'd do everything within my power to protect them. *Everything*. Not like her!"

I carefully filed away what I had just heard about kids so that we could come back to it later. First, I had to process all the rest of this somehow. My head was pounding. It was too much. Besides, all I wanted to do was hold him.

Carefully, I slid toward him and stroked his back. He turned and buried his face in my shoulder, sniffling. I moved closer so that I could wrap my arms around him, but he stiffened. He was too worked up from talking about his past to allow so much physical intimacy.

Take it slow, my inner voice warned me. *He can't learn to walk until he knows how to stand.*

"I'm glad you told me all of this," I whispered in his ear. "I understand. I'll be patient. Someday, you'll heal enough that you'll be ready to let me touch you."

He rested his forehead against my shoulder. "It'll never happen. I've been this way for too long. I'll never stop freaking out about being touched."

"Yes, you will," I promised in a confident voice. "Someday. I don't care how long it takes. You can have all the time in the world."

"Time!" he cried contemptuously, leaning away from me away so that he could look me in the face. His eyes were filling with tears. "Time," he repeated slowly. "Time is exactly what I don't have."

Panic welled up within me. My palms began to sweat. "Why?" My voice was flat.

He gritted his teeth, still staring at me.

There was a lot still unsaid here, and it weighed heavily on my heart. "Danny? Tell me what's wrong! Right now!"

"I can't."

"Yes, you can. You have to, in fact." This time, I wasn't going to let up. He'd said so much tonight already, but I wanted to know the rest. I *needed* to know the rest.

"I'm afraid you'll jump up and run away and never come back." His voice was trembling, and another tear was forming in the corner of his eye. He blinked it back hastily.

"Has that happened before? Did someone run away when they heard this?"

"Yeah."

My heart squeezed at the pain in his voice. "I'm not running anywhere. I promise." Under no circumstances would I run away from him. Not if the house was on fire.

His mood changed abruptly once again. "Never make promises you can't keep," he snapped, striding to the window, where he turned and scowled at me with what looked like rage.

"Just tell me what's wrong," I pleaded.

"Fine!" The defiance in his voice was scathing. He crossed his arms, uncrossed them to run his hand through his hair, and then crossed them again. It was several minutes before he finished fighting some inner battle. "Okay," he said at last, sighing in resignation, the fight leaving him. "I'll tell you."

My heart was in my throat, and I'd bitten down on my lower lip so hard I tasted blood. "Well? What is it?"

"I'm HIV-positive."

"What?" The words seeped into my brain slowly before bouncing back, shooting through my gut, and landing in my stomach, where they're still sitting today. "What?" I asked again. "That's impossible. The only people who get that are…"

Prostitutes. Gay men. And junkies…

"I know what you're thinking right now," he murmured. "But it's not true. I didn't get it from drugs. I've never done any drugs in my life." He swallowed. My father gave it to me."

The panic that had welled up within me before was growing steadily now.

WHO CARES WHO HE GOT IT FROM? my inner voice screeched. *Run! Get away from him!*

Sweat beaded on my brow, and my whole body felt hot. For a moment, I thought I was going to pass out. A wave of nausea washed over me as I recalled all that long, intense French kissing we'd done. "YOU HAVE *AIDS*?" Even I didn't know exactly why I was shouting at him like a lunatic.

"Not exactly," he said calmly. "I'm HIV-positive. There's a difference. I'm healthy, no symptoms. AIDS will develop eventually, but until it does, I can live a completely normal life."

"BUT IT'S *CONTAGIOUS*!" I screamed. "We've known each other for nearly a year, and you never said anything! HOW COULD YOU DO THIS TO ME?"

He sat back down on the bed. "Don't panic," he said quietly. "You really have nothing to worry about. You don't have it. There was never a situation where I could have given it to you. I promised to watch out for you, and to warn you before things ever got dangerous. And I always keep my promises. Always!"

"You should have told me!" I was still shouting at him. I couldn't help it.

"I know." How many times had he sighed over the course of the evening? Cautiously, he put an arm around me. "Is this okay?"

He was actually asking permission. My instinct was to shake him by the shoulders for even asking and then try to cuddle with him... Except...

I felt myself stiffen under the weight of his arm.

For the first time ever, I felt uncomfortable in his presence. I wanted to get out of his room—get away from him.

Sensing my discomfort, Danny withdrew his arm. "You can go if you want." His voice was perfectly composed.

Every cell in my body was tense, prepared to flee. I felt like a coiled spring. *Run*, my inner voice said again. My internal warning system was shrilling and blinking in every color of the rainbow. Frantically, I looked around the room, evaluating all the ways I could escape this nightmare.

"You can leave," Danny repeated. "It's okay."

That was my cue. I leaped up far too quickly and nearly ran into the hallway. Danny followed me out but stopped a safe distance away, arms crossed again. His expression was blank, giving no indication of what was going on in his mind. "It's okay if you leave. But don't be scared. You don't have it. Really. You're healthy."

I realized in horror that my hands were shaking as they pulled on my shoes and retrieved my purse from the hook on the wall. Then I stopped for a second and looked back at Danny one more time. I wanted to say something, but I couldn't think of anything appropriate.

"You can come get your stuff on Monday while I'm at the gym," he said quietly, making a motion in my direction. "That way, you don't have to run into me." He was extending his hand, and I couldn't stop myself from flinching away. He let out a soft, joyless laugh, and I realized he was just reaching for the doorknob behind me.

That's all it took to make me incredibly embarrassed by how I was acting. But I couldn't help it. I was terrified.

"Should I drive you home?" Danny asked, opening the door for me. "You're so worked up. Simon and I can drive your car down to you in the morning."

Without replying, I slipped past him, taking meticulous care to avoid any physical contact. I ran out of the apartment, down the short, tiled hallway of the building, and out the front door. I unlocked my car remotely mid-run and finally collapsed in the driver's seat, gasping for air. It took me three tries to start the car.

When I did, I backed out of the parking spot, tires squealing—something I never would have managed if I'd been deliberately trying to do it. My hands were so slick with sweat that they were slipping off the steering wheel. Radio on full blast, both windows down all the way, I maneuvered the Mercedes onto the highway. Oncoming traffic kept honking at me, which drove me insane—until I realized I was driving with my headlights off.

My phone beeped. I pulled it out of my bag and read the message.

Please send me a short text when you get home.

I just want to know you made it home safe.

Worried. Thanks.

I started laughing hysterically. The guy had some nerve. I felt like throwing the phone right out the window. Suddenly, I realized I was about to drive off the road and yanked the steering wheel back at the last second.

Jesus. Maybe I really shouldn't be on the road in this condition.

I stopped at the next rest area I saw, parking haphazardly across two spaces, and stormed out of the car. My head was threatening to explode from all this information I was incapable of processing, and my legs started moving of their own accord. I started running, aimlessly, through the darkness. Danny had told me so much tonight, opened himself up to me so much, difficult though it was for him—and I'd just left him. Alone.

All at once, I realized I could run as much as I wanted, or drive to Alaska, or hide in the farthest corner of the Earth, but this nightmare would always catch up to me. Maybe not today, or tomorrow, but someday, it would catch me. Stopping in my tracks, I planted my hands on my knees.

Think, Jessica! Think!

I racked my brain for all I had ever learned about HIV. They'd covered it in school once. "The gay plague," the kids had called it. Suddenly, I remembered the modes of transmission: unprotected sex, sharing needles, blood transfusions…

Kissing, no matter what type, was completely risk-free, and so was living in the same household as an infected individual. Step by step, I went through the past year with Danny in my head.

We'd drunk from the same bottle, we'd eaten together, and I'd come into contact with his sweat. But none of that was dangerous. The virus wasn't transmitted through saliva or sweat.

Oh my God. When we fell off Maya...

We'd fallen off, and he'd begun to bleed. And when I'd tried to help him… His violent reaction suddenly made perfect sense. He'd been protecting me.

Now I understood why he'd tried so desperately to keep me at a distance all this time. His abusive childhood had only been *part* of it.

I ran my hands through my hair in frustration. What else did I know about AIDS? It was an autoimmune disorder that destroyed the immune system little by little, sometimes over the course of years. It remained asymptomatic for a relatively long time, so it would be impossible to tell that someone had it—but as soon as they started showing symptoms, they often went downhill fast. How did someone actually die of AIDS, though?

I didn't know, but it was probably terribly painful and horribly lonely.

The realization threw my thoughts right back to Danny.

How did he feel right now, after I'd just run off after I'd explicitly promised him I wouldn't?

What the hell was I even doing here in this godforsaken parking lot?

I began walking back to my car slowly but picked up the pace when I remembered my windows were open and my purse was sitting on the passenger seat. Or, at least, I hoped it was still there. If not, well…whatever. After tonight, I couldn't imagine myself worrying about trivial things like that.

It was all still there—nobody else was in the parking lot. Suddenly ravenous, I picked up my purse and headed for the vending machines beside the restrooms, where I bought a candy bar and a drink.

There was a condom vending machine beside the men's toilet with a sticker reading, "Stop AIDS now. Wrap it up!" I didn't know whether to laugh or cry. It was too much irony. On a sudden childish impulse I put some coins into the condom machine and pulled out a small box.

Just then, a greasy-haired man with tattoos all the way to his neck stepped out of the restroom and hissed, "If you still need those tonight, I'm ready, baby!" He waggled his tongue obscenely.

I gave him the finger before tearing the box open, slipping one foil-wrapped package into my pants pocket, and dropping the rest in my purse. Then I walked away from the building and pulled out my phone. Although it was the middle of the night, I dialed Christina's number.

She couldn't have been asleep, because she answered on the second ring, sounding totally awake but worried.

"Tina!" I cried into the phone. "Something's wrong—"

"What happened?" She was instantly on full alert.

"Danny..."

"What? What happened?" she cried, nearly hysterical.

"He has... He's... Oh...G-God!" I stammered.

"He told you," Christina said in a dry tone.

Of course. What kind of naive little girl was I? I should have known she already knew. "Why didn't you ever tell me?" I shouted at her. "He has *AIDS*! You knew, and neither of you fucking egomaniacs ever said a word to me! Why?"

"To protect him from people reacting like you," she said coldly.

"You're both insane!"

"Are you with him?" She sounded worried.

"Of course not! I left!" All at once, I felt completely ridiculous.

She exhaled heavily into the receiver. "Jessica." The urgency in her voice reminded me a lot of Danny. "Sit down and listen to me very carefully."

"I'm sitting," I snapped, dropping into the grass.

"This situation has always existed," she said, speaking slowly and clearly. "The knowledge you have now doesn't make it any realer than it was before he told you."

It took a while for her words to seep into my agitated mind. "What do I do now?" I asked in desperation.

"Keep going as you were. Nothing has changed, apart from one thing in your head. I've been living with him for two years now, and I've never been at risk. At least not from AIDS," she added dryly.

"But you don't *sleep* with him!" I shrieked.

"Neither do you," she retorted.

Fury rose up within me. Did she always have to know about everything between me and Danny?

"Jessica," she said, still calmer than me by miles. "A known danger is much easier to face than the vague risks of everyday life."

Really? Was that true? "What do I do now?" I repeated.

"Do you remember the promise you to made me just after we met?"

I nodded, though she couldn't see it through the phone. She responded anyway. "Trust me," she said in a voice as soft as butter. "If you break that promise, I'll find you. No matter where you hide, I'll find you. And you should be far more worried about that than catching anything from Danny."

I turned her words over in my head. The situation had always existed. He'd had the virus in his blood all these months we'd been together. The fact that I knew about it now didn't increase my risk of infection. Probably just the opposite.

"Jessica?" Christina jolted me back to reality. "Go back to him. Please. I'm going to hang up now. I need to call him."

Still lost in thought, I stuck my phone back in my purse. I needed to change my CB radio handle from "Unicorn" to "Nightmare" as a way of reminding myself of this nightmare I would never escape. It would keep following me, hunting me down, from that day on. Probably for the rest of my life.

By the time I pulled up in front of Danny's apartment building again, it was nearly morning. As usual, the blinds were open, so I could see that the lights were off inside, though that didn't necessarily mean Danny was actually asleep. He often kept the lights off when he was at home. He'd once told me that the darkness made him feel safer. For some reason, that made sense to me now.

My parking spot directly in front of Danny's bedroom window was still free, and I started maneuvering my large car into the space. Normally, that wouldn't have been a problem, but right now I just couldn't do it. I was confused and exhausted.

"Crap," I muttered, adjusting again. So much for three-point parallel parking. More like forty-two-point. "Fuck!" I shouted, slamming my hand against the wheel. If I kept lurching back and forth like this much longer, I'd wake Danny for sure—if he was asleep, anyway, which I highly doubted.

Finally, I gave up. The back of the car was sticking way out into the narrow street and would definitely be a problem for traffic. Whatever. Let the neighbors flip out in a few hours. I had other problems.

I removed my shoes at the door and crept into Danny's apartment in my socks. Then I slipped into the bathroom to change into my sleep shorts and T-shirt. At first, I wondered if I should sleep on the couch so I wouldn't wake him, but I decided against it.

As it turned out, Danny was still awake. He was lying on the bed with his arms folded behind his head. "You came back," he remarked dryly. The streetlamp outside the window gave me enough light to see his face by. There was no joy on it. Not even relief.

"Of course I came back."

Slowly, he sat up in bed. "Why?"

"Because I love you."

"That's pretty stupid of you."

"Maybe, but that's how it is," I said. "Even if you were a man-eating alien from the planet Klendathu, I'd still have come back."

"Why?" he repeated, shaking his head. He seemed to be directing the question at himself, but I answered it anyway.

"Because I love you. More than anything. More than my life!"

Danny got up from the bed and walked past me into the living room. I followed him out, carelessly dropping the clothes I was still carrying to the floor.

He pressed his forehead against the windowpane. "I'm going to die. You're aware of that, right?"

"We all die sometime," I said, trying to keep my tone light.

"Yeah," he growled. "Some younger than others."

"Danny, you're healthy. You could be healthy for years to come. By the time you start to get really sick, they'll have found a cure."

"Or not," he said quietly. "They research cancer treatments like crazy, but nobody's interested in us. So I have to live with the knowledge that I could die at anytime."

114

"None of us know when we're going to die," I whispered, though I knew Danny's life already held acute awareness of his own mortality.

He was silent for a moment, still staring out the window. "What kind of parking job is that?" he asked suddenly. "You can't leave it like that."

I shrugged. "I couldn't get into the spot."

He grabbed his jogging pants off the couch, slipped them on, and walked to the door barefoot. "Give me your keys. I'll park it properly."

I gave in, rummaging around in my purse before pulling out the key and holding it out to him. He reached for it, and our fingers touched. We both stopped short, and our eyes met. Suddenly, all of the pent-up emotion from the past few hours exploded around us. The electricity would have been enough to power half the city. The need to touch him was overwhelming.

Danny felt it, too. I snatched the car keys out of his hand, tossed them into the corner along with my purse, and wrapped my arms around his neck, firmly pulling him in.

We stood there silently for a while, gazing deep into each other's eyes. My pulse began to race, and I felt him breathing faster, too.

He opened his mouth to say something, and I used the opportunity to press my lips against his. He returned the kiss hesitantly, and my hands slid slowly over his shoulders toward his chest. He flinched and grabbed my wrists in a vise-like grip, holding them in place behind my back.

"We can't do that," he murmured against my lips.

"Oh, you'll see how we can in a minute!"

He laughed softly. "Don't be silly. I don't even have condoms in the house."

"Let go for a second, please?"

He released my wrists with great reluctance. I picked up the pants I'd left on the floor after changing, reached into the pocket, and held up the little foil square triumphantly.

"Oh, please!" He rolled his eyes. "No way. It's too dangerous."

"I don't care," I said, deliberately using the phrase he was so fond of. But it wasn't entirely true. Of course I was afraid, but the fear would always be there, and I didn't intend to let it get between us forever. So I turned a deaf ear to my inner voice, which was frantically trying to remind me that I'd bitten my lip bloody just a little while ago.

"Jessica."

"Shh," I said, kissing him again. He let it happen but stopped returning the kiss. Cautiously, I let my hands glide over his chest. I felt him stiffen, so I stopped. Instead, I reached for his hips, pulling him against me. I felt his erection and slid my hands back over him. He drew in a sharp breath and held it. His eyes were closed, and his lower lip was trembling slightly. I let my hands travel slowly.

He stepped away from me quickly, practically fleeing, retreating until his back was against the wall. I followed him. "Don't back me into a corner," he practically begged.

I guided him by the elbow back to the middle of the room. "You're going to have to trust me tonight," I whispered, my lips at his neck.

"The c-car," he stammered. "I have to repark the car." It was his last desperate attempt to prevent the inevitable.

Slowly, I pushed him toward the bedroom. "Fuck the car!"

***

The piercing sunshine and birdsong streaming in through the open window woke me. I blinked into the bright light. Then I realized that my head had been on Danny's chest, and I immediately let it sink down again as I inhaled deeply. Warmth and contentment enveloped me, and I wished more than anything that the moment would never end.

His even breathing told me he was still asleep, so I took the opportunity to watch him. I found myself wondering, once again, how a person could get away with being so beautiful. Then again, he wasn't exactly getting away with much of anything in life.

Our night together had been anything but brusque and emotionless, which had probably been because he'd let me set the pace, which I thought was a huge demonstration of trust. Even so, he'd held my wrists the entire time, only releasing them once he'd put enough distance between us that he felt halfway safe again. It wouldn't have bothered me if it hadn't been so frustrating that I couldn't touch him in all the ways I wanted to.

He was still wearing the T-shirt he'd had on the day before, too. I'd tried to take it off of him twice, but he'd resisted vehemently. Having the material between us bothered me—I would have liked to touch his bare skin. Cautiously, I ran my fingers across his chest. Even that feather-light touch was enough to make him twitch and snap his eyes open.

For a moment, he stared at me in confusion but then his expression grew tender. "Good morning," he rumbled.

"Morning," I said, giving him a kiss on the cheek and stroking his arm with my fingertips. He made a contented snuffling sound and turned the inside of his arm toward me so that I could touch him there. I felt him shiver in pleasure under my fingers, and it made my heart leap for joy.

"How are you still sleeping?" I asked. It was already eight. Normally, at this hour on a weekend, he'd be out running or training.

"It's just so nice," he murmured, stretching languidly.

That was my cue. I sat up and bent over him. He returned my kiss, but when I laid my hand on his thigh, he bolted upright.

"What happened last night can never happen again." His eyes sought mine, locking with them. "Do you hear me? It's too dangerous!"

I quickly laid my index finger against his lips. "Stop. Don't say anything. Don't ruin it, please."

To my relief, he fell silent immediately.

I didn't understand what the problem was. Everything had gone well, much more easily than expected. The used condom was knotted neatly and safely packed away in the bathroom trash can. We'd both washed our hands afterward, a rather unromantic detail we hadn't wasted any time discussing. I'd even managed to keep myself from thinking about the disease.

But now reality was crashing in with monstrous force. Thanks, in part, to Danny's words.

Apparently placated by my reassurances, though, Danny reluctantly rose from the bed. "I'll go park your car properly, and then I'm going to take a shower." He tromped out of the room, and all at once, I felt sick. The whole situation was crashing back over me like a wave, making me seriously nauseated.

Deep breaths! Count to ten!

Why was I in such a panic? There was no way anything could have happened. I had to get myself under control before he came back. I couldn't let him see my fear, or else he'd never touch me again.

Jumping out of bed, I stepped into the fresh air coming through the open window and started doing yoga.

Inhale, upward salute. Exhale, downward-facing dog. Inhale, cobra. Exhale, child's pose...

Danny returned to the bedroom and eyed me skeptically as I stood there in my pajamas, stretching my hands toward the heavens. He didn't say anything. Neither did I. The sight of him standing there left me completely speechless. Naked, except for a towel around his hips, he reached down and fished his clothes out of the pile of rubble that had once been his dresser. I kept gaping at him. I'd never seen him like that.

He gave me a taunting grin. "Everything okay?" he asked, raising an eyebrow.

He knows perfectly well what effect he has on women, I suddenly realized. He knew all he had to do was snap his fingers and any girl would fall for him. But Christina was right: he didn't snap. And, as of yesterday evening, I knew why.

While Danny made breakfast, I took a long shower. Maybe I was hoping it would allow me to escape reality for a few more minutes. But it didn't quite work. I sat down at the breakfast table with damp hair. Danny was wearing a red—blood-red—T-shirt, and his own wet hair was uncombed as ever. When he leaned in to pour my coffee, he smelled like shower gel. I chewed my toast listlessly.

For a while, we sat at the table in silence, only the radio playing in the background. It was an uncomfortable silence, as though there were an invisible wall between us.

"Well, ask your questions already," Danny said at last. "Not talking about things or tiptoeing around them won't change the situation."

My hands cramped around the coffee cup in front me. Goodbye, beautiful illusion of a carefree life.

"Things here aren't all sunshine and roses!" Christina had said to me once. Thanks a lot, Tina. She could have gone ahead and expressed herself a little bit more clearly back then.

My list of questions was practically infinite, so I decided to start with the most harmless one. "Who all knows you have HIV?"

"My parents, of course. Christina, Jörg, Ricky, Simon... My boss at the gym knew, and Dogan, my trainer, knows, too. Nobody else."

"Dogan knows? But he still took you to the world championships? Isn't that dangerous? Didn't you run the risk of infecting someone?"

Danny shook his head. "That would be practically impossible. My blood would have to spray directly into an open wound on my opponent's body—and it would have to get there within a fraction of a second, because the virus dies immediately in the air. There's probably a better chance of getting struck by lightning."

"But, you still stopped doing knockout fights. Was it because you didn't want to take that risk?"

"Not right away. Not until after the world championships. Everyone got tested before that, and after, things got difficult. Some event organizers banned me from participating in bigger competitions once they found out. So I decided it would be easier if I switched to light contact."

He put his bare foot on the seat of the chair, drew his knee up to his chest, and rested his chin there.

He's creating a protective barrier between himself and you, my rational mind informed me. I needed to make sure he didn't withdraw completely.

"How long have you had it?"

"Nobody knows exactly. I didn't have any symptoms after I was infected, or at least none that I noticed. Some people get something like the flu when they first contract it. But even if I'd had that, nobody would have thought it unusual. Worst-case scenario, I got it right at the beginning, when I was eleven..."

"When your father started doing that to you," I murmured, finishing his sentence.

"Right. I assume that's what happened."

"Is that bad? Having had it longer? Because of the incubation time?"

"It's not exactly incubation time," he explained clinically. "They call it the latency period. It's the stage where you have the virus and can infect others, but you're completely healthy. It doesn't affect me physically at all. Nobody can predict when it'll break down my immune system enough that I develop AIDS. Everyone's totally different—with some people, it happens within a few months. But there have been a few cases where it took almost fifteen years. There's no standard."

I was afraid the coffee cup would shatter under the pressure of my grip. "So maybe it will never happen to you?"

"That doesn't happen." His voice was calm and collected. "If you have HIV, you get AIDS. There's no way around that."

"And then? What happens then?" It came out as a whisper.

"You get symptoms. You get sick. Could be anything—nausea, dizziness, skin diseases, colds. Your immune system just hits a wall." He described it like he was talking about how clouds form in the sky. "Eventually, it develops into full-blown AIDS. If you're lucky, it kills you fast. If not, you waste away miserably for months, even years."

My lips were trembling. I shut my eyes for a moment and wished myself far, far away, to some sunny Mediterranean beach. "What exactly do you die of?"

"That's different for everyone, too. A lot of people die of lung infections or tuberculosis. Or some other harmless disease, because your immune system can't handle it anymore. Isn't that pathetic? Croaking from a cold?"

I shook my head, appalled at his crude choice of words. But he probably had to talk like that. It was his way of dealing with it, of taking some of the horror out of the whole thing. "How did you find out?" I asked quietly. I couldn't make my voice go above this volume. "That you had it?"

He stood up and began clearing the table. I sensed that I was treading on dangerous territory. "My father told me. Just after I moved in here. He called. Told me he was sick, wanted me to visit him. But I refused. So he told me over the phone. Just like that. That I'd been infected for years and was going to die soon. Just like he was." He banged the dish he was holding into the sink with a loud clatter and crossed his arms. Abruptly, he closed his eyes, and tears began running down his face.

"My dad knew the whole time," he whispered. "He had to have known. He'd been messing around with prostitutes for years. It didn't stop him. Sometimes I think maybe he infected me on purpose."

"Jesus!" That was all I could think of to say. Things like that didn't happen. Surely, *surely*, there was no way that actually happened.

Standing, I went to him, uncrossed his arms, and then drew him in gently. He buried his tear-streaked face in my hair, resting his forehead against my cheek, shoulders shaking. I stroked his back comfortingly, feeling his tears drip down into my cleavage and soak my T-shirt. I didn't care. My fear of becoming infected had given way to boiling fury at Danny's father, a person I didn't know and would never meet, and yet I hated him more passionately than anything in the world. My rage continued to swell, growing ever hotter, and remained my constant companion.

"See?" he sniffled. "My life is one giant catastrophe. I told you. I didn't want to drag you into it. I'm so sorry. We'll never be able to have a normal relationship."

"Sure we will," I said stubbornly. "You saw that last night."

He gave me a helpless look. Tears were still swimming in his eyes. "I don't mean *that*. We'll never be able to have children. We'll never have a future."

I had to smirk. "You're twenty years old, and you're thinking about children? Most guys don't have kids until they're in their thirties. A lot could happen between now and then."

"But I really, really want kids." His voice was equally stubborn.

"So do I, but not yet. Things will be different in ten years. By then, they may have a cure. By then, they may find a way for HIV-positive people to have healthy children. By then—"

"I'll be dead."

"Stop. Don't even think things like that!"

He gritted his teeth.

"Have you been to an HIV counselor?" I asked.

"Yeah. But it's been years."

"Then let's go to one together. Please."

He ran a hand over his face, wiping his tears away, and took a moment to compose himself. Before my eyes, he transformed back into the calm, confident person I knew. "What do you think you'll get out of it?"

"I think I'll get information out of it."

His silence lasted a little too long—I could tell he was against the idea.

"Please," I said. "I need to learn how to deal with this, too."

"Okay." He nodded, suddenly determined. "I still know a few places. I'll call around tomorrow and find out where we can get an appointment."

I stretched up on tiptoe and kissed him on his lips, which tasted of salt. "Thank you. You're the best."

"I'm an idiot," he said. "I never should have gotten you into this whole mess. Instead of just warning you, I should have stayed away from you!"

"Stop blaming yourself." I poked him in the chest. "I'm an adult, I can make my own decisions. Your father's the one who made you feel all of this guilt. Don't let him continue to have that kind of power over you!"

He mumbled something under his breath.

Out of the blue, I told him, "I trust you, Danny. Completely and totally, in every respect. But you have to trust me, too. And if I think it's not dangerous for us to sleep together, then please accept that."

"But it *is* dangerous!"

"Everything in life is dangerous. I might go outside and get killed by a falling roof tile. Or run over by a mail truck. Or maybe I'll get heat stroke."

He shook his head and rolled his eyes. "Why don't we wait until we've talked to the counselor, and then decide from there?"

That seemed like a fair compromise. I didn't expect they'd recommend chastity. "Okay."

Danny took my hand and pulled me closer. "Last night, I realized I can. Trust someone else, I mean. For the first time in my life. Up until now, I always thought trusting other people was a mistake I would never make. I never thought I'd be able to let someone else get so close to me—physically and emotionally." He looked down at the floor. "I trust you completely and totally, too," he said. "I just need to work on putting it into practice. Be patient with me."

I nodded and squeezed his hand to tell him that I understood, and that it was okay. Of *course* putting it into practice would take time. "Let's go for a walk," I said. "So you can tell me what happened with your mom, and why you think it was your fault."

Back at my parents' house that night, I lay awake in bed for a long time, barely restraining myself from booting up my computer and reading everything I could find about HIV. I was deliberately avoiding it, because I knew it would only make me crazier. I'd have rather discussed it with Christina, but we hadn't crossed paths since I found out.

And that wasn't all that was bothering me.

The story he'd told me that morning was still echoing in my head. Danny had told me he was responsible for his mother miscarrying his younger brother, and he'd said it calmly, like it was the most obvious thing in the world. As though there were no reason anyone would think otherwise.

How could his parents say something like that? He'd only been ten. I could just see him standing there, at his family's house in America, holding his heavily pregnant mother's hand, begging to go back outside for a minute to look for his dog, who'd run off.

I could hear his father scolding him, refusing to let him leave. Of course Danny had ignored him and darted off. But how could he have possibly known that his mother would keep hold of him, that she would lose her balance and fall down the stairs? Not even an adult would have anticipated such a thing. How could they expect it of a child?

I tossed and turned. My head was pounding, and every time I closed my eyes, I saw a flaxen-haired boy with blue eyes...stretched out on a bed, counting the minutes and wondering if he could risk moving, even an inch, just to turn onto his side.

By the time I finally dozed off, it was already nearly morning.

I'm running and running. Up an endless staircase reaching into the radiant blue sky. But the faster I run, the faster the steps collapse. They're falling apart one by one, up from the bottom, until the destruction catches up to me and the stone beneath my feet crumbles.

I reach out for the comforting blue of the sky, but the steps drag me down instead. Now I'm falling and falling, and no matter what I do, I can't find anything to hold on to anymore.

Chapter Thirteen

August 2000

The three of us went out to buy Danny's new dresser. Back at home, we worked together to assemble it and put his clothes away.

Christina was so happy I'd gone back to Danny on Saturday night that when I first walked in, she'd thrown her arms around me and squeezed me for more than a minute. She hadn't even mentioned the destroyed furniture. She knew Danny's temperament, and anyway, it probably wasn't the first time he'd reacted that way to an emotional situation. It was his way of dealing with the rage he carried around in the pit of his stomach.

That Friday, I drove straight over to the martial arts center after work. A few of Danny's students were taking the orange-belt exam the following day, and he wanted to go over everything with them once more. Christina was coming to watch as well.

I didn't see her in any of the chairs surrounding the main ring, so I figured she was in the back, in the area Danny reserved for his students.

I spotted him from across the room. He was standing on a mat, surrounded by his students. "Feint left, kick right. No, don't step in between," he said. "Feint, down, kick. No step. Good, just like that. Make sure to hit with your shin…" Once he was more or less satisfied with his students' side kicks, he turned to give me a kiss. "Hey. Tina's back there somewhere."

Danny's training style was the exact opposite of Dogan's. He never raised his voice or showed impatience. He used positive reinforcement to motivate them, not pressure. Not one of his students had failed a test yet.

I saw Christina sitting on a mat near the wall. She was wearing black shorts and a light-colored training jacket, which was zipped up all the way to her chin. I went over and dropped down beside her.

After exchanging greetings, we sat in silence for a while, watching Danny. He was standing on his right leg and had his left raised high above his head, kicking it into the air to demonstrate how to shoo an opponent back. He was left-handed and preferred to kick with his left leg as well, so at times he had to rethink a little when showing his students how to do things. At first, I'd been completely baffled by the idea of anyone being able to kick almost vertically in the air like that, but by now it was normal to me. We often spent evenings at the center, with Christina and I sitting comfortably on a mat in the corner while Danny either worked with his students or practiced on his own.

He'd taken on so many new students and added classes to his schedule so quickly that it had become a full-time job. Even so, he still went off to do photoshoots almost every weekend, sometimes for two or three days at once. His phone rang constantly during the week—students were always calling to ask him questions, and his agent often called to tell him when his next shoots were, how to get there, and what to wear to them.

"I wanted to thank you again," Christina said, seemingly out of the blue.

I blinked in surprise. "For what?"

"For coming back to him."

I couldn't help smiling. "You don't have to thank me for that." I gave her a long look. "To be honest, I didn't do it for you."

"Of course not, but I'm still incredibly happy about it. Please don't be mad at him for not telling you sooner. He wanted to tell you right from the start, but Jörg and I both worked to convince him not to. We wanted so badly for it to work out for him for once."

"I'm not mad at him, Tina," I assured her. "He warned me often enough, and he tried to keep me away. But I wanted to be with him."

"Well, thank you," she said again. "For accepting me. Any other girl probably would have made him choose."

"Tina, if I'd made him choose between you or me, he'd have chosen you."

Christina regarded me thoughtfully, as though trying to decide whether she could tell me the truth. "Maybe in the beginning," she conceded at last, "but those days are over, and you know that. If you asked him to choose right now, he'd pick you."

I thought about it for a moment and realized she was probably right. "Tina," I said, reaching for her hand, "I would never force him to pick between us. I wouldn't force him to do anything. How could I?"

She still had that scrutinizing look on her face "So he's told you everything? About his past?"

"Yeah, I think so." At least, I hoped that was all of it.

She looked pleased. "Good. Then you'll be hearing about it often. In detail. Talking about it is important to him."

"I'll always listen," I promised. "Do you guys discuss it a lot, too?"

She nodded. "Yeah, we talk about everything. He knows my past, and I know his. We don't have any secrets from each another." She fell silent for a moment. "I want to let you in, too," she said suddenly. "I mean, I don't want to have any secrets from you anymore, either. Can I tell you my story?" She gripped my hand tightly.

"Of course you can."

She pulled me a little farther into the corner and turned so that her back was to the rest of the arena. I did the same. Christina bit one of her fingernails uncertainly. "It's not easy for me to talk about," she whispered. "But I'll try."

"Okay," I said. "I won't interrupt. I'll just let you talk."

She gave me a grateful smile. "The funny thing is," she began, "everyone always says I have nothing to be ashamed of, but I still can't manage to look people in the eye when I talk about it." Still chewing on her nail, she looked down at the ground and said in a monotone voice, "I was seven, my sister was ten. My mom didn't know anything about it at first. My dad would wait until she left the house. She'd go out with her friends every Thursday, and then he'd come and get us and take us to the bedroom with him.

"At first, he only did it to Caroline, but he'd make me take all my clothes off, sit in a chair beside the bed, and watch. Later, he started touching me, too—putting his fingers between my legs, making me touch him, forcing his penis into my mouth. But he only took my sister to bed with him. Until one day, she ran away and left me behind."

I wanted to ask why her sister hadn't taken her along, but I didn't want to interrupt.

Christina seemed to read my mind, though. "You're probably thinking that going through something like that would create a deep bond between two sisters, but it was just the opposite for us. She hated me, because she had to get in bed with him every time, and I got to just watch. When she was thirteen, she ran away and never came back. I haven't seen her since.

"After that, I had to take her place in bed with him. My mother began to suspect something was wrong, but she didn't do anything about it at first. She stopped going out in the evening, but he still found opportunities to be alone with me—when she went shopping or to the doctor or whatever. And she was in contact with

Child Protective Services a lot, searching for Caroline, but there was no sign of her anywhere. Never has been."

As if a dam had burst, tears began running down her cheeks. Her large eyes narrowed, and her mascara began to smear. She was still staring at the section of mat between her feet, clutching my hand tightly.

"He made me undress completely every time," she went on tonelessly. "My father never hit me the way Danny's did, but he took photos. He'd make me sit on a chair with my legs spread, and then he'd take pictures of me from every angle for what seemed like forever..." Hearing quiet footsteps, she fell silent and quickly wiped her tears away. Danny had come up behind us, and now he reached out to touch Christina's hair.

"Everything okay?" He looked worried.

I knew he was exceptionally sensitive and had incredible emotional radar, but this still completely astonished me. He couldn't have seen from the training area that Christina was crying—it was too far away, and we were facing the wall. And yet here he was, as if we'd called out for him. The emotional connection between the two of them must have been so strong that he'd felt her pain, or at least suspected it somehow.

"Everything's okay," I assured him, giving him a look to indicate he could leave. "She was just telling me—"

Grasping the situation immediately, Danny nodded and disappeared as quickly as he'd arrived.

Sniffling, Christina cleared her throat to continue. "I had to put on my mom's heels and bras." She struggled to get the words out. "It was all much too big for me, but he loved seeing me walking around in it. He took pictures of that, too..." Her thumbnail was already bleeding, but she kept biting it anyway. I closed my eyes. I'd actually thought that nothing could shock me after Danny's story, but now I knew better.

"Did your mother do anything about it?" I asked quietly.

She nodded. "She found out three years later. She divorced him and left with me. But she hated me from that day on. For destroying her marriage, and for the fact that my sister had run away."

I snorted in fury. Unbelievable. You'd think a mother would stand by her children unconditionally.

"I was at the end of my rope, I was dead inside. I started cutting myself, with razors, just so I could feel that I was still alive. Sometimes I even poured salt into the wounds so they'd hurt more. And then, when I was fourteen, I ran away. Hung around the train station, got into drugs. Just hash at first, but I graduated to heroin pretty quickly. That started a whole vicious cycle: I'd sleep with some sleazeball in order to get heroin, and that would disgust me so much that I'd take even more heroin.

"Back then, I was firmly resolved never to go through something as horrible as sex unless it was for money. If I had to put up with all of that, I thought I should at least get paid for it. Eventually, Child Protective Services found me, but I ran away again and again. They found me a group home and a therapy group for severely traumatized children. I refused to stay put in the home, but for some reason I gave the self-help group a chance, and that's where I met Danny."

She turned and looked at me intently. Her eyes were red from crying. "He probably saved my life. As we became friends, he hounded me into rehab and took me back to the group home. Then he helped me press charges against my father...who ended up only getting six years." She swallowed hard. "Can you imagine? Six years! They couldn't prove what he'd done to my sister, and they hadn't been able to find the photos. And the fact that I hadn't pressed charges until much later made it even more difficult. He might parole out even sooner for good behavior."

My thoughts turned to Danny for a moment. After the whole nightmare of his own father's trial had finally ended, he'd gone through the same crap all over again with Christina.

She closed her eyes and wiped her face with both hands before continuing. "I moved in with Danny two years later. Back then, I was already almost totally off the drugs, but he still stuck me in inpatient rehab for nearly eight months. I hated him for it, begged him not to do it, threatened to end our friendship, but he insisted. Today, I'm grateful he did. When I got out, I was totally clean, but he still took me back there this year to reinforce it all. But you know that part of the story."

Cautiously, I drew her close, buried my face in her hair. "Thank you, Tina," I whispered. "Thank you for telling me. Ever since I met you guys, I've wished I could be part of what you have."

She jerked away from my embrace and stared at me, looking baffled. "Jessica," she said. "You've been part of it for a long time. You've become just as much my family as Danny is. I love you, too."

I grinned and pulled her back in. "I love you, too, Tina." After a while, I added, "And I love Danny. With all my heart. You don't have to worry—I'll never leave him. Promise. No matter what happens, I'll stay with him."

It was the truth. I loved Tina, and I loved Danny more than anything. I would travel this road with him until the end, even if it was the last thing I did in my otherwise-meaningless life.

***

I'd been having a hard time concentrating on work all week long, so I left early on Friday and went out riding before going to Danny's. Silently, I closed the front door behind me and stepped into the hallway. I'd been expecting Danny to be home as well, but he didn't come out to meet me, which wasn't like him at all. "Hello?" I called.

Christina came out into the hall. "Jessica, come in. Danny's still at work."

"His car is parked outside."

She walked over and hugged me. "Really? He didn't come inside. Maybe he's in the yard?"

"I'll go check."

Christina disappeared into her room again, while I set my purse on Danny's dresser and walked through the living room to the terrace. The deck chairs were positioned neatly around the outdoor table, and there was nobody on the lawn, either.

A soft whistle let me know that I wasn't alone. I looked around, curious. It took me a while to find Danny. "What the hell are you doing on the roof?" I called. "Come down!"

"No," he said. "You come up."

I barely suppressed a sigh and wondered how he'd gotten up there. Then the green trash can beside the attached garage caught my eye. I climbed up onto it and then onto the garage roof, one knee at a time. From there, I hoisted myself up one level higher, to where Danny was sitting, on the roof of the apartments. It was easier than I'd expected.

The gabled roof wasn't especially steep, but I still crawled over to Danny on all fours, too afraid to stand up. The tiles were very warm, but tolerably so. If the sky hadn't been cloudy half the day, I'd probably have gotten blisters on my hands. "What are you doing up here?" I repeated as I settled in beside Danny.

"Watching the sunset," he said, kissing me on the cheek.

"From here? Funny, I could have sworn your apartment had windows."

"But you can only see the *spot* from here." He pointed between two trees, out into the distance. He was right. The view was breathtaking. We could see past all the rooftops and far out into the fields. But what was *the spot*?

"What are you talking about?"

"Over the hill to the left of the cemetery, there's this one place where it looks like the sky and the ground are connected. The Gateway to Heaven." He scooted closer and turned my chin in the right direction. "There."

I had to admit he was right. There was a place where the horizon seemed to fade gradually until it disappeared altogether. "I see it," I breathed.

"And my soul spread far its wings, and sailed o'er the hushed lands as if gliding home." Danny's whisper sent a shiver down my back, and the hair on my arms stood up.

"Sad, but beautiful," I said quietly.

"That's my favorite part of 'Night of the Moon.' It's a poem by Eichendorff. It's about reuniting those who have been separated. The boundary between Heaven and Earth dissolves, allowing passage back and forth between the two worlds. The dead can come to the living, and vice versa. But it only works when the horizon comes close enough to the ground, like it does out there."

"I don't believe it."

Danny gave me a questioning look. "Um, it *is* just a legend."

"Not that." Confused, I tried to sort out my thoughts. "The day we met, while I was on the Ferris wheel, I recited the first verse of that exact poem! And you came over and talked to me half an hour later. And now here we are, talking about that poem. Crazy, huh?"

Danny only shrugged. "I don't think so. People get premonitions all the time. They just don't realize it because they're busy thinking about a bunch of other crap."

"A premonition?" This was getting far too spiritual for my taste. "About what? This conversation? Or meeting you?"

"Who knows? Or maybe it was—"

At that moment, the roof window a few feet away from us opened, and a woman with wild, curly hair poked her head out. "Good Lord, Danny, why can't you sit under the roof like normal people?"

"It's nicer up here," he said. "Want to join us, Britta?"

She rolled her eyes. "Oh, sure! Should I bring tea and cookies, too?"

"Yeah, great idea!" Danny agreed merrily.

I heard her mumble "You get down from there!" as she closed the window.

"Is she serious?" I asked.

"I hope not." Danny grinned. "I hate tea."

"Bullshit. Everyone likes tea."

"I don't." He gave me an apologetic look. "Bad experiences."

"With tea?" I looked at him doubtfully.

"Long story," he said with a dismissive wave before turning to me. "Anyway, you should remember what you thought about all this today, and then pay closer attention in the future. Then you'll notice things like that more often. Premonitions, signs, moments of serendipity, whatever you want to call them. Maybe they'll help you someday."

"I don't understand. Help me with what?"

Danny was silent for a while. The light around us began to change, becoming reddish and somehow surreal. "Someday," he said, "when I'm not around anymore. When you're near the horizon, you'll be near me, too.."

"Stop it," I broke in, a shade too gruffly. "You're giving me chills."

"Just remember it, Ducky. Just in case."

"We shouldn't even be thinking about stuff like that."

"I know."

The window opened again, and Britta leaned out. She had neither tea nor cookies. "Get down from there, now!" she called, waving her hands in our direction. "If our landlord sees you up there, you'll be in a lot of trouble."

"We're going!" I said, to placate her. I gazed out one last time toward the horizon, toward the blood-red sun, and then dropped to my knees and crawled back to the garage.

Danny lay down on the warm roof tiles. "I'll be right there. Give me five minutes."

Chapter Fourteen

September 2000

Erika Blumhardt glanced nervously at the clock. Just one more appointment left for the day. A young couple who had scheduled last month. Erika suddenly regretted having agreed to see them. Even though they weren't due to arrive for another fifteen minutes, she couldn't take her eyes off the parking lot outside her office window. She caught herself shifting from one foot to the other in agitation. Why weren't they here yet? Why did everyone always show up at the last minute?

To be fair, she'd been getting annoyed at little things a lot more frequently lately. Especially work-related things. She'd been working in social services for fifteen years now, the last ten in AIDS therapy, and it hadn't been like this at all before. The people who'd come to her seeking help hadn't infuriated her. Deep down, she knew it was wrong of her to feel this way about them, but she couldn't help it. The people who came to her were just so irresponsible. In principle, it didn't matter to Erika at all that they put their own lives at risk, but they endangered people around them as well. It was like Russian roulette, except that some of the people involved didn't even know they were part of an immoral game.

She'd never have seen it that way before. Back then, she'd just felt sorry for her 'patients,' as she'd secretly called her clients. Nowadays, when an HIV-positive man told her he'd had unprotected sex with the sobbing, terrified woman sitting beside him and only told her about his condition afterward, she'd think of her own daughter.

They came in wanting to know if there was anything they could do about it, and yes, it was possible to do something about it, but most of the time she felt like screaming at the guys to think with their brains and not their other organs. The thought of Yasemine ending up with a guy like that made her want to climb the walls.

Yasemine's birth had changed a lot of things. Everything, actually. Erika had changed. She knew that her new attitude made her the wrong person for this job, and she resolved yet again to speak to her supervisor, to lay her cards out on the table and ask to be transferred. This just couldn't continue. She was already furious with her next clients despite the fact that they weren't even late yet, just because she wanted to get back to Yasemine. Maybe she should call the nanny?

The knock at the door jolted her out of her thoughts. She strode quickly across the room and opened the door.

"Erika Blumhardt," she said, shaking the young man's hand first. He was tall, blond, and unusually attractive. The dark blue of his eyes was fascinating, and she caught herself staring into them a second too long. She hadn't caught his name. Hastily, she turned to the young woman and shook her hand as well. The girl was more ordinary-looking, slender, with large brown eyes in a pale face. Her chestnut-colored hair was slightly stringy and reminded Erika of the fat, ancient pony she'd owned as a child. She introduced herself as Jessica.

"Come with me," Erika said. "Have a seat at the table." The couple followed her to the back of the room, and she gestured for them to sit.

It's the woman! Ever since she'd started working there, she'd secretly played this game, guessing which of her clients was the infected one. She was almost always right. This time, it was easy. "What can I do for you?" she asked in a pleasant tone, sneaking a glance at her papers to remember the man's name. *Danijel Taylor.*

"We just wanted to get some information," the girl said. "About the disease. Transmission and all of that." She struggled a little to get out the words. She seemed nervous. Her partner sat silently, arms crossed, relaxed but reserved. He seemed to wish he was somewhere else. He probably found the situation unpleasant. The partners often did.

"First of all, let me give you some pamphlets you can read later, on your own time. One of my business cards is in there, too. You can call me anytime if you have any other questions or need help."

The young woman slipped the stack of papers into her bag. A moment of silence followed.

"I'll start by telling you about the disease. Feel free to interrupt me if I cover anything you already know, or if you don't understand anything I say." Erika barely suppressed a sigh. Clients like these were the absolute worst. Came in without actually knowing what they wanted, so she had to tell them anything and everything. This could take a while.

"HIV infection progresses through three stages: the acute stage, the latency stage, and then Acquired Immunodeficiency Virus, or AIDS. The acute stage occurs a few weeks after a person is first infected. The virus multiplies rapidly in the person's body, and his or her own immune system weakens as it attempts to fight the disease off. The acute stage is often mistaken for the flu, because the symptoms are very similar: fever, lack of energy, and nausea, for example. Some people don't experience any symptoms, though. Eventually, the body manages to stabilize the virus level, and the immune cells slowly recover, so the symptoms subside. That's the second stage, known as latency, where the virus is still gradually multiplying within the person's body, but he or she experiences no physical effects."

She stopped and looked at her clients. Jessica was listening attentively, but Danijel seemed bored. She was almost hoping one of them would interrupt. "On average, the latency stage lasts no more than ten years, though there are exceptions in both directions. A few patients remain HIV-positive for a very long time without developing AIDS, and a few develop AIDS just a few months after they are first infected."

"Hang on," Jessica said. Erika saw the glimmer of hope in her eyes. "You just said that some patients are HIV-positive without it developing into AIDS? So it's possible to never get AIDS?"

Erika suppressed another sigh. This was usually the moment when she felt the most empathy for her patients: the moment where she had to dash their hopes.

"No, that doesn't happen. At least, not yet. Researchers are working on it. As of right now, everyone infected with HIV will eventually develop AIDS. Just not necessarily within that ten-year time frame I mentioned. It may take more than ten years in a few patients, but it's more frequently faster than that. It progresses differently every time, depending on the patient, on his or her immune system and physical constitution.

"Our best available treatment option is called AZT. It was originally developed to fight cancer, so there's quite a bit we still don't know about its effect on HIV. But there also aren't any other options out there for prolonging the latency stage. Patients complain about its severe side effects, though, and most people don't stay on it for long. So, right now, it's mostly a question of when the infection occurred, and how long the latency stage lasts."[1]

---

[1] *Modern HIV treatment regimens involve a combination of medications, known as HAART therapy; AZT alone is now primarily used to prevent virus transmission from mother to child. At the time Danny was receiving treatment in Germany, though, patients only began HAART therapy once their T-cell count had fallen below three hundred and fifty. Until then, they lived without medication, unless they were able to tolerate AZT.*

Jessica drew in a sharp breath, seemingly processing what she'd just heard. Danijel was still placidly sitting there with a perfectly neutral expression on his face. Erika might as well have been explaining how cough drops were made.

There it was again—the rage. Who did he think he was, sitting here acting all indifferent and superior? He probably thought his good looks would protect him against infection. She knew these types of men. Arrogant to the bone. Barely stopping herself from shaking her head, Erika resolved yet again to talk to her supervisor about being transferred.

"As the person's viral load slowly rises over time, it weakens their immune system even further, lowering the number of T-cells they have to fight off disease. When the person's T-cell count drops below two hundred, they're considered to have full-blown AIDS. The person may develop symptoms similar to the ones they had during the acute stage, only this time, the symptoms don't go away, so there's no mistaking it for the flu. With their immune system weakened like that, the person may develop what we call opportunistic infections—infections that a healthy person would be able to fight off easily, but that may prove fatal to someone with AIDS."

The girl nodded. At least one of them was actually paying attention. "The problem is that we don't know when exactly he was infected. He's never had symptoms. All we know is that it was sometime between the ages of eleven and thirteen. Probably closer to eleven—that's the most logical option."

He? Erika blinked in surprise. She certainly hadn't expected that.

Lost that bet.

"How old are you now, Mr. Taylor?" she asked, trying not to stare at him. There was something about him she found alluring.

Good God, Erika, she chided herself. *This kid's young enough to be your son!*

"I'm almost twenty-one. So, according to your statistics, it's about time for me to get on with dying." His expression was still neutral, but there was no mistaking the cynicism in his voice. It didn't faze her, though—she was used to such reactions.

"As I said, it's just a rough guideline. It can progress very differently from one person to the next. What are you doing to prolong the latency stage? Do you take AZT?"

"Not anymore," he said dryly. "I did for a while, years ago, but I couldn't tolerate it. I just work out a lot and eat right, and so far that's worked well. I'm already boosting the statistical average." A hint of a smile played on his lips, taking the sting of sarcasm out of his words.

"How were your most recent blood tests?"

"Very good," he said quickly. "Can you tell us about transmission risks?"

"Of course." She cleared her throat and gave him a stern look. "You use protection during intercourse?"

"We're not idiots," he retorted.

He was really starting to get on her nerves. Even beautiful people couldn't just treat people however they wanted and get away with it. "If you already know everything, Mr. Taylor, what exactly is it you're looking for here?"

"Tell me something I don't know yet," he said. "Or even better..." He squinted accusingly at his girlfriend. "Tell *her* that it's still possible to get infected no matter how careful you are!"

Aha. The truth was beginning to come out. The woman was the driving force behind this appointment. Erika had to smile—just like that, she began to like the young couple. He seemed genuinely worried about his girlfriend. That was so refreshing after all the men she'd seen, the ones she would have to protect her daughter from. With couples like those, she was usually overdramatic in describing how careful they needed to be. She'd exaggerate on purpose to scare them, to force the infected partner to face the facts.

These two, on the other hand, seemed like they were being more careful than necessary, so there was no need to exaggerate. In fact, she suddenly felt like she needed to de-escalate their fears.

"HIV is relatively difficult to transmit," she told them. "There's only an infection risk if infected bodily fluids—primarily blood, semen, or vaginal fluids—come into direct contact with open wounds or mucous membranes. The virus is most frequently transmitted through unprotected sex between men. Living with an infected person is absolutely not dangerous.

"Sleeping together in the same bed, kissing, sharing food, none of those are a problem. Intercourse using proper protection is fine, too. The risk associated with unprotected oral sex is negligible, provided you avoid swallowing bodily fluids. The only other thing you should avoid is sharing razors or toothbrushes, but that's just to err on the side of caution—the virus dies almost immediately upon contact with air."

Jessica gave Danijel a triumphant look. To Erika, it almost looked like the girl wanted to stick her tongue out at him. He, on the other hand, didn't look pleased with the response at all.

"Isn't it foolish to have sex despite all the danger?" He raised his eyebrows. "That's gross negligence!"

"No, not at all!" Erika shook her head. "You, as an HIV-positive person, have a right to a completely normal life. From a purely legal standpoint, you're not even obligated to tell your partner that you're infected!"

"But if I infect her, from a purely legal standpoint, I'll be on the hook for it."

"Not now that she's aware that you're HIV-positive, and as long as everything between you is consensual. Don't paint such a grim picture. Most new infections occur within the drug scene. Worldwide, HIV is transmitted far less frequently through heterosexual intercourse than through blood transfusions.

"Even if worse comes to worst and the condom breaks, there's no reason to panic: it's unlikely the infection will be transmitted, and even that small risk can most likely be prevented through what's known as post-exposition prophylaxis, or PEP. The person takes HIV medication for four weeks, and it prevents the virus from taking hold in the body. It works almost every time."

"Great," the boy retorted sarcastically. "Sounds fantastic. So *sensible!*"

"I'm telling you how it is," Erika said gruffly.

The young woman looked thoroughly satisfied with the conversation thus far, but Danijel seemed more annoyed than anything. This time, Erika didn't even bother trying to hide her sigh of resignation. There was just no pleasing everyone, no matter how hard she tried. Maybe she should move to a beach somewhere and sell souvenirs. Then she'd have a better shot at making the people around her happy. She snuck a glance at the clock. Just after five. She needed to pick up Yasemine.

"If the two of you don't have any other questions, I think I'd like to stop here. As I said, you're welcome to call me any time." With that, she sprang to her feet. She wanted to see her daughter, and she didn't care anymore whether she came across as impolite.

***

138

Everything we had just heard slowly began working its way into my brain as we walked across the parking lot.

Ten years, she said. Ten years on average.

Then AIDS developed. Ten years… Danny would be twenty-one in December.

Ten years. The number was rotating in my head. How was he staying so calm?

Because he knew that already! He came to terms with it long ago.

I couldn't process it. It was too much. Much too much.

My feet stopped working. We were only halfway to the car. Danny took another three steps before he realized, and then he turned around to look at me. "What is it?" he asked suspiciously.

"She said ten years," I whispered.

"No, no, no." He reached for my hands. "Stop getting worked up about that. It doesn't apply to everyone!"

"It's a statistic based on facts." I couldn't hold back my tears. Danny wiped them from my cheeks with his thumbs.

"It's an average. Averages are for average people. Am I an average person?" He gave me a challenging look.

I shook my head. No, he was anything but average.

"See?" He smiled in satisfaction. "It doesn't apply to me. I'm healthy, I'm in great shape, I eat right. I'm ten times more physically fit than most people are during the best years of their lives. That way, I'm constantly signaling to my body that I'm healthy, and it reacts accordingly. If I sat around thinking about the disease all day long, I'd end up getting sick."

He tapped his forehead. "That's the power of positive thinking. Your attitude makes all the difference. A little while ago, I read about an experiment where they brought some people who were allergic to carnations into a room with a big bouquet of carnations. So they all started to sneeze like crazy…and then they were told that the flowers were plastic." He gave me a meaningful look. "You see? The people had allergic reactions because they thought they would. So I do the opposite—I always act like I'm completely healthy. We can't give the disease an inch. That's our only option." He sighed. "Or, at least, it's the only option I can handle. We have to live like everything is normal. You and me both, Ducky. Can you do that?" His eyes bored into mine hypnotically.

"I'll try."

139

He nodded. "Good."

"I don't get it, though. You said you don't even take medication. Why not? Are you insane, or are you just a complete idiot?"

He snorted. "It's not that simple. I took Retrovir at the beginning—it's a brand of AZT. But I couldn't stomach it. I puked nonstop for three and a half months, I lost twenty-five pounds, I was sleeping twelve hours a day, and I was sweating like a pig all the time. I couldn't play sports, couldn't live anything like a normal life. I barely made it to school during that whole period. It was like I was already sick, with no end in sight.

"And then I stopped taking it, and just like that, I felt fine again. I just didn't want to do that to myself anymore. The vague hope of living a little longer wasn't worth the guaranteed loss of quality of life. I decided I wouldn't take any medication at all as long as my T-cell count was still over three hundred."

The explanation sounded plausible enough to me. I just hoped he got checked regularly. "How often do you have your T-cell count checked?"

"My last test results were fantastic, but that was a while ago," he admitted. "It's been almost two years. But I feel fine. Nothing's changed since then, I can tell."

"Listen," I said. "I'll go along with all of this, but you need to have that test done regularly. However often the doctor says you should. And you need to talk to him about whether it's okay for you not to take medication."

"Okay," he agreed. "I need a new doctor anyway. Mine retired two years ago. I'll make an appointment...on one condition."

"What?"

"You have to go with me and get yourself tested for HIV."

I was speechless for a moment. "What? W-why? That's silly. There's no way anything happened that night."

"It's not about that night," he said, letting go of my hands and crossing his arms. "I know you don't have it. But you went into such a panic about it, and I don't want you even a little afraid when you're with me."

"Oh. Well, then, I'll do it," I said lightly, trying to suppress my budding fear. If I was so sure I didn't have it, then why were my palms suddenly sweaty? Why was my heart racing? Why did I feel like I'd do anything to avoid having to take that test?

Because you're crazy! my inner voice snapped at me. *You dance with death every day and act like it's the most natural thing in the world.*

I waved my hands in front of my face, shutting up the voice and waving away all the mental images suddenly flooding my head—images of the night Danny and I got close.

Too close!

Danny furrowed his brow in concern. "Everything okay?"

I hid my worries behind a smile. "Of course." My voice was a shade too high. "Why wouldn't it be? Make an appointment for both of us, and I'll take the stupid test. Why not?"

"Okay," he said, but he kept watching me. Reading my thoughts, I was sure. That was probably why he insisted on me taking that dumb test. He knew how afraid I really was.

He took his keys out of his pocket and unlocked his car. "We need to focus on the positive things we talked about back there."

"Which were?"

He suddenly smiled. "Erika said it was okay for us to have sex."

"Wonderful," I grumbled. "When I say it, you cover your ears, but when she says it, it's gospel."

"She knows what she's talking about!" Danny opened the passenger-side door for me, biting his lower lip to suppress a grin. "Anyway, it's not like I have no personal interest in it."

"Hmph." I raised one eyebrow. "That's not how it seems to me. These past few weeks, you've been shooting me down nonstop."

"I just wanted to protect you." He looked contrite. "It won't happen again."

"I'll believe it when I see it." I hardly dared hope anything would change in the future.

"As long as I can hold your wrists while we're doing it, I'm good," he admitted, still trying not to grin.

"You can," I promised. I put my hands on my hips and shook my head. "That stuff with your dad really gave you issues, didn't it?"

"I know," he said. "And it's amazing that you know that and you're still with me." With that, he walked around to the other side of the car, got in, and started the engine.

Sighing, I dropped down into my seat. "Erika was totally into you."

"I noticed." He rolled his eyes. "Sick, right? She's old enough to be my mom."

"Speaking of moms…"

"Yeah?" His voice was wary.

"So you said your parents aren't dead…"

His body stiffened, and his hands cramped around the wheel. "Yes, I did say that." He took his eyes off the road to give me an appraising look.

"I want to meet her!" I blurted out.

"What?" he shrieked, completely forgetting about the street for a moment. We veered dangerously close to the guardrail, and he had to yank the steering wheel around, causing the car to skid. We swerved back and forth a couple of times before he got it back under control.

"I just want to meet your family," I muttered, gripping my seat. "That's no reason to kill us both."

"No way!" he growled, still clenching the wheel. "Never, not ever, not a chance, forget it!"

"Why not?"

"My father's in jail. If he ever gets out, I hope it's in a body bag. Wild horses couldn't drag me anywhere near him."

"I don't mean *him*," I assured Danny. I'd decided never to use the word "father" to describe the man. It was just wrong. "But I'd at least like to meet your mom."

Danny sniffed irritably. "I told you: my mom's been making up her own reality for years now. She's nuts."

I stood my ground. "I don't care if she's nuts. I want to meet her."

He rolled his eyes again. "Fine. But don't say I didn't warn you."

"It can't be that bad," I said optimistically.

He ignored the remark. "I'll let her know we're coming to Rottweil this weekend."

Wait, Rottweil? You mean she still lives in the same house?

I dismissed the thought. If Danny didn't think he could handle it, he'd have said so.

***

142

A very slender woman opened the door to Danny's childhood home and stared at us. She was exceptionally pretty, with light blond hair pulled back in a tight ponytail and blue eyes that seemed huge in her slim, pale face. They probably would have been gentle eyes if they hadn't been darting around like a hunted animal's.

"Come in, hurry," she said, pressing herself against the wall so that we could get past her into the house, and then hastily shutting the door behind us. Nervously, she glanced back and forth between us.

"Hi, Mom," Danny said. "I wanted to introduce you to Jessica."

She beamed at me. "So nice to meet you! I'm Marina. Come in, come in." I gave Danny a triumphant look before we followed Marina through the expansive entrance hall. "How nice of you two to finally come by." For a moment, she appeared to be debating whether to shake my hand, and then seemingly decided against it.

It was an older house, with dark tile floors and white stucco walls. To my right, an oak staircase led to an upper floor. I shuddered, recalling how Danny had said the stairs had creaked when his visitor was on his way up to his room. What was this like for him, being here in the house he grew up in, where so many horrible things happened? But maybe the house itself wasn't as traumatizing with *him* gone, I reasoned. I *hoped.*

Marina led us into a large, open-plan living room, with a new-looking couch positioned behind an expensive marble table. I peeked over at the kitchen area, and the floor tiles and the counters were marble as well. Money had apparently been one thing the Taylors hadn't wanted for. The centerpiece of the room was a large fireplace, where a huge fire was crackling away, despite the heat outside.

"Would you like something to drink?" Danny's mother asked.

"No," Danny said.

"Yes," I said at the same time.

Marina walked over to the large living-room windows and stood there for a moment, rubbing her arms. "Terrible weather, isn't it?" She looked over in our direction, but her gaze seemed to fix on a point above our heads. "It's been snowing all day," she said, turning back to the window. "I hope it stops soon! The cars can barely make it up the street, it's so icy out... I don't know why they haven't come and plowed it yet..."

I gave Danny a look of confusion. It was September.

He tapped his forehead and then rotated his finger at his temple to remind me that his mother wasn't all there. Almost automatically, I stepped behind Marina and looked out at the street to try to see what she was seeing. Someone slowly drove by in a convertible with the top down.

"I'll make you two some tea," she said, turning. "You must be frozen."

"Just water for me, thanks," I said, glancing down at my shorts and sandals. Danny was wearing shorts, too, along with an American flag T-shirt. Feeling slightly uncomfortable, I sat down on the couch and looked around, taking in the room. There wasn't a speck of dirt anywhere, nothing out of place. Everything in the room had been polished until it gleamed. I didn't see any photos or personal effects anywhere, either. All in all, the room seemed cold and emotionless.

Marina brought my water in a crystal-clear glass and sat down beside us. "So, tell me!" she said lightly, as though we'd known each other for years. "How are you both?"

"We're fine. I'm glad I'm finally getting to meet you."

"Has Danny ever told you about America?" Her eyes lit up. They were nearly the same unusual blue as her son's.

"A little," I replied. "He said you had a beautiful house with a pool."

"It *was* beautiful, yes." Her voice took on a rapturous note. "We lived way outside the city. All alone in a big meadow. At night, you could hear the grasshoppers chirping everywhere. Danny was very successful in swimming and track back then." She launched into a full report of his childhood athletic achievements. Her memory was phenomenal—she knew his best throw, his longest jump, his fastest swimming and running times.

"My husband and I thought he'd grow up to be quite an athlete. He was such a promising young talent." Then Marina stopped, giving Danny an accusatory look. "But when we came to Germany, he just threw it all away. Without a pool at home, practicing was too much trouble for him, so he quit. I'm afraid he was always a bit on the lazy side." She brushed a long strand of hair behind her ear with trembling fingers.

I blinked at Danny in confusion. It was news to me that he'd done other sports before, and I couldn't imagine why Marina would call him lazy.

"I quit for other reasons," Danny replied in his own defense. "Mainly because I switched sports. You know that—every time I entered a competition, you had to sign a permission form."

Marina nodded. "Of course I know that, Danny. It's okay. Sports just aren't everyone's thing."

Danny took a breath, getting ready to defend himself again but then seemed to decide there was no point.

But a world championship and a coaching career counted as "successful" in my eyes.

"He's a very successful athlete," I piped up. As I spoke, I touched the table, absently tracing the pattern of the marble with my fingertips.

Marina jumped up and hurried to the kitchen, returning a moment later with a can of disinfectant. She sprayed the table and wiped it down with a soft cloth. For a moment, I wondered if she was going to spray me as well.

Danny rolled his eyes and crossed his arms.

"Sorry," she murmured as she sat back down again. "Liam will be home from school soon, you see. He's been so susceptible to germs ever since that terrible accident. I have to keep everything completely clean, or he'll have problems with his immune system. His is deficient, you know."

I nodded, because I wasn't sure what else to do. *Who the hell is Liam?* Danny had never mentioned a sibling…

"Mom." Danny spoke with deliberate slowness, as if to someone who didn't catch on to things very quickly. Which she probably didn't. "You're mixing that up. The one with the autoimmune disorder is me."

She laughed, almost hysterically. "You really ought to show a little more compassion. Oh, Danny and Liam," she added to me. "They've never gotten along, for whatever reason." She looked at me for a long moment with a sad expression on her face. "I don't think Danny's ever forgiven Liam. Liam's the reason we had to come to Germany—he was so sick when he was born, and the doctors here are just better. Danny would have rather stayed in Atlanta. He had his friends there, and his sports…and he never got over the fact that he couldn't bring Rex with him."

"Rex?" I gave Danny a blank look. He shook his head and rolled his eyes again.

"Danny's dog. We had to leave him behind, because we couldn't bring him on the plane." Marina seemed genuinely sorry about it.

"The plane wasn't the problem." Danny turned to me. "We couldn't take the dog with us because my father killed him in a rage."

I glanced between the two of them in alarm and took a large gulp of water.

Marina turned pale. "Danijel!" she snapped. "How can you say such things? Your father would never have done such a thing. He loved you!"

"Oh, yeah, he sure did." Danny's voice dripped with sarcasm. "In his own special, perverse way."

Suddenly, I realized coming here had been a bad idea. Guilt wracked me—for insisting that Danny bring me.

Without replying, Marina stood up and walked across the room, dropping into a rocking chair in the corner. She rocked back and forth incessantly, seemingly staring right through us, as though she'd forgotten we were there. I reached for Danny's hand, intertwining my fingers with his in the odd way we always did. He watched his mother silently.

Marina ran her hand softly down her flat stomach. "Two more weeks," she whispered tenderly. "The baby's coming in two weeks."

"Um, congratulations," I said.

Danny shook his head and scowled at me. I gave him an innocent shrug. "I think we'd better go," he said. I'd never seen him this irritated.

"Don't you two want to look around? I'd like to show Jennifer the house."

"I'd like to see it," I told Danny quietly, ignoring the fact that she'd called me by the wrong name.

He jerked his hand away. "Have fun," he replied bitterly.

Marina gestured for me to follow. I trotted along behind her, down the hallway and up the stairs. They really did creak. I shuddered again.

She brought me to Liam's room first, of course. Colorful wooden letters spelling out "Liam Fynnley" were glued to the door. This family had a thing for unusual name spellings.

Marina opened the door almost reverently. It was clearly a boy's room. Soccer-themed sheets on the bed. A poster of Britney Spears above the desk. A small glass case held a handful of trophies. I walked over and looked at them more closely. They were for kickboxing.

"Liam does kickboxing, too?" Strange. The two of them ought to have gotten along well.

Marina looked confused. "What? No. Liam plays tennis. He's been playing since he was young."

"Oh." I peered at the trophies again. Almost all of them had two small figurines on them, with one kicking his leg into the air almost vertically and the other ducking away. I didn't see tennis rackets anywhere. Deciding maybe it was better not to ask any more questions, I straightened and looked around some more. Although the room was lovingly arranged down to the last detail, there was something cold and lifeless about it. The bed looked like no one had ever slept in it, the notebooks on the desk were new and blank. Stealthily, I opened the large closet, and discovered to my shock that it was empty.

Marina was busy straightening the bed, though it was already far too neat.

Danny must have gotten lonely downstairs, because he followed us up after all and came into the room, joining me beside the open closet. He noticed my confusion. "Come on, I'll show you my room." He closed the closet doors and was just reaching for my hand when his mother ran over to him.

"Are you crazy?" she shrieked. "Keep your hands off!"

Danny raised his hands immediately, yielding. "Okay, okay," he said. "I won't touch anything else."

Marina sprayed every inch of both closet doors with the disinfectant and wiped them down several times. I felt like snatching the can and the towels from her.

Danny took my arm and pulled me to his old room, which was at the end of the hallway, between the bathroom and a hall closet. It was quite a bit larger than Liam's room, and it was the complete opposite in almost every other respect as well. Everything in here was complete chaos—from the looks of it, nobody had set foot in the room since Danny had left home. The blue sheets wadded carelessly at the foot of the bed had a thick layer of dust on them. Several kickboxing awards hung on the walls, and there was another glass trophy case, but the trophies inside were arranged haphazardly, as though a few were missing here and there. The slanted ceiling was paneled in wood.

All in all, it was a cozy room, one a teenaged boy would feel comfortable in—if it weren't for that big closet that instantly made me remember everything Danny had told me. I looked back at the unmade bed, at the dark-brown wooden frame, the headboard with the posts in the corners…

Suddenly I felt like I couldn't breathe. My throat was closing up—I had to get out of that room before I suffocated. I didn't dare look at the floor, for fear of

147

seeing traces of blood. It felt like that monster was going to come stumbling drunkenly into the room any second. I could even smell the stench of alcohol and cigarettes, could hear the little boy crying out desperately for the mother who never came.

I practically ran from the room, dragging Danny behind me. We ran smack into Marina, who was standing in the middle of the hallway like a ghost, staring into Liam's room. When she saw that we were holding hands, she let out a shriek and stared at me in horror. "That will kill you, Julia!" she hissed. "Didn't he tell you?" All at once, her eyes took on a look of hysteria. "DIDN'T YOU TELL HER?" she screamed at Danny. "Are you trying to kill her? Are you trying to kill us all?"

Danny took a deep breath, forcing himself to remain calm. "Mom, don't panic. The virus can't be transmitted this way. Nothing's going to happen to anyone."

"The virus!" She clapped her hands over her mouth. "Heaven help us, Liam will be home from school any minute now!" She ran back into Liam's room to retrieve the disinfectant and began meticulously spraying down every place we'd been standing.

I stared at Danny in disbelief. He shrugged, his face remaining expressionless.

"Let's get out of here," I said. We went back down the creaking steps, and I brought my glass back to the kitchen. Marina followed us.

"You're leaving already?" she asked, her voice completely changed. "Don't you want to meet Liam?"

"Maybe another time."

She nodded and sat back down in her rocking chair.

"Bye, Mom," Danny said, but his mother had forgotten we were there. Her eyes were fixed on that point above our heads once more, and she was rocking back and forth. Back and forth. Back and forth.

We breathed a sigh of relief when we got back outside into the sun.

Danny gave me a challenging look.

"What? That went great," I said, forcing brightness into my voice.

He raised his eyebrows and wrinkled his nose.

"Seriously," I said. "I like your mom. She's funny."

"She's completely nuts!"

"I like her anyway," I insisted as we got in the car. "She can't help that she's crazy. Those were hard times for her, too."

Danny muttered something under his breath in English.

"He didn't really kill your dog, did he?"

"He did. Drunk as a skunk, he bashed his head in with a stick, right in front of me. At least he didn't suffer."

Don't think about it, Jessica! For God's sake, don't think about it!

I felt like I needed to say something. "For a while, I was actually wondering why you'd never mentioned your brother. Then I figured it out." I fell silent for a moment, my heart twisting in my chest. "Liam is the baby your mother miscarried."

His silence told me I'd guessed right.

"I'm really sorry," I whispered. "About your dog, about Liam, about…everything."

Danny pursed his lips, seemingly fighting back his emotions. Then he nodded curtly and started the engine.

Chapter Fifteen

September 2000

Tamara Yvonne Müller knew it was him. There was no way a second person with that weird name lived in the area. She wasn't sure whether she'd have recognized his voice if she hadn't seen his name. Probably not, since it had been three years already. They'd gone to high school together. The girls had swooned over him, but he'd ignored them all. He'd only noticed her, Tara. Long, dark hair, dark eyes, a face like a china doll's, with perfect skin and a model figure. She was still dreaming of making it big in the fashion world, but for the moment, she was stuck working in this stupid doctor's office, wasting her exceptional talents. She had no doubt that her talents were exceptional.

Tara had seen him as her big chance. She'd known that he modeled—for catalogues, magazine ads, sometimes even billboards. They could have been the perfect couple.

And for a couple of weeks, they had been. They'd met up outside school and gone out in the evenings. He'd brought her home with him once, but it hadn't gone anywhere—they'd just made out for a while, and then he'd chucked her out again, this time for good.

Despite everything—despite his weird standoffishness, despite the way he'd shot her down several times in no uncertain terms, and despite the fact that he'd spent hours every day on that stupid sport of his instead of spending time with her—she'd been willing to look past it all.

In the hopes of getting just one opportunity to go with him to a photoshoot.

But, instead, he'd thrown her out like a pair of pumps with broken heels.

She was still furious with him after all this time. And it was all because of that thing with the underwear. He'd told her he'd been offered a gigantic contract as an underwear model for the biggest label in the business, and he'd turned it down. Because, as he said, he'd felt uncomfortable about it. Felt uncomfortable!

And then, all this time later, this call to the doctor's office had come in.

When she'd heard why he was calling, she'd almost fallen out of her chair. This man named Danijel Taylor said he'd been HIV-positive for a number of years, and that he was looking for a new doctor so that he could get regular blood tests. *HIV-positive?* Had he not booked an appointment for his girlfriend at the same time, Tara might have assumed he was gay.

Had he recognized her? Highly unlikely. He'd always called her Tara, like all of her friends in high school had, and she went by her full name here at work. Anyway, who even listened to the receptionist's name when they called to make an appointment? And Tamara Müllers were probably a dime a dozen.

So she'd scheduled appointments for them both on Thursday morning. She would draw blood from the girlfriend, Jessica Koch, to have it tested for HIV, and from Danijel for a complete blood workup so he could find out how he was doing. And then they'd come in to speak to the doctor the following week.

***

She recognized him immediately. "Good morning," she said in a friendly tone when they walked in. When she saw the girlfriend, she nearly burst out laughing. This Jessica was almost a head shorter than him, and she certainly didn't measure up to him in any other respect.

That's *what he dropped me for?* her injured pride piped up. *You've got to be kidding me!* Her anger at him swelled all over again—but she was at work, and she kept her expression perfectly neutral.

If Danijel was surprised to see her here, he didn't let on at all. In fact, as he handed her his insurance card, he acted like he'd never seen her before. Tara entered his information into the computer and then handed them each a new-patient form. "The waiting room is back there," she told them with a smile. "Please just fill out the form, and then I'll come get each of you one at a time."

Hand in hand, they walked off in the direction she'd pointed. Tara shook her head in disgust. Public displays of affection were so ridiculous. She took her time getting everything ready for the blood tests, took a phone call, and then headed for the waiting room. She'd start with him.

"Mr. Taylor, please," she called. He stood up, gave his girlfriend a kiss, and followed Tara into the examination room.

"Have a seat, please," she told him. "We'll get started in just a moment." He sat down obediently, and she snuck a glance at him: expensive brand-name sweater, deliberately mussed hair, looked like he was going straight from here to another photoshoot. The fact that he might actually be doing exactly that, and taking that ordinary girl with him, infuriated Tara. As she prepared the needles and put on gloves, she wondered whether she should continue pretending not to know him. Hmm. She decided against it.

"Which arm?" She sat down across from him with a friendly smile, and a pleasant scent of shower gel and aftershave wafted over to her. She crossed her long legs provocatively and leaned in to give him a good view down her low-cut neckline. She called it a success that his eyes flickered down to her cleavage for a moment before regarding her face skeptically. The look in his unusually blue eyes was so icy, it nearly froze the blood in her veins.

"Doesn't matter," he said, sounding suspicious.

She put a tourniquet around his left arm and inserted the needle. "How are you, Danny?"

"Great." He never let her out of his sight for a second. "How are you, Tara?"

So he *did* remember her!

"I'm great, too," she trilled. *I have a boyfriend. He's Italian, he's gorgeous, way hotter than you. His name's Angelo Lamonica.* She didn't say it out loud, of course. It would have sounded childish. "I didn't think you knew who I was anymore," she added instead.

"Sure, I do," he said slowly. She had the oppressive feeling that she was shrinking steadily under his accusatory stare. "I just didn't know if you still wanted me to know who you were," he added.

The first syringe was full. Tara removed it from the needle and capped it carefully before attaching the next. "Why not?" she purred just a little too gently. "I'm not holding a grudge."

Goddammit, why did I say that?

She heard him sigh deeply. "Tara, listen, I really had my reasons. It didn't have anything to do with you. It was a really long time ago. Can't we put it behind us? I have other things to worry about right now."

I can imagine, she thought viciously. *If I were HIV-positive, I'd have other things to worry about too.* She didn't say it—she was at work, she couldn't say things like that. Discretion was mandatory in her line of work. So she just nodded and went on filling the third syringe.

"I'm sorry if I hurt you, Tara," he said, seemingly out of nowhere.

She looked up in surprise. His eyes were gentle now, almost tender, and just like that, she remembered why she'd fallen in love with him back then. Her heart sped

152

up a little, and a swarm of butterflies fluttered through her stomach—but she quickly drowned them in anger. Who did this guy think he was?

"I was done with you anyway," she snapped.

"Good, then," was all he said.

She pulled the needle out of his arm, put a Band-Aid on it, and extended her hand. "The doctor will discuss everything with you next week, Mr. Taylor." Her tone was cold and formal.

"Thanks, Tara. Take it easy. See you."

She smiled cynically at his attempt to pretend they were friends. "Have we met before, Mr. Taylor? I don't recall."

Out of the corner of her eye, she saw him shake his head as she walked out to fetch his girlfriend. She used disposable gloves for that procedure, too, just to be safe. You never knew. Tara wished she could ask the girl why she'd decided to get tested for HIV, but her curiosity would just have to wait until their next appointment.

***

Tara shifted nervously on her high heels. Danijel and his girlfriend were back, and Tara was getting more and more impatient. Today, she had to tell Danijel's girlfriend her test results were negative and then bring Danijel in to see the doctor. Maybe she'd finally pick up some good intel then.

"Ms. Koch, please," she called into the waiting room. "We'll just go into the examination room for a moment to discuss your results." Of course, he trotted along behind her. *Like a dog*, Tara sneered in her head. "Alone, please," she added, a little annoyed.

"He can hear the results," the girl insisted.

Tara shrugged and pulled the door shut behind them, more for appearances' sake than because she really cared who overheard. "Your test results were negative," she said curtly. "Mr. Taylor, please come to examination room three. The doctor is waiting for you there."

Tara saw the girl turn pale, and it took her a couple of seconds to realize why. It took every ounce of willpower she had to suppress a smile and pretend she hadn't seen the girl's reaction.

Apparently sensing his girlfriend's terror, Danijel pulled her into his arms and whispered, "Negative means you don't have it. Everything's okay, you're healthy!"

Tara could practically feel his furious eyes on her as he followed her into the examination room. Jessica walked back out to the waiting room.

"Sit down, Mr. Taylor," the doctor said as soon as they entered. "I've just taken a look at your medical records."

Tara gathered up a few instruments, drew fresh paper out across the examination table, and then let the instruments fall to the ground. She knelt down to search for them, moving with deliberate slowness.

"It says here," the doctor began, "that you received treatment with AZT for a brief period in 1996, and then again briefly in 1997."

"That's right," Danijel said.

"But for just three months each time."

"Both times, I stopped taking it because the side effects were too severe."

Wuss, Tara thought.

"To be honest," Danijel went on, "I feel fantastic right now. I'd like to hold off with medication for as long as possible."

Tara stood up to disinfect the instruments and sort them into the drawers. In the mirror, she saw the doctor nod. "Not to worry," he said. "Your blood work results are fantastic—if you don't want to take medication, you have my full support. At the moment, there's no real need for it. Your T-cell count is over 500 per microliter of blood, which is great—you shouldn't be experiencing any symptoms. We'll go over your viral load results in just a moment, but first"—this was where the doctor gave the patient a look of warning, Tara knew—"I want to stress how important it is that we test you at least every six months, preferably every three, so that we can keep an eye on those T-cell counts. Once they start going down, we'll have to take action. If they fall below two hundred, that's classified as AIDS."

"Okay," Danijel said. "I'll come in for tests every three months."

"As regards your progression..." The doctor laid a printout on the table. "I don't have any information on when you were first infected. Do you know when and how that happened?"

Tara's heart began to race. She held her breath in anticipation.

"Would you mind if we discussed that in private?" Danijel asked.

The doctor blinked at Tara, as though he hadn't even realized she was still there. "Of course," he said. "Ms. Müller was just leaving."

Oh, how she hated Danijel Taylor!

First, he scorned her, then, he made her look bad in front of her boss.

This wasn't over yet.

She left the room with a friendly smile.

***

The perfect opportunity finally came around noon. Tara's coworker had left Danijel's file in the cabinet and run out to pick up some lunch, leaving Tara alone in the office for a few minutes. She would have to be quick.

Fingers trembling, she pulled out the file and opened it. *Bingo.*

The info she wanted was quickly found: He'd just gotten out of a rehab clinic a couple months before. So he really was a junkie.

She skimmed the rest of the text quickly and discovered, to her surprise, that he'd actually been at the rehab clinic to accompany someone else. But then again, his insurance had covered part of his expenses, which was highly unusual for someone just there as a companion. Apparently, he'd gotten therapy there, too—but for trauma, not addiction…

She heard footsteps outside and hastily shut the file. Crap. She wasn't going to get anywhere this way.

As she shut the cabinet, she decided that it didn't matter anyway. Drugs, trauma, whatever—he'd been in rehab, which made him a junkie, end of story. She'd go to her boyfriend and tell him all about Danijel. Normally, she didn't especially like Angelo's aggressive, violent temper, but this time she could use it to her advantage. She knew Angelo hated gay people with every fiber of his being, and she planned to make use of that, as well.

This weekend, she'd tell him her very own version of the Danijel Taylor story, and then her ex would learn his lesson.

Chapter Sixteen

November 2000

Danny's students had convinced him to take part in a three-day full-contact tournament. They'd said they wanted to watch him in the ring so they could learn from him, and that argument had won him over.

The tournament started on Thursday evening, and it was being held near the town of Sinsheim. Since Danny didn't feel like driving an hour each way every night, he got hotel rooms for Christina, me, and himself. Dogan had come as well, not wanting to miss the opportunity.

There were several fights each evening, all knockout. I was a bundle of nerves the whole time. Having Christina gripping my arm nonstop and murmuring, "Oh God, oh God, oh God," under her breath didn't really help the situation.

During the next-to-last fight, Danny started getting tired and losing concentration, and ended up taking a hard kick to the face. Blood began streaming down his temple from a wound above his right eye, and the fight was interrupted.

He was still hanging from the ropes, gasping, with Dogan mercilessly barking strategy instructions in his ear, when the ring doctor came over to treat the wound.

Five stitches, without giving him time to sit down, and with no anesthetic. It was all I could do to keep Christina from running over and holding Danny's hand, at which his opponent probably would have died laughing right on the spot. I, on the other hand, was mostly afraid he'd end up with a scar—the doctor was sewing him up quickly and indifferently, as if they were in a war zone.

After that, somebody wiped the blood off the mats and signaled for the fight to continue.

Danny ended up winning, wound and all, and advanced to the final round. He won the last fight easily, practically without trying, but he still insisted he wasn't making a return to full-contact competitions. Despite my constant worrying, I was somehow disappointed, too.

On Sunday, Danny was actually exhausted for once. He skipped his morning run and slept until nearly nine—both of which were extremely unusual for him. We had a long, leisurely breakfast at the hotel before checking out and heading for home.

***

One night the following weekend, I lay stretched out on Danny's bed, thumbing through a magazine. Christina was in her room, painting her nails, and Danny was watching TV in the living room. Leika was curled up on the rug in the dining room, dozing. To an outsider, we'd have probably looked like we'd fallen out, but nothing could be further from the truth.

Although we were each in a different room, doing our own thing on this Friday night, we were one. If I'd felt like having company, I could have gone into the living room and cuddled with Danny on the sofa. He'd have greeted me with open arms. I'd have been perfectly welcome in Christina's room, too. It was wonderful to belong somewhere, to feel like I was part of a community. I felt good, more comfortable than I had at almost any other time in my life. Our lives were hardly free of problems—our future far from rosy—but all three of us were determined to make the best of it. As long as we were together, nothing could shake us.

In the middle of this languid reverie of mine, Danny came into the room. "I'm going out," he said, sitting on the bed to rub my neck.

"Now?" I grumbled. "It's already almost nine. Where are you going?"

"Nine is early on a Friday night," he said defensively. "Ricky just called. He and Simon are going out for a drink and then to a club. They want me to come along for once. Like old times."

I rolled over onto my back to give him a look of outrage. He laid his hand on my collarbone. "You could at least ask if I want to join you," I growled.

He shook his head. "Sorry. Guys' night."

I grabbed his hand and used it to pull myself up. "Let me guess: you're going to play your stupid number-hunting game again?"

He shrugged apologetically. "It'll probably end up happening, yeah."

I rolled my eyes. "Dirty cheater," I muttered, insulted.

Danny took my face in his hands, looking deep into my eyes. "It's all just for show," he whispered against my lips. "You know that. I'm not going to call any of them."

My breathing sped up, and my outrage faded as quickly as it had developed. *Goddamn, how does he do that?* "That's true. You didn't call me either," I retorted, looking a little hurt.

"I would have. Really. I promised I would."

"Those poor girls, sitting around waiting for your call for days on end, crying their eyes out." *Like I did*, I added in my head.

He laughed softly. "Oh, come on, it's not really that bad. You survived."

"Barely, though. Seriously, those girls are getting their hopes up, and you're just playing with them. It's not fair."

He shrugged again. "Nothing about my life has ever been fair."

So this was his way of dealing with the fact that he thought his life was unfair? Well...I could accept that. It could have been a *lot* worse.

"Go on, then," I muttered, pushing him off the bed. "Get out of here. And don't you dare lose that stupid game!"

"Thanks, Ducky." He gave me a kiss. "You're the best. Don't wait up—I'll probably be late."

A few moments later, I heard his car start, and I turned back to my magazine. I knew he would come back to me, and I knew he was mine. He would always be mine.

I read for a little while longer, took Leika for a walk, said good night to Christina, and went to bed. As I was lying there, I thought of the guys walking around with a girl on each arm at that very moment. Smiling, I shook my head. The thought didn't make me jealous in the slightest.

It was definitely a scream, but I wasn't sure if I'd dreamt it or if it had come from outside. Yawning, I rubbed my eyes and checked the radio alarm clock on the nightstand. It was just after three, and the other side of the bed was still empty.

Still half-asleep, I rolled over onto my side, but then I heard the bedroom door open. It wasn't Danny in the doorway, but Christina. The light from the hallway flooded the room, and I could see her wide eyes. She was clutching her pillow tightly against her chest.

"Danny?" she whispered into the dark room. She looked like a five-year-old, not like a woman of nearly twenty.

"Danny's still out," I whispered back.

"When's he coming back?" Her voice was thin and wavery—she'd clearly been crying.

"I don't know. It could be a while yet."

"Okay," she squeaked, turning to go. "Sorry I woke you up."

"Tina?" I called after her, and she stopped uncertainly.

"Yeah?"

"If Danny were here right now, what would he do?"

She hesitated for a moment, before finally admitting, "He'd let me get in bed with him."

I raised the blanket and patted the mattress decisively. "Come on."

She didn't have to be asked twice. She switched off the hall light and crawled into bed with me.

"What do I do?" I asked quietly.

"Nothing," she whispered back. "Just be there." She turned her back to me and snuggled in close. Even though the window was open and it was cool in the room, I was only wearing cotton short-shorts. Our bare legs were touching, and her mostly bare bottom was pressed against my lower body. Danny's body radiated such heat in bed that I was always warm enough. He usually slept in a T-shirt and boxers, and when I imagined her pressing herself against his pelvis like this, I found it nearly impossible to believe that there was nothing erotic about it, as he had once assured me.

But then I discarded the thought with a sigh. It didn't matter.

Tentatively, I wrapped an arm around Christina. Her entire body was completely tense, and every so often she let out a heavy sob. I brushed a few stray hairs out of her face, the way Danny would have. The way Danny did with me, too.

At that moment, I realized just how much my life had changed in the past few months. I could barely remember the last time I'd given any serious thought to who paid rent and who paid utilities around here. Thinking about such banalities almost made me laugh out loud. Problems like those were part of another life, a life I had once thought was real, but now knew was just a distorted version of reality. This, right here, was reality: an abused girl who had just gotten out of rehab a few months ago, sobbing, half-naked, in my arms, waiting for my boyfriend to get home.

Had I actually once thought it was unfair that someone would pay the bills for someone else? In this lifetime? Absurd. It was just absurd. Far more absurd than lying beside a former drug-addicted prostitute in my HIV-positive boyfriend's bed while he was out flirting with other girls at the club.

I snuggled closer to Christina, burying my face in her soft hair. I'd never felt better in my life. I'd never been so emotionally fulfilled.

By the time Danny crept into the room, barefoot, it was nearly dawn. If he was surprised to find me lying there holding Christina, he didn't let on. He came around to my side of the bed and climbed in. Carefully, I let go of Christina, who was sound asleep, and turned in his direction.

"Hey," he murmured, kissing me.

"Hey," I said. "How many?"

"Fifteen. Fourteen for Ricky, nine for Simon. Winner!"

I kissed his forehead and gave him a thumbs up. "I'm proud of you. Sweet dreams."

He rolled over and curled up a little, and I scooted in against his back. Whether it was because I'd had Christina in my arms for the past few hours or because I was just that tired, I don't know, but for a moment I forgot our unspoken agreement and wrapped an arm around his waist like it was the most natural thing in the world. Within a fraction of a second, his body was stiff as a board, his breathing rapid and shallow. I froze in horror, not daring to move again.

After a while, he began to relax, and I laid my hand on his stomach. Immediately, he put his arm down over mine to prevent my hand from sliding any further up.

I made a mental note. *Touching stomach: okay. Touching chest: not okay.* Well, it was a start, anyway. Even small victories were victories. Tentatively, I began stroking his stomach, first with my thumb, then with my entire hand, covering a tiny bit more ground each time. He let me do it but kept the barrier firmly in place. His breathing was ragged.

"Danny," I whispered softly in his ear. "Everything's okay." Our code word again.

Suddenly, he took my hand, and I was sure he was going to push it away. Instead, he laced his fingers with mine, guided my hand underneath his T-shirt, and laid it on his bare chest, over his heart. He pressed my hand down firmly and maintained a tight grip on it, making sure I couldn't move it an inch.

I knew how much courage that had taken him, and I could only imagine the internal struggle he'd gone through before he'd been able to take that step. That knowledge alone made his tiny gesture so special that it moved me to tears. Without moving my hand, I shifted upward a bit and pressed my tear-streaked cheek to his.

160

He took three more deep breaths and let go of my hand. I held it still, keeping it right where it was, feeling his heartbeat. It took him a long time to calm down again.

I'd been planning on waiting up until he fell asleep, but I didn't make it. I probably fell asleep long before he did.

He woke me with a gentle kiss on the nose. "Good morning, Ducky," he said, brushing my cheek with the back of his finger.

"Morning." I stretched languidly and turned over. The other side of the bed was empty. "Where's Tina?"

"She got up a little while ago. She's out walking the dog, and she said she'd make us breakfast when she got back." He smiled at me. "So we can stay in bed a little while longer."

It was his way of thanking me for the previous night.

"Woo-hoo! Three cheers for Christina!" I pumped my fist in the air jovially. "I love that woman!"

"Yeah, I love her too!" he called, raising his own fist. "Christina's the best!"

"What'd you just say?"

"Hm?" He shrugged innocently. "The best?"

"Before that."

"Christina?"

I pinched his side. "Before that! You know what I mean!"

"Ohh." He yawned theatrically, stretching like a cat. "That I love her? You know that already."

"Get out of my bed, you dirty traitor!" I pinched him in the ribs to shoo him away.

"It's kind of my bed too," he whined, letting himself roll off the bed on his side before coming around to leap in again on mine. Before I could react, he jerked my pajama shorts off and threw them into the corner of the room.

"You're an ass!" I stuck my tongue out at him. He reached out to pull my top off as well, but I held it down and gave him a provocative look. "You first!"

His mood shifted instantly. "No!"

"Please?" I took the hem of his T-shirt between my fingers.

Hesitantly, he shook his head. "No."

"Danny," I pleaded, "there's nobody here. Just us. Nothing else matters. Everything's okay!"

"Okay," he said uncertainly. "Give me two minutes."

"You can have two hours if you need."

He took another deep, shaky breath and closed his eyes, trying to collect himself. It took him five minutes. I simply sat there, waiting, still holding the hem of his shirt.

"Okay," he repeated at last, raising his arms. I pulled the T-shirt up over his head with a fluid motion and handed it to him—throwing it into the corner with my shorts seemed unfair. He stuck it under the pillow.

I let my eyes travel over his body. Powerful chest, soft, flat belly, not an ounce of extra fat anywhere, muscular arms, hairless torso. He reminded me of Michelangelo's David.

Although the urge to touch him was almost overwhelming, I restrained myself—but I also decided that I wasn't going to let him hold me down today, the way he always had. Before I could tell Danny that, though, he seemed to read my mind, and he lay down behind me.

He sank down onto his back, and I rolled onto his chest. Arms propped against the bed, he eyed me skeptically.

Cautiously, I ran my fingertips up his arm toward his shoulder, feeling goosebumps rise. *Take it slow*, my inner voice warned. *One step at a time. Not much further to go now.* I did the same thing again, only with my entire hand. Then I let my fingertips drift across his chest, barely touching him until I reached his stomach. Touching his stomach was okay, or at least more okay than his chest.

Danny had his eyes closed and was taking deep, slow breaths. I knew he was mentally counting to ten over and over again, doing the concentration exercises he always did before kickboxing tournaments. That was okay with me—it was still another huge step in the right direction. He was reluctant about it now, but eventually he'd get used to me touching him this way, and maybe someday he'd even learn to enjoy it.

What would he have been like, I wondered, if his father hadn't done all this irreparable damage to him?

His relief was practically palpable when we heard a knock at the door and Christina trilled cheerfully, "Get up, you two! Breakfast is ready!"

Chapter Seventeen

December 2000

Danijel Alaric Taylor didn't want to turn twenty-one. He didn't want to leave his childhood behind, not while it still owed him so much. He felt like getting up and doing something completely childish, like running across a river in tennis shoes, even though the temperature was below freezing. Something more daring would be even better—balancing on a tenth-floor balcony railing, for example. He loved heights, and he loved adrenaline.

Jessica and Christina had realized those things for themselves a few days before when they'd gone up to the top of the TV tower: the girls had waited one floor below while Danny went up to the highest platform, where he'd clambered up onto the railing until the security staff had dragged him back down by his sweatshirt.

That was probably how the girls had hit upon the idea of buying him a ticket to go bungee jumping for his birthday. The vacation they were all taking in the mountains was the perfect opportunity. He'd gone bungee jumping once before, as a teenager, and now he could hardly wait to do it again.

He waited impatiently for dawn to arrive. His gaze drifted to the hotel window. He didn't like the fact that it was closed, nor the fact that they were on the third floor. If someone came through the door, he'd have nowhere to run. Fight or flight. If he had the choice, he'd always pick flight. Not because he was afraid to fight, or even because he was worried about being injured—he'd been used to pain since childhood, and was able to block it out almost entirely—but because he'd learned early on that fighting back generally made conflicts worse. The more passive you remained—the more silently you removed yourself from the situation—the better things turned out for everyone involved.

Only now did it occur to him that, even if he were on the first floor with the window open, flight wouldn't be an option. After all, he couldn't just leave behind the two girls lying here in bed with him. So "fight" would be the only option open to him. He'd face any battle for those two, no matter how impossible the odds. He'd die for either of them.

A cynical smile played on his lips. As if it mattered whether he'd die for them. His life wasn't worth anything anyway.

He rose to his feet quietly. The fact that a girl was sleeping on either side of him made him break out in a grin. Never in his life had he dared dream of actually having a serious girlfriend who knew about his situation. Not in this lifetime. And the fact that she was so okay with Christina was practically a miracle. He'd always taken it as a foregone conclusion that no woman in the world would accept his connection to Christina—a reaction he could certainly understand. How was he ever supposed to explain to a girl that it was okay for him to sleep in the same bed as his best female friend, but that he'd have a problem with his partner doing the same thing?

And yet, from his point of view, the explanation was a perfectly simple one. It wasn't just that he knew with absolute certainty that she would never touch him in the wrong place—it was more that she was a part of him. She was like his twin sister, like a mirror image of himself. He knew she was an attractive woman, he was aware of her assets, but he wasn't attracted to her. He didn't believe in higher powers or any of that other spiritual crap, but he was still absolutely sure that Christina was his soulmate.

He wondered briefly whether he ought to take Leika out before he went running, but then he decided she'd be all right to wait—they'd stayed up late the night before, and she'd been out right before they'd gone to bed. He wanted to run a little faster than normal this morning, to see if he could finish his nine miles in under an hour. Working out was the best way he knew of getting undesirable thoughts out of his head. And he'd been having a lot of those lately.

Danny slipped into the bathroom and did a quick check behind the door. He hated his own stupid habit of checking behind the door whenever he entered an unfamiliar room, but he'd never managed to shake it.

After brushing his teeth and changing into his workout clothes, he left the hotel room.

Outside, he settled into an easy jog at first, and then gradually increased his speed. He turned his music up as loud as it would go. Still too quiet. Even with the blaring music and the fact that he was practically sprinting, the thoughts crept back into his head.

Most days, he kept the obsessive-thinking carousel well under control, stopping it with pure optimism and positive attitudes. But on emotional days like this one, it started turning again.

Ten years, the woman at the AIDS info center had said. AIDS developed after ten years, on average. He'd managed to alleviate his girlfriend's fears about that statistic, but he hadn't convinced himself with his own arguments. He knew he was well above average in many respects, but he had deficits in others.

Did that make him average overall?

Danny wasn't sure. Even if he'd been absolutely sure he was well above average in every respect, that wouldn't have stopped the disease. AIDS would still have turned up eventually, there was no question of that, and "eventually" probably wasn't too far off in the future. He'd already come to terms with the fact that he wouldn't see his thirty-first birthday. What choice did he have but to accept it? If he made it to thirty, he'd be ecstatic.

The thing that really bothered him was that he'd be leaving people behind. Christina. He had plans for her. He wanted to secure a future for her so that she'd be okay without him. She'd get there—she was going in the right direction.

And then there was Jessica. Thinking of her made him run a little faster. Getting involved with her had been a mistake. A mistake he'd made for purely egocentric reasons.

At first, it had only been a game. How could he have guessed that she was so taken with him? How could he have suspected it would work between them, despite all clear indications to the contrary? How could he have known such a deep emotional bond would form between them? Was it possible for one person to have two soulmates in life?

Never in a million years would he have thought he was even capable of loving another person more than he loved himself and Christina.

But what was his love even worth? He'd loved his mother deeply, the way all sons did. And how had that turned out? He'd ruined her life, and now there was no place in her world for him. Since Liam's death, she'd spurned him and his love. And then there was Rex. He'd loved Rex with all his heart, but his love for the dog hadn't saved it.

No, his love wasn't worth anything. His love was dangerous.

And his trust? He'd never trusted anybody the way he trusted Jessica. He'd never dreamed a day would come when he'd voluntarily allow someone else to touch him, and now it had happened. He knew in his heart that they could trust one another unconditionally, but his head was still struggling to make it happen. Danny ran even faster. One day, he knew, he would break Jessica's heart. He kept weighing the alternatives over and over, trying to figure out how to minimize the damage.

Would it be better to break up with her now, or to wait until fate separated them? Which would she be able to handle better? Normally, he could guess what she would think about any given thing, but not with this—because she didn't know the answer herself.

He'd run far too fast, finishing his first four and a half miles sooner than planned, so he turned around and began running even faster in the other direction. When he got back to the hotel, he was completely drenched in sweat.

He opened the door, grabbed his phone, and whistled softly for Leika. She ran up to him, wagging her tail, and let him scratch her ears. The prediction he'd made to Jessica about becoming best friends with the dog had long since come true. Leika was still very young, not even three years old. As much as he loved the dog, he secretly hoped he would outlive her. He knew it was twisted, but the thought of having at least that much time left was strangely comforting somehow—at least it was *a* lifetime, if not exactly the one *he* should have gotten.

Jessica and Christina were still dead to the world. Danny put Leika's leash on before quietly leaving the room and heading down the stairs. He never used elevators if he could help it—the tiny, cramped space reminded him of a coffin.

As they walked, he read the messages on his phone: countless birthday wishes from his students, his friends, Jörg, the other children from the home. He flipped through them quickly for now, planning to reply later. His mother hadn't written, and Danny knew not to expect a message from her later, either. It was the same every year.

Disappointed, he put the phone away, though he was suddenly so furious that he felt like chucking it across a field. His brother, who had never lived, was all she ever thought about. Not wanting to scare the dog, he suppressed the urge to kick the wooden fence surrounding the nearby cow pasture.

Danny shook his head, trying to clear the unpleasant thoughts away. What he needed now was a cold shower and some distraction. There was plenty of snow on the Tyrol mountaintops. He, Jessica, and Christina would be going up there later. A cable car ride, that would be perfect today. If he was lucky, they'd get a gondola all to themselves, and then maybe he could climb out a little. Just a little, so that the girls didn't have heart attacks. He was in the mood for heights, and he urgently needed adrenaline.

Chapter Eighteen

January 2001

We started for home with heavy hearts. We'd stayed longer than planned, maxing out the vacation time I'd saved up. Though we'd booked one double room and one single, we'd all stayed together in the double every night.

The martial arts center was closed over the holidays, and Danny had gotten a coworker to take his classes for the rest of the time.

He'd also been putting off photoshoots right and left, and had to schedule them all for the end of January. As soon as we got back, he started packing his bags all over again, planning to leave the very next day for two weeks of catching up on modeling jobs in Karlsruhe.

His students complained when they learned they were stuck with the sub for the rest of the month, and Danny began to realize that there weren't enough hours in the day for both jobs. He was also driving Christina to work at the gym three times a week, but I started handling at least that part for him.

Generally, he enjoyed coaching more, but modeling paid a lot better, so he refused to cut his hours on either. Stubborn as he was, he kept on trying to do everything at once.

We hadn't had a second alone during the entire vacation—Christina had been around day and night. When we finally got into bed the evening we got home, I practically jumped him.

He let me remove his shirt without protest. He was doing well with that by now, and he didn't have a problem with touching, either—at least, as long as I gave him time to prepare.

He laid on his back and eyed me warily as I sat down on him. It was a long time before he managed to let go of my wrists, but he finally did, spreading his arms out to show me that he trusted me, that I had free rein. Feeling him trembling as he attempted to suppress his rising panic, I made sure not to bend over him too closely, so that I wouldn't restrict his freedom of motion any more than necessary.

When I returned from the bathroom, Danny was already dressed again. He was lying on his back with his eyes closed, clearly fighting back the childhood memories welling up within his subconscious. Submitting to me like that had been difficult for him, and I wanted to give him a few minutes to himself.

It was then that I made a huge mistake.

I just wanted to switch off the light, and to do that, I had to climb over him. I supported one hand on his left forearm, swung my leg over to straddle him for a moment, and held his right wrist with my other hand. Holding him down like that was a complete accident, and I didn't stay in that position for more than a second, but it caught him completely off guard.

That one moment was long enough. He cried out and jerked himself upright so fast that I went tumbling backwards onto the floor.

As I climbed back into bed, stunned, he wrapped his arms around his knees and began sobbing loudly, rocking back and forth. He couldn't help it—his past had come back to him with such force that he was left completely defenseless. He sat there like that for several minutes, crying helplessly.

I stared at him in shock. "What? What is it?"

He shrugged, seemingly confused himself by his own reaction. "I don't know."

Years later, I came across a report saying that it was common for people who had been abused as children to burst into tears after sex without being able to explain why. According to the report, they usually experienced it for the rest of their lives.

If that information was out there back then, we certainly weren't aware of it. His violent reaction was frightening to both of us.

I sat down beside him, took him into my arms, and let him cry it out, murmuring words of encouragement all the while. "It's okay, everything's okay. It was an accident, I'm so sorry."

"Nothing happened," he said in a distraught voice. "I know that, but I still can't stop bawling."

After a while, Christina joined us in the bedroom, sitting on the other side of Danny. She stroked his back silently, without asking any questions. It took what felt like years for him to be able to look at me again.

"I'm sorry." He wiped his eyes with the backs of his hands. "I'm so screwed up. Even if I lived to be a hundred, it wouldn't be enough time for me to learn how to be halfway normal."

I snorted in outrage. "You don't have to be sorry for anything! You're perfect just the way you are. I love you. I've never gotten along with normal people, anyway."

The three of us slept in one bed again that night, with the windows open, despite the cold. Christina and I cuddled up close to Danny so that we could benefit from his warmth, and we had two thick down comforters on top of us. We wouldn't have been cold had we been in Antarctica.

Chapter Nineteen

February 2001

Angelo Lamonica flipped the collar of his jacket up and braced himself against the icy wind. It looked like it was going to snow.

He hated having to walk to work. Actually, he hated work in general. He'd much rather have stayed home, made himself comfortable at the computer, and spent the day looking at naked women…or maybe gone to the gym and lifted some weights, primarily to impress Tara.

Just thinking about Tara got him hot. Angelo knew girls like her weren't for long relationships. They were good for spending the night with every so often, and that was all Angelo was interested in. Not that he'd tell Tara that, of course. He'd keep the relationship going for as long as he could, though he suspected she was actually into guys of a completely different variety. Guys like Danijel Taylor, who were the exact opposite of him. Guys who were born with a silver spoon in their mouths and never had to lift a finger.

Success was practically a given when you had the financial means. Being attractive made it even easier. Angelo knew that full well. He, too, had been blessed in the looks department: he was tall, muscular, with smooth olive skin, long hair that he usually wore tied back. His biceps were impressively large, thanks to years of working out and plenty of protein shakes. And he had a collection of fierce tattoos.

His most recent acquisition was a fire-breathing dragon he'd had done across his shoulders. He was looking forward to showing it off to the girls at the pool that summer. And God help anyone who gave him any shit about it.

It didn't take much to make Angelo Lamonica mad. And when he got mad, he got violent, compensating for his lack of technique with sheer aggressiveness.

Of course, he had one key advantage over his opponents: he had no scruples. Hitting a guy when he was down didn't bother Angelo in the slightest. He'd keep right on going without batting an eyelash. In fact, that was when he really hit his stride. He loved the sound of bones crunching and the sight of blood spraying. Craved it, almost.

That was probably the main difference between him and his best friend, Pete. Pete wasn't any less prone to violence—he could send guys to the hospital with the best of them—but he experienced no emotion whatsoever when it happened, and if it didn't happen, Pete was okay with it. Not like Angelo, who was practically addicted to violence, spent his weekends doing whatever he could to provoke it. Unfortunately, the opportunities didn't always present themselves...

So how fortunate was it that Tara had come and told him about this Taylor guy?

Angelo had seen him before often enough—on the street, at the mall, wherever. He hadn't known the guy's name, and they'd never spoken, but Angelo couldn't stand him anyway. He was just too good-looking and drove too fancy a car. Angelo didn't even have a license at the moment, thanks to a DUI, which only magnified his envy. Something about the guy had always gotten under Angelo's skin, but he hadn't been able to put his finger on it.

And then Tara had told him what she'd found out about him at work. She wasn't supposed to pass information like that on, but Angelo had sworn on his life that he wouldn't tell anyone else.

Of course, he hadn't kept the promise. How could he? If they wanted to give him a proper beatdown, they needed backup. You never knew what people like Taylor were capable of.

All Tara wanted was for Angelo to intimidate the guy a little. Her pride had been injured, and she wanted revenge. Angelo found that childish and ridiculous. His motive was simple: he hated fags. Especially sick, junkie fags like Taylor. The way they lived was disgusting enough, and now this one was bringing the plague into Angelo's hometown. His hatred knew no bounds. And if he could impress Tara at the same time, so much the better. That'd earn him another hot night with her. It had been far too long since the last one.

The fact that Angelo and his buddies had already spent the last eight weeks staking out the guy's apartment and never run into him didn't make the situation any better. He was itching to let off steam already, but Taylor had seemed to be on permanent vacation. Apparently he had the money for it.

When they'd finally spotted Taylor again at the end of January, Angelo had called in sick just to be on the safe side. He faked his way to a doctor's note that gave him nearly a week to spy on the guy. Now he knew where Taylor parked, when he worked, when his girlfriend came and went. That guy had a lot of nerve, lying to that girl so he could use her to hide his interest in men.

That wasn't Angelo's problem, though. The main thing was that he knew when and where the guy went running every morning: across the fields, and then a short distance through the woods. At ass-early o'clock, when normal people were still in bed. But that would be perfect. They'd just have to drag him off the path a little deeper into the woods...

Patience, Angelo. Just one more day.

His team would be ready, provided that none of them overslept. Lazy jackasses.

Angelo rubbed his hands. Whether from the cold or in anticipation, he wasn't sure. He stepped into the large warehouse where he worked and called out a cheerful "Good morning!"

His coworkers turned and stared at him, dumbfounded. Nobody there had ever seen Angelo Lamonica in a good mood.

Chapter Twenty

February 2001

I was starting to get antsy. I stepped through the terrace door into the small yard, scanning the adjacent country road for what felt like the hundredth time. I was alone in the apartment. Christina was spending the weekend with her friend Natasha again, probably because she felt like Danny and I were due some alone time.

It was almost eight thirty. I'd already finished walking the dog, and breakfast was waiting on the table. Sure, Danny had left a little later than usual, but he still ought to have been home by now. He never ran for more than an hour.

Just as I was about to grab Leika again and go walk the trail to see if we ran into him, just to ease my troubled mind, I heard the front door to the building close. I breathed a sigh of relief, annoyed with myself for freaking out so easily.

Before he could reach the apartment door, I opened it for him—and gasped.

His white shirt was spattered with blood. His nose was bleeding as well, and one of his eyes was swelling up. He walked past me, holding up a hand to stop me from saying anything. "Just don't ask any questions."

"What happened?" I asked anyway.

"What does it look like? I got in a little disagreement."

"Yeah, I can see that. And it looks like you lost." He'd come home from kickboxing with injuries now and again, but I'd never seen him like this.

He growled something I didn't catch.

Instinctively, I reached toward the gash above his eye. "Let me see that, I think you might need stitches…"

He shrank away. "Hands off! Blood!"

I'd forgotten the obvious for a moment, the way a person sometimes forgets that the Earth has gravity.

Danny pulled off his soiled shirt and jogging pants, wadded them up into one big ball and stuffed them in the trash can. "It's not that bad. It'll heal on its own. I've had worse, and they all healed just fine without stitches." He hastened to the bathroom.

I was too panicked to do anything but sit there in the kitchen, listening to the sound of the shower. After a while, he emerged with wet hair and fresh clothes, and joined me at the table. His eye was black now, but his nose had stopped bleeding. He'd bandaged the gash over his eye carefully, so that it would heal without leaving a scar. The bleeding lip, on the other hand, he simply ignored. I gave him a worried, expectant once-over as he bit into a piece of toast.

"What?" he asked, chewing.

"What happened?"

He sighed in resignation. "A couple of guys jumped me in the woods. I guess they weren't fans of mine."

"Who the hell were they?"

"Oddly enough, they didn't introduce themselves."

I was starting to get annoyed. "Can't you be serious for five seconds?"

"I am."

"How many of them were there?"

"Five, maybe six. I dunno, I forgot to count." He smeared some butter on a second piece of toast.

"Five or six?" I made a face. "You told me once that you'd be able to take five guys. So where'd they go, the ICU or the cemetery? Or were they all heavyweight boxing champions?"

He set down his toast and gave me a penetrating stare. "You need to listen more carefully. I said that I *could*, not that I *would*."

A sense of foreboding crept over me. "What's that supposed to mean?" I pushed my plate away. I'd lost my appetite.

"The Bible says, 'If anyone slaps you on the right cheek, turn to him the other also.' You should eat, Ducky."

"You're messing with me, right?"

"A little." He placidly reached for his toast again.

"Danny!" I snapped, snatching the toast out of his hand. "What the hell did you do?"

He reclaimed his breakfast. "I played dead. It works in the animal world. The animals lose interest and go look for a new victim."

"You didn't even defend yourself." It was a statement, not a question. "Why?"

He merely shrugged, leaving the question unanswered. Suddenly, I realized why he hadn't put up a fight, and why he probably never would.

Force of habit.

He'd learned as a child that it was better to let unpleasant things happen to him without resisting. The less he fought back, the less painful it ended up being for him. Despite all the martial arts training, self-defense still wasn't something he was capable of.

"Why did they do it? Did they have a reason?"

That was the moment when his carefully crafted mask of nonchalance fell away. He threw his toast down onto the plate furiously, crossing his arms. "They *knew*, Jessica!" He chewed on his bleeding lip. "They knew. They called me a junkie faggot and told me to get the hell out before I infected their village with the gay plague."

I sat bolt upright, horrified. "How? I haven't told anyone. I haven't!" I put one hand over my heart and raised the other. "I swear!"

"I know."

"But nobody else would know…"

"Tara," he said. "Tara Müller. The doctor's assistant. I know her from high school. We… Um, well… She wasn't one of the girlfriends I've told you about, but…um, I guess you could say I dumped her. And apparently she's still upset about it."

I threw my hands up in exasperation. "Why didn't you say anything when we were there? We could have had the tests done somewhere else!"

Danny shrugged, looking perfectly relaxed again. Sometimes he and his endless patience drove me insane. "It was too late by then anyway."

"Fantastic," I grumbled. "So now what? What do we do?"

"Eat breakfast?"

"About those guys!" It was all I could do not to scream at him. "We have to find out who they are. Report them to the police. Kill them. Something!"

"We don't have to do anything. I can't imagine it will happen again."

"What makes you so sure?"

Danny stirred a spoonful of sugar into his coffee and sighed. "I'm not. I just don't know who they were, so there's not a lot we can do." He ran a hand through his hair, one of his trademark gestures, and I gasped in horror when I saw that his entire left arm was scraped, from his wrist to his shoulder.

"Jesus, what did they do to you? Drag you across the asphalt?"

175

"Something like that, yeah. Can we drop this now?"

"From now on, when you go running, you're taking my dog with you," I decided. "She'll watch out for you. She doesn't let anyone get anywhere near me."

I smacked a hand to my forehead at the thought of a six-foot-tall world-champion kickboxer needing my medium-sized dog to protect him. Everything about this situation was so wrong. I shook my head, secretly resolving to pay sweet little Tara a visit at work sometime soon.

Chapter Twenty-One

March 2001

It was the first Friday in March. Christina, Danny, and I were sitting on the terrace holding a powwow.

"This can't go on, Danny," I exclaimed. "This was the third time!"

"Really, Danny," Christina chimed in. "They'll probably kill you next time."

Danny was staring holes into the sky, his arms folded. Apart from the greenish shine around his right eye, he had no visible injuries, but they'd nearly broken his wrist this time. It was seriously sprained, and every movement seemed to cause him pain.

Nothing had happened on the days he'd taken Leika with him, but she and I still stayed at my parents' house during the week, so he went running alone then. And they'd been waiting for him again one morning.

The second time, they'd jumped him late at night, while he was on his way home from work, practically dragging him out of his car and into the bushes. They'd bullied him for a long time that night, twisting his arms around behind his back, calling him a disease, threatening to make his life hell if he didn't move away.

He looked annoyed. "So what would you two suggest I do?"

"Go to the police," I said.

Danny scoffed and rolled his eyes.

Christina scooted over beside him and took his uninjured hand in hers. "Please, Danny," she said, looking at him anxiously. "I'm scared of them. What if Jessica and I come home one night, and they're here waiting for us? Please, go to the police, for me!"

Danny sighed. "Okay. I'll go on Monday."

"Thank you!" She threw her arms around his neck and kissed his forehead, giving me a triumphant look over the top of his head. I nodded to her in admiration. She knew how to handle Danny and his stubbornness. I was glad she was there.

"I got a job!" she suddenly blurted out. "A real, full-time job!" We blinked at her in surprise. "What? I need to become more independent. I mean, I can't live at your place forever," she said, glancing between Danny and me.

At *our* place? "Tina, this place is yours and Danny's," I reminded her. "But that's great news about the job!"

"That's fantastic," Danny cried, hugging her. "I'm so proud of you. I knew you could do it. Tell us all about it!"

"I start in September. It's at a boutique down in the village. Within walking distance, even." She beamed. "Now nobody will have to drive me to work!"

"Did you already sign a contract and everything? Without saying a word to us?" I asked.

She nodded happily before running into the apartment and returning with a piece of paper—her contract. It offered her a full-time job once she successfully finished a trial period.

"Wow, Tina, this...this is amazing!" I couldn't hold in my excitement. She'd really done it! She'd gotten away from the streets, away from the drugs, back into a normal life.

"And after I finish the trial period, I'll be earning enough money to start renting my own place." She glanced between us expectantly.

"Tina." Danny furrowed his brow. "My plan is to buy you a condo. I want to know for sure that you'll be set up."

She stared at him in disbelief. "You're nuts!"

"No, I'm totally serious. Just give me a year or two to put some money aside, and then I'll have enough to get you a two-bedroom place. Call it a congratulations gift, something to motivate you to work hard at your new job." Danny glanced over at me. "I hope that's okay with you, Ducky?"

"Of course," I said. "It's your money. You can do whatever you want with it."

"Why would you do that?" Christina shook her head, uncomprehending. "Buy a condo for the two of you."

Danny pulled her in gently. "Tina..." He hesitated. "You know that me buying a condo for myself wouldn't make sense. But, someday, when I'm gone, you'll need a place to go."

That was the second time Danny had mentioned having to leave us behind someday. My throat began to close up. There it was, the topic we avoided at all costs. Though we never talked about it openly, it was always there. Like a pulsating wound festering away beneath the skin. Sooner or later, it would have to burst open. I felt like stuffing cotton in my ears so I didn't have to hear him talk about it anymore.

Christina stuck out her lower lip, and her green cat-like eyes filled with tears, seemingly out of nowhere. "I don't want you to buy me an apartment!" She sounded like a stubborn child. "I don't want anything from you. I just want you to stay. You can't leave me!"

The lump in my throat grew, and I blinked away the tears forming in my own eyes. I realized all over again how much I loved Christina and how wrong I'd been about her in the beginning.

Danny pulled her onto his lap and wrapped his arms around her. As she nestled against him, her low-cut top slipped down even further, exposing her bare breasts. But it had stopped bothering me long ago. "Tina, honey." Danny pressed her tear-streaked cheek against his neck. "I'm not going to leave you. I'm going to be with you for many years. By the time I die, you'll be married with kids, and you won't need me anymore."

"Then what's the apartment for?" she snapped.

"Because that's how I want to do it!" Danny insisted. "You're my family. Someday, I want what belongs to me to go to you." Then he glanced over at me and added, "I'll think of something for you, too. You should have a place in life after my death."

I shook my head.

"I'll always need you, Danny," Tina sobbed.

He brushed her tears away with his thumb. "You'll get along without me just fine, but there's enough time before all that." He pushed her off his lap with a friendly but firm motion. "Go on, ladies, get ready. We're going out for dinner, and then we have to do something to celebrate Tina's big news."

Enough time. A phrase I would often recall later on—when it had become clear that we would never have enough time.

As we left the restaurant, we decided to just go out for a quick cup of coffee and skip the partying. Christina hardly drank anyway, and I could certainly understand Danny's aversion to it by that point.

Christina ordered herself a latte, and Danny and I got cappuccinos.

"Should we go to Cannstatt on Saturday?" Danny asked abruptly. "The spring festival's starting."

"Ooh, yes!" I cooed, and Christina clapped her hands in excitement.

"That's where you two met," she remarked.

I nodded. More than a year and a half ago, on an October night that seemed like it had been in another epoch.

"How romantic. But I'm not coming with you."

"Of course you are, Tina," Danny said, suppressing a smile. "Our first meeting wasn't all that romantic."

"Nope. Not happening." Suddenly, she straightened in her chair.

Danny noticed immediately. "What's up?"

"Shh," she whispered. "You guys hear that?" Then her expression hardened, and her face turned pale. She stole a glance at two older women sitting nearby. "They're talking about us."

Danny and I listened as well, holding our breath.

"Absolutely scandalous! I can hardly believe something like that lives here!"

"It's not safe anywhere anymore."

The older of the two, a white-haired lady with a perm and glasses, peered in our direction. "They ought to deport him before he spreads the gay plague all over the place!"

The other woman, a chubby lady in a hideous flowered blouse, hissed back, "Is he gay? Well, he obviously sleeps with women, too."

I swallowed hard. Didn't they notice that we could hear them?

"I heard he's a junkie." Miss Perm actually pointed at us. "Junkies, all of them. They're probably all infected with it."

The other woman looked over and realized we were all three staring at them open-mouthed. Hastily, she turned her back to us and continued the conversation more quietly.

"Let's go," Danny murmured.

"No, I'm gonna go kick their asses!" Christina snapped, but Danny pulled her back. I was still speechless.

Danny paid our bill and herded us out to the car. We followed in sullen silence. I was so furious, I thought I was about to explode. Danny started the car.

"I'm going back in there for a minute!" I suddenly decided.

"Ducky, there's no point. Just forget it."

I jumped out before he could drive off.

"I'm coming with you," Christina called, leaping out of the car as well. Danny shut off the engine again, muttering something that sounded like "Damn women." I was fairly sure he didn't mean the grannies in the cafe.

Without really knowing what I was going to say, I headed straight for the older women's table, pulled up a chair, and straddled it. Christina followed my lead.

"So we ought to be deported, hm?" I asked in a biting tone.

The two old ladies stared at me in astonishment.

"Because we're diseased, hm?" Christina added in the same tone.

"Not you two," Miss Perm said, trying to appease us. "The young man who was sitting with you. He's a junkie."

"That's not true at all." Christina gave them an affectionate smile. "I'm the junkie."

The women seemed confused, and then began glancing around for help from the cafe staff.

Christina leaned in, fixing her piercing green eyes on the woman in the flowered blouse. "I wonder what it's like to be a guy who knows he's going to die, and instead of sympathy and understanding, all he gets is stupid comments from stupid old women."

"Let's go," Miss Perm said to her friend.

"It's his own fault," the other woman said defensively, evading Christina's accusing gaze. "People shouldn't live like that!"

Christina's expression changed from one moment to the next. If I hadn't known her, I might have thought the look on her face was genuine. She glanced around the table, eyes wide. "I was raped as a child," she suddenly cried, actually managing to squeeze out a couple of tears.

"W-What? You were... what?" The granny in the hideous blouse clapped her hand to her mouth. "My God. That's horrible!"

I played along. "We can only pray the guy didn't have the gay plague, too. Otherwise, you'll die!"

"I think he had it." Her lips trembled. "I'm diseased! I'll have to be deported!"

I grasped her hand theatrically. "We'd better leave the country immediately, before it spreads all over the place! It's not safe anywhere anymore!"

Christina slumped over the table and burst into tears. Wow, she was good.

"We didn't mean it like *that*," Miss Perm said, as the other woman desperately waved the waiter over. "We were just saying—"

I got up and pulled the "sobbing" Christina to her feet as well. "Let's go. We're bothering them, I think. We'll just go find another cafe where nobody will pick on us."

"Your situation is totally different!" Miss Perm was standing now, hands on her hips in indignation.

"Oh, yeah?" I asked cynically. "Is it? How sure are you about that?" Without another word, I put an arm around Christina's hunched shoulders and walked off, leaving the old women standing there in confusion. If they thought about what we'd said for even a minute, that was already a success.

When we got outside, Christina straightened and raised her hand, laughing. I grinned and gave her a high-five.

Danny started the engine again when he saw us, and we got in, still giggling. "Better now?" he asked.

"Totally!" we exclaimed in unison.

***

Danny and I really did end up going to the spring festival without Christina—there was no convincing her to join us. Despite everything we said to the contrary, she thought there was something romantic about the trip, and that she had no business being there.

We got back home just before midnight. The house next to the apartment building was all lit up, with paper lanterns hung everywhere and loud music blaring into the street. Normally, we had no problem finding space for even our two large cars, but tonight, the entire street was packed.

"I'll park in the lot outside the cemetery, and we can walk," Danny said. It was a very warm night—we were both in T-shirts—and the walk sounded more fun than inconvenient.

182

Danny shut off the car, and we strolled along, hand in hand, down the quiet, narrow street leading past the cemetery.

"We've got company," Danny suddenly murmured to me.

I looked around in confusion. I didn't see anything for a long time, but then I twisted around and spotted two shadowy figures behind us, off to one side. Another two shadows were moving to our left; the high cemetery wall was on our right. Anxiously, I tugged on Danny's arm, but he kept walking calmly, without picking up the pace in the slightest.

Within seconds, they had us surrounded. "Hello, you two!" A large, dark-haired Mediterranean-looking guy stepped in front of us.

"Do you all really have nothing better to do than stalk me half the night?" There wasn't a trace of nervousness in Danny's voice. He just sounded irritated.

"We've been waiting for you," the dark-haired guy said. I put him in his mid-twenties, maybe a little older. "Since you've parked so far away, we thought you might like some company."

"Thanks, but we're fine on our own," Danny growled. "You guys are really starting to get on my nerves." He tried to walk past them, but three of them moved in to block our path, and the other three stepped in behind us. They were all about the same age, all dressed in black, and I noticed that every one of them was wearing black gloves.

Cowards! I thought furiously. If they were brave enough to beat Danny up, they ought to brave enough to at least take the risk of coming into contact with his blood.

The Mediterranean turned to me, smiling. "Angelo," he said politely. "Who are you?"

"Go to hell," I snapped.

He took a step closer to me. Danny tried to move in front of me, but two of the guys standing behind us grabbed him, one for each arm.

"Wow," he said admiringly, glancing around. "Six against one again. Respect."

Angelo casually motioned for one of the guys behind us to come forward. "Pete," he said, "why don't you explain to our friend here one more time what we want. He seems a little slow on the uptake."

I considered telling them Danny was a black belt in karate and a second-degree black belt in kickboxing, but decided against it. They wouldn't have believed it, and even if they had, it would have only made them even more eager to fight him.

There was an older man walking his beagle on the other side of the cemetery. When he spotted the group of men in black, he turned right around and hurried off in the other direction before I could even take a breath to call out to him.

Pete stepped forward. He was half a head shorter than Angelo, with an ugly, crooked nose that looked like it had been broken several times. He pushed back his black wool cap before grabbing Danny's chin between his thumb and forefinger, forcing Danny to look him in the face. "We want you to get your sick faggot ass out of here. Pack your shit and fuck off."

"I'm not going anywhere."

"You sassing me again?" Pete stared at him threateningly. Danny stared right back.

Goddammit, Danny, you really are an idiot, I muttered in my head. *Don't make them any angrier than they already are. Look at the ground or something. At least act like you're afraid. Give them what they want. Maybe then they'll leave us alone.*

"Fuck you." Danny never took his eyes off the other man.

Pete lost the staredown and took a step back—and then suddenly wound up and punched Danny in the face.

I closed my eyes. Did I really have to watch this?

When I dared to open my eyes again, Danny's nose was bleeding heavily. He squinted one eye shut for a moment, blocking out the pain, before hocking the blood up and spitting it on Pete's leg.

Pete leapt back in disgust. "He fucking contaminated me! Don't do that again, you nasty little dicksucker!" He moved in again, this time ramming his fist into Danny's stomach.

Danny probably wasn't impressed—he was able to tense his abdominal muscles up enough that he probably barely felt the blow. But they weren't done with him, not by a long shot. Danny still had one guy holding each of his arms, so he was rooted to the spot. I noticed the one on the left had a sinfully expensive leather jacket with a skull embroidered on the back. Maybe that would make it easier to identify him later.

Two of the guys had positioned themselves a few feet away to keep watch, but there wasn't a soul around to come to our aid anyway. Suddenly, I was glad Christina hadn't come with us. This would have been absolutely horrifying for her.

Angelo stepped over to Danny, taking his chin in hand the same way Pete had done. Abruptly, he barked out a laugh. "Check it out," he called jovially. "I never noticed this before." He traced the faint scar on Danny's face with one gloved finger. Then he wrenched Danny's head around so the others could see his left cheek as well. "Someone got to him before we did." Angelo kept running his fingers over Danny's face, inspecting the other side as well. "A real shame," he said. "Spoiling such a pretty little face like that. Tsk, tsk. That wasn't very nice at all. Go on, tell us, who was it?"

"None of your fucking business!"

The two other guys yanked Danny's arms back farther, causing him to inhale sharply. One of them had probably hit his injured wrist.

Angelo moved in even closer. "Who was it? I asked you a question."

"Go to hell!"

Angelo smashed him in the chin with the back of his hand and then rammed his elbow into Danny's ribs. "Don't get lippy, now," he chided, raising his index finger. Then a smile spread over his face. "I know!" he cried. "I bet it was your parents. Just after you were born, when they saw that ugly mug…"

Damn, I thought. *How did he hit the nail on the head like that?* I hoped it was enough to provoke Danny into fighting back. He was breathing hard, seemingly struggling to keep himself under control. *Why in the name of God is he controlling himself at all?*

"…because they didn't want you even then," Angelo added.

"Jesus, Danny!" I called to him. "Kick him in the damn face already!"

For a moment, it looked like he was about to do just that. He flexed the muscles in his arms, shifting his weight to his right leg. But just at that moment, Angelo laid his hand on Danny's collarbone, sliding his hand slowly and provocatively over Danny's chest and stomach. Then he ran his fingertips back to Danny's shoulder.

"You wouldn't do something like that, would you, sweetheart?" Angelo lisped affectionately.

Danny tensed up under Angelo's touch, closing his eyes to quell his rising panic, and I knew they would be able to do whatever they wanted with him now—he

185

wouldn't even try to defend himself. All those fights where I'd seen him take his opponents down without batting an eye, and now he was just standing there as though rooted to the spot, letting a few thugs beat him to a pulp. Again.

I cursed under my breath.

"Did you say something, baby?" Pete had moved in next to me.

"Oh, shut up," I hissed.

"How about we bring her home with us tonight?" Pete called to Angelo. "I can think of a few things she'd be good for." He made a vulgar motion with his fist at his mouth.

"Stay away from her!" Danny snarled.

Angelo glanced between the two of them in amusement, clapping his hands almost euphorically. "Bingo!" he exclaimed. "We finally found his weakness. Looks like we're going to have a whole lot of fun tonight."

Realizing his mistake, Danny bit down on his lower lip.

Angelo sidled in beside me. "Okay, kitten, off we go."

"You stay away from her." Danny's tone had changed. He wasn't just annoyed anymore—this was a threat. The two men holding him noticed the change as well. The shorter of the two had gentle, pale-blue eyes, and I wondered what the hell he was doing with the rest of them. Although both men whooped and cat-called along with the others now, they immediately tightened their grips on Danny and broadened their stances so they could dodge any kicks. A broad-shouldered, unshaven guy who had been standing guard came back to provide reinforcements, posting himself a few feet behind Danny with his arms crossed.

I suspected I knew what would happen now. They'd provoke him until he snapped, presumably because it was a lot more fun when the victim was desperately attempting to defend himself. And if they had to use me to make it happen, that was what they'd do.

Angelo pressed himself up against me. He smelled like cigarette smoke and cheap aftershave, and practically radiated dominance. My heart sped up. "Or what?" he asked Danny in a belligerent tone. "If we decide we're gonna have a little fun with her, what are you going to do about it?"

I saw Danny shift his weight again, almost imperceptibly, this time to the back. At the same time, he swept his gaze around the scene, seemingly listening for movement behind him, mentally gauging the distance between himself and each of the others. I was secretly relieved—this wasn't going to take much longer after all. Danny had reached his boiling point. When it came to me, he never hesitated long.

"I'm not warning you again. Get away from her. Now." Danny had clearly made up his mind to fight. The comment wasn't a real warning so much as a method of distraction.

Angelo let out a loud laugh, putting an arm around my shoulders and groping my breast.

Danny freed himself with a single jerk of his arms. The two guys gripping him lost their balance and stumbled forward, and Danny ducked back and away from their grasping hands. The unshaven guy behind him took a step forward, and Danny launched his leg up, twisted around in the air 180 degrees, and smashed the back of his foot into the guy's face. There was a loud cracking sound, and the guy collapsed in a heap.

Pete and the two guys who had been holding Danny, having recovered their footing, all rushed in to grab him again. One of them clamped down on his arm, but Danny gripped the guy's wrist and flipped him over his back, sending him crashing to the ground. It was the one with the kind blue eyes. He immediately stood up again with a groan, but didn't dare attack again.

Pete grabbed Danny in a bear hug from behind, and the guy in the expensive leather jacket made the mistake of approaching from the side. Danny launched a couple of side kicks at him, hitting him in the stomach, and rammed his elbow into Pete's face at the same time. Pete let go to cover his face with one hand—and try to stop the bleeding.

The sixth guy, who had been standing guard, ran off without a word.

Angelo, watching the scene from a safe distance, suddenly gripped my arm tightly and pulled me in front of him, using me as a kind of human shield. "If you take one more step," he shouted at Danny, "I'll break her—"

Without hesitating, Danny smashed into Angelo's side with full force, missing me by a hair's breadth. He hadn't been listening—any interest he'd had in talking things out was long gone. Angelo flew back several feet, landing on his back with a scream. Before the Italian could get to his feet, Danny pulled him up by the collar and punched him twice in the face.

Blood spurted from Angelo's nose. "Have you lost your mind?" he wheezed.

Danny stopped short for a moment, then put his hand around Angelo's throat. "Touch my girlfriend one more time, and you die. I promise you that." He gave

Angelo a penetrating stare. Then he pushed Angelo's head down to about hip height and jerked his knee up into the other man's ribs. The sound of crunching bones mingled with Angelo's tortured screams.

Danny let him drop to the ground before looking around again. About ten feet away, Leather Jacket was struggling to get to his feet again. Pete was hunched over, hands propped against his thighs, spitting blood onto the ground. There was no sign of the others.

I stepped over to Danny. "Well, then." I couldn't help the grin growing on my face. "Not bad."

"He put his hands on you." Danny sounded frustrated.

"Don't worry. Nothing happened. Everything's okay."

"What do we do with him now?" Danny nudged the toe of his sneaker into Angelo's side. The other man whimpered softly. I shrugged, and Danny squatted down beside him. "Great friends you've got there," he remarked dryly. "They just ran away."

Angelo groaned as Danny reached for him and pulled him into a half-sitting position. "You broke my ribs!" he moaned.

"I know," Danny said. "Unfortunately, you'll live."

"You little shit stain. Nobody breaks my ribs and gets away with it. You'll pay for this, you goddamn faggot!"

Danny let go of him abruptly, and Angelo again curled up into a ball on the ground.

"He's okay," Danny told me. "If his ribs had punctured his lungs, he wouldn't be able to bitch that loudly." He wiped away the blood still trickling from his nose with the back of his hand. I pulled a tissue out of my purse and handed it to him. He cleaned his nose and did what he could about the blood on his hands. Inspecting them briefly, he decided it was dry enough that it was no longer dangerous. Most of it probably wasn't his anyway. I took the blood-smeared hand he extended to me, and we started for home.

"That was good," I told him. "They won't try that again."

"Don't kid yourself. Now they're more pissed off than ever. They're just getting warmed up."

After Danny's performance, I could hardly believe they'd keep going after him. "You think so?"

"I'm positive. Guys like that are all alike." He thought for a moment. "If they come near us again," he added, "they'll regret it."

"Yes, Danny!" I patted gently him on the chest. "That's exactly the right attitude."

***

"There's someone at the door for you, Danny." Christina looked confused. Danny had just returned from running, I was still in bed, and Christina was making breakfast. By the time we'd gotten home the night before, she'd already been asleep, so she hadn't heard about our ordeal yet.

Danny came to the door, still wearing his sweaty running clothes. The woman waiting there for him didn't waste any time with pleasantries. "You broke two of my son's ribs last night!" she screeched.

He ran a hand through his hair a little sheepishly. "I… Yeah… Sorry."

"Don't think I haven't heard," the woman hissed in her shrill voice, gesticulating wildly. "I know all about you. You're a dirty drug dealer, and now you've committed assault! Two broken ribs, two teeth knocked out, and I don't even know what else! I'm reporting you!"

"I'm truly sorry," Danny said again, apparently unperturbed with her threat of police.

She began panting even more heavily. She probably thought Danny was laughing at her.

I pushed my way up to the door and shoved him aside. "I'm not sorry," I hissed at the woman. Now that I was look her in the face, I could clearly see it was Angelo's mother. The resemblance was uncanny. "Your darling little boy and his friends have already assaulted my boyfriend three times now! Six against one. And they threatened me and groped me, too. Anything that happened to your *boy* was in self-defense." I began shutting the door.

"I'll have you arrested!" she shouted hysterically into the closing door.

I opened it up a crack again. "Oh, please. Go right ahead. Have a wonderful Sunday!"

"What the hell was that?" Christina took a bite of her eggs, her eyes wide.

"Have you completely lost your mind?" I snapped at Danny. "Did you actually just apologize to her?"

He shrugged. "I dunno…" He hesitated. "Maybe I overdid it a little last night. I didn't have to break his ribs."

"You did nothing wrong! Let her go to the police. No judge in the world will think we started it."

"When he sees the results, he might."

"Hello?" Christina broke in, chewing. "Are you going to fill me in or what?"

"Our dear Danny finally saw reason," I announced proudly.

Chapter Twenty-Two

April 2001

We decided to visit Maya before I drove back to my parents' house one Sunday evening. We spent a while walking through the fields with her, and we rode her together on the way back, as we often did.

Danny had been letting me sit behind him more and more often when we rode Maya. I'd always been careful about keeping my arms loosely wrapped around his hips, sometimes laying my hands on his thighs, and making sure not to touch him too much. Today, I wanted to go a step further.

"Get ready," I warned him before pushing my hand underneath his T-shirt and stroking his stomach. He didn't react badly, so I let my hand drift upward. I felt goosebumps break out on his skin, but he remained completely relaxed.

We did it! I cheered in my head. I slid my other hand up his shirt and embraced him softly enough that he wouldn't feel restrained. I laid my cheek against his shoulder. "Danny?"

He kept the reins loosely in one hand. "Hm?"

"I like you."

He laughed quietly. "Yeah, that's one way to put it."

"What, don't you like me?"

"I love you."

I purred contentedly. "I'm glad I have you."

"I'm glad you have me, too," he replied.

"I'm happy, you know? Everything is just the way it should be. We're together and happy, Christina's clean and getting ready to start a new job, and those guys aren't going to bother us anymore. Everything's good."

"Yeah," Danny said. I could tell he was holding something back.

"It would be the perfect happy ending to a movie," I remarked, cuddling up against his back.

"There are no happy endings in real life."

"Then we'll make one ourselves," I insisted.

"Maybe it's not such a bad idea," he murmured. "Maybe we should just stop here and go our separate ways."

Shocked, I had to restrain myself from gripping him more tightly.

This wasn't the direction I'd wanted the conversation to go in. Not at all. "Is... Is that what you want?" I asked breathlessly.

"I didn't say I wanted it. But it would probably be the wisest thing to do." He was silent for a while. "I'm dragging you into all this crap," he went on. "Those idiots aren't going to leave me alone, and for some reason I just don't have a good feeling about Christina. But none of that is the biggest problem—the real problem is me. We can ignore it all we want, but one of these days, we're going to run smack into it."

"Maybe we won't." I tried to remain cheerful. "Where's your optimism? You're young, your T-cell levels are great. We just have to wait for them to find a cure."

"Who knows how long that will take? It's a race against time that I'll never win."

"They'll find a way to keep the disease in check until they can treat it," I insisted. But I had no idea who exactly this vague "they" were. "Soon, HIV-positive people will be able to live totally normal lives and have healthy children, and eventually they'll eliminate it entirely."

"Maybe you're right."

I couldn't tell whether he said it because he actually believed it, because he didn't want to dash my hopes, or because he just desperately wished it could be true.

I heard the weird rattling sound an hour later, just as I was about to drive out of the village. The car was making some very unhealthy noises, and taking it onto the highway didn't seem like a good idea, so I drove back to Danny's. I yanked the apartment door open and stomped into the living room.

He blinked at me in surprise. "Did something happen?"

"Yeah." I sulked. "My car sounds like it's about to fall apart. Here, come listen." I threw my keys at him without warning, but he caught them in one hand at the last moment. His reflexes were amazing.

Listlessly, he shuffled out of the apartment, still barefoot, and I stepped over to the living room window.

Christina came out of her room. "Thought I heard you back." She stepped up beside me at the window. "Why so angry?"

"There's no way my car is just acting up all of a sudden. Not on its own. It was those guys."

Danny drove the car around for a few minutes before parking it again and sliding underneath it. After a while, he came back inside.

"Well?" I asked testily, like I'd been expecting everything to be fixed.

He shrugged. "I'm not a mechanic, but I think there's something going on with the exhaust system. Anyway, you can't drive it home like that, not until we've had it looked at."

"Great." My mood sank to a new low. "How am I going to get to work tomorrow?"

"You can take my car."

"What, and you're just going to walk to work?"

"My first class isn't until nine. I'll just go running a little earlier so I have time to take the car in and drive it to work once it's been cleared by a mechanic." He lifted his keys from the hook on the wall and held them out to me. "Be careful," he warned. "Mine's a little zippier than yours. And the chassis is lower, so don't drive over any curbs."

I rolled my eyes and snatched the keys from his hand. "I know how to drive," I muttered. "And my Benz has 150 horsepower. I'm sure I'll be just fine in your sad little BMW!"

"With 190 horsepower, plus chip tuning," Danny said. "The brake is the one in the middle."

"I love you, too." I gave him a kiss on the cheek and left the apartment, unlocking his car as I walked. Still furious, I dropped onto the leather seat in a huff, and then moved it forward about a foot and a half. Scowling, I wondered how Danny could stand the car's weird blue interior lighting.

Then I took a deep breath. The car smelled like vanilla and Danny. My mood lifted a little. As soon as I drove off, I could tell his car really was a lot more powerful than mine, and it made me a little uneasy. Almost too cautiously, I maneuvered the doomsday machine back to my parents' house.

My mom met me in the hallway. "Hey," I said.

"Jessica! Do you want some dinner?"

She asked me that every time I came home on Sunday evening, and I always gave her the same answer: "I ate at Danny's."

"Alexander's mother called," she said cheerfully.

"What did she want?"

"She asked what you were doing this summer. You've been invited to go with them to Italy if you want."

Back when Alexander and I were together, I always went with him and his family on vacation. They spent four weeks at the same campgrounds in Grado every year.

"Oh, Mom," I sighed. "Alex and I broke up. And we're staying broken up. Why would I want to go on vacation with his family?"

"I'm sure it would be fun," she said, trying again.

"I don't get four weeks of vacation from work," I pointed out. "And I might go somewhere with Danny." Though we hadn't actually talked about how we were going to spend our vacation time this year.

"Well, you can always change your mind," my mother insisted.

***

I drove Danny's car back to him on Monday after work. He wasn't home yet, which made me worry my car would be in the shop for a while. Hopefully the damage wasn't too serious.

Christina and I made dinner—whole-wheat pasta with cheese sauce and a mixed salad—and then cleaned up the kitchen. I cursed like a New York cab driver during rush hour the entire time. "We have to do something about those thugs! Now they're demolishing our cars, too? We can't let them get away with this!"

"Wait until Danny gets home," Christina said, trying to placate me. "Maybe something really did just break."

"One of these days, I'm going to claw Tara's eyes out," I promised myself aloud. Christina and I had visited Danny's ex at work twice now—once to call her out, and once to speak to her boss. She'd denied any involvement, of course, but she'd still been written up, because the doctor believed us and remembered that Tara had been in the room when he'd spoken to Danny.

Danny didn't get home until late in the evening. "What was wrong with my car?" I asked in greeting.

194

"You're going to laugh," he said. "Nothing was wrong. Those jokers threw two cigarette lighters into your tailpipe. They were just sitting in there rattling around. It took the guys at the garage forever to figure out what was wrong."

"Fantastic," I said. "I *knew* they were responsible. So now what?"

Danny shrugged. "We don't have any proof."

After dinner, he admitted, "Your Mercedes star was broken off this morning, too. I didn't want to tell you, and I had it replaced right away, but that probably won't be the last time. They stole my antenna a few days ago as well."

He hadn't told me about that.

"Pathetic cowards," I growled. "Now they're too afraid to run into you, so they're taking it out on our cars."

Danny nodded. "Which was to be expected, I suppose. Let's just wait and see what happens. We'll go to the police if we have to, though I don't think anything would come of that."

Chapter Twenty-Three

May 2001

Rather than driving straight to Danny's one Friday, I stayed in Stuttgart to meet up with Vanessa. She was spending the weekend at her parents' house, so we went out to dinner and a movie. She told me all about her boyfriend, Chris, whom she'd met in Munich. That explained why I hadn't seen or heard from her in weeks. Strangely, I hadn't missed her at all. With Christina and Danny at my side, I didn't seem to need anyone else.

"I'm going to marry him," Nessa declared. "Chris is definitely the kind of guy you marry." I rolled my eyes. Every time Vanessa fell in love with a guy, she always called him the 'kind of guy you marry.' "How are things with you and Danny?"

"Great," I said. "Everything's great." There was so much Vanessa didn't know about Danny. I'd have liked to tell my former best friend all about how my Mercedes star had been broken off fourteen times in the past few weeks, how either Danny's or my car antenna was always missing, and how he'd found a nail in one of his tires just a week before.

But I didn't tell her any of it. Nor did I mention the group of guys who'd ambushed him and beaten him up several times. Telling Nessa any of that would have meant explaining why it was all happening. I knew I'd have to tell her about Danny's illness once it developed into AIDS, but I wanted to wait until then. I had no desire to sit there listening to her yammer on for hours about how dangerous this was, how stupid could I possibly be, and didn't I know there were other fish in the sea?

So I kept silent and felt a pang of envy as I heard all about how perfect her relationship with Chris was. In the back of my mind, I decided to meet up with Vanessa even less often in the future.

By the time I got home, picked up Leika, and set off for Danny's, it was well past midnight. When I parked my car behind Danny's BMW, the whole building was dark. Christina and Danny's blinds were open, as usual, so I could see that their lights were all off. The apartment above theirs was dark as well, but that was normal—Britta and her husband, Holger, both worked a lot, so they were almost always asleep long before this.

Danny, on the other hand, was almost always awake until the wee hours of the morning. He considered sleeping more than five or six hours a waste of time. But tonight, he seemed to have turned in relatively early, by his standards. Unless, of course, he was just sneaking around in the dark again.

I saw it on the way from the car to the building: a gigantic cloth banner stretched out from one corner of the building to the other, with blood-red capital letters spelling out:

DIE, FAGGOT

My throat burned like I'd swallowed a hot iron.

I glanced around quickly, but of course the perpetrators were long gone. Tears of rage and indignation welled up in my eyes. Why would they do something like this? Why? Wasn't it bad enough that he really was going to die? Our wounds were already far too deep—why did they have to pour salt in them?

I tried to pull the banner down, but I couldn't reach it.

How the hell did those goddamn assholes get that thing all the way up there?

I wanted to take it down without even mentioning it to Danny, but I didn't know where I could get a ladder at this hour, so I supposed I had no choice but to wake him.

I crept into the bedroom and discovered Christina on my side of the bed, asleep in Danny's arms. The sight of them was touching. It seemed like it had been a million years since she'd last come to his bed.

Danny woke up right away when I approached them. There were advantages to his being such a light sleeper—it never took more than three seconds to get him out of bed. I gestured for him to come with me, and he got up and followed me outside.

"Bad news," I warned him as I brought him out front.

The terrible banner came into view.

"Wow." He nodded, almost in admiration. "Impressive. They're really serious about this."

I'd been afraid he'd flip out, but he was perfectly calm. Far too relaxed for my taste, in fact. I eyed him skeptically.

"This is the second one this week," he explained.

"You've got to be kidding."

"No, really. And that's not all. Check this out!" Barefoot and wearing only boxers, he padded across the street to his car. I followed him, filled with dread, and he pointed to the hood.

Death to queers!

It was scratched deeply into the paint.

"I'm sick of this!" My voice was far too shrill, and my stomach was tying itself into painful knots. How could he stay this calm? "Police! Now!"

"Tina and I went and filed a report yesterday," he told me. "They said there's almost no chance they can do anything without proof. We'll have to think of something. Either I'll hire some kind of security service to watch our cars, or we'll need to do it ourselves."

We went back into the building and fetched a ladder from the basement.

"Speaking of police reports," he said, grinning. "I received a copy of the one made about me. I'll show you in a minute." He leaned the ladder against the building and climbed up seven or eight rungs to reach the banner. I could only shake my head in amazement yet again. Not because he was climbing a ladder barefoot in the middle of the night, but because even this ridiculous situation wasn't enough to spoil his good mood.

The cord holding the sheet up was glued to the building facade. Danny yanked that side down, and then he climbed back to the ground. Together, we yanked the other end down and wadded the thing up before throwing it in the Dumpster.

The police report was sitting on the kitchen table. I picked it up and read it over. "Well, at least it was worth it. Two broken ribs, two teeth knocked out, a broken arm, and a ton of bruises. Nice job."

He gave me a concerned look. "I went too far, didn't I?"

"More like not far enough. You don't feel bad about it, do you?"

"It was an accident. I wasn't deliberately trying to hurt them." He folded his arms. "Except Angelo. I broke his ribs on purpose."

I nodded, wondering how things would have turned out if Danny had actually been trying to hurt the others. "They were deliberately provoking you, Danny. Nobody has to just sit there and take that."

"I have an appointment tomorrow to bring the car in and have the hood repainted," he said, changing the subject. "After that, I'll go to a security company and ask them to watch our cars for a couple weekends."

Chapter Twenty-Four

June 2001

When I left the office, I saw Danny's car parked right in front of the door—polished until it shimmered in the sun, as always. Danny was leaning against the hood. I wasn't surprised that he was picking me up from work on this particular Thursday.

"Happy birthday, Ducky," he said, taking me into his arms. "We're going to your place so you can pack your things and pick up your furball, and then we're going on vacation."

"What? We can't do that. I have to work tomorrow."

"No, you don't." Danny gave me a wolfish grin. "You have the day off. I called your boss. We'll be gone until Sunday."

"You what?" Somehow, he'd managed to throw me for a loop yet again. My shock turned into excitement. "Where are we going?"

"It's a surprise. Bring a swimsuit."

After a nearly eight-hour drive, we arrived at a spa on the Adriatic Sea.

We spent our time on the beach, mostly in the water. Danny was an excellent swimmer, and running around half-naked in front of strangers didn't bother him one bit, as long as there was no danger of anyone touching him. Christina had stayed home, since the vacation was Danny's birthday gift to me, and it was probably for the best. She never got undressed in front of strangers. As revealing as her clothing was at home, she was extremely modest in public. The few times we'd managed to convince her to join us at the public pool, she'd insisted on wearing a T-shirt. She'd told me once that heroin had been the only way she'd had the courage to go with random johns and take her clothes off in front of them.

There hadn't been a single incident while the security company was monitoring our cars. But the trouble had started up again once Danny dismissed the monitors. Angelo and his buddies must have realized they were being watched.

But all that felt miles and miles away. Because it was.

"Jessica." Danny's voice broke into my train of thought as he rolled over onto his stomach. The two of us were stretched out on a large cotton blanket spread across the soft sand, enjoying the warmth.

My eyes drifted to Danny's back, to the fine, light scars gradually fading from view beneath his deepening tan. Two or three more days of sun, and they would be almost completely invisible—at least until winter, when they would stand out once more, painful reminders of what his father had done to him—and the nightmare that would one day catch up to us. I would be at Danny's side when it happened, there was no question of that. And I knew Danny would never leave me of his own free will, although I wasn't sure how exactly I knew that. I just did. I knew it the way you know you need air to breathe, or that the sun provides warmth.

"Are you even listening to me?" he asked.

"Um, no," I admitted. "I was busy."

"Ah. Doing what?"

"Looking at you and wondering whether it wasn't a little unfair that you were this much better-looking than everyone else in the world."

He raised a skeptical eyebrow. "Well, I can repeat myself if you're finished with that...? I'd like to go to Atlanta this summer."

Oh. "Do you have relatives there?" *It's so far away...*

"Yeah, an aunt. My father's sister. Actually, I go every year, sometimes even twice a year. I just didn't go last summer because I was at the retreat with Tina."

Was he asking me for permission or something? "Danny, it's your home. You can go whenever you want, for as long as you want."

"Well, I want you to come with me."

"What?" I didn't believe my ears. "Those flights are super expensive."

"I'll pay your way, of course. And we can both stay with my aunt. Tina won't be coming, because she's starting her job." He sat up. "I'll pay your return flight, too, of course," he added with a grin. "In case you were worried I was going to leave you there."

My stomach tensed up. I'd never been on a plane before—I was afraid of flying—and the prospect of spending twelve hours in a plane sent me into a panic. "How long are you going to be there?"

He shrugged. "Six to eight weeks? I know you don't get that much vacation, but you could fly out and join me for a little while."

Join you? Fly out alone? My inner voice ran away screaming at the very idea. Then again, being without him for that long sounded even worse.

"I don't know," I said hesitantly. "Why don't we wait until next year? Once my temporary contract is up, they're hopefully going to hire me on full-time, and I could just take a couple of months off before I start. Then we could both go for eight weeks." Maybe I could weasel out this way. "That way, I wouldn't have to fly alone," I added. "I've never flown before."

He scooted up next to me. "Jessica," he said, giving me a meaningful look. "I'm worried I won't get a chance to visit home after this year."

"Where would you get a stupid idea like that?" I snapped. "Of course we will!" At that moment, I decided once and for all that I wasn't going to join him in the U.S. this time around. Not because I didn't want to—I just wasn't going to throw oil on the fire by catering to what I thought were completely unfounded worries.

"It's just a sort of feeling," he said, struggling to put it into words.

"Well, we're going to do it the way I said," I told him. "You go alone this year, and next year, I'll go with you, and we can stay however long you want."

Danny pursed his lips, and I could tell he was gritting his teeth. He wasn't happy with the arrangement, and he seemed to be trying to decide whether to keep arguing his point. Finally, he sighed. "Whatever, okay. But that means I'm going to be gone eight weeks. Tina's stable enough that she can get by without me for that long."

"That's okay," I said, wondering how the hell *I* was going to survive all that time without him. A lump formed in my throat at the very thought. "Don't worry about Tina. I'll check on her. When she starts work, I'll sleep at your place for the first week to make sure she gets up on time."

"Thanks." Danny shifted around to sit up, cross-legged. "But you should take a vacation somewhere, too. While I'm gone."

I told him about Alexander's parents' invitation, expecting him to be totally against the idea. "I guess I could always go down there for a bit. Vanessa and her new boyfriend are invited, too."

"Sounds like a good idea." He never ceased to surprise me. "Yeah, do that. A break would do you good."

"A break?" I repeated. That sounded like he meant... "From you? That's not what I was saying!"

"Not exactly from me," he said easily. "From the rest of it. All the drama, my problems, my illness." He pondered for a moment and then nodded, looking even more convinced. "Yeah, you should do that. A few weeks of normal teen life. Go out, go to parties, have fun." He paused, then added, "But no drinking, okay? Otherwise, you'll end up half-naked in some guy's bed again…and it might turn out differently the next time. Not all guys are like me."

I nodded a little sheepishly. "No alcohol, promise."

Danny stood up and put on his blue-striped T-shirt again. "Let's go back to the hotel. I'm starving."

I rose to my feet as well, shooed Leika off the blanket so I could roll it up, and trotted after Danny. I didn't like the turn the conversation had taken, but there was no going back now. "Aren't you worried about me going on vacation with my ex-boyfriend?" I asked him.

Danny stopped and gave me another one of his X-ray looks. "What exactly should I be worried about?"

I shrugged hesitantly, thrown off by the question. "That I'll fall in love with him again? That I'll get back together with him, or end up in bed with him?"

"No," he said slowly, "I'm not worried about that. I trust you completely, and I'm confident you would never abuse my trust. I don't doubt your love for a second."

I smiled. "And you have no reason to."

"I know." He held out his hand, and I took it. "Just like you know that I won't look at anyone else the entire time I'm away."

I knew that. I didn't doubt his love, either.

***

When we returned on Sunday evening, there was a brand-new mountain bike waiting for me in Danny's basement, a gazillion-speed model with a gorgeous aluminum frame. The price was easily in the four-digit range. Of course, he'd bought it for me just so I could keep up with him on bike rides. It was the most expensive bike I ever had.

Chapter Twenty-Five

July 2001

The day before a big martial arts youth competition, Danny stayed at the center all afternoon, and well into the evening, going over key strategies with his students.

Christina and I were hanging out on the couch watching TV, stuffing ourselves with chips and getting crumbs all over the floor—our favorite type of Friday night. Suddenly, we heard an ear-splitting clattering sound, followed by a loud thump.

Christina shrieked and latched on to my arm in panic. "What was that?"

"I don't know. I'll go look."

Leika ran into the living room, equally panicked, and hid under the table, whimpering. I had to peel Christina off me so that I could go investigate.

I padded into the hallway and looked around. Everything seemed normal, but something had definitely broken somewhere in the apartment. Christina followed me out to search as well, and soon we found it: a fist-sized rock sitting in her room, surrounded by shards of broken glass from the shattered window.

Groaning, Christina cautiously made her way to the stone and read the note wrapped around it. Without a word, she handed me the piece of paper and walked out of the room.

On the crumpled paper, large capital letters spelled out:

GET OUT OR WE'LL *REALLY* GET NASTY!

"Now what?" I gave her a look of despair as she returned with a dustpan. "This has to stop!" They'd hung up another one of their charming banners just the week before. Our landlady had already called once to ask whether we couldn't handle our disagreements in a more civilized way.

"That does it!" Christina put her hands on her hips and set her jaw. "They've gone too far this time. I'm going to call Ricky and Simon. And Patrick—he's another friend of Danny's and mine. And Giuseppe. I'll have them all meet up here next Friday and bring someone else with them if they can. Those jackasses have been coming on Fridays a lot."

"What are you going to do?"

"Turn the tables on them. We'll ambush them when they arrive, and then they'll really be in for it."

Something didn't feel right. "Shouldn't we ask Danny first?"

"Whatever, he'll think it's a great idea! He offered to watch the cars himself before. That would have meant ambushing them, too." Christina was like that. Once she got an idea into her pretty little head, she considered it a done deal, and everyone had to play along.

"Do we really need that many people?" I gave her a doubtful look. After all, Danny had been able to handle the whole group by himself last time.

"We need that many people," she said. "Two more would be better. We need to be able to hold them all—we can't let any of them get away."

"And then?"

"Then they'll get the shock of their lives. When our boys are finished with them, they won't come back." A gleeful Christina immediately set to making calls, while I set to work taping over the broken window.

Half an hour later, she returned, beaming. "It's a go!" she crowed. "They're all coming—Ricky, Simon, Giuseppe, and Patrick. And they'll bring a friend, too. So, with Danny, that'll be six to six, if the others bring their whole group... And we'll be there, too!" she added proudly.

"Danny will certainly be delighted," I said sarcastically.

"Let's wait until tomorrow to tell him, after the competition," she said, closing the blinds on her window. I hoped Danny wouldn't notice when he came home. "Deal?"

"Deal," I said, shaking her hand.

***

The guys were posted around the building: Danny and Simon in front, Ricky and Giuseppe in the back, and Patrick and some guy named Sven in the bushes near the cars. They'd forbidden me and Christina from leaving the apartment. We'd been waiting for more than two hours now, but we were still fairly confident they'd show up.

Danny had immediately noticed that the blinds in Christina's room were closed, of course, but he hadn't given it much thought. Or, at least, he hadn't suspected it had anything to do with thrown rocks until we'd told him about it. Surprisingly, we didn't have to work to convince him that Christina's plan was a good one—he liked the idea immediately. Knowing that Christina could have been hurt if she'd been in her room enraged him so much that we'd been afraid he might go looking for the guys immediately. Instead, he'd contented himself with having the broken windowpane replaced.

Now they were all sitting in their hiding spots, dressed in black, exercising patience. Danny was most likely bored to death. Sitting still wasn't exactly one of his strong suits. Christina and I were equally impatient, even though we were posted in the most comfortable place.

It was long after midnight when we heard a soft whistle from near the cars—the signal we'd agreed upon. We pressed ourselves to the window, but it was too dark to see anything. Despite what we'd agreed, Christina and I went outside.

They were running like scared rabbits, the cowards. Five of them. I saw them scurrying off in every direction, with our guys in hot pursuit. I scanned the area, looking for Danny. He and Simon were chasing a pair of the thugs. Danny, the faster of the two, left Simon in the dust and caught up to the two offenders effortlessly.

He took the first one down with a running jump kick square in the back—a move that would have immediately gotten him disqualified from any competition fight. The guy went sprawling to the ground, and Danny ran right over him to stop the other one the same way.

Pulling the second one up from where he'd fallen on the ground, Danny twisted an arm behind the guy's back and pushed him toward the apartment building. He'd left the first guy—Pete, I now saw—for Simon, who struggled to drag him back as well.

Giuseppe hurried over to help, and together, they at least managed to keep Pete from running off. Danny had one of the two who had been holding him the last time, while Sven and Patrick had the unshaven one. Ricky had gotten hold of Angelo. The only one they hadn't caught was Mr. Leather Jacket—apparently he hadn't come this time.

Even together, Simon and Giuseppe had a hard time with Pete. He fought like a rabid dog, swinging his fists with abandon. They flew in every direction. Although we'd planned on just holding them once we caught them, Simon and Giuseppe started punching Pete. They didn't have a choice—Pete obviously wasn't going to go down without a fight.

All at once, Danny elbowed the one beside him in the stomach so hard that the guy spent the next several minutes struggling to breathe. Then he kicked Pete in the hollow of the knee at an angle, sending him tumbling to the ground. Another kick in the side, and Pete was down for the count—now Simon and Giuseppe just had to drag him behind the building as planned. At least Pete hadn't lost any more teeth this time around.

Danny almost seemed to be having fun. I wasn't sure whether I found that good or worrying. He was always so impulsive. Once he'd lost his temper, it was difficult for him to rein it in again.

Sven and Patrick had no trouble keeping their guy under control. His nose was bleeding, and he was cursing like crazy, but he'd stop trying to fight back. Ricky and Angelo, however, were fighting tooth and nail. Angelo was the last to get behind the buiding, but it didn't look like Ricky would manage to drag him off alone. Patrick ran to help him, and Tina and I followed.

"Tonight was the last time," Ricky bellowed at him, smashing his fist into Angelo's face yet again.

After that, everything happened much too fast.

"Ricky! Watch out!" I heard someone shout—I think it was Simon.

The warning came too late.

Angelo had pulled a hunting knife from his pocket and stabbed Ricky in the side. Immediately, he drew the knife back to attack again, but before he could, Danny landed on his arm, saving Ricky from a second hit.

Danny grabbed Angelo's wrist, twisted his arm around behind his back, held it in place with both hands, and kicked it. Angelo's forearm snapped like a twig.

"Call an ambulance!" Danny roared at us. I hadn't brought my phone outside with me, so Simon pulled out his own and called the paramedics.

Ricky sank to his knees, pressing his side with both hands to staunch the bleeding. Christina and I sat down beside him, and she pulled off her sweatshirt and held it tightly against his wound. Simon laid a comforting hand on Ricky's shoulder, and I looked back at Danny.

I'd thought he couldn't get any angrier than he had been the last time these guys jumped us.

It turned out I was wrong.

He snatched the knife from the hand of Angelo's useless arm—his forearm was pointing away from his body at an absurd angle. Holding the knife in his right fist,

Danny punched Angelo again and again with his left. There was nothing coordinated about his blows anymore—he was just letting off steam.

As Danny shoved Angelo up against a tree, Christina came to her senses.

"Danny! Stop!" she screeched. "You're going to kill him!"

Ignoring her, Danny closed his free hand around Angelo's throat and slammed the man's head against the tree. Angelo was no longer in any condition to stop the assault.

"I told you people!" Danny snarled. "Do it again, and you die!"

Angelo raised his good hand defensively. "I didn't touch your girlfriend, you psycho!"

"No, you just rammed a knife into my friend's stomach." He slammed Angelo's head against the tree again. "I decided to add that offense to my promise."

"You're a complete nutjob!" Angelo whimpered, his voice cracking.

"Knife attack," I heard Simon say on the phone.

"Stop it, Danny!" Christina screamed beside me, she but didn't dare let go of Ricky's side. "You really are going to kill him!"

Suddenly, sharing Christina's concerns, I stood up to go over to him. But I was so dizzy my knees were threatening to give out.

Wait a second, my inner voice advised.

"I'm not as crazy as you think," Danny replied in a dangerously quiet tone. "I just like to keep my promises." With that, he released Angelo, but the other man was far too dazed to run away.

Danny took Angelo's uninjured arm, stretching it out and pushing the sleeve back. In a flash, he switched the knife to his left hand and took Angelo's wrist in his right. When he held the point of the knife to Angelo's arm, Angelo's eyes widened, and he gaped at Danny for a moment before violently jerking away.

Danny slapped him upside the head in response. "Hold still!" he snapped. "You're only going to make it worse."

Angelo obeyed.

Danny brought the knife back into position and cut a four- or five-inch incision into Angelo's forearm. Then he used his teeth to pull up his own sleeve and cut his own arm with the knife, which was already smeared with both Ricky's and Angelo's blood.

What on earth was he doing? I watched in rapt horror.

He'd sliced his own arm far more deeply than the Italian's. Blood began streaming down his arm. Everyone else stood there like wax figures, watching the scene.

No.

I closed my eyes. I knew what he was planning to do. When a person carried death within themselves like Danny did—every day, everywhere he went—and had the power to pass it on to others, did they ever find themselves tempted to do it?

A look of horror came over Angelo's face as he realized what Danny was doing. "Hey, wait, man, no! Don't do this!"

"Then you'll see how it is." Danny's voice was calm and composed, almost friendly. "Maybe you'll be as lucky as I've been, and you'll meet nice people like you guys. It's twice as much fun with friends like you." He raised his bleeding arm into the air.

Finally shaking myself into action, I stepped behind Danny and carefully touched his injured arm. "Danny, don't do this," I whispered.

"Do something already, you stupid fucking cow!" Angelo barked at me.

Suddenly, I hated him so much that I let go of Danny. The man had beaten my boyfriend, left hate messages, and threatened me with far worse things.

But that wasn't the reason I stepped away. I knew Danny. He'd never do something like this. He just wanted to scare Angelo.

"I can't do anything!" I put on a helpless expression. "He's insane. You know that!"

Danny reached for Angelo's arm again, straightening it out, and then drew his own arm dangerously close.

"Please, man!" Angelo begged. "Don't do this, you could seriously kill me! I'm sorry! We'll leave you guys alone. Please!"

Seeing the glowing rage in Danny's eyes, I wasn't quite as sure that he wouldn't do it.

I reached for his arm again, but a hand came down on Danny's shoulder from behind. "Danny, no!" It was Ricky. "No," he repeated softly, pulling Danny away. "He's not worth it."

Danny took a deep breath before turning away and dropping into the grass. Ricky and I sat on either side of him. Panting with relief, Angelo sank back against the tree.

The ambulance arrived two minutes later, and three police cars pulled up a minute after that.

As the paramedics loaded Ricky up and called in a second ambulance for Angelo, the police surrounded the rest of us. Realizing how many of us there were, they called for backup as well.

One by one, they took us to their cars to search us. Hands on their own weapons, two of them approached Danny, who was still sitting on the ground and bleeding heavily. Realizing he was still holding the knife, Danny tossed it away demonstratively and landed in the grass. Danny raised both hands. "It's okay. I'll come with you."

"Keep those hands up," one of the men snapped at him. "Get over to the vehicle and put your hands on the hood, feet apart."

Danny pointed to his still bleeding arm. "Can I clean this up real quick?"

"No," was the man's gruff reply. "That can wait."

Danny smiled pleasantly. "It would be the sensible thing to do. HIV-positive, you know?"

The policemen exchanged a look of uncertainty. "Okay, then," another one said. "Do you have something to bandage it with?"

Danny rolled his eyes. "Yeah, of course, I never leave the house without a first-aid kid."

"Don't get lippy." A cop hit him in the back and shoved him toward the police cars, but then handed him a gauze bandage from the first-aid kit in his trunk.

Danny carefully bandaged his arm before obediently putting his hands on the hood of the car. The policeman roughly pushed Danny's legs apart with his foot and patted him down. I could see Danny gritting his teeth. They didn't search me or Christina, most likely because they didn't have a female officer present.

A few minutes later, the reinforcements they'd called in arrived in the form of a van. They divided us all up among the available vehicles, putting Christina, me, Danny, Simon, and two of the thugs into the van and the others into the cars. Suddenly exhausted, I let my head sink down onto Danny's shoulder.

"Watch out," he whispered. "I'm covered in blood." I didn't care. I reached for his hand, wishing more than anything that we were at home in bed.

The guy across from us bent toward us. I recognized him as the one with the pale-blue eyes. "I'm Kevin," he said.

"Nobody cares," Danny grunted.

"I just wanted to say that I didn't know anything about the knife, and I think that was wrong of him. I'll say that down at the station."

Christina gave him a friendly smile. "Thank you. That's nice of you."

Kevin clapped Danny on the knee. "You guys put up a good fight."

Danny rolled his eyes. "Just shut up already."

The cops pushed us into the station and kept us there the rest of the night, taking our statements one by one. In the end, two of the other guys spoke up for us, saying that Angelo had pulled the knife without warning and stabbed Ricky, and that Danny had reacted in self-defense.

In the end, nothing at all happened. Nobody was charged, and the incident was dismissed as a "bar fight" that had unexpectedly escalated into a knife fight.

Ricky was amazingly lucky—Angelo hadn't struck any organs. The wound would heal without a problem, leaving him with nothing but a small scar.

Angelo, however, was in the hospital for more than two weeks. His broken arm was a complex splintered fracture that required several surgeries, and he had a severe concussion as well as whiplash. His nose was broken, and his spleen was ruptured, but the injury was encapsulated, so he hadn't had any internal bleeding and they'd managed to save the organ.

On top of that, one of the ribs Danny had broken the last time was cracked all over again.

Astonishingly, he and the others all expressly refused to press charges, even though the hospital staff repeatedly advised him to do so. He preferred to drop the whole thing.

After that night, there were no further incidents.

Chapter Twenty-Six

August 2001

Danny's flight left at 5:30 in the morning on a Thursday. He took a taxi to the airport—we said our goodbyes the previous Sunday. Even though we hardly ever saw each other during the week anyway, I missed him terribly. It was one thing when I knew he was nearby, in a place I could get to in half an hour by car. Having him on the other side of the world was something else entirely. I just didn't feel complete without him. He was part of me, my other half, my elixir of life. Without him, I had no drive, no motivation, no happiness. It was like someone had taken the oxygen out of the air. By the end of the first day, I already deeply regretted having let him fly out there alone.

His first text arrived that evening:

> *Landed! It's ungodly hot here, but beautiful. I'm home!*
>
> *I miss you already. I'm never flying without you again!*
>
> *Love you*

The message triggered a whole mess of contradictory feelings within me. First, I was happy that he'd gotten there safely—I'd secretly been in a panic wondering if the plane would crash. But it saddened me as well. He was *home*. But…wasn't this sort of his home, too? Here, with Christina and me?

The more I thought about it… What exactly kept him here? Why hadn't he gone back long ago? It occurred to me that I'd never asked him. He'd come to Germany because of his parents, but they obviously weren't his reason for staying. He never saw his mother anyway—he was probably much closer to his aunt halfway across the world. I decided I'd bring it up when he got back.

I started fantasizing about moving to America with him someday. In fact, I'd go immediately if he asked me to. I didn't really care where we lived. I'd follow him to the Himalayas or the Yukon, if that was what he wanted.

At any rate, I was definitely going with him next year, and I'd leave it up to him whether we stayed eight weeks or eight years. I'd combat my fear of flying through sleeping pills if necessary. Danny was claustrophobic. If he could manage to spend hours cooped up in an airplane, with no way of getting out for fresh air, I could face my fears, too. Maybe he was just used to it by now. He'd flown back and forth so often as a child that it had probably become normal to him. He could help make it normal for me.

***

It wasn't until several days after he left that I discovered the envelope Danny had secretly stowed in my car. He hadn't been able to resist leaving me several hundred euros, along with a note reading,

Vacation money—not for alcohol!

Typical Danny. Rather than risk any protest from me, he'd avoided any discussion at all by stashing it in my car to be found after he'd left.

My packed suitcase and I waited in the running car for Vanessa. Alexander was parked nearby with his giant trailer attached to his car. He was staying longer than the rest of us, so he was driving his new trailer down, intending to leave it there for good. They needed to get their speedboat down to Italy as well, as they did every year, so Alexander had installed a towing hitch to the back of my car for the boat. I figured it wouldn't be a problem, since I wouldn't have to make many turns on the highway. My mind strayed briefly to Christina, who was planning to spend a couple days with Natasha. She said she didn't mind being home alone for the rest of the time I would be away.

I honked again, and Vanessa and Chris finally emerged. Beaming, Nessa bounced down to the passenger seat beside me and introduced me to her boyfriend. I liked him immediately. He was friendly, good-natured, and seemed genuinely interested in Vanessa. After we exchanged a few pleasantries, Nessa sent him off to Alexander's car.

Vanessa and I were both wearing short shorts and sandals. We both stuck our sunglasses up into our hair and rolled down the windows, and suddenly I was in a fantastic mood, almost euphoric. Vacation with friends! With totally normal friends who didn't hang out in the dark at night because they thought it was safer not to turn on the lights. People I could take into an elevator or grab jokingly without sending them into a panic. People whose company I could enjoy without thinking about a million different things, like accidentally hugging them or accidentally closing the window or accidentally coming into contact with their blood. It was a vacation from AIDS.

I was even looking forward to the 500-mile drive down to Italy. With the boat trailing behind us, and Alex and Chris in the car in front of us, we got on the interstate and rushed toward the sun and the sea.

When we arrived, we all helped Alexander set up the trailer, and then we figured out our sleeping arrangements. Vanessa and Chris got the berth underneath the roof of the trailer, while Alexander and I took the fold-out pallets on either side of the dining table.

Then we filled the boat's minibar and pulled the boat down to the harbor together, where we guided it into the water. As we made ourselves comfortable at the bow with our provisions, Alexander steered his Bayliner out to the open water. I clung to the railing, wind tearing at my hair as the boat shot through the waves. I heard Vanessa screeching and giggling at the spray hitting our faces. I was in a fantastic mood, and I had to admit this was a pretty good group.

A few minutes later, the droning sound of the engine died away, and Alexander threw the anchor overboard. "Somewhere around here, the water is so shallow that you can stand up in it," he told us as he joined us, holding a couple of beers. "We're directly over a sandbar."

"It's beautiful here," Vanessa cooed. Apart from a smaller boat a mile or two off, there was no one else in sight.

"Can I drive later?" Chris asked, bringing his beer to his lips.

"Sure. I've got a license, so everyone on board is allowed to drive." Alexander grinned broadly. "But let's go swimming first." He let down the ladder attached to the rear of the boat.

Vanessa held a bottle of beer out to me. "No, thanks," I said, shaking my head.

"Why not?"

"You have to ask?" Alexander called derisively. "Blame that boring dude she's with."

I suppressed a grin. The accusation was so many miles away from the truth that I couldn't even take it seriously.

Vanessa shrugged. "If she doesn't want any…" She handed me a Coke.

"So are we going swimming or what?" Chris pulled off his shirt, chugged the rest of his beer, and threw the bottle out to sea in a high arc.

"Hey!" I frowned at him. "Don't do that!"

The others stared at me in confusion. "Do what?" Chris asked.

"You can't just throw that in the sea. Go get it!"

Alexander stepped up beside me. "Jessica, chill out. Just because the guy you're dating is uptight doesn't mean we all have to be."

Uptight? Danny was a lot of things, but uptight wasn't one of them. He still would never have thrown his trash in the ocean, though. And, thanks to him, I'd become more mindful and attentive, as well. I realized with something like satisfaction that the naive, thoughtless Jessica of old no longer existed.

"Fine, I'll go get the bottle myself," I said, standing.

"Chris, seriously," Vanessa said. "I don't think you should do that, either. We're civilized human beings here."

"Fine." Chris wrinkled his nose before climbing over the railing and jumping into the water. There was practically no current around here, so he reached the bottle in just a few strokes and swam back to the railing with it in hand. After taking the bottle from him and setting it on board, Vanessa climbed down to join him in the water.

"Well, great," Alexander muttered. "Now the guy's not only poisoning *your* mind, he's gotten to my friends, too."

"Alex, cut it out," I said. "You know perfectly well that throwing trash in the ocean is wrong. If everyone did that—"

"But not everyone does it." He leaned against the railing beside me, staring sullenly down into the water. "These holier-than-thou Danny types are all over the place. I'm sure they'll save the world one of these days."

I turned toward him and grasped his arm. "I know you're angry at him," I said quietly. "But don't be. Things are the way they are. They're not going to change. If you want us to be friends, you're going to have to start by accepting the situation."

Down in the water, Vanessa started squeaking as Chris tried to dunk her. Alexander let go of the railing and wrapped his arms around me. "You're right," he said. "I just miss you so much sometimes."

I pulled him close and hugged him harder than I'd have ever dared with Danny. In that moment, I realized how often I thought about Danny, even at moments like these—and yet, at the same time, I also realized how much easier my life would have been with Alexander. I smelled his familiar aftershave, and suddenly I longed for the simple, normal teenage life I would have been able to have with him.

214

Why can't you be happy with this guy right here? What does Danny have that he doesn't?

Alexander released me, but only to tilt his head and lean in for a kiss. I jerked away. "Stop it!" I snapped. The question I'd asked myself only a split second before seemed utterly superfluous.

"So I don't have a chance?" He sounded sad. "No matter what I do, I've lost you?"

"You haven't lost me," I said. "We can be friends... If you accept that Danny and I belong together. That's your only chance of not losing me completely."

The sound of him grinding his teeth made me flinch. I would never have been happy with Alexander. Trying to would have been pure self-deception.

"Okay," he said, pursing his lips and nodding. "I'll try." Then he pulled his shirt off, climbed over the railing, and dove into the water.

For a moment, I stood there watching the spot where he had disappeared. Then I gave myself a mental shove and jumped in as well.

Chapter Twenty-Seven

September 2001

Danny and I wrote each other one or two texts a day, and he always called briefly on the weekends. Despite the huge distance between us, I could practically feel how happy he was through the telephone. He was back in his old life, the way things were before everything fell apart. He met up with old friends, driving out to the beach to surf with them on weekends, and enjoying the vibrant city in the evenings. More than once, I found myself worrying that he'd just decide not to come back. He had more than enough money to get set up over there, and he'd be able to do one or both of the jobs he did here in Germany.

Fortunately, my fundamental trust that he would never leave me was so unshakeable that it nipped my fears more or less in the bud each time I thought about it. Even so, I missed him desperately. It was getting overwhelming.

There was nothing left for me to distract myself from Danny's absence. I'd long since gotten sick of my "normal" friends—I wanted my partner back, with all of his quirks. As enjoyable as the vacation in Italy was, none of it had given me anything close to what I got from Danny. More than anything, it couldn't fill the hole in my heart created by his absence. Without him, I just didn't feel complete. It was like part of me had been torn away and exiled to the end of the world.

When I got home, I found everyday life harder and harder to manage—somehow, without his infinite zest for life, I just didn't enjoy anything anymore. Naturally, I kept my promise to stay with Christina for the first week of her new job, at the beginning of September. It was astonishingly easy for her to get up early every morning for work and keep to a schedule. She liked the work, and knowing how proud we were of her seemed to motivate her even more.

Leika and I spent our weekends with Christina, too, even though Danny wasn't there. Christina and I went to the movies, made dinner together, cleaned the apartment, and lazed around in the evenings in front of the television. At night, we'd curl up in Danny's bed together and joke around or tell stories. I reminded her about how she'd threatened to kill me when Danny and I had first gotten together. She laughed and admitted that she'd thought I was a total square—that she'd never imagined I'd be okay with the fact that she was part of Danny's life as well.

In turn, I admitted that I'd thought she and Danny were super weird, but I'd been so drawn to their personalities, their auras, that it hadn't bothered me.

216

Meeting them probably really did prevent me from becoming a petty, bourgeois stick-in-the-mud who wasted her entire life chasing material things.

We crossed off the days until Danny's return; on the final day, we started counting down hours, waiting for the taxi that was going to bring him back to us in the wee hours of the morning.

"It's here!" Christina suddenly cried, and we both ran outside to meet him, Leika barking wildly at our heels. I jumped into his arms from a dead run, never before and never since so happy to see another human being. Danny lifted me into the air and held me close for a full minute, only setting me down again so he'd have an arm free for Christina. She clung to him tightly, weeping for joy, like a little girl seeing her mother again after a long time apart. Leika yowled exuberantly until Danny finally found the time to greet her as well.

We stood outside for what felt like hours before finally gathering up Danny's bags and coming inside. The three of us snuggled into his bed, with Danny lying on his stomach, half on me, and Christina still clinging to his arm. He'd gotten very tan, and his hair was at least two shades lighter. As always, he was in a fantastic mood. We spent the whole morning looking at photos of his home country, listening to his stories, and peppering in our questions, before finally falling asleep all tangled together in a pile.

We were the weirdest little group in the world, but we were happy. Maybe we were naive, too, because none of us would ever have guessed that this would be our last summer together. If anyone had told us that, we'd have stared at them in disbelief, and then probably laughed in their face. At least, I think so. I should have just listened to Danny more carefully—what he said to me in Italy turned out to be true. His intuition was remarkable, and his gut never lied to him. But even considering all that, we'd never have imagined the circumstances that ended up separating us.

Chapter Twenty-Eight

November 2001

Even from far away, I could tell something was wrong. When I pulled up to his place, Danny was standing outside by his car, waiting for me. He didn't seem his usual self—the serenity he usually radiated had vanished. He shifted nervously from one foot to the other, running his hands through his hair again and again, like I was taking too long to park.

"What's wrong?" I asked.

"Tina's gone."

"Gone *how*?"

"She ran off," he snapped in a tone I'd never heard him use. He looked crabby and upset, two adjectives that didn't normally fit him at all. "She didn't come home last night, said she was staying at Natasha's. And she didn't come home after work today, so I called the shop, and they said she never showed up. She didn't call, either!"

"Damn." My heart began to thump faster. "Did you try her cell phone?"

"Of course I did, I'm not an idiot," he muttered. "Get in the car already, we have to look for her." Without taking the time to turn the car around, he reversed down the frontage road, tires squealing, to the main street.

"Where are we going to go? Where could she be?" I didn't have the first clue where to begin.

"I'm going to pay a visit to the dealer she always bought from. If she's just disappeared without saying a word to anyone, that's the only explanation."

Oh, God, my inner voice shrieked. *Why would she do something like this? She was doing so well! Something must have happened.* "You know where to find him?" I asked tentatively.

"Yeah, I think so." We drove to Stuttgart. The traffic didn't give Danny any problems, thanks to his complete disregard for other drivers and the two red lights he sped through.

"How do you know where to find her dealer?" I asked at last.

"Jesus Christ, I just know, okay?" He chewed nervously on a fingernail. Offended, I crossed my arms and turned away. "Sorry," he said after a while.

"It's okay." I put my hand on his thigh. "Let's go find Tina."

He rolled down a couple of extremely shady alleys I'd never seen before. After a while, he parked beside a trio of trash cans in front of an old warehouse. "Wait for me here," he warned as he got out, but I followed him through the open rolling gate leading into the warehouse.

A dozen or so younger guys were sitting around on the ground, all wearing jeans, button-down shirts and dark sweatshirts. A couple of them were smoking a joint, clearly in another dimension. The others peered at us with hostile expressions.

Danny went straight for a bald guy with a cigarette between his fingers. He was wearing a white ribbed undershirt, an open lumberjack shirt over it, the sleeves rolled up to reveal his tattooed forearms. I guessed he was in his mid-thirties. Apparently he was the guy to talk to around here.

"Was Christina here?" Danny asked in lieu of a greeting.

The guy shrugged. "Who's Christina?" I immediately suspected he knew perfectly well who Danny meant.

"You know," Danny snapped. "Tina. Little shorter than me, long, black hair, green eyes. Did she buy anything from you guys?"

The guy in the undershirt held out a hand and beckoned expectantly with his fingers. He wanted money. "Maybe if I think about it a little more, it'll come to me," he said with a contemptuous grin.

Danny smiled pleasantly for a moment and then suddenly snatched the man up by his collar. Even though the guy was a head taller than Danny and had probably seventy or eighty pounds on him, Danny managed to overpower him and push him up against the wall. Without warning, he punched the man several times in the face.

"So think about it!" he growled, pressing his forearm against the man's throat to hold him in place.

The guy tried to put his cigarette out on Danny's arm, but Danny used his free hand to slap it out of his fingers.

"Christ, can't you just give me an answer?"

Apparently, it was possible to make Danny angrier than I'd ever imagined. There seemed to be no upper limit to his rage. The realization frightened me. But out of the corner of my eye, I could see that the other men sitting around were slowly getting to their feet. I did a quick count. There were nine of them, and none of them looked especially puny. One reached for a nightstick.

Why the hell was Danny so impulsive? He usually threw money around without a second thought, but instead of just giving this guy fifty euros, he'd risked a brawl.

"Danny," I said in warning. But he'd already noticed the others. He slammed his shin into his hostage's side three times, at full force, leaving the guy gasping for air.

"Call your dogs off," Danny snarled. "Otherwise, you'll be dead before they can even get their hands on me."

My brain was working a hundred miles an hour, trying to picture how Danny was planning on killing him without a weapon. It wouldn't take the others more than a couple seconds to reach him. And he'd once told me it was practically impossible to kill someone with one blow, even for an experienced martial artist. The particular set of circumstances it would require almost never happened in real fights: the opponent had to be someone who knew nothing about martial arts, and he would have to be holding perfectly still so that you could hit him hard enough in exactly the right spot, down to a fraction of an inch. Besides, if Danny actually managed to kill him, would the others really just let us leave?

The guy in the undershirt didn't give Danny's words quite that much thought. He made a small motion with his index finger, and the others sat down again.

"Just answer my question," Danny repeated.

"She was here last night," he said, still wheezing. Danny had hit his lungs so hard he could barely breathe. Maybe he really had been afraid for his life, at least for a moment. "She bought some stuff from me and then stayed the night in the main building."

"Where is she now?"

"No idea. She left two hours ago. She was going home." His breath whistled loudly as he spoke.

"That wasn't so hard, was it?" Danny released him before retreating as fast as he could. There was a flurry of movement around us. Danny grabbed my hand, and we sprinted out of the warehouse. Without stopping for a second, he shoved me into the car, glanced around hastily, leaped over the hood, and jumped into the driver's seat. Then he locked the doors from the inside and jerked the car into reverse, slamming into one of the trash cans with a loud crunch. The car skidded for a moment, giving the men chasing us enough time to surround the car.

"Get down," Danny told me before shifting into drive and hitting the gas. I heard a deafening bang and the sound of squealing tires. Danny careened down the narrow alley at nearly sixty miles an hour, only slowing once we reached the main street.

"Were they just *shooting* at us?" I screeched.

"Why do you think I told you to wait in the car? Did you think they wanted to play Ping-Pong?"

I gaped at him. He shook out his left hand. His knuckles were bleeding. I was utterly speechless, incapable of even closing my mouth. Every time I thought I finally knew Danny Taylor inside and out, I discovered a new side of him.

"What?" He looked nervous, and he was still breathing hard. "Why are you staring at me like that?"

"One of these days, you're going to drive me over the edge!" I shook my head, struggling to compose myself. "You just hand yourself over to a couple teenagers like a lamb to the slaughter, even though they wouldn't have stood a chance against you. But then when things really get dangerous, and you have zero chance, *that's* when you go for it. Fantastic, Danny. Excellent strategy. I'm really impressed."

He snorted. "It's the only language they speak. If you go in there and say, 'Please, please,' you're toast."

"As soon as we have Tina back, I'm sending you to a self-help group to learn anger management in dangerous situations. Maybe learning to knit would do you good, or crocheting some potholders."

"There's just no pleasing you, either." He looked insulted. "'Don't just put up with this, Danny. Defend yourself already, Danny. Do this, Danny. Do that, Danny…'"

"I *would* suggest you make decisions based on the individual situations," I snapped, "but there's no point. When your temper gets going, your brain shuts down."

"Everything went fine," he said. "Now we just have to find Tina."

It began to rain—just drizzling at first, but then the clouds really opened up. We made our way home at a snail's pace, keeping an eye out for her. She had to be either headed home on foot or hitchhiking. I called Danny's landline several times, but there was no answer. Apparently, she wasn't back yet.

Somewhere along the rural highway, Danny suddenly slammed on the brakes and pointed out into the rain. "There she is."

She was soaking wet, frozen to the bone, and completely out of it as I ran to her and dragged her back to the car. "Tina!" I shouted. "Where were you? We were worried!" She just stared right through us without replying. Her pupils were pinpoints, and she could barely sit upright, which meant she'd probably just taken something.

She didn't say a word the entire drive home.

Danny carried her through the rain and upstairs to the apartment, setting her down in the living room. We pulled off her wet clothes, and I made her some hot chocolate. She drank it wordlessly, clutching the cup with trembling fingers, and then suddenly began scratching herself wildly. I knew what was happening. Heroin triggered the body to release histamines, which made you itch everywhere.

Danny sat down beside her and took her hands. "Just tell me why, Tina," he said tenderly.

"It's starting again!" she shrieked, crying and clawing at her sweatshirt. "It's starting again, just like before!"

I blinked at Danny in confusion. He shook his head, uncomprehending. "What's starting?"

"Everything, just like before." Christina's speech was slurred. She'd jumped right back in at a dose so high that she couldn't even talk properly. "It's the only way I can stand the pain."

"Should we give her something to help her sleep?" I suggested.

"No way," Danny said. "Medications on top of drugs could be dangerous. Let's just wait it out."

The three of us sat up half the night on the couch, until Christina began throwing up. She finally passed out from exhaustion in the early hours of the morning, and Danny carried her to bed. He and I remained on the couch, discussing what to do next.

"I'll call the clinic tomorrow and ask when I can bring her in," he decided. "She needs to go back. She's used at least twice—essentially, she has to start back at square one."

"Really?" I was shocked. "Surely, she can't be addicted again that fast."

"You can get addicted to heroin by using it just once," he said. "Not physically, but mentally. She won't have the willpower to keep herself from doing it again. You have to remember she was addicted for years."

"What does she mean about the pain? Does that make any sense to you?"

"Yeah." Danny sighed. "She had phantom pain for years—pain with no demonstrable medical explanation. At first, they thought it was rheumatoid arthritis, so they ran a bunch of tests on her, but everything checked out. It's all psychological. People who have suffered years of physical or sexual abuse get that sometimes—they have pain in places that have nothing to do with the abuse and that can't be explained medically.

"Others often dismiss the pain as nonsense, but it's completely real to the person experiencing it. Tina started getting it years ago. She started cutting herself to block it out. Used razor blades. Then she discovered drugs. Heroin is the quickest pain reliever out there. So that's how she got it to stop."

"That's horrible!" I buried my face in my hands. "Isn't there anything she can do about it?"

"Therapy," Danny said. "Therapy is the only thing that helps. But she did all of that before. It's just that…when damage has been done over years…you can't just talk it out of existence from one day to the next."

"Have you experienced something like this, too?"

"Phantom pain? No, I never had it. I never felt the urge to self-injure, either."

"You just let people beat you up every once in a while," I said gently. It was a poor attempt at a joke.

A smile flitted briefly across his face. "Masochism isn't really my thing, either, trust me." He sighed again. "I'll call Tina's psychologist tomorrow, too. She should start going back to therapy—she used to go regularly. Then all we can do is hope the rehab clinic takes her back right away."

"Let's go to bed." I took his hand and pulled him to his feet.

"I'll sleep with her," Danny said. "We'll need to go to a hardware store tomorrow and get some padlocks. We can't let her run away again."

Danny spent half the morning on the phone. Christina's psychologist promised to start coming by to talk to her every day, starting the following week. The rehab clinic didn't have space immediately, but they offered Christina a spot in their supervised group home for two months beginning mid-December. Danny agreed, and also got permission to come a couple of days later to join her for two weeks.

They also told him to focus on getting her to detox, so that she'd at least have the drugs completely out of her system by the time she joined them, and then they could focus on her psychological addiction. Her physical withdrawal symptoms shouldn't be too bad, they assured him—she'd only used twice, she wasn't really "back on it" yet, so cold turkey would be all right.

Danny canceled all of his appointments for the next few weeks. His modeling agency gave him a lot of grief for it, since all of his shoots were already scheduled, but Danny didn't care. A coworker at the martial arts center agreed to sub for him, though he wasn't exactly enthusiastic about all the extra work. Danny knew the decision would cost him both students and modeling contracts, but he didn't see any other alternative.

Finally, he called the boutique where Christina was interning and made an appointment with the owner. It took a lot of convincing on Danny's part, but he finally agreed to release her from her contract until the beginning of April.

Having done all of that, he drove to the hardware store and bought a handful of padlocks to keep Christina in the house for the next few weeks. Before he left, he snuck a glance into her room to make sure she was doing okay. She was fast asleep. He gave me the job of keeping her inside the house while he was gone.

She didn't come out of her room all morning, so I assumed she was still asleep. When Danny opened the apartment door, he was already fuming. He threw me an accusatory look. "The window in her room is open. She snuck out."

"*What?*" I hadn't heard a sound. "That's impossible!"

Sure enough, her window was open, and there was no sign of Christina. Danny turned right around and strode back into the hallway. "I'll get her. You stay here!"

"You're not going back to those guys, are you?" I screeched. I couldn't let him do that. I was far more afraid for Danny than I was worried about Christina.

"Of course I am!" he growled. "I might catch her on the way, but if not, I'll have to go there."

"Danny, it's way too dangerous!"

"I don't have a choice," he said. "I don't think you understand the severity of the situation. That's a drug ring. They have pimps, too. If they get their hands on Tina, they'll send her straight out to turn tricks. Then we'll never see her again." With that, he walked out of the apartment, leaving me standing there in the hallway.

I ran after him in a panic. "I'm well aware of how serious this is!" I called. "I was there yesterday. Why do you think I don't want you to go?"

Danny stopped in his tracks, came back, and wrapped his arms around me. "Don't worry," he said softly. "I used to go fight Tina's way out of there all the time. I'll be okay. Everything is okay."

He walked to his car without looking back. I stood there fighting back the tears welling up in my eyes yet again.

Chapter Twenty-Nine

November 2001

Christina Marlene Schneider breathed a sigh of relief when she heard the BMW engine fade into the distance. It wasn't the first time she'd been glad he'd left. He was probably off to the hardware store for the tools to lock her up in this room again. Normally, there was no such thing as having Danny too close—whenever he wasn't within reach, she felt like someone had violently torn a piece of her away. She loved him far more than she loved her own life, though that life had always been meaningless to her anyway. Knowing that she'd disappointed him and was causing him worry filled her with infinite sadness.

Even she didn't know why she'd done it. It had been a reflex, like a movie on autoplay that she was powerless to stop. The little packet of dirty white powder stuck inside her bra was still all she could think about. She decided to wait a little longer, just in case Danny suddenly came back for some reason. He'd searched her yesterday for drugs, of course, but she knew where to hide things from him. And she was well aware that he'd left Jessica behind to keep an eye on her.

But Jess would be no real obstacle. She couldn't sniff Christina out nearly as well as Danny could.

Christina didn't think she could hold out much longer. The cold had already begun to spread through her body, and she felt her mouth filling with hot saliva. Even her eyes started to fill with fluid. Her legs felt strange, like they'd been dunked first in boiling water and then in ice.

How could she have known that she'd get withdrawal symptoms after just that one fix? Of course, she'd known it was dangerous, but she'd been sure one time wouldn't hurt—she figured she'd be able to stop right away. After all, she'd done the stuff so often in the past, one time here or there wasn't going to make a big difference, right?

That had been her theory, anyway. Now she found herself forced to face the sad reality of the situation: she hadn't stopped at one. She'd had to go back for more the very next day.

They'd given her cheap street heroin, probably no more than 20 percent pure. The rest was all powdered sugar and plaster. Nothing like the stuff Danny had gotten her back in the day—90 percent pure, practically uncut. Serious side effects were rare with high-quality drugs like those, and she hadn't had to worry about track marks as much.

Not that she cared about that now, because she certainly wasn't planning on slipping back into that vicious circle. She was going to stop again, get back to her job, and get her life under control once and for all. She had no doubt of it. This had really just been a one-time slip, triggered by the news her mother had given her: her dad was getting out early for good behavior. He'd be free at the beginning of next year. Hearing that had brought the roof down on Christina's head. She couldn't take the knowledge that *he* would soon be able to come anywhere near her.

As if on cue, the pain had started again. It had been gone for so long, and then bam, out of the blue, it had started again. Pain that she would never wish on anyone...apart from her father.

It started in her head and shot through every nerve in her body, until she couldn't think, talk, or move. Doctors couldn't localize it, couldn't explain it. It's all psychological, they'd told her. Well, of course, that was the easiest explanation, wasn't it? The crazy girl with the messed-up childhood was just imagining it all.

Even if that were true, it didn't make the pain any easier to take. Besides practically paralyzing her, it put her completely on edge, so that all she wanted to do was run away. Which she had. Right back to the thing she knew would help block out this horrible pain inside her.

She stood up quietly and removed the little baggie from her bra. Danny had taken everything else: the needles, the syringes, the lighter. She couldn't even smoke it. Furious, she opened the package and begun snorting the contents.

Christina hated snorting heroin. It didn't have anywhere near the same effect, plus it seemed pathetic. "Too dumb to fix," everyone had called it. But too dumb to fix was better than nothing, and it would be enough to quell the withdrawal effects until she could get her hands on a fresh supply.

She supposed she'd have to go back and see Johnny again. Get herself a little something, probably more than yesterday. They'd give her the cheap crap again— there was no way of getting the high-quality stuff unless you threw buckets of money at the dealers like Danny had. And there was no point wasting her time hoping he'd do that again. The only reason he'd done it before was because, addicted as Christina was back then, the people at the drug counseling center had recommended against going cold turkey. Better to wean her off the heroin gradually, they'd said, so that she wouldn't have to go the medication route. And Danny had gotten her better stuff than she'd even known existed. Any junkie in the world would have gladly given a kidney just to experience it once.

Once you try smack, you never go back! Christina shook her head. She needed to concentrate on what was important here. Right now, she'd be happy to get even 5-percent junk.

She got dressed as quietly as she could, feeling the heroin beginning to work. The cold was fading, her eyes and mouth were dry again, and her legs didn't feel quite as weird anymore.

Then the rush hit her.

She stretched deliciously. Now nothing mattered. Her world would be perfectly fine for the next three hours—which was enough time to figure out how to get another fix.

"After the game is before the game," an old German soccer coach had once said. The minute you finished one, you had to start thinking about the next. It was even truer for junkies: after the fix was before the fix.

The window opened without a creak. Christina climbed out and slipped away from the apartment building, hunching over as she ran toward the street. She'd made it! She was free! Suddenly, she was filled with such euphoria that her heart was hammering in her throat. She wasn't sure if it was down to the heroin or her successful escape, but she didn't really care.

She ran to the main street but then decided to stay on a back road so she wouldn't run into Danny when he inevitably came looking for her. She stuck her thumb out whenever she saw a passing car, and it wasn't long before an old VW Golf pulled up beside her.

"Hi," she said. "I need to get to Stuttgart. Can you give me a lift part of the way?"

"Of course, honey." He unlocked the doors, and she climbed in. "I'm Robert," he said, pulling back onto the road. "What's your name?"

"Tina." She looked the guy over. He frightened her. Late forties, with thick, horn-rimmed glasses and greasy, parted hair. His shirt was snow-white. He smelled like cigarettes, and he reminded her of her father. Pretty much every man that had anything in common with that monster frightened her. She pressed herself farther down into her seat.

"What are you doing in Stuttgart, honey?" His voice was far too friendly. She needed to get out of there before she had a panic attack. All the heroin in the world wouldn't have kept her calm in this situation. Better to take a taxi, she decided.

Suddenly, she began to worry that Danny would notice her absence too quickly and get to Stuttgart before her. She'd get there faster with a taxi, and she'd still have more than enough money for several bags of H. She'd just gone to the bank yesterday, in fact. Having her own account and her own income certainly had advantages.

"Honey?" the guy beside her prodded.

Sweat beaded on her forehead, and she'd already bitten her thumbnail down to the quick. Seeing a traffic light up ahead, she prayed it would turn red in time.

Yes.

Before the car even came to a complete stop, she wrenched the door open and ran. She could hardly believe her luck—she found a taxi immediately. When she told the driver the address, he gave her a doubtful look. Apparently he knew the area.

She didn't care. That was the great thing about heroin: nothing mattered.

A couple of blocks from her destination, she paid the driver and got out. She didn't want to attract any attention, so she could get in and out as fast as possible. Clouded as her mind was, she still found herself getting nervous. There weren't just dealers inside that building—there were pimps, too. She'd already taken a serious risk by sleeping there the night before. This could get dangerous fast. The men in there thought of girls as playthings for them to use however they wanted.

In years past, she'd already experienced a few guys sending her out to turn tricks before deciding they didn't want to let her leave. How many more times would Danny manage to get her out of there again? Tears ran down her face when she thought about him, about how often the guys in this building had already beaten him up because of her.

This is the last time, Danny, she silently promised. *Once this stuff is gone, I'll quit and start living the life you want for me!*

She wasn't going to disappoint him again.

As she slowly approached the front entrance to the warehouse, she saw his BMW blocking the front gate.

Christina cursed. How had he gotten there so quickly? It pained her to realize how panicked he must have been to make such an obvious mistake. He knew the warehouse had a back entrance, but he'd still been too dumb to hide his car. Now, she could just slip to the back unnoticed while he waited in vain out front. It wasn't at all like him to be this inattentive, and she felt horrible about the chaos she had obviously unleashed within him.

For a moment, she considered just going over to his car and giving herself up, but she couldn't make herself do it. She needed the heroin.

With a heavy heart, she headed around to the back.

She was just turning the corner when someone grabbed her from behind, gripping her forearms so tightly that she knew there was no chance of escape. A wave of panic crashed over her, and she started screaming as loudly as she could. One of the hands released her arm and clamped down over her mouth. Christina thought she was going to suffocate.

"Shh, Tina, it's me," Danny whispered in her ear.

Danny! Her panic dissipated as quickly as it had come. At first, she couldn't quite decide whether to feel angry or relieved. Nothing was going to happen to her now, but she also wasn't going to get any heroin.

The anger won out.

"What do you want?" she shrieked. "Let me go! I'm going in there!"

"No, you're coming with me." As he steered her back to the front entrance, she realized he'd parked his car out front as a decoy—he'd been waiting in the back the entire time. She could have marched right up to the front entrance unnoticed. The revelation infuriated her even more.

"Why can't you keep your nose out of my business already? I'm old enough to make my own decisions!" She began taking swings at him.

"I can see that, Tina," he replied coldly. Still mercilessly clenching her arm, he herded her to the car before gently but firmly forcing her into the front passenger seat.

She thought about using the few seconds he needed to get to the driver's side as a chance to flee, but decided against it. He was much faster than her—she wouldn't get far. As he got in and locked the doors, she sat there, pouting, letting the tears flow freely.

"Just leave me alone!" she wailed. "I don't want to be around you anymore, I want to live my own life!"

"No problem," Danny said. "You're free as soon as you're clean. But not until then."

Chapter Thirty

December 2001

Christina hadn't spoken a word to us in a month. Danny and I had made the entire house breakout-proof. Every evening, he walked around the building, closed the old wooden shutters from the outside, and secured them with padlocks. The neighbors probably thought we were totally bonkers now. If they didn't already, anyway. After all, by that point, half the village had heard about Danny's illness—and the lifestyle he supposedly led. The fact that two women were always coming and going at his place probably didn't help his image much.

We didn't care, though. The people we were close to knew the truth, and they liked us the way we were. The rest of the world could kiss our behinds.

But things were still hard. One Sunday night, the two of us collapsed into bed late, completely worn out. Christina refused to sleep with us that night, preferring to pout in her room. And Danny was beyond stressed.

He hadn't gone running in days, nor had he been to the gym. Knowing that probably wouldn't change any time soon put him in a terrible mood. He grew more and more restless, searching in vain for ways to burn off his excess energy. He'd spend his evenings in his workout room, pummeling his punching bag and doing countless chin-ups and push-ups, and then he'd be all over me—only to realize afterward that it still wasn't enough.

Some days, he'd spend hours pacing the apartment, which nearly drove me out of my mind. For the first time since we'd met, I began to worry ever so slightly that living with Danny full-time might occasionally get annoying.

"Will you be okay sleeping like this?" I'd asked him the first time we locked the shutters. He'd locked his own window, too, afraid that Christina would try to make a break for it when he was dead asleep. I thought his fears were unfounded—Danny would have heard an ant crawling through his bedroom—but he was sure it was the only way.

"No," he'd said. "I doubt I'll be getting much sleep in the next few weeks."

This particular Sunday night was no different. Danny lay there, wide awake, nervously running his hand through his hair and drumming his fingers on the mattress.

"This has to stop, Danny," I told him. "Tomorrow morning, you're going running. She'll be okay without you for an hour." Stressful as the situation was, I was afraid he would explode if he didn't blow off a little steam.

"The worst is yet to come," he predicted. "Pretty soon, she won't allow us to keep her locked up."

So far, her physical withdrawal symptoms had been manageable. In the beginning, she'd mostly done a lot of throwing up, crying, and shivering. Danny had piled blankets on top of her, brought a TV to her beside, and slept in her room at night. Today was the first day she'd sent him out, which was why I thought she was starting to feel better—back when she'd been suffering so terribly, she hadn't wanted him out of her sight for a second.

"The worst is over, isn't it?" I asked.

"I don't dare hope that. You don't get off of smack that easily."

"She only did it three times."

"But she was hooked on it for years before. Plus, she hardly weighs anything, and she's not in a very good mental state, so it didn't take her long to get addicted again."

"Danny," I said. "You're going running tomorrow. I'll go to work late, and I won't let her out of my sight for a minute. Promise."

He sighed. "Okay. After that, you should probably wait a week before coming back over. What comes next won't be pretty."

Danny was right, as always. That same night, Christina marched into our bedroom. "I want out, now!" she shouted. "If you guys don't let me out of the goddamn house right now, I'll freak!"

"You're not getting out of here, Tina," Danny said calmly. "Whatever you do, you're staying here."

"Whatever" turned out to be running around in a circle like a madwoman. Danny got up and put on a sweatshirt and a pair of jogging pants. For a second, I thought he was going to take her outside, but then I realized he was just preparing for a long night.

Without warning, Christina ran into the dining room, grabbed a kitchen chair, and began smashing it against the front door. Danny grabbed her from behind while I took the chair away from her.

"I hate you!" she screeched, punching Danny. "WHERE DO YOU GET OFF, MEDDLING IN MY LIFE? DON'T YOU HAVE ENOUGH PROBLEMS OF YOUR OWN? Mind your own fucking business!"

Danny simply held her wrists and let her throw her tantrum. She kicked him, even tried to bite him. He only released her when she asked to go to the bathroom. Danny followed her, but she ran in and locked herself inside. She spent the rest of the night shouting and screaming behind the door. Danny remained sitting there with his back against it, while I tried to sleep because I had to work the next day.

But Christina was tireless in announcing how much she hated Danny and how much she wanted him out of her life. After an hour or so, I gave up and joined him on the floor. He was sitting there with his knees pulled up and his face buried in his arms, sobbing.

"She doesn't mean it," I said in an attempt to comfort him.

"I know that," he said. He rubbed his eyes, trying to compose himself. "She didn't make it, Ducky," he whispered. "We've lost her. My gut tells me we've lost her. We'll never get Tina back now."

"How can you say such a thing?" I was horrified. "It's just a relapse. She'll go back to the clinic, and she'll come out clean again."

Where was he getting these ideas? Danny was usually so optimistic—why was he suddenly talking like this?

He only shrugged, shook his head, and burst into tears again. We sat there, shoulder to shoulder, listening through the door. After a few hours, Christina came out and attacked Danny all over again. Together, he and I wrapped her in a blanket, fixing her arms and legs in place to keep her from hurting us, and took her to our bed. Danny laid behind her, holding her down with all of his strength. We covered her in a whole stack of blankets, but she kept shivering anyway. By the time she finally fell asleep, the sun was already up.

"Go run if you have the energy for it," I told Danny. I knew he'd lose his mind if he didn't—he was taking the whole thing to heart far too much. "Lock the door from the outside if you want. I'll stay in here with her."

"Thank you." Danny gave me a kiss on the cheek and slipped out. He would probably never be too tired to run. I heard him lock the door, and I prayed that Christina would stay asleep until he returned. Until then, I barely dared breathe for fear of waking her.

All at once, for whatever reason, I shared Danny's fear that we had lost her for good.

Even though I was very late to work, I left a couple hours early, claiming I had a headache—which I did, but it wouldn't normally have kept me from working. I was really only leaving because I was too agitated to concentrate. I decided I'd stop by Danny's for a while, and then I'd go home to avoid trouble with my parents for having been away so much during the week.

When I arrived, the apartment was astonishingly quiet. Danny had cooked the night before, and Christina was now sitting at the kitchen table, shoveling leftovers into her mouth with almost unnerving gusto. Danny was leaning against the island with his arms crossed, watching her every move the way he'd been doing for days.

"Hello, hello," I said, glancing between them, and then wrapped my arms around Danny. "How are you?"

"She's doing better," he said, answering a question I hadn't really asked. "The worst is probably over now."

"I asked how are *you*."

He shrugged uncertainly. He probably didn't think the quiet would last. I hugged him again before sitting down beside Christina. "And you, Tina?" Cautiously, I took her hand. "How are you?"

Christina was silent for a while, avoiding my eyes. "Sorry," she suddenly blurted out. "I didn't really mean any of the stuff I said." Then she stood up and put her plate in the dishwasher. For a moment, she stopped in front of Danny and stroked his arm. "Thank you," she whispered, and he nodded curtly before she left the room.

"See?" I cried triumphantly. "She's pulling herself together again!"

Not long after that, Christina's social worker came to talk to her. Christina was almost too compliant.

Exhausted, I drove home, silently counting the days until she could go to the clinic. Things would be a lot easier for Danny then.

***

The gym bag was sitting in the hallway, packed and ready. Christina was lying on her stomach beside it, clawing at the carpet. "Who the hell do you two think you are?" she barked at us. "I'm not going! You can't force me! You're not my parents!"

Danny had been trying to reason with her for a good two hours, and I was starting to lose my patience. We were never going to get out of here at this rate. The problem was, she was right. We really didn't have the authority to force her into rehab. We could drag her to the car by force—and were determined to do so if necessary—and haul her off to the clinic, but if she didn't stay there voluntarily, we didn't have a prayer. They wouldn't keep her there against her will.

"Tina," Danny began for the hundredth time. "There's no other way. If I leave you here now, you'll take off at the first opportunity, and then the whole thing will start all over again. How often have we done this already?"

"I don't want to!" she wailed. "Doesn't what other people want count for anything in your *fucking* egocentric world?"

"Don't be unfair, Tina," I scolded her. She was starting to wear away my already thin patience. We were only trying to help.

"Please, just let me go, please!" She'd switched gears—now she was playing the sympathy card. "Please!" She grasped Danny's hand. "If you really love me as much as you always say you do, then please just let me go now."

Danny remained firm. We both knew she was pulling out all the stops to get what she wanted. Which was heroin. She'd have sold her own grandmother for it.

"Different strategy," I hissed to Danny, and he nodded. I pulled her fingers free of the carpet, and he simply lifted her up and carried her out to the car. I walked ahead of them, carrying her bag, and opened the door to sit in the back with her.

She swung her fists at us wildly as Danny got in, locked the doors, and started the car.

"Tina!" I shouted at her. "Stop this shit! You're not getting out of here!"

"I HATE YOU BOTH!" She was back to screaming again. I tried to hold her hands down, because she kept reaching out to hit Danny from behind. "HOW DARE YOU?" she screeched at him. "I thought you were my *friend*! You said we would always stick together, that you would do anything for me! You lied! You're a disgusting liar, you just want to get rid of me!"

"It's not going to work, Tina," Danny growled back. "You're not going to change my mind. You can go ahead and hate me if it helps you, but I'm taking you to that goddamn clinic."

"I *do* hate you," she sobbed. "You're just like all the others. You want to ship me off somewhere to get rid of me. We're done! Things will *never* be the same between us. We're going our separate ways for good!"

I knew perfectly well that she didn't mean any of it, that she'd never leave Danny once she'd cooled off and her head was clear again. Danny knew it, too. Even so, I could tell how much her words hurt him—and that he felt like throwing her out of the moving car.

"Danny," I griped. "This isn't going to work. I can't hold her."

He stopped at the shoulder and beckoned for me to come up front to drive, while he clambered between the seats into the back. That worked better. I focused on the crisp female voice of the GPS up front, while Danny struggled with Christina in the back. When she was angry, she always reminded me of a Tasmanian devil. At least now Danny would have a chance to use up some of his excess energy.

Fortunately, there was hardly any traffic, so we made good time. After a while, I glanced in the rear-view mirror and saw Christina curled up on Danny's lap, crying, as he stroked her back. When I finally spotted the large building with the green wooden shutters nestled among the pines, I nearly cheered in delight.

I got out and opened the door for the other two. Danny pushed Christina out of the car, and she let herself fall to the ground like a sack of potatoes. Together, we got her to her feet again.

Danny raised her chin, forcing her to look at him. His blue eyes bored into hers. "You're going in there, Tina," he told her. "You're going to be good and do what they tell you. I'll join you in a couple of days. You can do this. As soon as you're halfway stable again, I'll bring you home. I promise!"

Christina was at her wits' end. She clung to his sweatshirt, gazing up at him through bloodshot eyes. "Please, Danny. Please don't. Please don't do this to me. Don't leave me here. I'm begging you, don't leave me here. You're the only person in my life, I love you more than anything, please don't do this to me. Don't break my heart. Don't leave me alone!"

If they kept this up, they were going to break each other's hearts.

Seeing us pull up, two attendants came out of the building and headed toward us.

"I'll be here soon!" Danny assured her. "I'll bring you back home, I promise! I swear on my life, I'll bring you back home!" He leaned in and gave her a kiss on the lips.

The attendants unclamped her fingers from Danny's sweatshirt and pulled her inside. Though she put up no resistance, Christina kept looking back over her shoulder and reaching out for Danny, as if hoping he would save her at the last minute.

After she had gone, he stood there in the parking lot for several minutes, staring after her, looking totally lost. I was almost afraid he would run in after her and bring her out again. "Come on," I said, taking his elbow. "I'll drive home."

Still staring at the building, Danny absently climbed into the passenger seat.

"You did everything right," I assured him. "She'll get over it, and she'll thank you later. Just like she did before. There was no other choice."

I could tell it hurt his soul to leave her behind like that. They were yin and yang, peas in a pod. Now and forever.

***

Danny spent his twenty-second birthday in rehab with Christina. He returned just before New Year's, and he and I drove up into the mountains, to the same hotel the three of us had stayed at the year before.

Danny hadn't said another word regarding that vague, foreboding feeling about Christina that had come over him that one awful night. His optimism had returned. It had been a relapse—those were always a possibility—but it hadn't been the end of the world. She'd be in rehab for a while, and then she'd start over.

He wanted that so badly.

Chapter Thirty-One

February 2002

Danny kept his promise and picked Christina up at the beginning of the month. She was emaciated and haggard, with none of the zest for life she'd always radiated before. And she'd told us why. Her father had gotten out of prison. That's what had triggered her relapse. She reminded me of a wind-up doll: she could walk and talk, but she was dead inside.

Hoping to distract her as much as we could, we took her out all over the place on evenings and weekends—the zoo, the local indoor pool, all kinds of festivals and events.

Danny took another two weeks off, ignoring his students' protests and earning himself a hefty fine from his modeling agency for breach of contract. He resumed guard duty, doing his rounds to all the windows outside the apartment every evening and locking us in like we lived in some kind of bunker.

One Sunday morning, Christina suddenly cheerfully announced over breakfast, "I think I'm out of the woods. I want to start working again in March."

Danny gave her a skeptical look. "You've still got time, Tina. You can start again at the beginning of April. I've worked it out with them. Just give yourself another four weeks."

She set her jaw stubbornly. "No, really. I'm over it. I want to work again. It was fun."

He shifted from one foot to the other uncertainly. "Okay. I guess we can drive out there tomorrow and talk to your boss, see what we can do."

As it turned out, Christina's boss put her off until April. Her psychologist gave us hope, though: she was doing well, and it was certainly possible that she was out of the woods.

The past few weeks had been pure stress. Danny hadn't even let Christina take the dog out by herself, and he'd slept with her almost every night. But things were finally beginning to look up again.

Until one morning in the middle of March, when we discovered that Christina had managed to silently remove the padlock on her window in the middle of the night and sneak away.

Chapter Thirty-Two

March 2002

Even as a child, Björn Wildermuth had known he wanted to be a policeman. Inspired by Colombo and Hercule Poirot, he'd pictured himself hunting down criminals someday, too.

His childhood dreams had only somewhat come true: he'd since learned that everyday cops' main responsibility was doing the dirty work. Today was no exception—and on his birthday, too. At least he wouldn't have to go to the girl's parents today. Not yet. What would he have said? "Hello, your daughter is dead. I don't suppose you have any coffee?"

He'd first seen the girl yesterday afternoon. It was his first dead body. Some junkie's girlfriend had found the girl in their apartment; she'd probably been lying there for three or four days already. The girl had had intercourse with the man shortly before her death, and the fact that she'd used right afterward, in his apartment, deepened Wildermuth's suspicion that he'd been her pimp. The stuff he'd given her had been bad somehow, so bad that she'd stopped breathing almost immediately.

The girl's body showed evidence of sexual assault as well—yellowish bruises on her wrists and on the insides of her thighs. Strange that the addict pimp hadn't done any of the bad heroin himself. Possibly just a coincidence, of course.

Björn's supervisor, Harald Mayer, was leaning toward negligent homicide, possibly even premeditated murder. Björn himself suspected that the girl had made herself available of her own free will, accepting these perverse little games as the price she paid for the dope she wanted so badly. He figured it was just bad luck that this particular batch had killed her—and maybe that was the kind of risk one had to take as a junkie.

Björn headed out for Besigheim. A guy out there had reported his roommate missing a week ago. The girl fit the description perfectly: his roommate had turned tricks and used heroin in the past, and now the guy was afraid she'd slipped back into that scene. He gave them a few tips on where the girl might be found, and with whom.

As he drove, Björn grew more and more nervous. *It's just the roommate*, he reminded himself, trying to calm himself. He really hoped this guy would be able to identify her. By the time the others at the station had managed to find her parents, Björn wanted to have a solid ID on this dead girl—because he had no interest in standing around in the morgue beside a hysterical, shrieking mother. It was bad enough that he was going to have to see the corpse yet again today.

The apartment was in a well-kept duplex with a small yard at the end of a quiet back road—probably an expensive neighborhood. Not exactly what he pictured when he thought of junkies. The building was large, with a white facade and old-fashioned shutters over the windows. Björn noticed there were padlocks all around the windows on the bottom floor. Someone was obviously paranoid about burglars.

He straightened his uniform and pressed the buzzer. The door opened almost instantly. When Björn stepped inside, the first-floor apartment door was already open, and a guy who looked to be a few years younger than Björn was standing in the doorway. He was tall and muscular, and he looked like he'd just gotten back from the gym. His eyes flew over Björn's uniform, and something like panic crossed his face. Maybe this girl was more than just his roommate? His girlfriend? The guy looked to be about the right age.

"Mr. Danijel Taylor?" Björn asked.

"Yes. What happened?"

"Officer Björn Wildermuth," he said, extending his hand. "May I come in?"

Taylor stepped out of the way, and Björn followed him into the apartment.

"What happened?" Taylor asked again.

"We received a call about the body of a young woman found in an apartment on the east side of Stuttgart. She looks like she might fit the description of the person you're looking for."

Taylor cursed softly in English.

"Let me stress that we are in no way certain of the identity of the deceased," Björn hastened to add. "She had no ID on her, so she may be someone else entirely."

Danijel Taylor ran both hands through his hair, seemingly struggling to maintain composure. "Did she overdose?"

"We're still waiting on the autopsy results, but it looks like it was a toxic reaction to heroin."

Taylor cursed in German this time and began pacing up and down the hallway. "Was she raped?"

How does this kid know that?

240

"There's no final report yet," Björn said. "But the possibility hasn't been ruled out."

"I can't believe this!"

He's going to freak out on me here in a minute ...

Björn attempted to comfort him. "It may not be her. Would you come with me to identify the body?"

"Yes," he said, chest heaving. "Just…let me change clothes real quick." He turned away, but then stopped and turned back almost immediately. "Whatever, I'll go like this." Then he turned yet again and walked off in the direction he'd come from. "Gotta call my girlfriend," he mumbled.

His girlfriend? So the dead girl really was just a roommate. Björn breathed a sigh of relief.

After making a quick call in the other room, Taylor took his keys from the hook beside the door. "Let's get this over with."

"Don't you want me to take you?"

"I'll drive myself," he said.

Even better, Björn thought. That would save him a trip back. And some awkward conversation. Now he'd have time to grab breakfast before he had to be back at the station.

The two men descended the short flight of stairs to the cold basement. A silver metal table waited in the center of the room, covered by a white sheet. The outline of a person was clearly visible underneath.

Björn stepped up to the table, while Taylor remained two steps behind him. To Björn, the other man seemed very composed, maybe even impatient. "Are you ready?" Björn asked him.

"Just take the goddamn cover off already!"

Björn pulled the sheet back and watched Danijel Taylor closely. He showed no reaction, no emotion whatsoever.

Goddammit, it's not her! Björn waited a moment before covering the body again. Then he noticed that Taylor's lip was bleeding. He kept running his tongue over it to lick the blood off.

"That's her," was all he said.

"Are you sure?"

"No doubt."

Björn began to worry. The other man suddenly seemed completely apathetic, disconnected from the world around him. Paralyzed, almost. "Are you all right, Mr. Taylor?" He reached out to give Taylor a friendly pat on the arm, but the other man pulled away almost furiously and strode toward the exit. Björn walked after him, two paces behind. "Can I bring you anything? Or drive you home?"

"My girlfriend's coming," Taylor replied.

"Do you need any help?"

Danijel Taylor shook his head and walked out of the morgue without another word.

Chapter Thirty-Three

March 2002

Apparently, I'd miscalculated somehow. I'd never manage to fit three more parking spaces into this layout. "Bea?" I called, and she poked her head up from behind her desk. "Bea, I'm not getting anywhere with this. Can you help me?"

She stood up and walked over to look at the large blueprint spread out on the desk in front of me.

"I need to get another parking spot in here somehow," I said, tapping the area giving me trouble.

"Hm." Bea measured the length with a drafting triangle. "There's enough space, but the angle wouldn't work."

My phone vibrated inside my purse. Very unusual for this time of day—it was only mid-morning. "Sorry, I need to take this." I looked at the display. Danny! My heart began to race. He hardly ever called me while I was at work, and certainly not in the morning. "Danny?"

The silence on the other end was far too long. "The police are here," he said without a word of greeting. "They may have found Tina."

"Is she okay?" I asked anxiously.

"This cop and I are driving down to the morgue to see if it's her."

Good God! "Where is it?" I practically bellowed into the telephone.

He gave me the address.

"Wait there!" I screeched. "I'll leave right now. Don't move!" *Oh, God, please let it not be her!*

"Jessica? Are you okay?" Bea gave me a concerned look. "You're white as a sheet!"

"They may have found Christina's body."

Dear God in Heaven, if you're up there somewhere, please let it not be her! Danny will never get through this!

"The girl who lives with your boyfriend?"

"Yeah." Suddenly jolted into action, I leaped up and grabbed my purse. "Bea, I gotta go. I'll be in touch later. Tell the boss."

She nodded. "I'll cross my fingers for you."

Me too. I'll cross my fingers for me. For Christina. For Danny! Please, God, let this be some other girl. Danny's gone through enough, please, please, not this too! Please let this be some other girl!

The whole way over, I sent one frantic prayer after another up to heaven, offering God all kinds of things if this girl could please just not be our Christina.

At some point, it occurred to me that, somewhere in the world, a mother might be sitting there begging God just as fervently for this girl not to be her daughter. I stopped praying.

I don't remember how I got to the morgue. I didn't have any idea where it was, and I didn't have a GPS or a map. I think I asked around. Regardless, when I got there, there wasn't a single available parking space anywhere, so I left my car in the fire lane. Danny's car was parked a little farther on.

Darting out of my car, I ran toward his. Then I saw him. He was running around and around his car. Again, and again, and again.

No. No. No!

I broke into a run and called his name. Oh, God, it *was* her.

Christina's dead! Why, God, why? Danny won't survive this! Why, God, why?

My heart was hammering in my throat and my stomach was one big clump of ice. "Danny?"

He didn't react.

"Oh, God, Danny! I'm so sorry!"

Without looking at me, he ran straight around to the driver's side door.

"You can't drive like this!" I cried.

His face was snow-white, and he'd bitten his whole lip bloody. Still staring blankly out into nothing, he ducked away and ran past me again. Suddenly, I was terrified he would just keep on running and never stop. I hastened after him, grabbed his arm, and pulled him back to his car.

"Get in. I'll drive." My voice cracked, and I realized I was in no condition to drive, either. Tears rolled down my cheeks as I led him by the hand to his car, pried his keys from his clenched fist, and opened the door for him.

Though I was blinded by tears and sobbing the entire way, I somehow managed to follow the GPS's instructions back to Danny's. My joints were like jelly, my insides were in knots, and I could barely swallow. Danny didn't say a word. His eyes were still focused out into the distance, and he kept right on chewing his bleeding lip.

Shock! my inner voice shrieked. *He's in shock! Get him to a doctor!*

But my hands were shaking so badly that I couldn't get the key out of the ignition. Danny had already gotten out and gone into the apartment.

I found him sitting cross-legged on the couch. His workout clothes were clinging to his body, and his socks were dirty.

"Danny!" I shouted. "Say something!"

He didn't say anything, didn't even move.

"This is hard for me too!" I stood there screaming at him, letting my tears flow freely. "It hurts me too! She was my Tina, too! My Tina! CAN YOU UNDERSTAND THAT?"

At some point, I started running around in a circle, the way he'd been doing before. I needed to do something. But what?

Call someone. You guys need help.

Where was my phone? I ran around the apartment like a madwoman looking for it, before finally finding it in my purse. I dialed Ricky's number.

"Ricky!" I shouted into the phone.

"Jessica! What's wrong?"

"Christina's dead. Danny's in shock. You have to come over here."

"Shit. What the hell happened?"

"She's dead!" I sniffled and wiped at my running nose.

"I'm in Berlin," he said nervously. "Can you put Danny on the phone?"

"No!" I snapped. Was the whole world against me or something? "He isn't speaking, because Tina's *dead*." I hung up and scrolled through my contacts to find Simon's number. His phone was off. Then I called Bea—I really needed to talk to somebody. "Bea, it was her. Christina's dead."

"I'm so sorry to hear that, Jessica," she said calmly. Probably because she was still at work. "Let me know if there's anything I can do for you two."

"I need the rest of the week off. Have them take it out of my vacation time."

"I'll let them know," she said. "Was it an accident?"

"I've gotta go. I'll be in touch."

My car. I needed to pick it up, or else it would be towed. Why hadn't we driven home in my car and left his in the parking lot?

Oh, that's right, because Christina is dead.

Everything was in chaos.

I knew Danny would never manage to get there and back, so I called my brother and asked if he could bring me to my car. Of course, he wanted to know why I'd left it somewhere in the first place. "I'll explain later," I snapped at him. Why was everyone so slow on the uptake? Thorsten would be off work early today, and he promised to come in two hours.

Two hours? What was I going to do with myself for that long?

What was I going to do with myself ever again?

Christina was dead. She would always be dead.

Then it hit me. Jörg. Call Jörg. Have him come out and look after Danny. He was Danny's case worker, he would know what to do.

I didn't have his number, so I ran into Danny's office and rummaged through everything in the room. No dice.

Back in the living room, Danny didn't look like he'd moved an inch.

"Where's your phone?" I barked at him.

He shrugged indifferently.

"You're a lot of help," I muttered.

After a while of frantic searching, I found his phone on the kitchen table. I went through his contacts and painstakingly added Jörg's number to my phone. I don't know why I didn't just use Danny's. Most likely because Christina was dead.

Jörg picked up on the third ring. "Pfisterer."

"Jörg? This is Jessica!"

"Jessica who?"

Jesus Christ, was everyone trying to piss me off? "Danny's Jessica. Christina is dead!"

Silence.

"Where are you two?"

"At Danny's. He's… I need your help!" I practically begged.

"I'm coming," he said. "I'm out and about right now. It might be an hour, maybe more. I'll be there as fast as I can."

What the hell was everyone doing for so long? This was unbelievable. I ran back to the living room. "Danny!" I yelled. "Stop this shit right now!"

Why are you screaming at him, too?

"Talk to me," I growled, taking a pillow and throwing it at his head. He didn't try to catch it or block it. I launched a second pillow at him.

It wasn't until long after that I realized I was in complete shock myself. At the time, all I could feel was anger. Furious and desperate, I knelt down on the floor in front of Danny and shook him by the shoulders. He didn't defend himself. I grabbed his face and forced him to look at me. His lip was completely shredded, and the eyes he'd once hypnotized me with now stared straight through me. There was no spark of life left in them, only fathomless emptiness.

"Danny," I pleaded, tears streaming down my cheeks. Without a word, he pulled me into his arms, laid his chin on my head, and stroked my back as I cried and cried and cried. Danny showed no emotion at all—he was a robot.

My phone beeped, pulling me away from Danny. It was Thorsten. He was going to be here soon.

Had it already been two goddamn hours? Where the hell was Jörg?

Slowly, I stood up. My stiff knees cracked when I stretched them. "I'm just going to go get my car real quick," I told Danny quietly.

No response.

"Jörg's coming over. He should be here any minute. You won't be alone for more than ten minutes. Will you be okay for that long?"

Danny nodded.

I gave him a kiss on his bloody lip. Even that, he went along with. And in that exact moment, it became clear to me that Danny would never be the same again. Something in him had broken and could never be fixed. The revelation made me burst into tears all over again. I stroked his blond hair. "I'll be back in two hours. Stay right here, whatever you do!"

It felt like I was leaving a ticking time bomb.

As I walked out, I started to dial Jörg's number, but I saw his car pulling around the corner. A sigh of relief rushed out of me.

My brother was already outside waiting. "What's wrong, sis? You look upset." He even sounded a little worried, at least by his standards.

"Can you please just shut up and take me to my car?"

He drove in offended silence all the way there. "Why did you leave your car at a morgue?" he asked, pulling up beside it.

"So you could ask stupid questions about it," I growled before yanking the door open and walking off without thanking him for the lift.

On the way back to Danny's, I called my mother to let her know I wouldn't be home for the rest of the week.

"Where are you?" she asked anxiously.

"Danny's. Something happened. I took the week off from work. I won't be home until Sunday."

"What's going on?"

"Nothing. I won't be picking the dog up. See you Sunday."

Before I could hang up, she asked, "It sounds like you've been crying. Did you two get in a fight?"

"No!" I shouted. Every nerve in my body was vibrating. "How could we fight when he's not speaking to me at all?"

My mother took that the wrong way, of course—how could she have known any better? "Maybe you ought to come home if he's being like that."

"The girl he loves more than anything in the world died."

My explanation only made things worse, of course.

"What?" she gasped. "But that's you, isn't it? You're his girlfriend."

"The other girl he—" I stopped mid-sentence, realizing I was digging myself into a deeper hole. "Just leave me alone." I hung up and added another name to my mental list of people I owed an apology.

Just like that, I felt completely drained. I wanted to go back to Danny, to get in bed with him, pull the covers over my head, and sleep for all eternity. And dream. Of a better world. One without illness, without rape, without AIDS, without death.

One with a healthy Danny and a living Christina. And unicorns grazing under rainbows beside laughing children with pink cotton candy.

Jörg's car was still in front of the building when I returned, and I thanked God for that as I stormed into the apartment. Jörg met me in the hallway with a finger to his lips. With quiet steps, he led me to the kitchen, where I collapsed in a chair, and he gave me some hot tea and a couple of chocolate chip cookies. As if I would be able to eat something.

"Danny's in shock," he said, peering closely at me. "And so are you."

"Did he talk to you?" I took a sip of the tea. Peppermint. Somehow, it reignited the few remaining sparks of life within me.

"Yeah, he did."

I blinked in amazement. "How did you manage that?"

"Years of experience. I'm a social worker. It's part of my job."

Listlessly, I nibbled on a cookie. Calling Jörg had been a better idea than I knew. "Where's Danny now?"

"In bed. I brought him some medication to help him sleep."

"You gave him sleeping pills?" *No fair! I want some too!*

"It's the best thing for him right now. He was completely out of it. I don't know if he'll be able to cope with this. It's too much for him. He's blocking it out right now, but he's going to have to work through it, or he'll never make peace with it. He needs to grieve."

"How do we make sure that happens?" Considering how he was today, I couldn't imagine him ever allowing himself to grieve.

"It'll come," Jörg said. "He'll go through a whole spectrum of emotions, which is a good thing. It's important for him not to get stuck at anger. The only thing that will help him is grieving. He needs to find that emotion, and he needs to stay in it for as long as he needs."

I nodded again.

"I'll pick him up tomorrow afternoon," Jörg went on. "We have a psychologist at the children's home—I'll take Danny there."

"He's agreed to go with you?" I was astonished. I never would have thought that was possible—but then again, I'd also learned by then that I would never know Danny well enough for him to stop surprising me.

"You should come, too," Jörg said with such conviction that I didn't bother contradicting him.

"What happened to her?" I asked. "Do you know?"

Jörg told me what Danny had told him. That it was possible Christina had been raped. That nobody knew why the drugs she'd taken afterward were bad. I think that was the worst part: that she hadn't just died peacefully. Those mental images would haunt Danny for the rest of his life. And me, too. As if we didn't already have enough horrible images in our heads.

Jörg fixed some noodle soup, and somehow I managed to get it down, one spoonful at a time. As unbelievable as it seemed, life really did go on. At least for the people left behind.

It was late in the evening when Jörg finally stood up to leave. "I'll leave my phone on all night," he promised. "If you need anything, call me. No matter what time."

"Thanks."

Jörg gave me a goodbye hug. What would I have done without him? I asked myself that question a lot later on, when it became clear that Danny and I were completely alone in the world. His father was in jail, his mother was useless, and his aunt was across the ocean. And my parents lived in a different world. They never would have understood any of this. They'd have dragged me back home to protect me from Danny.

We were alone, and we always would be.

I didn't bother changing for bed. I just laid down beside Danny in my jeans and sweater. Danny, who was curled up under the covers, asleep, had done the same. He'd taken off his dirty socks and thrown them in the corner, but he was still wearing his workout clothes. Silently, I stretched out beside him. He smelled like sweat. In all the time I'd been with him, he'd never once smelled like cold sweat, and he'd certainly never gone to bed without showering.

I gently pulled him closer. He woke up. Of course he woke up. It wouldn't have mattered if Jörg had given him ten pounds of sleeping pills—when someone got into bed with him, he woke up. He was traumatized in every corner of his soul, and Christina's death wasn't going to improve that.

He reached for my hand, laid it against his chest, and held it there for a while. Then he stood up slowly, walked to the window, and fixed his gaze on some imaginary point far off in the darkness.

"Talk to me, Danny." How often had I said those words to him today already, and how often would I have to repeat them in the future?

He turned to look at me, as if he'd just now noticed I was there. "Don't you need to get home?" he asked, confused.

Well, at least he'd said something.

"I took some time off work. I'm going to spend the rest of the week here with you."

He acknowledged that triviality with a nod and resumed staring out the window. "She was raped," he suddenly blurted out.

"They don't know that for sure," I replied weakly.

"All her life, that was the exact thing she was most afraid of. Why the hell did it have to happen to her, of all people? Again! What the fuck is wrong with this fucking world?"

"You know better than anyone that life isn't fair."

"I hate men! All of them! Only men are capable of shit like that!" His voice trembled with anger and contempt. "They ought to be taken outside and shot, all of them!"

"Not all men are like that. You're a man, too."

"If that's what it takes," he said bitterly, "I'll join them in front of the firing squad. I'll happily lead the way, waving a flag."

"You're angry," I remarked. "That's good. Don't suppress it. You have to let the anger out."

As if on cue, something exploded inside of him. He slammed his foot into the wardrobe door, and the wood splintered on impact. Then he pulled it back and demolished the other side with his other foot. Having seen him do this before, I knew he wouldn't stop until he'd turn the doors to kindling.

Well, if it helps...

Danny moved around to the side of the wardrobe and hit it again with a series of kickboxing-style side kicks. He didn't bother to set his leg down between kicks for extra momentum, but the blows were enough to send the wood flying in every direction anyway.

His bare feet were beginning to bleed, but I knew he was used to pain and was able to block it out. If he noticed it at all, it didn't seem to bother him. Maybe it even helped distract him from the emotional pain a little.

Once the wardrobe was in shambles, he left the room. I followed him into the living room, where he smashed the glass door on the entertainment center with his already-injured foot. Shards of glass clattered all over the floor.

"Danny, that's enough." Was he planning on destroying all the furniture in the apartment?

"You said anger was good!" He kept right on kicking the splintered door. I had to look away—the sight made my whole body cramp up. Blood was running down his foot. Never before and never since have I met anyone who bled as often as Danny, the very person whose blood was poison.

"It is, but that's enough now!"

"I'm just getting warmed up!"

Good Lord! How could one person have so much fury inside him?

As Danny strode barefoot through the shards, I closed my eyes, not wanting to see the glass slicing into his skin. He headed for the dining room table and shifted his weight to prepare for another kick. I dashed over and blocked his way. "That's enough!" I shrieked. "It's enough! She's dead. What you're doing here isn't going to bring her back!"

Danny wound up and slammed his fist into the wall just over my head. There was an audible crack, the sound of snapping bones, but he still fired off a second blow with the same hand—and then screamed in pain.

"Stop it! Now!" I cried, seizing his shoulders and pushing him against the opposite wall. "You're injuring yourself!" I pressed his back up against the wall with all my strength. Of course, he could easily have defended himself, or simply grabbed me and thrown me across the room, but I never worried about that for even a second. I knew he'd never lay a hand on me, no matter how out of his mind he was.

I pressed my forearm against his throat as hard as I could. I wasn't actually trying to choke him—I just wanted to get him to panic. Danny panicking meant Danny withdrawing into himself and freezing up, rather than Danny exploding in uncontrollable rage. I wanted to take advantage of that, to use his panic to help me get him under control. Even so, as I deliberately forced him into the corner, I felt guilty about it.

Danny slid down the wall so that he could duck out from underneath my arm and escape, but I pushed a knee down onto his stomach and pressed him to the wall with both arms, one forearm still against his throat. He began breathing faster as the panic welled up within him. For a moment, he shut his eyes and gasped for air.

"Why are you doing this to me?" he asked quietly, but I remained silent, focusing on keeping him in the corner.

His rage evaporated almost immediately. The tension dissipated from his body, and he collapsed into a ball, concentrating on taking deep breaths. I sighed in relief and let go.

He sat there, motionless, until I stepped away. Despite his injured hand, he managed to crawl on all fours to the couch, where he climbed to his feet and headed for the door.

Hurriedly, I squeezed past him and moved into the doorway. "Where are you going?"

"Please let me go!" He sounded desperate.

"Where?" I looked him over. His left foot was streaked with blood, his wrist was probably broken, and he was completely out of his mind.

"To where Tina got her heroin."

"What for?" To look for the guy who'd given her the bad batch? That could have been anyone—there was no way he'd figure it out. Didn't he know that?

Call Jörg!

I knew it was the best option. But I couldn't get to my phone without moving from the door.

"Because I want some, too," he said lamely. "It helps you forget."

Panic enveloped me. "No!" I crossed my arms. "Cut that crap out!"

"I'm not asking your permission!" he growled.

"You're not getting past me!" I planted my feet in the very center of the doorway.

He laughed softly. "You can't be serious. You want me to show you how I'll get past you?"

"You can't drive like *this*!" I waved a hand in his direction, not really sure if I was referring to his hand or his foot.

He scoffed. "I can, and I will!"

I stretched my arms out, propping my hands on either side of the door frame to block his path. "No way are you going out there to buy drugs." I tried not to sound nervous. "If you want to do that, you're going to have to punch me out of the way."

He scoffed again, turning away and stalking through what was left of the living room. Then he dropped onto the couch, pulled his knees up to his chest, and buried his face in his arms.

Once I was sure he was going to stay in that position, I went to the bathroom and fetched two wet washcloths. When he realized what I was planning on doing with them, he took one out of my hand and washed the blood off his foot. I wrapped the other one around his wrist, which had already turned a worrying shade of blue.

"It hurts so much!" Danny suddenly cried.

I knew he didn't mean his hand. He was talking about the pain in his heart, which I couldn't mend, no matter how it threatened to tear him apart. Filled with despair, he clutched his knees and rocked back and forth like a small child, crying over and over again, "It hurts so much! I can't breathe! It hurts. I can't breathe without her! I can't live without her!"

Now he'd gotten to the right emotion. He was past the anger, and now the grief was coming out. Long-term, that was the only thing that would help him, like Jörg had said. Anger couldn't heal wounds—only grief could. I needed to let him stay with that emotion, as painful as it was.

"Yeah, it hurts, Danny. But it will get better. Someday, the pain won't be so bad."

"When?" he asked. "When? I can't breathe like this."

"It'll get better, but it may take a while."

Danny looked at me. Tears were welling up in his eyes, which were darker than usual, and red from crying. "It's like part of me is missing," he whispered. "Like someone ripped a part of my heart out of my chest."

Tears began to stream down my face, as well. I didn't know whether I was crying because of his pain or because of my own. Probably both.

I pulled him into my arms, and he sobbed against my shoulder. We spent the rest of the night like that: sitting on the sofa, clinging to each other and crying for the loss of a person who had been an inseparable part of us both.

Chapter Thirty-Four

March 2002

When I woke up, Danny was still lying across me, fast asleep. I knew I'd never get him off of me without waking him up, so I just lay there quietly and waited. His breathing was even and quiet, his cheeks still flushed from crying, his hair stringy with sweat. But if someone had photographed him now, even as sweaty and tear-streaked as he was, he'd still have looked gorgeous.

Carefully, I brushed a few strands of hair from his forehead, and after a while, he opened his eyes. With uncharacteristic lethargy, he used me to pull himself up and looked at me. "Ducky," he said, giving me a kiss on the lips. It tasted like salt. "You looked after me. Thank you."

I raised a skeptical eyebrow and glanced around the trashed room. "I failed completely," I replied. "I'll make us some coffee, and then I'm taking you to the hospital."

"Hospital?"

"I think you broke your wrist."

"Oh!" Danny raised his swollen hand to eye level and peered at it in surprise, trying in vain to move it. "So I did. How did that happen?"

The coffee got us at least halfway going. We headed out, leaving the debris the way it was. Neither of us had bothered to shower or change. I don't think I even combed my hair.

We waited at the hospital for nearly three hours. Danny, with his head on my shoulder and my hand in his uninjured one, did nothing but breathe and wait for a nurse to come get us. At last, they X-rayed his injured wrist and put a cast on it, assuring us it was a simple fracture that would heal quickly.

We were silent on the drive home, as well. Danny was still holding my right hand and refused to let go, so I had to shift gears with my left, which was terribly complicated.

"What should we do with her room?" he asked as we neared his place. "I don't want it to remain completely untouched the way mine is at my parents' house, but I don't want to keep it artificially alive like Liam's. Does that sound dumb?"

"No, not at all. Let's sleep on it for a couple days, and we'll think of something. Something that isn't either of those options."

"Move out with me, Jessica. I don't want to stay in that apartment without her." His voice cracked. "Move out with me. I don't care where. You pick. Apartment or house, rent or buy, doesn't matter at all. If you like it, I like it."

"I'd love to move in with you somewhere." I wanted that so badly. Danny knew I dreamed of having a little house in the countryside. A nice green backyard, two dogs, children…

Which you two can never have together!

Shut up, I snapped at the voice inside my head. *Nobody asked your opinion.*

Why couldn't I silence that obnoxious voice inside me once and for all?

Do you really want to buy a house with him and then live in it alone as a widow?

Great. Now I was starting to argue with myself.

Yes, goddammit. I do. Maybe things will turn out completely different! With love, everything is possible. Never say never!

"Then that's what we'll do," he said. "Apartment or house? Rent or buy?"

"House. Buy," I said. "I want it to be forever."

"Okay."

It was so macabre. Christina was dead, and we were making plans for the future. But we needed that to convince ourselves that life hadn't ended for us as well. Tears rolled down my cheeks again, and Danny squeezed my hand tighter. "Let's wait until the summer," I suggested. "As soon as my contract ends, we can fly out to America, visit your home. For as long as you want. When we come back, we'll buy a house. I'll be earning good money then, so I can contribute."

"You don't need to contribute."

"But I want to," I insisted.

"We'll talk about that as soon as I'm in any condition to form reasonable arguments. Everything else sounds good to me." He let go of my hand and placed his hand on my thigh. The cast covering half his arm left only his fingers free. "Do you really think it'll stop hurting someday?" Danny looked deeply into my eyes— a sad imitation of that hypnotic gaze he'd once had.

"I'm sure of it. Time heals all wounds."

"But every wound leaves a scar."

It was certainly conceivable that Danny's wounds would never heal. How could they? At age ten, he'd been wrenched out of the life he knew, only to be raped and abused. He'd had to watch his own dog get killed. His own father had beaten him and manipulated him for years, and finally he'd landed in an orphanage at fifteen. Now his father was in prison, his beloved aunt lived in America, and his mother was crazy, not to mention completely uninterested in him. When he was almost seventeen, completely alone in the world, he'd been told over the phone that he had a fatal illness. His parents had even tried to blame him for his mother's miscarriage.

Thousands of miles from his home, traumatized and frightened, he'd lost his best friend, his anchor. He'd never be able to cope with that. It wasn't so much that Danny needed Christina—it was that she needed him. That fact had driven him, motivated him to deal with the injustices of the world somehow. If he couldn't save his own life, he hoped he could at least save the life of someone he identified with. Someone he loved.

And, in his eyes, he'd failed.

He needed to find a new purpose in life somehow, so that he wouldn't completely spiral out of control. And that was why we were making plans for the future.

I hoped and prayed he would be able to make peace with having lost Christina one day...and I wondered how much pain one person could withstand before it completely destroyed him.

Danny's pain would have been more than enough to destroy ten people living ten different lives.

Jörg was already waiting in Danny's apartment when we returned. He was horrified at the state of the living room. "Why didn't you call?"

I shrugged. "It all happened too fast."

After shooing Danny into the shower, Jörg began cleaning up the broken glass and furniture. I joined Danny in the bathroom so that I could change clothes and get ready for the appointment with the psychologist at the children's home.

"Great. We're already going to a shrink together," he grumbled as we got dressed. I was silent—I couldn't think of anything to say.

The doorbell rang. It was the police. Why couldn't they leave us in peace?

"I'll give you five minutes," Jörg sternly told the two officers in the hall. "Then that's enough for today. We have an appointment with a psychologist to get to." He guided the men into the dining room, and we all sat down amid the rubble.

With Jörg still cleaning up around them, the officers spent nearly half an hour asking the same questions over and over: Who did Christina hang out with? Was there anyone who didn't like her? Could we describe her dealer?

Danny answered all of their questions obligingly.

But I couldn't help wondering… How much more of this would he be able to take? They were sticking a knife in his open wounds and twisting it.

Worst of all, their suspicions had been confirmed: Christina had been raped. The police were investigating, looking for the man who'd given her the contaminated heroin. They had ruled out willful intent—junkies were often killed by toxic reactions, they said, and they also didn't know whether the man had used any of it himself. It was possible he had but his body had been able to handle it.

Eventually, Jörg asked the cops to leave. They promised to be in touch as soon as they knew more.

The next day, Jörg brought us back to the psychologist at the children's home. We went in one after the other to get everything off our chests.

That evening, we started piling the destroyed furniture in front of the front gate so that we could have it hauled away. Danny and I hardly spoke a word. Before, no matter what he was doing, he'd have had some witty remark at the ready, but now he was silent almost all the time.

He ordered new furniture from a catalog and had the delivery guys put it together. He didn't feel like doing it himself. Actually, he didn't feel like doing anything at all. The perennially optimistic and cheerful Danny, the guy who was always raring to go and full of crazy ideas, now sat in the living room in front of the television while other people put together his furniture. It didn't make sense.

This change was almost more than I could take. I wanted my boyfriend back. I felt like shaking him until he snapped out of it. But I couldn't even manage to get him out of the apartment. He just sat on the couch and waited. I knew he was waiting for the police to find out who had raped Christina and given her those drugs. I wanted the perpetrator to be caught, too, but I prayed to God that the police locked him up right away so that Danny couldn't get his hands on the guy. Secretly, of course, I'd have loved to see the guy torn to shreds, but I was terrified that Danny might end up in prison. Like his father.

The funeral was scheduled for a Wednesday at the beginning of April. It was a longer delay than usual, because the autopsy report needed to be finished first.

"I'm not going," Danny told me when we heard the date.

"What are you talking about? Of course you're going."

"Nope. Tina and I had an agreement. I didn't want her coming to my funeral under any circumstances, and she promised not to. She would have wanted the same. It wouldn't be right of me to go."

He was silent for a long time, lost in thought, as he so often was these days. "I don't like funerals," he went on. "They don't help anyone. Standing around at a cross to cry is stupid. I don't want you to go to mine, either." He gazed at me, trying to hypnotize me as he'd once done, but quickly gave up.

"Then I'll go alone," I told him.

He nodded. "You do that. If her old man is there, call me, and I swear to God I'll come out there and kill him."

I left the room so he wouldn't see me crying. What had happened to Danny? Would he stay this bitter and hateful forever?

We spent almost every evening in front of the TV, watching movies we could barely follow. Danny hadn't run or been to the gym in days, and he hadn't been to work, either. We sat there stuffing ourselves with fast food, holding hands in silence, looking out the window, and waiting until we fell asleep sometime in the middle of the night. If we got up at all, it wasn't until noon. Sometimes, we spent the entire day in bed. We didn't even bother getting dressed.

I dreaded Sunday evening, because I knew I'd have to go home. There'd be trouble at home, but that wasn't the reason. I was worried Danny would let himself go completely if I left him alone. Jörg was still coming by every day to bring us to the psychologist, but what would Danny do the whole rest of the day?

Chapter Thirty-Five

March 2002

I woke up sometime in the middle of the night and discovered that Danny wasn't beside me on the couch. I went to look for him in the bedroom, but he wasn't in bed, either. The computer was off. Danny's BMW was still parked in the same place I'd left it at the beginning of the week. He had to be in Christina's room.

I found him in her bed. He was lying on his side, covers pulled up to his chin, crying silently. When he saw me come into the room, he raised the blanket, inviting me to join him. We snuggled close in her room, in the bed that still smelled like her, and imagined that she might walk through the door any minute and smile at us.

"Why is life so goddamn unfair, Jessica?"

I'd been asking myself that more and more lately, but hearing it from him was frightening. If he started railing against Christina's fate, he'd eventually start refusing to accept his own, and then he'd be completely lost. I couldn't let him start asking himself why everything had turned out this way.

"You shouldn't think about things like that, Danny. We'll never get answers to questions like those."

He sat up in bed and began to cry again. "Why did she have to die?" he asked me over and over again. "She had her whole life ahead of her. Why her? Why not me? Why didn't I die? With me, it wouldn't have mattered. Why couldn't I have died in her place?"

I got out of bed and left the room, fleeing to the backyard to escape his words. It would have been just as wrong for Danny to die. Fate was a dirty, cold-hearted liar who played favorites at random, without caring in the slightest what was fair or what made sense.

Dawn was beginning to break when I returned to Christina's room. Danny was still awake, wiping his tears with his sleeve. "Why not me?" There it was again, that question I had neither the ability nor the desire to answer. "It wouldn't have mattered with me. I would have died for her so happily!"

***

Returning home very late in the evening, I tried to sneak off to my room without being noticed.

"Jessica!" my father thundered.

My parents were both in the living room. They were only still awake because they'd been waiting up for me. "Where were you?"

"At Danny's. I told you."

"You haven't been at work all week, and your certification exams are in September!"

Certification exams. Stupid words on lifeless paper. Were there actually people in the world who cared about stuff like that? "I took the week off," I said defensively. "I told you—something happened."

"We're not sure we believe it," my mother said, trying to be the mediator. "Who did you say died?"

"Christina! Danny's roommate and best friend!"

"What does that have to do with you?"

Was she serious? She actually didn't seem to believe me. But then, why would she? I'd never told her about Christina. Maybe I should have. "She was my friend, too!" I shrieked.

"What happened?" my mother asked. "Car accident?"

"Drugs," I replied curtly. "She died from bad heroin."

"Heroin?" My mother paled. "Jessica, what are you doing around heroin?"

"Nothing. But Danny's roommate used to be an addict."

"Oh my God!" My mother clapped her hand to her mouth in horror, fingers trembling. "He made such a good impression on us. Why would he be living with drug addicts? You said he had his own apartment."

Heat began spreading through my body. "You guys are completely misunderstanding this! It's his apartment, and he doesn't do drugs. At *all*. He just helped Christina because—"

"Well, you're not hanging around that *Danny* in the future," my father interrupted, pronouncing Danny's name as though it were an insult. "Apparently, he's not good for you anymore!"

"Not good for me?" I echoed in disbelief.

My mother gave me a sympathetic look. "He doesn't seem to be the right sort of company for you, Jessica. You should get back in contact with your old friends. You were so happy last summer, with Alexander and Vanessa?"

"I *am* happy!" I shouted. Traitorous tears rolled down my cheeks as if to belie my words. "I'm flying to America with Danny this year, and I might stay there for months!"

My mother shook her head in despair, and my father shouted back, "Fine! But until then, you're sleeping *here*. This is never happening again. You're staying at home and going to work and that's it! End of discussion!"

I squared my shoulders resolutely. "I'm an adult. I can do what I want."

"Be reasonable," my mother pleaded. "We've always given you so much freedom. You're being completely unfair right now."

"The funeral is on Wednesday," I said coldly, "and after that, I'm going to Danny's, and I'm staying there until he's halfway stable again. It could be a week, it could be a year. He really loved his best friend, you know." I spun around, leaving my horrified parents standing there.

Then I poked my head back into the living room and added, "I don't care whether it's fair. Life is never fair. You guys should probably get used to that."

Chapter Thirty-Six

April 2002

I took half a day off work and went directly from the office to Christina's funeral by train. Danny stayed home.

The funeral was a small, simple affair with an anonymous grave. Danny's expectations that Christina's father would show up hadn't come true. Her mother was there, along with Ricky, Simon, Giuseppe, Natasha, and me. That was the entire list of mourners.

Christina's mother, a small, delicate woman with sunglasses much too large for her face, appeared unmoved throughout the ceremony. Just before we left the cemetery, I went up to introduce myself.

"I'm Jessica," I said, extending my hand. Ricky remained close behind me. I think he probably knew what would happen.

"Mm-hm," she said absently. I wanted to ask her where she'd been all these years. Why hadn't she come to visit? Why hadn't she congratulated her daughter when she'd gotten her job?

"I'm so sorry about what happened to your daughter. She was my best friend."

She brushed my hand away, eyeing me as though I were some kind of hideous insect. "She wasn't my daughter," she said in an icy tone. "She was a cheap junkie whore." With that, she turned and flounced off toward the cemetery gate.

"You should be ashamed of yourself, you evil bitch!" Ricky called after her, and for a moment, I thought he was going to run after her and smack her across the head. He stayed with me, though, taking my arm and pulling me away with him. "Don't let that get you upset," he said. "There's no use."

My knees were trembling, and suddenly I was incredibly glad Danny wasn't there. It was bad enough that *I'd* had to hear that crap.

Ricky brought me to my car, like the second older brother he'd come to feel like to me, and promised to come by the following day with Simon. They'd done it several times already over the past week, trying in vain to shake Danny out of his lethargic stupor.

On the way home, I passed a stationery store, and on a whim, I stopped in to buy a couple of fat markers, along with a whole bunch of candles.

When I got to Danny's, he was sitting on the couch, staring at the flickering television screen. The whole scene was just so wrong. I couldn't get used to it, nor did I want to.

"How was it?" he asked without getting up, which wasn't like him either. He'd always met me at the door before, back when he'd been himself.

"Okay," I said. "Her dad didn't come."

He nodded and turned back to the TV. Sighing, I took the remote out of his hand and switched the television off. Then I grasped his uninjured hand and pulled him to his feet. "You said you didn't want Christina's room to stay how it was, and you didn't want it to look artificial." I pulled him into her room and handed him one of the markers. "So we're going to redecorate. She loved poetry so much—let's write something for her."

He agreed. He was still the old Danny in that regard: up for anything, with no discussion. The realization made me almost euphoric. Maybe he really would find his way back to his old self someday.

We spread the candles out around the room—on the table, the windowsill, the shelves, everywhere—and lit them. Once that was done, we sat down on the floor and started writing. Then we used the markers to immortalize our work on the white walls.

Danny took the space above her bed:

I am not dead,

I'm just changing sides

To be with you all

Wherever you go

I used the blue marker to write a few lines over the old couch in the corner:

The cold earth will not hold me,

I am no longer trapped

In darkness I found the light

And now I am free

Over the window, Danny wrote:

One last time you went

Far away over the clouds.

Now you shine down, heaven-sent,

And live on in my heart.

And together we wrote:

And with her died a thousand dreams.

Time heals wounds, but scars remain!

We did that all afternoon. Afterward, we snuggled into her bed together, stomach to stomach, and started telling stories about her. It became a kind of ritual—our way of handling our grief. Every evening, before we went to sleep, we lit all the candles, got into Christina's bed, and took turns telling stories about her. He'd go one night, I'd go the next.

Danny told me how he'd met Christina in that self-help group. She'd been totally distraught when she first started coming, and she'd sought him out from the beginning. At first, she'd just sat beside him; then, she'd started trying to get put into groups with him so that she could work with him. She'd clung to him like ivy, and he began taking her home with him after group meetings. They'd cook dinner together, eat, and talk. Over time, he'd become an ever-greater influence on her, and eventually, he'd managed to get her off the drugs. Then one day she'd come over to his place and simply stayed.

The next evening, I admitted to him that when I'd discovered Christina on his couch that first night, I'd been so jealous that I'd decided to hate her for all eternity—but the hate had quickly turned to love, because she'd been so much like Danny.

In turn, Danny told me that she'd hated me just as much at first, because she'd been sure I'd take him away from her and turn her newly structured life upside down.

I revealed how she'd threatened to kill me if I ever dared injure him, and I recounted the wise words she'd had for me when Danny had confessed he was HIV-positive.

He told me they'd talked that night as well. He'd been completely sure he'd lost me for good, but she'd promised him I'd come back to him within a few hours. And, as it turned out, she'd been right.

We called the game "Christina is…," and for the next eight weeks, we played it every evening I was at Danny's. It made us feel close to her, kept her alive in a way. Often, we spent the whole night in her room, falling asleep in each other's arms. Although I'd never have thought it possible, Christina's death brought us even closer together.

Never in my life had I been so close to another human being—emotionally close, not physically—nor have I been since. We were soulmates, no question. He was a part of me, and I was a part of him. I'd never need photos or other things to remind me of him. Danny lived within me, and I knew he would until my dying day.

We resided together in unconditional love, united through pain and cemented through the trust we'd worked so hard to build between us.

We were one, and we would remain so for all eternity.

Chapter Thirty-Seven

May 2002

Somehow, life went on. I went to work as usual, and Danny got back to his routine of running in the morning and then going to the martial arts center. He had modeling work as well, but he was spending less time doing both jobs than he had before.

His wrist healed quickly, and the cast came off. We kept playing *Christina is...* every night, until one evening, Danny said to me, "We should quit doing this. We need to start focusing on the future." Then, in English, he added something like, "Objects in the rear-view mirror may appear closer than they are." I suppose he meant that this experience would always have a hold on us as long as we kept looking back.

That evening, we lit the candles for the last time, and once they'd burned down, we left the stumps where they were. Then we said goodbye to Tina and left the room hand in hand. We closed the door together, both of us holding the doorknob.

Neither of us ever went back into that room again.

Danny started taking an active interest in his illness like he never had before. I don't know whether he was trying to distract himself from Christina's death, or whether he'd have gone through this phase either way. But I had an inkling that Christina's death was the cause. Before, he'd just been so optimistic—too optimistic for this.

I reminded him of what he'd said to me once upon a time: "We can't give the disease an inch. That's our only option." He said that's why he never acted like he was sick. And I reminded him of how he'd insisted that I go along with it. But now, all of a sudden, he was completely obsessed with AIDS. He read dozens of books, spent hours researching online, and met up with people he'd met on some Internet forum or other.

I started studying for my certification exams, and we, together, planned our trip to America. I knew my company would hire me on full-time as long as I passed my exams, so I'd asked my boss if I could delay my start date until January so that Danny and I could spend more time in America. My boss said he'd let me know no later than mid-August, so we wanted to be ready to buy our flights immediately after that. Danny had both a German and American passport, so at least he wouldn't have any problem staying in America for an extended period of time.

We started checking out houses together and worked out a clear idea of what we were looking for. We wanted to buy something as soon as we got back from America—we'd talked about it at length. Danny had decided he was okay with remaining in Germany, since he was pretty well situated here both personally and professionally. As long as I was willing to travel to America with him regularly, he was satisfied. This year, he wanted us to spend eight weeks at his aunt's house, and then go on a four-week backpacking trip across the country. "So you can see the world a little, Ducky," he said.

We went camping at Lake Constance almost every weekend, staying until late on Sunday evening every time. We couldn't stand being at home. It was just too empty. Whatever Danny wanted to do, I was fine with—I was just elated that he'd finally peeled himself off the couch.

***

At the end of May, Danny came across a website for an AIDS hospice in the Black Forest. He called me over as he was clicking through it. I stepped behind him, resting my arms on his shoulders as I read. He turned down his music, which was much too loud as always, and asked, "What do you think?"

Danny said it as though we were looking at a computer game he was thinking of buying. Instead, it was a private organization that took in people with HIV or AIDS and assisted them until they died. It gave me chills.

"You think you'd be interested in that?" I asked doubtfully. Casually chatting about this was a struggle for me. But he just wasn't the kind of guy to go to a place like that to die.

"No, I don't..." he said slowly. "But I'd like to go check it out. I want to know what it's like to die of AIDS."

Jesus Christ! Why? I don't want to know that! I took a deep breath.

"Are you sure? That's not even relevant to us yet."

"I need to know," Danny insisted. "And you need to know, too!"

"Danny, I'm not sure I really want to know."

"You should. You need to have advance warning, so you have plenty of time to run."

I shook my head, pinching him in the side. "That ship sailed a long time ago. You know that." I tried to make it sound like a joke.

"We'll see," he retorted. "They allow visitors on the last Sunday of every month. Will you go out there with me tomorrow?"

Every cell in my body rebelled against the idea. I didn't want to go, didn't want to see that. I didn't want to spend tomorrow in a hospice, surrounded by people marked for death. Death played far too great a role in our lives already.

"Of course I'll go with you," I said out loud.

After all, I'd already decided: door number two, forever and always. I had to go with him. I made my choice a long time ago.

Chapter Thirty-Eight

May 2002

Danny drove much too fast, as always, and the highways were so empty that we arrived pretty early. Visitors weren't allowed in until after lunch, so we spent a while strolling through the forest surrounding the beautiful half-timbered house.

"I'm scared to go in," I admitted.

"So am I," he said. "Trust me, so am I. I just have to know, though."

Danny had registered us in advance, and the head of the institute welcomed us warmly. "Just go ahead and look around," she told us. "You can go anywhere you like—everything's open today. Make yourselves at home."

No, I was *not* going to do that.

My heart was racing, but I tried not to let it show. I didn't want Danny to feel that all of this was weighing on me.

We started with a cautious stroll through the outside grounds. Danny looked curious and interested as he tramped around the property; I clenched his hand tightly, sometimes even closing my eyes as I prayed desperately that we wouldn't run into any of the residents.

I let him lead the way, and soon he started dragging me inside. Toward the residence wing. It was always easy for Danny to start up conversations with new people. This was no different. He entered their rooms, sat down on their beds, and started chatting with them as though he'd known them forever. I don't remember any of what they talked about, because I was practically willing my ears shut the whole time, and focusing all my energy on not running away screaming.

Death was a constant presence here, sitting in the rooms, clinging to the walls, floating in the air, written on the faces. We saw a girl of about nine with full-blown AIDS. She was covered with Kaposi sarcoma, a type of skin cancer common in late-stage AIDS patients. Her emaciated face reminded me of a skull, and I knew the sight of her would haunt my dreams for a long time to come.

A guy not much older than Danny passed us in the hallway, pulling his IV and limping like an old man. His face was covered with a red rash. Probably shingles. His hair was snow-white, his skin fragile as parchment paper. As he went by, he stared at me with eyes full of hatred. His expression told me in no uncertain terms that he found it completely unfair that he was sick and I was healthy. His nearly black eyes followed me accusingly, and a chill ran down my spine.

"Why are you healthy, and I'm not? Why?"

Danny kept stopping in his tracks and giving me worried looks. "You can do this, Ducky. Everything's okay. You just can't let it get to you this much. Pretend it's just a movie." He was the one trying to give me courage, when it should have been the other way around. I wanted to say something cheery to him in return, but I couldn't get a word out. We were as far away from "Everything's okay!" as it got.

We stepped into the nursing ward, where a woman was getting a blood transfusion. Her ear was full of telltale blisters. It took a lot of willpower to keep myself from scratching—the sight of them suddenly made me itch all over.

An older man was lying beside her, coughing continuously. There was a tube in his nose, and he was wheezing so badly, it sounded like he was going to choke to death any minute. Automatically, I began breathing more shallowly, not wanting to breathe in the air that had been inside his body.

All at once, I felt like I was choking, too. Desperately, I tugged on Danny's hand. "I have to get out of here, Danny!"

Without a word of protest, he turned around and led me to the exit. I was angry at myself, because I hadn't wanted to say anything, but it was all awful, too awful, and suddenly I didn't feel like I could handle any more of it. I was a teenager! I belonged at parties, not at my partner's deathbed!

I snuck a glance at the man beside me. He was young, athletic, and unbelievably attractive. The painful loss he had suffered had probably marked his soul, but it hadn't hurt his face any—nothing about him looked ill or injured in the slightest. I just couldn't get my head around the idea that he might someday end up like these people here, with white hair and hate-filled eyes, slowly wasting away. His optimism and his lust for life were just now returning. When I imagined him permanently becoming the bitter, frustrated wreck he'd been after Christina died, I felt sick to my stomach.

Suddenly, I felt like I was going to throw up. As soon as Danny got me outside, I fled to his car, gasping for air. Tears sprang to my eyes without warning, and Danny took me into his arms, regarding me empathetically. He was obviously well aware that I was hopelessly overwhelmed, nowhere near as self-assured as I'd made myself out to be.

"I shouldn't have brought you with me," he said.

"It's okay. I had to see it eventually. I need to learn to deal with it." But it wasn't okay, and I didn't want to learn to deal with it. I wanted a normal life and a healthy boyfriend. I wanted it so desperately it hurt. Why didn't we have ordinary problems like everyone else? Why didn't we ever fight about who left their shoes lying around, or who forgot to put the cap back on the toothpaste? Why didn't we have jealousy issues or normal doubts about our relationship? Why was everything about us so different from other couples our age? Why did I have to deal with so much sickness and death, when I was still so young?

Danny kept looking at me, seemingly reading my thoughts. I could see the wheels turning in his head, and I really believe that that was the moment when he decided:

"Maybe it would be best for everyone involved if I threw myself in front of a train."

There wasn't a hint of sarcasm in his voice.

"I'm so unbelievably sorry," Danny said, pushing me away a little. "I'm sorry I'm doing all of this to you. But I can't tell you how glad I am that you're here with me today. It's so much better than being here alone. Thank you."

"I just wish I could help you somehow." I wiped the tears from my eyes and fought back the nausea, which gradually began to subside.

"You help me more than you know." Danny leaned against his car. We stood there in silence for a while, lost in thought. "This is all my father's fault," he growled. "I hate him. I hate him so much!"

Slowly, I closed my eyes. "I hate him too." It was the understatement of the century. My whole body was flooded with loathing for this person I didn't even know, this person who had destroyed both of our lives.

"I'd have been able to handle anything else." Danny's gaze shifted back out into the distance. "Whatever it was, I'd have found a way to deal with it. There's nothing in life you can't get through, or at least work around. But the fact that he's sentenced me to death as an innocent man... I'm powerless against that." All at once, his eyes filled with tears as well. "Ducky, I meant what I said about the train." He lapsed into a thoughtful silence for a few moments. "Although...not a train. I don't want anyone else involved."

"Stop it, Danny, please. Let's go home." I tugged on his arm with a pleading expression on my face.

"I tried to kill myself once before, as a child," he began. "It was the summer I was fourteen. I slit my wrists with a razor blade. Both arms. I didn't actually want to die, though." He shrugged. "It was a cry for help."

"Did anyone find out?" Why was I even asking? The world was so unbelievably awful.

"My mom found me. She knew what I'd been trying to do, but she covered it up. A few sports drinks, a couple of bandages, a week or two of long-sleeved shirts, the end."

"So much pain and suffering could be prevented if the people in this miserable country would open their eyes and see what's happening around them. But they're just caught up in their own insignificant little problems, focused on their own pathetic existence. They could care less about the living beings around them."

Danny had said that to me. Long ago. Nobody had noticed the boy with the haggard expression far beyond his years, running around in sweatshirts for weeks despite the heat. Would I have noticed something like that? Was I as bad as everyone else in the world?

I shook my head. "But why?"

He misinterpreted the question. I could imagine only too well why he'd cried for help like that. What I couldn't get my head around was that nobody had done anything, not even his own mother.

"It was hell," he replied quietly. "When I hit puberty at thirteen, my father stopped molesting me. My body was changing in ways he didn't like. Plus, he couldn't get me to subjugate myself to him unconditionally anymore, and he hated me for it. At first, I thought things would get better, but instead they got much worse."

"What happened?"

"How do I explain this without you thinking I'm completely nuts?"

"Just tell me."

"You mean you already think I'm completely nuts, so one more thing won't make much of a difference?"

"No," I said emphatically, taking his hand. "I don't think that. I think you're the most admirable person on the planet, and I would never think you were nuts!"

A smile flickered across his face for a moment. "He started beating me regularly. A lot more than he had before—just whenever he felt like it, to make me feel his hatred for me, which I couldn't do anything about. Sometimes he whipped me up and down the room."

"And that was worse than sex," I concluded in resignation.

"Yeah," Danny said. "As horrible and perverse as all of that other stuff was, at least there was a little tenderness in it. A tiny bit of love, in whatever sick form. When that stopped, all that was left was hatred in its purest form. Not just when he was drunk, either. It was constant. Yeah, that was definitely worse. Much worse." He gave me a skeptical look. "Does that make any sense at all?"

"Yeah, it does." I'd seen the scars on his body often enough, knew each one individually. So I could well imagine how much hatred he was talking about. "You longed for love," I concluded. "I can understand that. There's nothing sick about that. It's normal."

He nodded. "I was really confused about it back then. For a long time, I thought there was something wrong with me."

Furiously, I kicked at a rock on the ground. "The only person who has something wrong with him is your father. I hope you know that?"

"Yeah, I think I do." Danny looked up at the sun, trying to blink away his tears. Yet again, I found myself dwelling on the painful question of how he would have turned out if his sadistic pedophile father hadn't done all of this permanent damage to him.

"Come on," I said, tugging on his hand. "Let's take a little walk so you can get yourself together, and when you're ready, we can drive home."

I'm running again. I'm running away. I know with absolute certainty that I'm running away. Fleeing. It's an escape!

Cold, hate-filled eyes are following me, black as the night I'm running through. They're sitting in a bony skull, picked clean of flesh. The eyes aren't actually eyes, they're holes that used to contain eyes. Blue eyes. But now the eyes are gone, the life is gone, the blue is gone. All that's left are emptiness and death.

And I'm running and running, but no matter how fast I run, it will catch up to me eventually...

Chapter Thirty-Nine

June 2002

We spent my twentieth birthday in the city. What started out as me picking out a new pair of jeans and some boots ended up as a marathon shopping spree—even though that wasn't usually my style, and even though we'd agreed Danny would just get me something small this year, since he was paying for our trip to Atlanta in September. Instead, Danny ended up buying me the most expensive riding breeches out there, with completely overpriced chaps to match.

After that, we drove out to Lake C to camp for the weekend. We pitched our tent in our usual spot, a secluded area in a wild meadow where dogs were permitted as well. The one disadvantage was that it was a long walk to the bathrooms, but neither of us minded that. On the plus side, it was right by the lake, and we had a whole section of meadow to ourselves.

A gigantic storm surprised us the first night. I sat bolt upright, frightened awake by the thunder outside, and then realized Danny wasn't in the tent. I wasn't surprised, though. He loved thunderstorms and other natural phenomena, and even at home he often got up in the middle of the night to enjoy them outside. I left Leika behind in the tent and tramped barefoot through the already swampy meadow. The rain was warm, but very heavy—I was soaked to the skin within seconds.

I didn't have to search for him long. I knew Danny's favorite spots, and even from far away, I could see him sitting there on the muddy lakeshore. He wasn't wearing shoes, either, and his wet T-shirt and shorts were clinging to his body.

Silently, I sat down in front of him, positioning myself between his knees. He wrapped his arms around me, and we sat there for a while, watching the storm. Nets of bright lightning crisscrossed the sky, tearing through the air with deafening cracks.

"I'm going to die," Danny said suddenly. "My goal was to get to at least thirty, but now I know I'll never make it that long. I won't even see twenty-five."

I turned to look at him, brushing my wet hair out of my face. "Why are you saying that? You're always optimistic—why are you talking like this?"

Danny shrugged. "Just intuition. All of a sudden, I started getting these weird feelings. It's not like I've consciously started thinking negatively or anything… I can't really explain it."

A chill ran down my back, and I began to shiver—it was like my organs were freezing inside my body. I remembered that vague feeling he'd gotten about Christina, when he'd told me that she was lost to us forever. I pressed my palms to my ears, squeezing the sides of my head, trying to forget what I'd just heard, to convince myself that it was all just words.

Long after the thunder had died away, I was still sitting there as though turned to stone.

Finally, Danny took my hands and put them in his lap. "I'm sorry," he whispered, gazing at me intently through the rain. "I won't say things like that anymore."

My heart began hammering wildly. He wouldn't say them anymore? That didn't mean he'd stop thinking them, only that he'd keep them from me in order to protect me. I began to panic. I've never been prone to panic attacks, but I had one that night. I clutched my throat and began to hyperventilate, terrified that I was going to suffocate. The more I breathed, the less oxygen I got. I wanted to scream, but I just didn't have the air.

Danny picked me up and carried me away from the place we'd been sitting, away from his panic-inducing words. I clung to his neck as he walked with me into the lake and set me down in the cold, waist-deep water. The panic evaporated instantly. My head was clear again; whatever premonitions I'd been having suddenly seemed surreal.

"Come on," Danny said, taking my wrist and pulling me along behind him, the way he liked to do.

We swam through the ice-cold water, fully clothed, in the middle of the night, in the pouring rain. Afterward, we ran back to the tent, threw our clothes in the grass, snuggled down underneath our blanket, naked and wet, and made love. We pressed our bodies close together, warming each other, and I prayed silently that this weekend with him at the lake would never end.

***

The long-awaited call came sometime in June: Detective Wildermuth informed us that they'd taken the man they'd been looking for into custody. He'd admitted to having lured Christina into his apartment with the promise of a fix, and then held her there against her will and sexually assaulted her twice. Afterward, he'd given her the contaminated heroin, though the police believed his assertion that he hadn't known it was toxic.

They'd gotten him on a number of other charges as well. He'd confessed to raping several other young girls and dealing large quantities of drugs. He also had a previous conviction for assault. This time, they gave him three years.

"Three years," Danny said bitterly. "Three goddamn years for a person's life. And then he'll get out and go strolling around in the world like nothing happened. And Tina will be dead forever."

"You can't think of it that way," I said. "It's not three years for a life. They didn't hold him responsible for her death. She took the stuff voluntarily. Think of it as an accident. Nobody wanted it to happen, not even that guy. It was an accident."

"Three years," Danny repeated. Then he turned his eyes toward heaven and spoke his first and only prayer. "Please, God, let me live that long! I promise you, as soon as he's out, I'll get him. And when I'm done with him, he'll be on his knees begging me to let him die."

Chapter Forty

August 2002

Just after mid-morning, my phone vibrated in my purse, setting off all my internal alarms. For a moment, I was tempted to reject the call, since I didn't recognize the number. "Hello?"

"Jessica Koch?" a woman asked.

"Yeah?" My voice sounded unnaturally high.

Oh, God, Danny's dead!

"Are you Danijel Taylor's girlfriend?"

"Yes. What happened?" I'd been asking that question far too often these days.

"He was in a car accident. He was admitted here in Bietigheim Hospital half an hour ago." The woman's voice was calm and pleasant, but the world began turning faster, and the office was spinning dangerously.

"Where is he?"

She gave me the address for the hospital, and I stormed out of the office before I'd even hung up. I didn't bother telling Bea where I was going. They'd probably heard my telephone conversation, because nobody called to ask why I'd just walked out.

The drive to the hospital seemed to stretch on for eternity. My head was buzzing. *Just a car accident,* I told myself, trying to keep calm. *He must be okay, because otherwise he wouldn't have been able to tell the people at the hospital to call you. They had to have gotten your number from him.*

It was amazing how well my rational mind was still working.

When I got there, I sprinted to the admissions desk. "I need to see Danijel Taylor," I wheezed. "Which room?"

The blonde behind the desk clicked around on her computer with a tranquility that nearly made my head explode. "Just a moment, please," she said, smiling. Then she reached for the phone and called one of the wards. It was several minutes before she addressed me again. "He's in the emergency ward on the fifth floor. It could be a while before he's moved to a room."

I took the stairs, too impatient to wait for the elevator. I ran down the hallway like a maniac until I reached the emergency department front desk. "My boyfriend was brought here," I panted. "Danijel Taylor. Can I see him?"

"He's in radiology," one of the nurses replied. "They're doing an ultrasound of his abdominal area, and then they'll need to take some X-rays. You can see him in an hour or two, as soon as he's been brought to a room."

"What? Two hours? He had them call me so I would come out here! Can't I just talk to him for a second?"

"I'm afraid not." She glanced through the paperwork, and her gaze fell upon a small note. "He said you'd be out," she murmured, half to herself, as she read. "Oh, right, it was about the car. It's out in a field, blocking a farmer's way. It's going to need to be moved. He said to tell you to have it scrapped."

"Scrapped? Why? The car's only four years old," I told her, perfectly aware that she wouldn't care.

She shrugged as if to confirm my suspicion. "That's what he said. Anyway, they need it out of there. You should call a tow truck." She told me where the car was. Danny must have been on the way to the gym.

And he wanted me to have his nearly new BMW scrapped?

Goddammit, Danny! This situation was absolutely too much for me. "How is he?" I asked the nurse.

"The doctors are still with him. He has a broken collarbone, a serial fracture of the ribs, and whiplash, along with a concussion. They're still examining him to see if he has any other internal injuries. I'll let you know as soon as you can go in to see him." With that, she walked away, leaving me standing there.

Internal injuries? That didn't sound like he was doing well at all.

Agitated, I walked up and down the hallways of the hospital until I found radiology. I briefly considered just walking in, but I didn't even know if he was still in there, so I decided against it.

Instead, I called Jörg again. I had his number now—it was a good thing I'd called him from my own phone last time. "Jörg?" I said. "Danny was in a car accident. I'm in the emergency ward, and they won't let me see him, but they want me to have his car towed."

"Wait there, Jessica. I'll be there in twenty minutes." Thank God for Jörg.

A moment later, the doors to the radiology department swung open, and two nurses emerged, pushing a hospital bed in front of them.

"Danny!" I called, rushing over. The nurses were kind enough to stop. "What happened?"

He was awake, and apart from a bloody scrape across the left half of his face, he looked uninjured, if a bit dazed. "Jessica!" He grabbed my hand immediately. "I was in a car accident."

Yeah, I knew that much already. "Are you okay?"

"Yeah. Couple broken ribs. They hurt. Okay besides that. Need to move the car." He spoke in quick, choppy sentences, and his breathing was shallow. He wasn't doing well at all—he couldn't even take a proper breath. I saw they'd given him an IV, and the bag hung above his bed. Immediately, images of the AIDS hospice flashed through my mind, and I felt another panic attack coming on. Danny noticed and tried to sit up so that he could get a better look at me, but finally he gave up and fell back onto the bed with a cry of pain.

"You need to stay lying down," one of the nurses admonished him sternly, pressing him down into the pillow. "He needs to have some X-rays done," she explained to me. "We're giving him the contrast medium intravenously. It may be a while. We'll let you know." She moved to push the bed again, and I began gasping for air.

Danny didn't let go of my hand. "Everything's okay," he said, trying to calm me down. "It was just a car accident. You hear me? A regular old car accident, nothing more. Everything's okay!" Speaking left him far too out of breath for "everything's okay" to apply. The nurses peeled his hand from mine and rolled him away down a hallway marked "Staff Only."

"I'll go get the car and come back," I called after him. I took several deep, slow breaths, the way Danny always did when he wanted to calm himself down. Car accidents could happen any time, there was no real reason to worry. At least, that's what I kept telling myself.

Just then, Jörg came down the hallway toward me. "How is he?" he asked before he'd even reached me.

I shrugged. "I only saw him for a minute. Broken ribs, whiplash, nothing life-threatening."

Jörg nodded. "Okay, let's plan this out, then. We'll call a tow truck, and then we'll drive out to the scene of the accident and figure out where to bring the car. After that, we'll go to your place and pick up a few things for him. He'll probably have to stay here a few days."

I agreed, and as we made our way to Jörg's Passat, he called a towing company and relayed the address I'd given him. Then we drove out there ourselves. The street was stick-straight, without a single curve for miles. There were no trees in the area, the streets were dry and clean, and it was obvious no other cars had been involved in the accident. There was just nothing there, no skid marks indicating he'd swerved or hit the brakes, not even any shards of glass. Danny had driven into the ditch for no reason. His car was upside down in the middle of a field, at the foot of the embankment leading up to the street. He hadn't even tried to stop.

"Good God," I murmured. "How the hell did this happen?"

Jörg parked near the ditch, put his hazards on, and got out to survey the scene. "I don't know, Jessica," he said, putting his hands on his hips, "but it's pretty goddamn strange. Danny knows how to drive. He should have at least tried to stay on the road."

"What do you mean?" I shrieked, almost hysterical. "Are you saying he did this on purpose?"

"No." Jörg gave me a stern look. "That's not what I mean. Why would he deliberately drive into a ditch?"

"Because he wants to die," I replied lamely.

Jörg shook his head decisively. "No," he repeated. "That wouldn't be like him. Do you really think he would do something like that without saying anything to you beforehand?"

Did I think that? No, I didn't.

Danny wasn't like that.

"You're right."

"And if you wanted to die, this isn't the place you'd pick," Jörg went on. "It looks more like he fell asleep at the wheel."

Now it was me doing the decisive head-shaking. "No way. Danny's the last person in the world to just fall asleep!"

"I hope he can tell us more later. Let's go check out the car."

Uncertainly, I followed Jörg down the embankment. "Oh my God," I breathed. "Nobody could survive this!"

And it would probably have been better for him in the long term if he hadn't survived it!

I pushed that ugly thought aside, along with the images of the AIDS hospice, completely disgusted with myself. We stepped up to the car. The roof was completely crushed, the windshield shattered. All the airbags had deployed. The tailpipe was sticking out at an angle from the back of the car, like an antenna. The driver's side door had been pried open. I rubbed my eyes and face in complete disbelief.

"There's no repairing that," Jörg remarked dryly.

"Let's take it to a mechanic. Please. Maybe there's something they can do."

Jörg looked at me like I'd lost my mind. "This car's completely totaled, Jessica."

"Mechanic," I insisted.

The tow truck came, and we followed it the short distance to the authorized BMW repair shop, where they unloaded the car and set it upright. It looked even sadder than before.

I stared in complete bafflement at the car I'd claimed I'd never liked. I remembered the night we'd met at the festival, when Danny had driven after me in this car and blocked my path. How he'd driven backward down the road afterward. And the night he'd put me in the back and taken me to his place because I was so drunk. Tears burned my eyes as I recalled all the long conversations we'd had underneath those diffuse blue interior lights.

I tried to open the passenger door, but the whole car was so bent up that it wouldn't budge. The loss of this car hurt my soul. Not just for my own sake, but because I knew how attached Danny had been to the BMW, even if he'd never have admitted it—after all, it was only a material possession.

The owner of the garage emerged from the office. "Mama mia!" he cried, throwing up his hands. "Five percent survival chance, maximum! Did the driver come out of there alive?"

I nodded.

"Mama mia," he repeated. "Must be a lucky kid. Fate really smiles on some people!"

My throat burned as though I'd swallowed fire, and tears ran down my cheeks. I couldn't take that much irony. Should I give him a quick run-down of Danny's life?

"Scrap it," I told him, turning away so he wouldn't see me crying.

Jörg climbed into the twisted metal through the pried-open door to get Danny's things from inside, and then took photos for the insurance claim. Hopefully Danny wouldn't ever have to see them.

The police report indicated that Danny had been going much too fast when he drove off the road—they estimated he'd been pushing a hundred miles an hour. He hadn't tried to brake or change direction. The BMW had rolled at least three times before coming to rest upside down. Nobody else had been involved, and there'd been no witnesses. Danny must have been completely alone on the road, which only made the whole thing even stranger.

A couple of people had called emergency services after driving past the scene. Nobody had stopped to check on Danny.

The paramedics hadn't arrived until forty-five minutes after the accident, which would have been enough time for Danny to bleed to death if he'd been more seriously injured.

In my head, I cursed everyone who had driven by without stopping, wishing scabies on all of them. Never in a million years would Danny have driven past an accident scene without checking to see whether he could help. It wouldn't have mattered to him where he was going or how much of a hurry he was in. But I'd already learned that life wasn't fair.

Danny's seatbelt had saved his life, but it could just as easily have turned out differently. As bad as the accident was, he'd come away with relatively minor injuries, which was probably a matter of pure luck.

He'd been conscious the whole time, until the ambulance arrived, but he'd been unable to free himself. His cell phone had been out of reach—he'd put it on top of the middle console, and the phone had flown through the car when it rolled. Jörg found it underneath the back seat.

They tested Danny for drugs and alcohol, but as always, he'd been completely sober.

***

When Jörg and I entered his hospital room, the head physician was already in there, talking to Danny. An IV was still hanging over Danny's bed, running painkillers into his veins, but he smiled when he saw us and made another unsuccessful attempt to sit up. This could get interesting. Broken ribs required at least six weeks of bed rest, and Danny couldn't even keep still for a few hours.

I sat down on his bed, so relieved to see him alive that I hugged him much too hard. "Please don't touch," he whimpered, raising his arms defensively. "Broken ribs really are hell."

"How is he?" Jörg asked the doctor, who gave him a skeptical once-over before apparently deciding Jörg must be the patient's father.

"He's stable thus far," the doctor replied. "We're going to keep him here for a couple of days to observe him and rule out any complications." He was somewhere in his mid-fifties, with white hair and a receding hairline, and he looked like the type of guy who never cracked a joke. "I'll come down to see you again this afternoon," he said to Danny before turning to go.

"Doctor?" Jörg stepped forward to stop him.

"Yes?"

I saw Danny give Jörg a scathing look.

"Did he tell you he's HIV positive?"

The doctor started. "No, but we would have found out. I'm sure it's in his file." He gave us a friendly smile, but I sensed that he felt caught out. He obviously didn't like it when friends and family meddled in his work.

"I just thought…" Jörg hesitated. "I thought you might want to check him thoroughly. His blood and all that. Maybe there's some kind of connection."

The doctor nodded. "No problem, we were going to draw blood anyway. I'll go ahead and order a complete workup. Nothing will get past us, don't you worry." Smiling, he left the room.

Danny gaped at Jörg in outrage. "What was that about?" He waved toward the door.

"You need to tell them things like that!" Jörg insisted.

"You heard him. They would have found out anyway."

"Well, then, there's no need for you to get insulted, is there?" Jörg wasn't about to let Danny upset him.

"What the hell happened this morning, anyway?" I put in. That was the real question here.

"A connection between HIV and a car accident." Danny snorted contemptuously, ignoring my question. "What a load of bullshit!" Immediately dismissing other people's ideas as bullshit wasn't like Danny at all. But since Christina had died,

Danny had said and done a lot of things I never would have suspected him capable of.

"What happened this morning?" Jörg asked, repeating my question.

"There was a deer in the road."

"A deer?" I gave Danny a questioning look.

"Yeah. You know, those brown animals that live in the woods. The males have antlers, and the babies are called fawns, and they have little white spots—"

"Danny, we know what deer are," Jörg broke in.

"Oh, well, good." He made a move to roll over onto his side but discovered he couldn't do that, either.

"So this accident was because of a deer?" Jörg pressed him.

"Yeah. It was just standing there, in the middle of the road."

"And why didn't you brake?"

"I did. It wasn't enough." He shrugged and looked at me apologetically. "The deer is okay, Ducky, don't worry!"

"Danny." Jörg gave him an admonishing look. "We saw the road. You didn't brake."

"I didn't? Oh… Then I just swerved. Maybe that was it." Danny had never been a good liar.

"You drove into a field at a hundred miles an hour without braking? Because of a deer?" Jörg raised his eyebrows skeptically.

"Why not? I like deer." He would have crossed his arms by now if the needle in the crook of his elbow hadn't been preventing it. We sat there for a moment, looking at him expectantly, and suddenly he grew furious. "Jesus Christ Almighty, so there wasn't a deer! Can't I get in an accident without everyone making a big thing out of it?" He tried to take a deep breath to grouch at us some more, but a pained grimace cut across his face. "If nothing else about the rest of my fucking life is normal," he went on in a quieter voice, "then let me at least get in one car wreck like a million other guys my age do."

Danny sank back onto his pillows, trying desperately to get enough air. Whatever he was keeping from us, now wasn't the time to press him for answers. Jörg seemed to realize that as well, because he changed the subject. "I took a couple pictures. There was really no salvaging the car."

"I know," Danny said. "I saw." Seeing our mournful expressions, he added, "Guys, it was just a car. It was fully insured. There's nothing to mope about."

"I liked that car," I admitted sadly. "And I know you liked it, too."

"As soon as I get out of here, we'll buy a new one," Danny assured me.

"Let us know when you hear your blood test results," Jörg said. Danny was long overdue for a checkup—it had been five months since his last one—because he hadn't managed to make himself go since Christina's death. But the last one had been so good that he'd had no reason to worry.

"You don't have to remind me of that," Danny told Jörg. "I would have done that anyway." Danny was unusually irritable, but it was probably just because he was in so much pain.

"You should get some sleep," Jörg decided. "Your Ducky and I are going to go get something to eat, and we'll be back later."

The doctor didn't return until that evening. He checked Danny's vitals and blood pressure, and seemed entirely satisfied with what he saw. A nurse had taken several blood samples that afternoon as planned, but the results hadn't come back yet.

We could see from the X-rays that three of Danny's ribs had snapped clean through, and a fourth was cracked as well. "They should heal without any problems," the doctor told us. "Fortunately, they're all clean breaks. The most important thing is rest. No physical activity at all for six weeks, and then start slow after that. After ten weeks, you should be right as rain."

Danny stared at him in horror, but the doctor ignored him.

"And it's important that you breathe with the pain, never against it. Don't hold back—take nice, deep breaths, even if it hurts. You need to keep filling your lungs with air—otherwise you may develop a lung infection, and we want to avoid that. The nurses will show you a couple of breathing exercises in the morning."

Danny closed his eyes, still trying to process the idea of six weeks without martial arts or running.

"Is there anything we can do to aid the healing process?" I asked.

"Well, it's better if he sleeps on the broken ribs at night."

Danny squinted up at the doctor doubtfully. "How is that supposed to work?"

286

"It will be very painful, but it compresses the broken ribs and helps them heal faster. Keep trying it, at least."

"Poor Angelo," Danny murmured to himself. "One other question: we were going to fly to America in five weeks…"

"Do you have trip cancellation insurance?"

"We haven't booked the tickets yet," Danny explained lamely.

"Then book them for a month later. Better safe than sorry." The doctor snapped his file folder shut.

Danny gave me a questioning look, suddenly seeming extraordinarily tired, almost resigned to his fate.

"Four weeks one way or another doesn't matter," I told him. "So we'll go a little later, who cares?"

"Okay," Danny murmured.

Now I really suspected something was off. Danny knew more than he was letting on. Normally, he'd never have just agreed to put off his vacation. Once he'd gotten something into his head, he generally made it happen, and it wasn't like him to let a couple of broken bones stop him.

Broken ribs are the most painful breaks of all, my inner voice said, trying to placate my fears. *He's got other things on his mind besides vacation right now.*

***

When I came into the room two days later, Danny was already sitting up in bed. His roommate had been discharged the day before, much to Danny's relief. Danny hated having strangers sleeping anywhere near him, and knowing that he was trapped in bed, practically immobile, with a man lying just a few feet away, had made the whole thing almost intolerable.

"Hey," he said when he saw me. "Wanna go downstairs with me?"

"Can you walk?" I asked uncertainly.

A crooked smile spread over his face. "I broke my ribs, not my legs. Of course I can walk." Very slowly, he stood up. His IV had been taken out the day before, so we were free to trot down the hallway hand in hand. But I still watched him out of the corner of my eye. "Ducky, can you quit with the looks already?" he asked when we reached the bottom of the stairs. Even in this condition, he'd still refused to take the elevator. "I'm fine, really."

It wasn't true, but complaining wasn't part of his repertoire. If he'd been fine, he wouldn't been walking so slowly. At my normal pace. "Ducky walking," he normally called it. For the next couple of weeks, Ducky walking was going to be our usual speed.

We got ice cream from the hospital cafeteria and went outside to sit on the back of a park bench, our feet on the seat, our faces turned toward the sun. "You're breathing wrong again," I scolded him. "You need to take deep breaths."

"I would if I could," he grumbled. "I swear, I've broken every bone in my body, including a couple of ribs...but four at once, plus a collarbone? Really sucks. How am I going to do this for six weeks? I hate sitting still."

"You'll be okay. We'll survive."

"I need to be in shape again by next weekend. I've got a three-day photoshoot in Karlsruhe. If it goes well, I'll get the contract, and then we'll both be financially set forever."

I poked at my chocolate-chip ice cream with my spoon. We'd never had to worry about money before. Ever since we'd gotten together, I hadn't had to spend a dime of what I made. He put gas in my car, paid my bills, bought me clothes, and paid for everything when we went out. I would've been happy to trade our problems for silly little money woes. I'd happily have given away everything I owned, worn burlap sacks and straw shoes, and lived on noodles and ketchup if it meant Danny could be healthy and Christina would come back to us.

"Set forever?" I repeated. "You didn't tell me anything about that."

"I only found out about it myself the morning of the accident." He crumpled his paper ice cream dish and tossed it across the bench, dunking it neatly in the nearby trash can. I didn't even try to follow suit—I hopped up and threw my dish from three feet away. It bounced off the rim and landed in the dirt. Annoyed, I picked it up and shoved it in the can.

Danny didn't manage to stifle his laughter.

"Were you on the phone while you were driving?" I asked.

"No. And even if I had been, I always talk on the phone while I drive. It's never made me drive into a ditch before."

Danny was right. Someone was always calling him—his modeling agency, one of his students—and he'd take the call while still expertly doing whatever he was doing.

"Okay, okay," I said in resignation.

Danny sighed. "I have to make another call in a minute, too. Dogan and the other teachers will have to divide up my students. Who knows if I'll ever be able to take them again?"

"Of course you will. They're just broken bones. They'll heal. That's all it is, isn't it, Danny?"

He was silent.

"Danny?"

He took my hands and pulled me closer. In the sunlight, his eyes glowed that dark blue that still fascinated me as much as ever. "Ducky!" He held me fast with his gaze—he was starting to remember how to do that. "Why are you questioning this? Have I ever lied to you? It was a car accident, that's all."

It was a fair point. Why was I doubting him? Our whole relationship was based on absolute honesty. Apart from that little white lie about his parents at the start of our relationship, he'd never been anything but truthful to me. Suddenly I felt guilty, and I made up my mind to trust him the way I always had. There was no reason not to.

"I do believe you," I assured him. I probably really was worrying about it too much. Car accidents happened every day, all over the world.

"Good." He looked satisfied. "Let's go upstairs. Ricky said he was going to come by later." He held out a hand so that I could help him to his feet. Then he wrapped his arms around me and hugged me as tightly as his destroyed bones would allow. "Don't worry about me," he whispered. "I'll be okay. You just focus on your exams."

Something about his whole demeanor should have set off my alarm bells, but it didn't. I stuck to my resolution and trusted him the way I always had.

I stayed until visiting hours ended, but instead of leaving then, I snuck around the halls for another two hours, and then hid for another hour in the family shower room. Now that he'd been moved off of the emergency floor, the nurses would only be checking on him every few hours—unless he called. Once the night shift started, and the day nurse had made her last rounds on Danny's floor, I crept down the dim hallway and slipped into his room. He was awake, listening to music, and when he saw me, he stared at me like he'd seen a ghost. His eyes were red, making me wonder if he'd been crying.

"Ducky. Where'd you come from?"

"Outside," I whispered, nodding toward the hall.

"Oh. You don't say. How did you manage to keep from getting thrown out?"

"Trade secret."

Without another word, Danny scooted to the edge of the bed to make room for me. That was one of the things I loved most about him. He would never have scolded me for doing something unusual or crazy. Quite the opposite, actually—he was usually eager to go along with wild ideas, and he thought of plenty himself. Even after we lost Christina.

I crawled into bed with him.

"You're completely nuts," he whispered against my lips.

"I got it from you."

He laughed softly. "Nice of you to imitate my best quality."

Despite the cramped hospital bed and his broken ribs, we managed to make love. He simply lay motionless on his back—the days of him getting panic attacks in that position were long gone. I could do whatever I liked with him now, even prop myself up on his wrists. Right now, I just had to make sure not to touch his left side. Afterward, I laid down on his right, and we fell asleep cuddled close together.

When the night nurse finally came around a few hours later, she was astonished to find two of us in Danny's bed. She threw me out, of course, and I spent another couple of hours slinking through the halls before returning for breakfast.

Danny shared his food with me, and afterward, I snuck into the kitchen and stole a second helping. Tiny as the portions were, Danny would have been starving even if he'd had a whole one to himself. Eventually, I drove to work and spent the day trying not to fall asleep at my desk before returning in the evening.

"Blood tests were okay," Danny said by way of greeting when I walked in. "My T-cell count has gone down, but it's still all right."

"How far down?"

"Still okay," he replied curtly. "Not bad enough that I have to start treatment. The doctor said I should let my ribs heal first and then have my own doctor do another test. Until then, I shouldn't worry."

"Well, that sounds sensible. How are you doing?"

"Bored to death. I want to go home. Maybe you should sleep here again tonight. If we're lucky, they'll catch us again and throw me out."

***

Danny was discharged from the hospital six days later, and I stayed over at his place for a while, accepting my longer work commute and my parents' annoyance as the price I had to pay. I left Leika with him during the day to keep him company. He took her for long walks and taught her all kinds of tricks, like "play dead," "give me five," and "roll over." The walks weren't really enough physical activity for him, but they passed the time. In the evenings, he helped me study for my exams.

After barely a week at home, he developed cabin fever.

I was standing in the kitchen making myself a sandwich when he called from the living room, "Well, if I didn't know what I was going to die of already, I'd certainly know now."

"Oh?" I called back. "Do tell."

"Boredom," he groaned. "Definitely boredom!"

"Nobody's ever died of boredom," I chided him, biting into my sandwich.

"They're definitely going to put 'boredom' on my death certificate as the cause of death," he insisted.

Of course he was bored. Normally, he would have spent the entire day at the gym—plus, he'd have gone running every morning and probably ridden his bike in the evening, and then he'd have had photoshoots on the side. And he'd had Christina around before, so he'd practically never been alone. He'd never spent much time at the computer or watching TV—he'd had far too much energy for that.

Now, he spent hours alone in the backyard every day, sitting on the grass because the patio furniture hurt his ribs, reading one book after another. He was looking forward to the weekend, when he'd get to go to Karlsruhe. He was planning on taking a cab there, and I knew he wouldn't let anything stop him from going, even if he had to crawl there yowling on all fours.

I walked into the living room holding my sandwich. Danny was lying with his stomach on the couch and his head and forearms resting on the floor. "What the hell are you doing?" I asked, chewing.

"Yoga, obviously."

"That's not yoga. That's ridiculous."

"Okay, then I'm doing ridiculous. Ridiculous is still better than nothing."

"Do you think that's good for your ribs?"

"Who knows?" he muttered. "What can it hurt? They're already broken. And I'm bored, bored, bored to death."

"Get dressed," I ordered him. "We're going out."

He wriggled down from the couch. "Yippee! We're going out! Where are we going?"

"Hm... The zoo?"

"Give me three minutes."

"Then I can deliver you to the bats, and you can go hang upside down with them."

"Bats sound good," he agreed. "Anything sounds better than bored to death."

Chapter Forty-One

September 2002

As expected, Danny landed the contract after his job in Karlsruhe. He was going to be part of a massive marketing campaign for a well-known brand of cologne. He was at the height of his career thus far. This one shoot would pay more than I earned in an entire year. And after this campaign, he'd be flooded with other offers. He'd already received several, but he hadn't signed anything yet.

My final exams went quite a bit better than expected. I went in well-prepared and came out feeling good. And my feeling had proven right: I ended up with an A-minus. The results smoothed things over between me and my parents after weeks of tension, and Danny was incredibly relieved, as well. Knowing how badly he wanted me to do well had motivated me a lot more than my parents' obnoxious nagging.

"You did great," he told me when he heard, circling his arms around me. "You've earned a free wish. Anything you want, it's yours."

"I don't want anything." My only wish was for him to be healthy and happy.

"But you deserve something nice," he insisted. "Pick something!"

"You're buying me a trip to America this winter. That's more than enough, really!" After a lot of back and forth, we finally decided to wait until the end of the year to fly out. It had been more than seven weeks since the accident, but Danny's broken ribs were still giving him far too much trouble. He'd done his breathing exercises every day in the beginning, until he could inhale normally again, and he'd slept on his left side every night despite the pain. So his X-ray results were all the more frustrating: two of his ribs were still completely broken, and the other two were deeply cracked. The doctor ordered him to rest even longer and strongly discouraged him from taking pain medication so that he'd immediately feel when he was overdoing it.

Danny hadn't taken painkillers even once outside of the hospital, and he'd stopped doing sports entirely. But none of it seemed to be helping, which was unusual. Normally, he recovered quickly from broken bones and other injuries.

On one particular Saturday morning, he sat down at the computer after breakfast and, a little while later, called me over. I sat down on his lap and looked at the screen. He was clicking around on a car dealership's website. "Pick one out," he ordered.

"One what?"

"A car, Ducky, what else?"

"What would I do with a car? I already have one."

Danny sighed and cursed under his breath at how slow I was. "*I* need a car," he explained. "If I don't get mobile again, I'm going to lose my mind."

"So why do you want me to pick one out? Are you buying two?"

He turned to give me a look of annoyance. It wasn't like him to be so testy. "Are you doing this on purpose?" he asked.

I shook my head, and he sighed again. "Okay, let's try this one more time. I want to buy myself a car, and I want it to be one you like, because eventually, it'll go to you."

I was starting to suspect where he was going with this, but I played dumb. When had he gotten so pessimistic? "Why should I get your car? You need it yourself."

He pushed me off his lap and stood up. "You should start getting used to the idea that I'm not going to live forever." His voice was dangerously quiet.

"Danny... Is there something I don't know?"

"Why can't you ever do what I tell you and just pick yourself out a fucking car?" he snapped.

"Because I don't want a goddamn car," I retorted in an even icier tone. Why was he cursing at me so often these days? He'd hardly ever cursed before. He'd cracked jokes, he'd laughed all the time, he'd messed around. But since Christina had left us, he'd started to curse.

When I think back to this conversation now, I feel terrible for Danny and I regret the way I acted. He'd wanted to buy me a car because he loved me, and because he wanted his worldly possessions to go to me. But I was just too pigheaded to accept that he wouldn't be driving the car until it was ready for the junkyard. I really wish I had just gone with him to find a car. Not because I'd have gotten a new car—but just to make him happy. But that day, all I wanted was for him to stop thinking so negatively.

"Fine," Danny said at last, looking offended. "Then I'll pick out a car I like, and you'll just have to take what you get."

"By the time I get your car, it'll be an antique, and I won't want it anymore anyway."

Danny shook his head, running his hand through his hair, and then crossed his arms. "What am I going to do with you?"

All at once, I knew. "There's something you're not telling me. You know more than you're admitting." He hadn't said anything all this time because he wanted to protect me. He'd only reveal what he knew once he was sure I'd be able to handle the truth, or else he'd wait until there was no getting around it anymore.

"I'm going out to buy a car now. Are you coming with me?" He took a checkbook out of the drawer.

"So you're just going to go shell out a ton of money on a new car right now, today? Why can't you get a used one?"

"I can't stand buying stuff other people have already used."

"That's completely stupid!"

"Oh, yeah? Why? Because a new car wouldn't be worth it for me anymore? It would just be wasted on me?" His voice was cold, accusatory.

"I didn't say that."

"But you were thinking it!"

"That's not true!"

"What were you thinking, then? That it's a waste because I'll just drive it into a ditch or wrap it around a tree? I'm not stupid! I'll get it fully insured!"

"I think it's stupid of you to spend that much money on a car when we're planning on buying a house together next year!"

Danny snorted. "I can get both. I'll put a smaller down payment on the house, and I'll pay it off over a longer period." With a look of pure frustration, he added, "Oh, wait, I forgot. I won't have enough time to pay it off. I have a fatal illness, don't you know."

Why were we fighting? We'd never fought before, not once.

"I just thought we were going to buy these things *together*," I said, trying to steer the conversation in a different direction. "I thought that was what you wanted, too."

"When has anyone ever cared what I wanted?" he asked bitterly.

"I care, Danny! Don't blame me for your life!"

"What are you going to do with a house all to yourself? Do you want to live out the rest of your days all alone in there, a sad, old widow? Maybe you should buy a house with someone you can actually live in it with."

"*You know what?*" I screamed at him, mainly to keep him from noticing that I was close to tears. "Just go get your goddamn car!"

"Yeah, I will." He said it calmly and firmly, without raising his voice. Without another word, he stomped past me and grabbed the house keys from the hook on the wall. Then he turned around and threw me a furious look. "When I'm dead, it'll be your car, and you'll be mad at yourself forever because you didn't come with me to pick it out yourself." Then he stalked out, slamming the door behind him.

Hurt, I took a deep breath, then ran to the living room window and wrenched it open. "Danny, you don't have to walk!" I called. "Take my car!"

"No, thanks! I'm happy to walk!"

Furious, I banged the window shut again. Now he was dead set on tromping down the road with broken ribs. Mules were cooperative by comparison. I sank to the floor in resignation, already regretting not having gone with him.

Danny was gone the entire day. Sometime in the early evening, a pitch-black BMW with a red license plate came rolling up the street. It was the follow-up model to his old car. Lower to the ground, with the same external fog lights. Danny parked on the side of the road—a three-point parking job, something I'd never manage. Sighing, I walked out and planted myself on the sidewalk, hands on my hips.

Danny got out, grinning broadly. "Well, what do you think?" He was in a fantastic mood again.

"Gorgeous," I replied sarcastically.

He rattled off a series of technical specifications, but I was only half-listening. "I think it's great," he concluded.

"You're driving around in a car worth as much as a two-bedroom condo. Very sensible, Danny. Great work there!" I patted him on the shoulder to underscore my words.

His euphoria evaporated immediately. "You're right," he admitted. "That was dumb of me."

"Sure was. But hindsight...you know."

Danny gave me a sad look. "I should have just given you the money instead of buying myself a car. You and your new partner could have used it as a down payment on your house."

I rolled my eyes.

"Why didn't you tell me that before?" he asked accusingly.

"What new partner? Who says I'll ever want to be with anyone else? Danny, stop planning my future without asking me!" I didn't want to hear any of it. There was no place in my head for life without him.

"Ducky, I have to plan your future. I don't have one of my own." He thought for a moment. "I'll put the purchase order and all the documentation in the glove compartment, and I'll actually take care of my stuff for a change. That way, the car will stay like new, and after I die, you can sell it. It'll be worth a couple thousand less, but you'll be able to handle that—I've got more than enough in my bank account. It'll all be yours. Use it to buy a house. For you and your family... Yeah, that's a good plan. What do you say, Ducky?"

I walked back into the apartment without a word and left him standing outside.

Chapter Forty-Two

October 2002

His broken ribs just weren't healing. Although Danny was supposed to keep resting, he'd started running in the mornings again, determined to get back to his old life. But the weeks still dragged on endlessly for him, until finally, at the beginning of October, he said impatiently, "I'm going out to the gym. I want to see if I can do at least a little. You want to come?"

A sense of foreboding crept over me. Even walking up stairs and vacuuming were painful for him—there was no way he was going to kickbox in this condition. But I knew there would be no talking him out of it, so I agreed.

"You drive," he said, pressing the keys into my hand.

"Danny, one of these days, you're going to have to get over your fear of driving." Ever since the accident, he'd refused to drive with me sitting beside him. I didn't want to drive that battleship of a car, and I found his refusal ridiculous as well, since he was perfectly capable of driving on his own.

"I'm not afraid of driving, I'm afraid of getting in an accident with you in the car." He went around to the passenger side. Now wasn't really the time to argue about this, I decided. Danny was already setting himself up for disappointment at the martial arts center, and accepting he would have to wait even longer to start training again would be hard enough for him.

Sighing, I got behind the wheel. I had to admit that the car really was fun to drive, though I felt pretty overwhelmed by its size.

Danny's mood brightened considerably as we stepped into the gym. Immediately, he headed for the two rings at the back. I tried not to look toward the corner where Christina and I had sat so often, watching him.

Dogan came over and hugged Danny. He'd called several times, wondering how we were doing and when we'd finally show our faces around here again.

"Got ten minutes?" Danny asked. "I want to see if I'm ready to start again."

"Of course, Dan. For you, always. I've been waiting for you for weeks." He seemed genuinely delighted to see Danny—which made sense, since he was Dogan's best employee *and* most successful student.

Dogan swung himself up into the ring and somersaulted over the ropes, the way Danny had often done in the past. Entering the ring like that was a tradition of theirs. At that moment, I hated Dogan for doing it.

Danny pulled off his shoes, socks, and sweatshirt, and climbed into the ring far less elegantly. After a short warmup, they started fighting, and within about a second, I could tell it wasn't going to work. Danny didn't have a chance in hell. He was focusing so hard on blocking out the pain that he didn't manage a single hit. He was far too slow, as well, and in noticeably worse condition. His left leg had always been his most effective weapon, but now he just couldn't get it into the air. Dogan went very easy on him, but when he landed a blow that was more implied than anything, Danny held up a hand to interrupt the fight.

"What's wrong, Dan?" Dogan bent forward, peering at his student intently. It was totally incomprehensible to him that Danny could neither parry his attacks nor launch any himself.

Panting heavily and covered in sweat, Danny fell backward against the ropes. "Just give me a quick break." He struggled to get himself together again and recoup his strength.

"You're not healed up yet," Dogan said.

"Let's go," Danny said, giving his trainer the sign for the next round. Immediately, he took another blow. He stumbled back but used the opportunity to try his best tactic: he feinted a low kick at his trainer's shin, and when Dogan moved to block it, Danny launched a high kick at his temple. He got the leg up, but he shrieked in pain as the blow connected. Thrown back by the force of his own kick, he skidded backward and lost his balance, landing flat on his back with another shriek.

"Everything okay?" Dogan quickly knelt beside him and held out his hand.

I buried my face in my hands, trying to hold the burning tears back. Danny, my Danny, who could have easily taken five guys at once a year and a half ago, was now lying flat on his back with his arms splayed out, unable to get to his feet. At that moment, I knew with absolute certainty that he would never get back to his old condition.

Danny refused to let Dogan help him up. If there was one thing nobody could break, it was his endless supply of willpower and his boundless pride. He would keep both of those until his death. He would find a way to die free and unbroken.

Slowly, he turned over onto his stomach and crawled away on all fours, only managing to straighten once he was outside the ring. After he'd gotten dressed again, he went up and shook Dogan's hand. "Thank you," he said. "For everything. Tell my students I'm sorry. I can't do it anymore."

"Dan, what...?" Dogan blinked at him, but Danny turned away without explaining and left the gym for the last time.

I murmured something about being in touch and then hastened after Danny. When I finally caught up, he was already standing beside his car, wincing in pain, his right arm pressed against his ribs and his left hand supporting his weight against the door. His breathing was ragged, the air whistling in his lungs. "I can't drive," he said quietly, suppressing another shriek of pain as he dropped into the passenger seat.

"Does it hurt a lot?" I asked as I maneuvered what I secretly thought of as Danny's new battleship out of the parking lot.

"No, not at all." He forced a smile. "I've never felt better." Then he pressed his forehead against the window and stared out in silence.

I hadn't even finished parking the car when he got out and ran into the house. I locked the car and slowly followed him inside. I wouldn't have to run any longer, I realized. The nightmare had finally caught up to us. The day I had always dreaded had come. It would all be downhill from here. We were skidding toward the chasm—and there was no stopping us.

As expected, I found Danny in the bedroom. He was lying on the bed, wailing into his pillow. He'd left the door ajar, and I pushed it open so I could go in and sit beside him. "Danny, I'm so sorry," I said, stroking his back. "It was just too soon. What did you expect with two broken ribs?"

"Can you please just leave me alone for a while? I need to try and deal with this somehow." He pulled the blanket up over his head and went back to crying.

Sighing, I got up and called Leika over so that we could go for a walk. How many times had I sighed in the past few weeks? Would it ever stop?

After just a couple of minutes, I returned to the apartment, but the BMW was gone. I found a note on the kitchen table:

Back before midnight.

Don't worry. I'm fine.

The note was in English. He was slipping into English more and more often lately, both in speaking and writing. It was a sign that he was really distracted.

As I waited, I spent a long time staring out the window, first into the yard and then out to the horizon. There was still no sign of Danny when I went to bed. It was nearly midnight when I heard his car pull in.

"Where were you?" I asked as he walked into the room holding a paper bag. Before I'd even finished asking the question, I knew the answer. "Oh, God, Danny. No! Don't. Please, please, don't do this!" Rage boiled up within me like lava inside a volcano.

"If I'm going to die anyway, it might as well at least be painless." He sat down on the floor and shook the contents of the bag out beside him.

My anger evaporated as quickly as it had come, turning to fear and worry. "That stuff really will kill you, I hope you know," I whispered, pointing to the foil packet of white powder.

"Heroin itself isn't actually harmful," he protested. "Most of the damage comes from the stuff they cut it with."

"Which is also in there."

"In this crap, yeah," he said. "But I ordered some better-quality stuff that doesn't mess up your body as much. They said I could pick it up next week. It'll be enough to last me until I die."

"God, Danny!" I cried. "What's happened to us? Am I supposed to praise you now because you can afford better drugs than the rest of the world?"

"You're not supposed to do anything. This is my decision." He went and got a coffee spoon, dripped a little citric acid onto it, and shook the white powder on top. Then he held a lighter underneath the spoon.

"Danny!" I screamed at him. "Quit this shit!"

"I'm not going to ask your permission, and you're not going to be able to stop me, either!" He pulled out a disposable syringe and a needle, and then he put them together.

Suddenly, I began to panic. "Do you even know how to do that? It's dangerous!"

"Did you know," he said as he drew the now-liquid heroin into the syringe, "that the most dangerous thing about fixing is that you might contract HIV? Funny, huh?"

"Hilarious. Do you know how to do that?" I repeated.

"Even half-dead junkies can manage it. It can't be all that hard."

"You can't shoot that stuff right away. It could kill you. You're supposed to just smoke it at first." At least, I thought that was how it worked. Hadn't the girl in *Zoo Station* said that at some point?

"I'm sure as hell not going to start smoking. That's gross. Anyway, this is such a low dose that it won't be a problem. Plus, I'm just injecting it under my skin, not straight into my bloodstream, so the effect won't be as strong."

I shook my head desperately. "You really have lost your mind."

"I know, but dying is easier when you're crazy." Danny pinched the skin on his right forearm, stuck the needle into the fold, and emptied the entire syringe without hesitation.

We waited for several minutes. Nothing happened.

"How do you feel?" I asked after a while.

Danny shrugged, more slowly than usual. "Pretty dazed. Everything's kind of surreal. And I'm nauseous."

"Serves you right," I grumbled, but he wasn't listening anymore. He dropped over onto his side and lay there, half curled up, on the floor. He was in about the same position as Leika, who was lying in her basket on the other side of the room. Both were asleep. It was restless sleep, not very deep, but at least they were sleeping. I wanted to sleep, too—to dive into another world and forget everything around me. Part of me wished that Danny had given me some of that stuff. If it helped you forget even half as well as he'd once said, then I wanted some, too.

It was nearly dawn when I took my blanket off the bed and joined him on the floor. Despite how warm it was inside the house, he was ice-cold. I snuggled up close to him and threw the blanket over us both. It was the first and only time he didn't wake up when I lay down beside him.

Leika got up from her spot as well and curled up against Danny's other side, as if she wanted to help me warm him up. I watched the two of them, listening to their breathing as I waited impatiently for the sweet relief of sleep. Not daring to take my eyes off Danny, I kept dozing off and immediately startling awake again. I was too afraid he might have been poisoned the way Christina had.

It was almost noon when he finally opened his eyes. He'd never slept that late, in all the time I'd known him.

"How do you feel?" I asked immediately.

302

Danny stared at me blankly for a minute or two before finally managing to sit up slowly. He shook his head in confusion. "I feel like I got trampled by a herd of water buffalo. What happened last night?"

I gave him an accusatory stare. "You shot yourself up full of that crap!" I pointed helplessly at the remains of his drug binge.

"Yeah, I remember that. But after that? What happened after that? I can't remember a thing."

"You went to sleep. That's all."

"I slept until now? That's crazy. Sleeping tablets are a joke compared to this stuff." In fact, he still seemed really out of it. It wasn't like him to take so long to wake up.

"Danny, please don't ever do that again," I begged. "Please. I sat up half the night worried sick about you."

"I haven't slept that well in years," he said evasively, wobbling to his feet. "If you need me, I'll be in the bathroom—I'm sick as a dog. I guess I need to think all of this over some more."

Chapter Forty-Three

October 2002

Someone was shaking my shoulder, and I resisted, trying not to wake up. I'd been sleeping soundly and peacefully, dreaming something nice that I couldn't remember anymore. All I knew was that I wanted to get back to that dream. I hadn't been sleeping very well lately, let alone having nice dreams. But the shaking didn't stop.

"Ducky. Wake up, Ducky."

"Mmph. What time is it?"

"Half past one."

"In the afternoon?" My eyes snapped open in horror.

"In the morning."

"God, let me sleep, then," I groaned, burying my head in my pillow.

"It's a beautiful night," he whispered. "It's totally clear, and it's warm enough that you don't need a jacket."

"And you want me to get up in the middle of the night for that?"

"Yeah."

"Jesus, Danny… You really are a lunatic."

"I know that," he replied quietly. "I've never claimed otherwise. Are you getting up or what?"

I rose to my feet, tugged one of Danny's sweatshirts over my head, and put on my sneakers. Grumpily, I followed him into the yard, knowing he wouldn't let me rest until I did. Leika joyfully hopped along after us. Danny had spread a blanket out on the grass, and now he stretched out on it, folding his arms behind his head and gazing up at the stars.

How often did he do this?

It really was an unusually mild night for mid-October. I laid my head on his stomach, and we sat there staring out into the night sky in silence: Danny lost in thought, me trying not to fall asleep.

"I have to tell you something…" he began. I straightened up. Danny sat up, as well, pulling me in between his knees. He wrapped his arms around me and laid his chin on my shoulder.

"What?" My stomach cramped up. Involuntarily, I drew my bare legs in to my chest.

"The car accident didn't…just…happen," he admitted in a whisper. Subconsciously, I'd known as much for a long time.

"What really happened?"

Danny took a deep breath. "Something happened to me. From one moment to the next."

"What? Oh, God! Like how?" Was this exactly what I'd feared?

"It was like something broke inside my head, like the string on a bow. And I was paralyzed for minutes afterward. I was completely aware the whole time, I saw my car go off the road and felt it flip, but I couldn't react. My whole body was just frozen."

I squeezed my eyes shut. "Danny, that might have something to do with your disease." Ironically, we never called it by its name. There was no "AIDS"—there was only "your disease."

He held me tighter. "Ducky, I know it has something to do with that. I know my body, and something's very, very wrong with it. That's why I didn't want to go to America with you. I was afraid we'd be out in the middle of nowhere, and it would happen again, maybe even worse next time. And then you'd be totally alone on an unfamiliar continent."

"You should have told me that right away at the hospital!"

He nodded. "I know, but you had your exams coming up. Not exactly a convenient time for such an awful diagnosis. I just wanted to be sure you wouldn't be distracted."

"Excuse me? You risked your life because of my stupid exams? What planet are you on?"

Danny remained completely calm. "Jessica, I'm as good as dead. You're all that matters now."

"Stop that!" I shouted. "It could have been something totally harmless. A stroke, for example."

He scoffed derisively. "So we're at the point where having a stroke at the age of twenty-two sounds like something to be happy about?"

"Don't keep assuming the worst. It could have been a coincidence." I knew it was a weak argument as soon as I said it. Where were all the straws when I needed to grasp at them?

"It wasn't a coincidence. My T-cell count went down fast between February and August."

"Back at the hospital, you told me it was okay. Were you lying?"

"They were okay, but they were a lot lower than normal. They went from over 500 to around 250. In such a short time."

"Because of Christina," I murmured. "It's because of Christina."

"Who are we kidding?" he blurted out. "It's finally happening. There's no denying it anymore."

Deep down, of course, I knew he was right. His body had always been his greatest asset, in every respect. He knew himself, and he knew when something was off. If he hadn't been absolutely sure about what was happening, he would never have done heroin…and I never would have let him.

We were world champions at pushing things out of our minds, and now we were battling for time. For each month, each week. Someday, we'd be fighting for each day.

"You need to go to the hospital," I said. "Get yourself all checked out, start HAART therapy.[2]"

"I have a photoshoot next week. The money's too good to cancel. I'll go in after that."

"A photoshoot? That's not important! Go in on Monday!"

"I'll go next week. A couple days either way won't matter. I'll just do this one last job, and then I'll quit."

"Why do you have to quit?"

"Because I'm a druggie with AIDS, and eventually they'll see that. Anyway, I don't feel like doing it anymore. I have too much money as it is. I mean, I bought a

---

[2] *Highly Active Antiretroviral Therapy involves treating the HIV patient with a combination of at least three different substances. Successful HAART therapy inhibits virus reproduction. Reducing the patient's viral load reduces the risk of AIDS developing, alleviates HIV-related symptoms, and restores the immune system long-term, if not always completely.*

new car even though I'm about to die. Tina doesn't need an apartment anymore, and there's more than enough there for you. So why should I?" His voice was sad, but he didn't seem frustrated.

"I don't like it when you get in this mood," I said petulantly.

"I'm just being realistic, Ducky!"

"Go to the goddamn hospital and get the goddamn therapy instead of sitting around here whining!" I shrieked at him yet again, knowing full well that this was a long way from whining. He was being completely levelheaded about the whole thing, resigned to the inevitable in a way that frightened me.

"I will," he assured me. "At the end of next week."

"Monday!"

"End of next week."

I smacked him furiously. "How about you think about me a little bit once in a while?"

Danny got angry then. Really angry. Angrier than I'd ever seen him get at me. He rose to his feet as well, eyes glittering. I'd never thought of his eyes as cold or icy, but at that moment, they were. "You're actually asking why I'm not thinking of you?"

"Yes, goddammit!" My voice sounded hysterical. Leika fled into the house. "Go to the hospital! Stop being so goddamn egotistical!"

He stepped up to me and laid his index finger against my chest, the way Christina had once done. "You're all I think about," he said dryly. "For a long time now, everything I've done has been about you only. You're the only reason I'm even still here!"

"If you want to go back to Atlanta, then be my guest. I won't stop you!" I bit down on my lips until they began to bleed. Why were we fighting again?

"You're the reason I'm still *breathing*!"

"Leave me alone!" I wailed.

Danny spun on his heel and stalked off into the apartment. I knew he was going to go do more heroin. It had been two weeks since the first time, but he'd done it again last week. I sank down onto the grass in despair. It was too warm out for me to hope that I could just freeze to death right here.

After a while, Danny came out again and sat down beside where I was lying. "I'm sorry," he said, stroking my hair affectionately. "I didn't say anything for so long because I didn't want you to fail your exams. I don't want you screwing up your life because of me."

I pretended to be asleep, trying to ignore the burning in my throat that came from holding back tears. All those weeks, he'd been alone with this terrible secret, alone with his fear, just because of my stupid test. I felt horrible—I wanted to curl up and die right there.

After a few moments, Danny lifted me in his arms and carried me inside.

***

Danny had his primary care doctor arrange for him to be admitted to the hospital, and we set off six days later, bags packed, in miserable moods. They scheduled CT and MRI scans, as well as X-rays of his head and his broken ribs, which were still causing him pain. They also arranged for several blood samples to be taken and sent off to a large external laboratory. Basically, they were going to check him from head to toe, until they figured out what had caused his episode in August.

They also decided to start him on HAART therapy. In the best-case scenario, it would fight off the virus so well that his HIV-related symptoms would go away and his immune system would stabilize long-term. Danny thought the therapy was unnecessary, since he didn't have any symptoms, and he didn't expect the therapy to do anything for him besides cause side effects. His primary care doctor had recommended the therapy solely because his T-cell count had dropped below 250—they always decided to start therapy based on lab counts, not on how the patient felt, which Danny argued was ridiculous. But I insisted he go along with it, firmly convinced that it would stop the disease. At least one of us had to keep the hope alive.

We went to his room and unpacked his things together, still not saying anything. Danny was in luck: the other bed in his room was empty.

"I hate it here," he grouched, breaking our silence.

"You're doing this, and I don't want to hear another word about it!" I was hell-bent on getting my way this time. If he didn't want another argument on his hands, he'd have to stay here.

Danny stuck his tongue out in between his teeth, crossed his eyes, and imitated me. I picked up one of the bananas lying on the table and chucked it at him. To my relief, he caught it effortlessly in mid-air—he still had his old reflexes. I was used to being able to throw anything at him without worrying that it would hit him, but now I realized I should probably be more careful about that.

"Great," he moaned. "Now you're throwing monkey food at me. What next? You got a little bow tie for me to wear? Maybe a collar and leash? I'm already being used for lab experiments." He'd always had a dark sense of humor, but it had been a lot less cynical before.

They took countless blood samples that day. Urine samples, too—it was probably standard procedure to drug-test HIV patients. Even though Danny hadn't done any heroin in days, and he'd only ever injected it under his skin, they found traces of it anyway. I was almost glad they did, because he'd never have told them of his own accord, and I thought it might be important for them to know when treating him. They were planning on starting HAART therapy that very evening, and while he was in the hospital, the medications would all be administered intravenously to make them more tolerable.

A nurse came in and introduced herself as Regina. She was tall and slender, with long, dark hair, no more than five years older than Danny. He seemed to like her immediately, which gave me hope. He had to get through all of this one way or another, as much as he hated it.

I stayed with him all day. At one point, Nurse Regina returned to insert his IV. She automatically used his left arm, though that was the one Danny probably needed more. He didn't say anything.

I knew safety came first, but it still hurt my soul to see her put on disposable gloves before inserting the needle into Danny's vein.

They're all acting like he's contaminated...

He is *contaminated,* my inner voice shot back.

"That'll stay in for as long as you're here," she told him. "If it starts to hurt, just tell me, and we'll switch arms." That would never happen. Danny would grit his teeth and take it all without ever complaining. Nurse Regina hung the IV bag on the hook above his bed before removing her gloves and stroking Danny's forearm tenderly, a friendly gesture that stayed in my memory—probably because it was one of the few instances of human kindness I witnessed in the hospital staff. Everyone besides Nurse Regina treated him like an object they were studying, not like a human being desperate for help.

Later on, the doctor came into the room. He greeted us, flipped through Danny's file, and shook his head. "Heroin addict," he remarked dryly. "Well, you shouldn't be surprised."

I drew in a sharp, angry breath, but Danny shot me a warning look, and I held my tongue. I don't know whether he liked the doctor's version better, or if he just assumed nobody would believe his story. Out of respect for his wishes, I wrapped myself in a cloak of silence, furiously biting my lip.

"If you experience any withdrawal symptoms, let us know right away and we'll put you on methadone."

"I don't think that will be necessary," Danny replied politely. "I'm not addicted to it, I've only done it a couple times."

"Of course!" the doctor agreed with a patronizing smile. "All addicts say that. That's the problem with addiction."

Danny sighed, capitulating. "If I need anything, I'll let you know." I didn't like the way he was just accepting whatever these people assumed. Where had his stubbornness gone?

"We'll X-ray your ribs tomorrow, and then we can do the CT scan after that, and your MRI appointment is scheduled for next Friday."

"Thanks," Danny said, and the doctor wished us a good evening without any real friendliness behind it and left the room.

"You can do this," I told Danny, sitting down on his bed. He was chewing his fingernails and looking at me helplessly.

"What happened?" he asked. "My numbers were all great for years, everything was okay, and then all of a sudden everything went to hell. Why?"

Tina!

"Maybe it would always have seemed that way to us. Even if this hadn't happened for another eight years, we would have felt like it had been sudden."

"It's because of Tina," he said. He'd known too, of course. "Losing her threw me for such a loop that the disease found a foothold. My body was too busy grieving to keep up its defenses."

I nodded, pursing my lips. People were prone to developing physical illnesses after becoming psychologically unstable. Even harmless little colds were more likely after highly stressful situations. When people were spiritually in balance and happy with their lives, they had much better chances of staying healthy.

Danny took my hand and drew me close. "I'm so sorry," he whispered. "I didn't do this on purpose. I wish so much that I could have stayed with you longer."

***

"How are you doing?" I asked when I came to the hospital on Wednesday. Danny had adjusted the bed to a sitting position and was staring out the window.

"Wonderful. Puking is a whole new way to start the day. I'm sure it's a lot more effective than working out."

"Be patient, Danny," I said. "As soon as you've gotten used to the medication, that will stop." I sat down beside him and leaned in to give him a kiss, but he turned away. He'd never done that before in all the time I'd known him.

"My ribs still aren't healed," he said. "One still has a big crack in it. The doctors say it might stay that way. My body's too busy dealing with the therapy and can't be bothered with unimportant things like ribs." He shrugged his free shoulder. "Whatever, who needs intact bones?"

"Danny, stop," I warned him.

"Oh, right, and my numbers got worse, of course. My T-cell count's nearly down to two hundred. Do you know what that means?"

I shook my head. I wanted to run out of the room screaming, but instead, I focused on trying to swallow the lump that had suddenly formed in my throat. I couldn't, though—it was too big.

"That means I'll probably develop full-blown AIDS any day now. The opportunistic infections should be just around the corner. Isn't that great?" He raised the arm without the IV in the air and did a fist pump. "AIDS at twenty-two! I did it! Isn't life wonderful?"

"Danny, stop," I said weakly.

"Stop what?" He raised his hands questioningly.

"Just stop. Stop being so cynical!" I wanted to yell at him, but I was completely drained, and it came out in a whine.

"But you haven't heard the best part yet!"

"What else?" I tried in vain to brace myself, swallowing the lump in my throat over and over. But it never went away. Ever. Years later, I went to several different doctors about it and had my thyroid, tonsils, and cervical spine examined, only to discover that it was psychological.

Abruptly, his mood changed. His cynical rage vanished, and he seemed to collapse into himself, burying his face in his hands. I immediately wished he'd go back to being cynical. "The CT scan found something."

"What?" I couldn't get anything else out—my voice simply failed.

"They don't know yet. The MRI on Friday will tell us more. In the meantime, they want to do a viral analysis of my spinal fluid. They think it's probably an infection."

"Okay." I forced myself to breathe. "Don't panic. We'll just wait for the MRI. If it's an infection, that's not bad. Infections are treatable."

He nodded.

"Did the doctors say it was bad?" Was I screeching? Why was I screeching?

"They just said I'd have to wait for the results. They don't have any idea."

Great. Now we were going to sit around wondering for two days. How were we supposed to take all this waiting? "Okay. I'll be here. And Jörg is coming over later. I'll tell him to be here, too."

He nodded again, fighting back the tears welling in his eyes. "This isn't the way I pictured it," he whispered. "I've gone through all the different ways to die in my head. Lung infection, tuberculosis…hell, even the flu. My biggest fear was getting that Kaposi sarcoma. If other people could see I was sick, that would be more than I could take. But now it's all turning out way different. I'm going to die of a brain tumor."

"Who said anything about a tumor?" I cried. "They were talking about an infection! They can treat infections."

Danny scoffed. "Jessica." He took my hands and gazed at me with a pleading expression. "I'm so scared of what's going to happen. I'm completely freaking out!"

So am I! Trust me, so am I!

"You're not alone." I squeezed his hand, scooting closer. "We'll get through this together. Whatever happens, I'll be here for you. You're not alone."

Danny began to sob. He drew his knees up to his chest, laid his head against them, and cried, his shoulders shaking uncontrollably. Helpless, I stroked his back, his hair, but he just didn't stop.

Neither of us heard the knock, so Jörg simply let himself in. He blinked in alarm when he saw us. "The CT scan found something," I explained quietly.

"Shit."

Danny stared silently at his hands.

"The MRI is Friday. They won't know any more until then." *Please come*, I mouthed silently.

Jörg nodded to me as he sat down on Danny's bed and put his arms around him. The show of affection only made Danny cry harder. He was gasping for air, nearly hyperventilating. "I'll call a nurse," Jörg decided. "They should give him something to calm him down."

"That's stupid," Danny spat. "I don't need anything to calm me down. I'm already dying! Don't I get to at least cry about it?"

Jörg grabbed his shoulder and gave him a penetrating look. "You can cry," he said. "As much as you want, for as long as you want. But when you're done crying, you pull yourself together and continue this fight. Got it?"

"What for?"

Jörg shook him almost roughly. "I asked if you got it."

"Yeah, got it," Danny sniffled. Yet again, I was amazed at how well Jörg was able to handle him.

Just then, the hospital telephone on the nightstand rang. Danny shook his head, indicating that he didn't want to take the call, so Jörg answered it. "Hello?" he said. "Just a moment, I'll ask him." He hit mute, took a deep breath, and turned to Danny. "It's your father."

"What the fuck?" Danny wailed. "How does he know I'm here?"

"Your mom probably told him," Jörg pointed out.

"Uh-huh. And how does *she* know where I am?"

"She's your mother, Danny," Jörg said. "I had to tell her. She should be given a chance to visit you."

"She won't come anyway!" Danny scoffed again. His eyelashes were wet with tears, his eyes bloodshot. "And what does *he* want with me?" He gestured at the phone in disgust.

"He says he wants to talk to you."

Danny stretched out his hand and waggled his fingers. Jörg handed him the receiver and unmuted the call.

"What?" Danny snarled into the receiver. After a while, he added, "I'll see you in hell, you fucking asshole!" Then he threw the phone down.

***

Somehow, I managed to survive until Friday. I was floating around in a kind of trance, spending every free moment with Danny, secretly sleeping in his bed at night.

One night, my parents invited me out to dinner to celebrate my exam results. They waited for me for almost two hours and tried to call several times, but I was at the hospital with my phone off and had completely forgotten about them.

"What on Earth is wrong with you?" It was a question I had gotten used to hearing from my mother.

I gave the same answer as always: "Nothing." What was I supposed to say?

My boyfriend, whom you guys love so much, has AIDS and is in the hospital. He'll probably die soon, just like his drug addict of a best friend did at the beginning of the year. Oh yeah, he's started doing heroin, too, but that's not how he got HIV. His father gave it to him. There was nothing he could do about it.

They'd never believe a word. I hadn't taken him to my parents' house since Christina died. My parents assumed I was so out of it because he and I were fighting all the time, breaking up and getting back together. I let them keep on thinking that. It was better than the truth.

Contrary to all expectations, Marina came to visit Danny on Thursday evening. Ricky was there, too, and he and I went out to the hall to let the two of them be alone. She talked about Liam nonstop, but at least she came.

***

Jörg, Ricky, and I waited in Danny's hospital room while they did the MRI. It took forever. A radiologist had come in all the way from Stuttgart to look at his X-rays, which we found very alarming.

"Why is this taking so long?" I asked for the fifth time, chewing my thumbnail.

"I don't know," Jörg replied nervously. He'd been pacing up and down the room for over an hour now, and it was driving me crazy. Ricky kept going out to smoke one cigarette after another, something he usually only did when he was out clubbing.

After what felt like a thousand years, Nurse Regina wheeled Danny's bed into the room. She squeezed his hand briefly and patted his shoulder. "The doctors will be right in to talk about everything with you." She smiled.

"Thanks," Danny said.

"Danny!" My voice was shaking. "How was it?"

"A breathtaking experience. Claustrophobia makes it even better. Really gives you an idea of how you'll feel later on, in the coffin."

Why can't you just stop that?

A group of five doctors came in then, four men and a woman. The mere sight of them was enough to make us all panic. All but one were wearing the blue coats that marked them as chief physicians. They positioned themselves around Danny's bed, stacks of files and photos in their hands. Danny sat up straight as a board, watching them tensely and trying to keep calm. I just hoped he wouldn't flip out.

"Mr. Taylor," one of them said. "We have your results."

"Yeah?" Even in that one word, I could hear his voice trembling.

The doctor's gaze wandered from me to Ricky, and then to Jörg. "Is it okay to discuss this in their presence?"

"Otherwise they wouldn't be here," Danny growled.

The doctor cleared his throat. "Well, we were fortunate to have the support of our colleague from Stuttgart. The images weren't easy to interpret. HIV-related leukoencephalopathy can be difficult to identify for sure, but we're fairly sure that what we're dealing with here is progressive multifocal leukoencephalopathy, brought on by your underlying condition.

"PML is very rare, and almost always occurs in people with immunodeficiencies, such as HIV or multiple sclerosis." He peered at Danny, who was sitting silently, arms pressed against his body. "The strange thing is that your T-cell count is still quite good. PML normally doesn't develop until a patient's immune system is already weakened. That's not the case with you, which is why you haven't had any HIV-related symptoms. But just because something is highly unusual doesn't mean we can rule it out. Nothing is impossible in medicine," he added.

315

"Great," Danny said. "So what does that mean for me?" He was outwardly calm, but his posture was stiff, and his fingernails were digging into his bare arms. His black T-shirt emphasized how pale he'd gotten as well.

"We don't expect you to experience any more episodes like you had in August, but we still strongly recommend that you stop driving. Other symptoms will likely begin in the near future, but they will come on very gradually."

"What symptoms?"

"There are different types," one of the other doctors explained. "Some people experience language deficits, memory loss, or blindness. In others, it affects the peripheral nervous system, resulting in weakness, tremors, muscle twitches, or loss of motor skills. Personality changes and panic attacks can occur as well. Based on your episode in August, Mr. Taylor, we assume that your nervous system is affected, but that's pure speculation."

"Sounds like a great time either way," Danny remarked dryly, shrugging. "Who cares? You take what you get."

"Is it operable?" I asked.

The doctor gave me a sympathetic look. "This is an infection, there's no way of operating. We could try to push a few of the lesions back, but that would involve a great deal of risk. The surgery would cause irreparable brain damage. And the patient might fall into a coma, or might never wake up from the surgery at all."

"So then what happens now?" Jörg asked.

"As different as the two types of PML are, they generally end the same. Dementia, hallucinations, seizures, possibly total paralysis. Eventually, most patients end up in a persistent vegetative state or need to be put into a medically induced coma, and then they don't wake up. Some die before that as a result of a stroke or a brain hemorrhage, or because their respiratory system becomes paralyzed."

Jump out the window, Jessica! You're on the sixth floor, you'd have a good shot at dying immediately!

"How will you treat him?" Through the fog in my brain, I heard that Jörg's voice was breaking as well. Someone took my hand. It was Ricky.

"Unfortunately, we don't have a lot of options." It was a doctor who had remained silent up until that point. "We'll have to hope that the HAART therapy works and his T-cell count remains stable. That's the only way we'll be able to slow the progression of the disease."

316

"How long do I have?" Danny asked.

The doctor ignored his question. "We'll also start him on risperidone and camptothecin," he told Jörg. "They can cause very serious side effects, though, so he'll have to remain in the hospital for the duration of the treatment. But together with the other medications he's already on, they could help."

"Could?" Jörg looked like he might punch the doctor. "*Could* help?"

"Nobody knows for sure. There haven't been any large-scale or long-term studies. We could also try putting him on topotecan, but that would be highly experimental, and also controversial. It may have even resulted in some deaths."

"How long?" Danny repeated, looking impatient. He kept running his hand through his hair.

"Mr. Taylor, may I introduce Dr. Ohrnberger? He's our psychologist, he'll be helping you during all this."

Danny scoffed. "Oh my God, I don't need a shrink. What I need is a miracle."

"Think it over," the doctor advised him. "He'll be available any time you need to talk."

"How long?" Danny asked for the third time. He was about to lose all patience.

"Three to fifteen months."

Silence…

"What if the treatment works?" Jörg's voice sounded like it was coming from another planet.

Three months…

Jump, Jessica! Jump out the goddamn window! Do it now!

"Then it'll be fifteen months. That's the best prognosis we can expect at this time," was the doctor's monotone reply.

My brain twisted up in knots and then, with computer-like objectivity, determined that fifteen months was more than three.

"Good God," Jörg said. Ricky released my hand and walked to the window. Did he want to jump, too?

Danny's going to die!

Suddenly, my throat closed up. I stormed over to Danny's bed and threw myself across it, grabbing Danny and clinging to him tightly. I felt him pull me close, felt his fingers clenching my sweater.

What am I even doing here?

"Bring the girl out," one of the doctors said.

The girl? Do they mean me? Who am I, anyway?

"She's in shock, bring her out with you."

Had I been screaming?

Someone tugged on my arm. I clung to Danny even more tightly, and Danny held me close. "Let go of her, goddammit!"

Two of the doctors started pulling me away. Suddenly, Ricky was there, unhooking me from Danny. "I'll take her with me," he said quietly, and Danny let go.

"Out!" Danny suddenly cried into the silence. "Everyone out!"

Ricky led me past the window.

Jump already!

"I said, everyone out!" Danny snapped. He threw his blanket on the floor and pointed to the door. "I don't have time to say everything three times!"

Is he making jokes? Like always?

Someone had thrown a water glass at the wall. It could only have been Danny.

Three months! I'll be alone! Alone. ALONE! Alone...

"*Get out, all of you!*" Danny screamed. "OUT!"

***

They gave me something to help me sleep and kept me there overnight. Jörg told me the next day that I'd thrown myself to the ground, screaming. I didn't remember any of it.

I tried desperately to go back and see Danny, but they wouldn't allow it. He'd flown into a rage and spent the entire day throwing any and all hospital staff out of his room. They refused to allow me in there, and they never took their eyes off of me for a second. They probably didn't want to risk having two crazies in the same room.

Jörg wanted to drive me home—to my parents' house—but I didn't have the strength to explain to them where I'd left my car, so he took me to Danny's apartment instead. Jörg stayed the whole night, catching a few hours of sleep on

318

the couch. What would I have done without him? Danny'd been right when he'd said Jörg was the best thing that could ever have happened to him. Even though Danny hadn't needed a legal guardian for years, even though he wasn't being paid to do any of this and it actually wasn't his problem at all, Jörg was there. I was so glad he was—without him, I knew, Danny and I would be completely alone in the world. Without Jörg, I would have gone crazy that night: alone in the apartment I had once been so happy in. Back when it was still filled with laughter and life. With optimism and excitement. With Christina and Danny.

I tried to call Danny about once every minute, but he didn't answer. The nurses told me they'd given him something to help him sleep. They'd sedated him.

They didn't let me visit until the next afternoon. Jörg had dropped me off at the hospital in the morning on his way to work, promising to return in the evening. I spent hours pacing up and down the hallways, waiting. I didn't even manage to let go of my car keys—I needed something to hold on to. By the time they finally let me into the room, I was nearly out of my mind.

Danny was sitting on the bed, arms crossed despite the IV, staring out the window as always. A Nurse Angela was with him, trying to reassure him.

Where's Nurse Regina?

I would have much rather had her there than this other nurse, to whom neither of us really felt a connection.

"Oh, come on, Danny," she said, smiling at him tenderly. "It's not that bad here. We'll all try our very best, but you'll need to put yourself in our hands and do as we say!"

Oh, no! My inner voice sounded the alarm immediately. *Wrong choice of words, and completely the wrong tone.*

Danny was practically hysterical as it was—I knew he wouldn't be able to handle this much intrusiveness. Giving up control like this.

The nurse cheerfully winked at him and left the room. Danny still didn't say anything, but I could see the wheels turning in his head. He gritted his teeth.

"Don't do anything stupid, Danny," I said quietly.

As if on command, he threw the blanket back, swung his legs out of the bed, and yanked the IV needle out of his arm, pressing his pillow against the crook of his elbow for a few moments to stop the bleeding.

I let out a groan and reached for his wrist, but he raised his arms defensively. "Let me be, please."

I obeyed. In moments like these, I just had to leave him alone. There would be no getting through to him anyway. I knew him well enough to know that he wouldn't talk to me now.

Moving quickly, he stuffed his things into his bag, pulled on a hoodie, and slipped into his sneakers. Then he left the room and headed toward the stairs. I trudged along behind him in resignation. At the end of the hallway, he walked straight into Nurse Angela's arms.

"Mr. Taylor, where are you going? You need to stay in bed!"

"I'm going home. Give me the letter that says I'm discharging myself against doctor recommendations. I'll sign it."

Nurse Angela gave him a friendly but firm smile. "No, no. You're not going anywhere. I won't allow it."

"Try and stop me."

She promptly grabbed his arm. Danny simply shook her off and began walking again, but Angela wouldn't give up that easily. She ran to catch up with him and grabbed him from behind, wrapping her arms around him. Frantically, she shouted to another nurse to call the chief physician.

"Let me go!" Danny shouted, but she remained stubborn. I could see his expression changing, his rage gradually turning to panic. He felt like a trapped wild animal, I knew. Suddenly, I felt completely sorry for him, and I reached for the nurse's wrist.

"Leave him alone, goddammit!" I cried, roughly yanking Angela away from him. Danny shot me a brief look of extreme gratitude before taking the car keys from my hand and running for the stairs.

"Aren't you his wife?" Nurse Angela snapped.

"I am." The less explaining I had to do, the better. This little white lie would help us out of here.

"Then why are you letting him leave?" She furrowed her brow, energetically stomping the floor with her Birkenstock. "This is his only chance. He'll die otherwise."

"He's going to die either way!" I shouted at her. I had to restrain myself back from hitting her. "And if he'd rather do it outside of this pathetic hospital, that's his choice!"

The chief physician arrived, but I fled down the steps as well, trying to catch up to Danny. But when I got to the parking lot, my car had already disappeared.

Dammit, Danny!

Fortunately, I managed to hail a taxi immediately, and I frantically gave the driver Danny's address. Back at the apartment, my car was still nowhere in sight, so I went inside, grabbed Danny's car keys, and took his car. I knew where I'd find him. My intuition always led me back to him. He'd never had trouble finding me, either. Sometimes it felt like he could read my mind.

I was right: the Mercedes was parked at the old mill, near the paddock. I left Danny's BMW beside it.

He was sitting cross-legged underneath the big linden tree in the meadow. His pony was lying next to him, letting him scratch her ears. As I approached, she stood up and trotted contentedly back to her stall.

Danny began picking daisies so that he wouldn't have to look me in the eye. Slowly, I sank down onto the grass. "Hey."

"Hey," he replied tonelessly, not looking up.

The evening sky was fading to red. We sat across from one another in silence. After the devastating diagnosis we'd gotten two days ago, what was left to say?

All of Danny's attention was devoted to plucking the petals off one of the daisies.

"You're not planning on going back to the hospital?" I asked. I already knew the answer—I just wanted to break the silence.

"I don't think it makes sense."

I nodded. "I thought you might say that."

"What good would it do?" He turned his reddened eyes to mine. I couldn't remember them being any other way anymore.

"It would be a chance, at least," I said, not sure I believed it myself. Would fifteen months in a hospital really be better than a couple months at home?

We lapsed into silence again for a while, until suddenly he announced with total conviction, "I can't do it, Jessica!"

A chill ran down my spine. "Can't do what?"

He gazed into my eyes. "Hand myself over to strangers in the hospital. Eventually, I won't be able to do anything on my own. They'll be feeding me, washing me, dressing me. You know? I'll be at their mercy. I can't stand the thought of that."

"Is that what this is about? You're afraid the things your dad did to you might happen again?"

"Yeah, that too."

I understood his worries, unfounded as they were. "That won't happen," I assured him. "They're hospital staff, they don't do things like that."

"It was my father," he said quietly, plucking his next daisy. "Fathers don't do things like that, either."

I winced and laid my hand on his arm. "It won't happen again. I'll watch out for you and make sure of it. I promise."

"Okay," he said. "Supposing I accept that. I go back and let them treat me. Where will it end? Sooner or later—probably sooner, you heard them—I'll need full-time care. I won't be able to get out of bed, might not be able to talk or think. Ducky, you know me. I love sports, movement, action. What good would living like that do me?"

"Maybe it won't end up like that."

"Oh, come on." Danny laughed quietly. "Who are you kidding? What do you think is going to happen? Do you think Jesus Christ himself is going to waltz into the hospital and miraculously heal me, and then I'll just stroll on home, perfectly healthy?"

"Probably not," I admitted.

"One more time for the record: I'm going to end up needing full-time care."

I wanted to contradict him, but he was right. Who was I kidding, apart from myself? "Okay, then, that's how it is." I tried to sound composed.

"Do you really want that? Do you want to come to the ICU day after day, read aloud to me, change my IV? Then go home and darn a couple of socks, and do it all over again the next day? Do you, at twenty years old, really want to watch your life partner die? Is that what you want?"

Was that what I wanted?

"Who can guarantee that I'll even die quickly?" he went on. "I'm not very lucky in things like that—otherwise I'd have died in that car crash, like I should have. But no, I had to survive. My guardian angel probably would have been a lot more useful to someone else, but as usual, nobody asked me. With my luck, it'll be drawn out for years. Do you really want to do that to yourself?"

"Danny. I made my decision. Door number two, you remember? It will always be door number two!"

His eyes found mine, held them. "I won't let you. My life has already been ruined. I'm not going to ruin yours as well." Then his gaze shifted to the setting sun off in the distance. "I always wanted children. A son I could be close to. A daughter that looks like you. We would have given our children everything. Whenever they were worried or upset, they'd be able to snuggle up in bed with me, without ever having to worry that I would touch them inappropriately." Danny's voice faltered, and he swallowed hard. "We would have been really great parents."

"Yeah, we would have," I whispered, my eyes filling with tears.

"I never had a chance in hell," he suddenly blurted out. "A lot of people claim that everyone is responsible for their own lives, but is that really true? I've accomplished so much in my life, and if I'd had time, I would have been able to accomplish a whole lot more. But I don't have time. Fate didn't give me anything like the chance to start a family. My dad destroyed my future and my life when he started climbing into bed with me." Tears rolled down his cheeks. He wiped them away with his sleeve. "But your life isn't ruined, Jessica." He looked at me intently. "I want you to have everything you want. A little house in the country, a husband, children... You'll have wonderful children. I'm not letting you waste your life on terminal care."

"Danny, I—"

He put his finger against my lips. His eyes glowed with determination. "I'm. Not. Letting. You. Just because you fell in love with the wrong guy once in your life and made the wrong choice."

"I didn't make the wrong choice!"

He ignored my protest. "Please, promise me that you'll never stand at my grave and cry over me. I want the same agreement with you as I had with Christina. Be happy without me."

"I don't think I can."

"Make a big bonfire. Burn everything you got from me. Find a nice, caring man and be happy with him. Forget you and I were ever together. Promise me you'll go right on living as if I had never existed!"

"Danny—"

"Promise me." He hypnotized me with his inhumanly blue eyes. Suddenly, he knew how to do that again.

"I promise."

"Good!" He gave me a kiss on the lips, looking satisfied, and thought for a moment. "I'm going to die," he said. "I accepted that a long time ago. I'm just so sorry that I dragged you into it. But I'm also infinitely grateful that you stayed at my side. I never dreamed I'd have that." He laid his hand on my cheek. "Thank you for that."

I pressed my face against his hand. "Thank you," I said quietly. "I've never lived so intensely as I did these past three years. I've learned so much about life. This will shape me forever."

He nodded, pressing his lips together, and withdrew his hand. I sensed that he wanted to say something else.

"Danny? Why are we having this conversation in the dark at the stables? Why do I get the feeling you're trying to say goodbye?"

He took a deep breath. "I've accepted the fact that I have to die. I've been resigned to my fate for a while. And I'm not afraid of death, either. What I'm afraid of is forgetting who I am, who you are. I want to carry you in my heart when I die."

My throat closed up even more, and my stomach twisted.

"I don't want you to watch me waste away from this miserable disease and have those images haunting you forever. I want you to remember me the way I am now, not the way I'll be on my deathbed. When you think about me years from now, I want you to picture me the way I've always been."

I nodded earnestly. "Okay."

Smiling, he said, "I'm not going to risk it happening any other way."

"What do you mean?"

Danny took my hands in his, holding them tightly. Through his long lashes, he let his gaze travel up my body. "The whole time we've been together, I've never asked you for anything, and I didn't plan on ever doing it. But today, I have a request."

"Yes?" I didn't want to hear it. Whatever it was, if he was prefacing it like this, it couldn't be anything good. I wanted to pull my hands away and use them to cover my ears, but he held them fast. "My request is that you accept my decision."

"Which is?" I couldn't breathe. I wanted to leave, to get some air and space, but he didn't let me budge an inch.

"I want to make my own decisions about when and how I die."

"What?"

He unleashed the full, overwhelming power of his gaze and put all his desperation and pain into this one word: "Please!"

No. NO! No, no, no. NO, my inner voice shrieked when the words sank in. *NO! Never. NO!*

"Please, he repeated.

NO!

"Okay," I said tonelessly. What else was I supposed to say?

"Thank you," he whispered, finally releasing me. Immediately, I pulled my hands back and jumped up, dropping back down into the grass a few feet away. It was starting to get cold, and the grass was already damp, but that wasn't why I was shaking. The chill came from the inside—I'd have been freezing in the heat of summer. Even though it was pitch-dark by now, I could still see Danny sitting in the meadow, looking up at the stars.

I don't know how long we sat there in that paddock, together but each of us alone with their pain.

I'm not running any longer. There's no point anymore. I'm standing beside the ocean. It's dark blue, and though the waves are very tall, its gentle color draws me in. The beach is covered with large, sharp stones, but I know I have to cross it. The sky is gray, heavy as lead. I know that my life is over, know it with an absolute certainty that keeps me from being frightened. I am going to die now, and that's okay. I just have to walk into the ocean and drown.

I set off without giving it a second thought. As I walk, the path behind me crumbles away. There's no going back. It doesn't matter, though. I wouldn't have turned around anyway. Death draws me in, like a galloping wild horse I can't get off of. I reach the shore and throw myself into the waves. Immediately, the current pulls me down into the ever-darkening blue. Even though I always knew what awaited me, I am suddenly terrified, and I start to scream. No sound comes out of my mouth. The water is too dense, too blue. I can't get any air. The blue blurs into pitch-black. I scream and scream and scream...

"Jessica?" Someone was holding me tightly, pressing me close to them. I recognized Danny by his scent. I couldn't see anything, because I still had my eyes squeezed shut, wildly determined to drown. "Jessica, wake up, you're having a nightmare!" He shook me gently, and I sat up, confused.

"Where am I?"

"With me," Danny said. "In bed. You fell asleep in the meadow, so I brought you home."

"Was I that fast asleep?" I hadn't been aware of moving at all.

"Apparently. It was a long day."

"What time is it?"

"Five thirty. You have to get up soon," Danny said. "You've got work. And sometime this evening we'll have to go get my car."

Work? Was today really Monday? Friday afternoon was burned so deeply into my memory that I couldn't believe it had already been several days since then.

Then I remembered our conversation at the paddock, and I thought I was going to be sick.

"How are you?" he asked.

I scoffed, annoyed. I should have been the one asking him that question. "I feel nauseous. I'll call the office later and tell them I'm sick. I can't go in like this."

Danny nodded. I couldn't imagine ever being able to concentrate on something as banal as work ever again. Resigned, I laid back down, only to realize I couldn't fall asleep again. Danny seemed to be feeling the same—he stayed sitting up in bed, his eyes once again fixed on that point only he could see. I gazed at him for a long time. He was so unbelievably gorgeous, nobody would have ever suspected that he was deathly ill and taking hard drugs. Would I ever get tired of looking at him? Most likely not. The time we had left together would never be long enough for that.

I scooted closer and began to undress him.

As we made love, he looked into my eyes and said, "Marry me."

"What?" Completely perplexed, I pushed him a little ways off me, and he stopped moving.

"Marry me!" he whispered into my ear.

My heart was threatening to explode. I loved this man more than anything, and I wanted more than anything in the world to marry him. But what future would we have? The idea of being a widow at twenty terrified me. My silence went on too long. He guessed what I was thinking, and he didn't say anything else.

Yes, I'd wanted to say. *Of course I'll marry you!* But I hadn't been able to get the words out.

Danny was curled up beside me, asleep again. Cautiously, I touched his shoulder. It was almost eight—unusual for him to still be asleep at this hour. "Danny." He woke up immediately and turned over onto his back. I rested my chin on his bare chest. "I'm sorry about earlier. Of course I'll marry you."

He folded his arms behind his head and looked at the ceiling contemplatively. "No, you're right. I don't want you to be a widow at your age. And you're supposed to live as though you'd never met me once I die, and you can't do that if you have my last name." Carefully, he nudged me away. "Anyway, I don't know if it would work."

"If what would work?"

"As a way of you inheriting my stuff. I think you have to be married at least three years for that to work. I'll look it up and figure out a way to transfer everything to you."

"Danny, I don't want your stuff. Stop saying goodbye to me all the time! I want you to stay with me!"

He gave me a gentle smile. "I'll stay as long as I can. After that, you'll get it all. Tina... The money for her apartment, take that also, as a down payment on a house for you and your family. Sell the car to help pay for it, too. The papers are all in the glove compartment as promised. You should get almost as much for it as it was worth new."

"I would never sell your car."

"Sell it," he ordered. "You'll just drive it into a wall anyway."

"Hang on. Which of us totaled the last car?"

Danny didn't take the bait. "I'll leave you Maya, too. I know you'd rather have a horse you can really ride, though. Use some of the money to buy yourself one. Maya can stay at the old mill—the children's home will pay for the upkeep, and the girls will take care of her. But I want her to belong to you, so that you can make those decisions."

"You've already arranged all of that?"

"Yeah."

I shook my head in disbelief.

"I actually wanted to give you an apartment, the way I'd been planning to do for Tina, but I don't think it would be a good idea. You're choosy, and I know you want a house. There's not enough there for that, but it should cover half. Find yourself a smart guy who loves you and will pay the rest."

"Stop planning my life for me already."

"You need to be taken care of after I'm not around anymore."

"BUT YOU ARE AROUND!" I suddenly screamed at him. "I don't want to hear any more about it! Stop telling me goodbye over and over again!" Full of despair, I left the bedroom, slamming the door behind me. Why wouldn't he leave me at least a glimmer of my illusion that everything was okay?

"I'm just going to do it!" he called after me. "If you don't want to hear about it, then I'll do what I think is right!"

Chapter Forty-Four

November 2002

Danny was a completely different person. As soon as he'd accepted his fate, his cynicism and bitterness vanished—he was as cheerful and fun as he'd been before, radiating an unbelievable love for life and almost infinite motivation to experience everything he (still) could. Having made the decision not to stay in the hospital helped him feel like he was in control, which made him a lot less afraid of the future.

We drove to the Italian coast in the middle of winter, parking in the middle of the beach and sleeping in the car with the heat running. As wonderful as it was, it was exhausting as well—I had no idea where Danny was getting all of this energy. He dragged me from one experience to the next without stopping. Since he'd completely discontinued HAART therapy, he was free of the side effects as well, so he felt fantastic again. Even though he'd showed no signs of either physical or psychological withdrawal during his entire hospital stay, he couldn't get enough of the drugs now.

Now that the doctors had told him he didn't need to expect a repeat of that episode in August, he'd started driving with me in the car again. He didn't want to risk going to Atlanta with me, though. Italy was as good as it was going to get. "You'll need to be able to get home without me if anything happens," he kept saying. He didn't think I was capable of finding my way around a different continent by myself. I didn't mention the fact that I'd never manage to find my way home from Italy, either.

On Sunday evening, he dropped me off at my parents' house. "You want to come up for a minute?" I asked.

He shook his head. "It was a long drive. I'm tired."

Alarm bells went off in my head immediately. In the more than three years I'd known him, I'd never heard him say those words. "I'm tired, too," I said, not letting my worry show. "I'll come over after work tomorrow, then." We said our goodbyes, and, as I was getting out of the car, he handed me an envelope and a debit card.

"I wasn't able to transfer my savings to you," he explained. "It didn't work. So I put everything in a new account. The PIN number is in the envelope. You can take whatever you need from there. The balance is six figures, so you'll never be able to take it all out at once with the card, but your name is on the account, so just go to the bank and close it out. I've kept enough for myself to cover what I need. The rest is yours."

I took the card and the envelope, nodding. There was no getting around the fact that he was going to die. If he wanted me to have his savings, so be it. I didn't want to fight about it anymore. "Okay. Thank you."

"You'd better go get it right away. Right after I die, at the latest. I don't want my dad getting wind of it and trying to get his hands on it."

"What would he do with it?" I asked. "He's rotting away in jail. I don't think he'd care about money." Danny's father had developed AIDS years ago and had all kinds of health problems. I desperately hoped he died before his son. Danny deserved at least that much justice.

He just shrugged. "He can't use it, but I wouldn't put it past him, even if it were just to get one over on me."

"I'll get it in time," I promised and got out of the car, putting the card into my wallet as I walked into the house with Leika. I waited to open the envelope until I reached my room, and I saved the PIN to my phone. There was a poem in the envelope as well:

Where You Will Find Me

Do not come to my grave,
You will not find me there,
Cast your grief aside,
Cold earth cannot bind me.

I ride on the winds
That visit you on summer days.
I will discover the oceans,
Be the waves that carry you to shore.

Now I am the sun's brightest light
To drive away your dark thoughts.
I am in every voice that speaks
To cloak you in hope.

So come not to my grave,

You know I am not there,

If you seek me, do not look down,

I am, like you, so near the horizon.

I read the poem a second time, and then a third, and suddenly the uncertainty I'd been feeling turned to fear. Had this vacation been a goodbye? Why had he given me access to his bank account today, of all days?

"I have to go again," I called to my parents as I ran down the stairs. "I'll be back tomorrow night!" I grabbed Leika's leash, and she followed me to the door.

"Jessica!" my mother shouted after me. "What's going on with you? You've been acting so strange lately!"

"I'm fine, just forgot something!" I started my car with trembling fingers and raced toward Danny's house. My parking job was, once again, ridiculous, but I didn't care. When I burst into the apartment, panicked, Danny was sitting on the couch in a jogging suit, watching TV. He raised an eyebrow at me, and suddenly I felt like an idiot.

"Sorry, I don't know…" I shrugged, sighing. "I thought… Oh, I don't know why I came."

He smiled when he realized what I'd been worrying about. "You thought I was going to get into the tub and slit my wrists?"

"The thought had crossed my mind, yes."

"That's silly. Bleeding to death takes way too long."

"Danny, was I right to worry?"

He patted the couch beside him. "No," he assured me, as I sat. "As long as I'm feeling okay, don't even worry about things like that. When it gets to that point, I'll let you know beforehand. I promise."

I thought back to the decision he'd made at the AIDS hospice in the Black Forest. If he was prepared to take his own life, then so was I. "I'm in, then!"

He stared at me like I'd completely lost my mind. "Excuse me?"

"You heard right! If you slit your wrists, I'm slitting mine. If you throw yourself in front of a train, I'll follow you. If you take sleeping pills, I'll take just as many."

Danny leaped up from the couch. "Get out," he growled.

"I'm serious! You said you love sports and action, and you don't want to live without them. I love you, and I don't want to live without you!"

"But I'm sick. I don't have a choice. I would love to go on living, but I can't. You can, and you will!"

"No. I'm going with you."

"Get the hell out," he said in a threatening tone, pointing to the door. "Take your dog and go, and don't you dare come back!"

"No," I said again, just as coldly.

"We're done. It's over." His voice was icy. "I don't care what happens, you're not coming near me again!"

"You probably think doing that would be brave of you. But that's not brave! It's completely stupid! It's just plain bullshit!"

As he always did when I started screaming at him, he simply left me there, storming out of the living room and slamming the door behind him. I hugged one of the pillows to my chest and began to sob. Why did he refuse to see it my way? We were normally on the same wavelength—he understood what I was feeling without me even having to explain it—and now he was reacting like this.

On my way into the bedroom, my gaze fell on the kitchen cabinets. Danny had written something across the wood in black Sharpie.

Wrong or right,
Courage or madness,
Meaningless and futile,
The countdown begins ...

One must always
Travel the last path alone.
Though you remain behind,
I will carry you with me in my heart!

Sorry, Ducky.
I'm so sorry!

I burst out sobbing again and sank to the kitchen floor. He'd never take me with him. He was going to leave me behind in this shitty life, and he even thought it was the right thing to do.

Rage built up inside me. How come he got to decide and I didn't? What gave him the right to make decisions about my life?

I straightened again and went after him, but he had locked the bedroom door from the inside. "Danny! Open up!"

"No. It's over. I don't want you anywhere near me anymore."

"Let me in!"

"No. Go home."

"My dog is in there with you, you idiot!"

"I'll bring her to your place tomorrow. Goodbye, Jessica!"

Furiously, I hammered the door with my fists. "Open the goddamn door!"

"I don't love you anymore!" he called out.

"Oh, cut it out. You're a terrible liar, don't even try!"

"I cheated on you. There's someone else!"

"Danny, open the door."

"I've been seeing her for two years now, and you didn't notice a thing. You can hate me now."

"I forgive you. Let me in!"

"I've been going to a brothel every Monday evening for the past three years!"

A flash of fear hit me. Not because I believed what he was saying in the slightest, but because he was alone in the room. He could be doing God knew what in there. Did he have sleeping pills with him? Or razor blades?

"Open the door, or I'm kicking it in!" I sounded hysterical.

"Go ahead and try!"

I'd seen Danny kick a few pieces of furniture, and splinters of wood had always flown everywhere. When I did it, nothing happened. I kicked it again. Then I heard motion behind the door. My heart sang with relief, but then I realized he was pushing the dresser up against the door.

"Open the fucking door!" I kicked it a third time, with no results.

"What is it about 'I don't want to be with you anymore' that you don't understand?"

There was nothing left in me. I collapsed to the floor in tears.

After a while, I heard him push the dresser away, and I waited for the door to open. But he just sank down against the other side of the door. We spent the entire night like that, back to back, crying. Separated by a door. Even though I could hear him sniffling, I knew he would never give in. He was more bullheaded than I was, always had been.

The sun was already beginning to rise when I gave up. "You win, Danny. I accept your decision. I'll stay in this stupid goddamn life and pretend I'm happy."

I heard him stand up and unlock the door. He came out and sat down again on the floor beside me. Then he took me in his arms. "I'm just trying to protect you."

I buried my face against his chest, sobbing. "Just how do you picture all of that happening? Should I act like everything's fine? Get married, happily ever after, and name my son Danijel?"

"No, that's exactly what you shouldn't do! You need to find a way of dealing with it. I already told you my strategy: make a big bonfire, burn everything—to help you let go of the pain and the anger. And someday you'll be able to think about me again. I mean, I don't want you to forget me completely, of course. I want you to remember me, but I want you to do it with a smile." He lifted my chin, forcing me to look at him. "Someday, I want you to think about me and tell your children about me, smiling, and then say, 'It sure was nice with that crazy guy, but now everything's great just the way it is!' Don't let yourself get trapped in bitterness or frustration. You'll find your path, Ducky."

"You're completely insane."

"Yeah, we've been over that. That's not going to change." He took my hand. "I'm going to die. And I want you to grant me my last wish: find yourself a guy, get married, and have kids. Make sure he's an average guy. Average guys are easier. They're more approachable and more predictable. They don't force you to dance to the beat of their own weird drum quite so much."

At the time, I thought Danny just couldn't stand the thought of me getting together with someone who was as attractive and special as he was. In retrospect, though, I realized that he was simply right.

He looked at me for a long time before he said, "After I die, don't think about me anymore until you can do it without it hurting. I guarantee that you'll be happy you're alive then. I promise you!"

***

When I got to Danny's place on Friday evening after work, I found him sitting on the floor with a cord around his arm, injecting the heroin directly into his bloodstream for the first time.

It took effect faster than usual, and instead of making him tired, it gave him a rush. Gleefully, he grabbed my wrist and pulled me out into the darkness, just like the old Danny. We ran and ran through the dark forest and strolled through the cemetery, reading the gravestones.

Danny became obsessed with sneaking into the cemetery at night and hanging out by the graves. Sometimes we spent half the night there, despite the cold, biting wind. I don't know what he was looking for there, but I really hope he found it.

Chapter Forty-Five

December 2002

In mid-December, we drove back to the mountains of Tyrol. We were planning to spend Danny's birthday up there and be back by Christmas. It was around then that he stopped going running in the mornings. It wasn't that he wasn't able to anymore—he just didn't care as much about staying in tip-top shape. He didn't see the point any longer. Instead of tramping around outside in the cold morning, he preferred to stay in the hotel bed with me a little longer, snuggling and talking.

We did a lot of hiking during the day. That was enough to burn off his extra energy. Even though he'd gotten out of shape—by his standards—I still couldn't keep up with him by any means. He dragged me up to all the highest peaks, where we enjoyed the view for a while before making our way back down. We tried skiing once, but I made such a fool of myself that I immediately lost interest.

"Let's go up there," Danny said, pointing to the gondola lift. There weren't many people there, so we waited until we could get a car to ourselves. It traveled a very long distance, high up over the mountains, stopping again and again for several minutes so that people could enjoy the view and take pictures.

Out of nowhere, as we were above a gorge, Danny took off his jacket and opened the window. I wasn't surprised, since he'd enjoyed climbing halfway out of the cars when we'd come here the year before last—but this time, he went all the way out. My heart began to race as I saw him clambering out. He stood in the window opening, holding the roof for support. Once he was sure he had his footing, he let go.

"Yeeee-haaa!" he bellowed into the wind, which tore at his sweatshirt as he stretched out his arms. He reminded me of Leonardo DiCaprio on the Titanic. He made no move to come back inside again—he stayed that way for half the ride.

He's completely lost it!

For a long time, I toyed with the idea of just pushing him off, weighing the pros and cons carefully. Danny would lose valuable weeks or months of life, but he'd be able to die unafraid... He wouldn't know what was happening until it was too late. But I couldn't do it. He trusted me so much, and I just couldn't bring myself to abuse that trust.

Danny climbed all the way up onto the roof. I leaned out the window. "Come inside. Please."

"I'm not going to fall."

"Danny, quit screwing around and come back in!"

"Ducky," he called. "This is what I want to do. I want to die like this. In free fall!"

"But not now, please!" I shouted back. Out of the corner of my eye, I saw him getting to his feet. My heart was hammering in my throat. I couldn't see him anymore—my neck didn't bend quite that far. The people on the ground beneath us had stopped in their tracks and were pointing up at us. A crowd was forming. Off in the distance, I saw flashing blue lights.

"Danny, come in," I screeched. "Otherwise, I'm coming out!"

That worked. He was predictable in such things. He swung himself back into the cabin, feet-first. His fingers were ice-cold, but he was radiant with joy. "I can do that. Just jump once, and there's no going back. Plus, you have time on the way down for your life to flash before your eyes."

"I'm happy for you," I said bitterly. "They're here because of you," I added, pointing to the police cars below.

"Dammit. We need to get out of here, or they'll stick me in a loony bin because they think I'm some suicidal maniac."

"Danny, you are suicidal, and you've always been a maniac. Maybe they really should take you in."

The police followed our car, lights flashing, until the gondola went over another mountain. They wouldn't be able to follow us straight across, but I was sure they'd be waiting on the other side. The mountain beneath us got taller, the distance to the ground significantly shorter. Our car stopped for a moment at the top. Danny leaned out the window to estimate the height.

"Let's get out."

I looked down as well. The thick, soft blanket of snow was at least ten feet underneath us.

"You truly are insane," I grouched.

"Come on," he urged me. "I really don't want to run into the police. I guarantee they'll arrest me." He swung his feet out the window and turned around to look at me again. "Just jump. I'll catch you." Without hesitating, he jumped down, even though he still had a cracked rib. Shaking my head, I climbed out the window as well, but I didn't just leap out like he had. I hung down from the window frame, legs dangling, eyes squeezed shut, and then let go.

Danny caught me as promised, spinning around on his heel to absorb the shock, and set me on my feet. Then he took my hand, and we ran down the mountain, in the direction the police had come from. I wished I could see their faces when our empty car reached the station. The thought made me laugh out loud.

Danny kept pulling me onward. He could have run on and on quite effortlessly, despite the deep snow. Only when we reached the foot of the mountain did we finally stop, gasping for breath. Then we slipped in among the other tourists on the hiking trail, strolling along with them as though nothing had happened. The police apparently thought we'd both jumped to our deaths: there were helicopters circling the mountains for hours afterward, probably looking for our bodies.

"That was great." Danny beamed.

"Let's not do that again. Are you okay?" I asked.

"Of course! I never want to get so sick that I can't jump out of a cable car."

"You are so crazy!" I said yet again.

"That's what you love about me. That's why you decided to stay with me. Because I'm different, I have passion. You don't like boring people. You wanted a guy you could experience things with, not stand around at his deathbed holding his hand."

Chapter Forty-Six

December 2002

We spent Christmas completely alone—we didn't feel like being around my family or going to any parties. We drove to a gas station to buy junk food and ate it in a parking lot with the stereo blaring, not caring about the happy families sitting around their Christmas trees nearby.

"I hope I can get through it all somehow," Danny said to me that night in bed, looking worried. "I think it's starting."

"What's starting?"

"Little things. A while ago, my foot twitched so hard that I stalled the car. My left hand was numb for almost two days, and I feel like my whole body is shaking all the time." His tone was indifferent, as though he were listing off problems with a computer.

"Why didn't you say anything?" I hadn't noticed any of that.

He shrugged. "I didn't want to cause any panic. I have to get another MRI in January, so I wanted to wait until then."

"I'm not going to panic!" I exclaimed, sounding much too shrill. "But you have to tell me things like that. Talk to me, there's no reason for you to go through it alone. You have to tell Jörg, too—you can't keep secrets from us."

He pressed his lips together and nodded.

I wrapped an arm around him. "I'm not going to leave you alone. No matter what happens. Whatever the future brings, we'll handle it together." Then I laid my head on his stomach and added, "I don't regret anything. Not one day, not one second. If we could turn back time, I would choose you all over again."

"Thank you," Danny whispered.

"What would have become of me without you? I'd have ended up just another sheep with no idea of what life was all about. Seriously, Danny, I'm so unbelievably glad I met you."

We had tears streaming down our cheeks almost all the time these days. We often didn't even notice anymore. Like now. If he hadn't wiped my tears away with his finger, I wouldn't have realized I was crying. It wasn't important, anyway. The important thing was that we were managing to keep on living a normal life, or at least a normal as possible. The important thing was that we spent this day happy. And then the next one, and then the one after that.

A sharp scream awoke me that night. I jolted upright in bed, frightened. Danny was sitting up beside me. His shirt was soaking wet, and he was trembling all over and gasping for breath.

"What's wrong?" I exclaimed, shocked, and turned on the lamp on the nightstand. "What happened?"

"Panic!" His breathing was ragged and shallow. "Panic! I can't breathe!" He clutched his chest in agitation, tearing at his T-shirt. I hastily scooted over and pulled his hand away.

"No, no, no. Shh, calm down!" I loosened his cramped fingers. "Breathe here," I said, putting his flat hand on his stomach. "Down low. Breathe deep against your hand."

"I can't," he wheezed.

"Yes, you can. Don't talk. Breathe."

Danny obeyed. We sat there for what felt like forever, focusing only on breathing in and out, until he finally calmed down a little. He kept his eyes shut, concentrating on taking deep abdominal breaths.

"I'm going to die," he said abruptly, opening his eyes and locking them with mine. His eyes were as blue as ever, gleaming with the same lust for life. They didn't fit his words. "It doesn't matter what we do. I'm going to die!"

"I know."

"What will it be like?" he asked. "Not the disease, I mean. Actually dying. Will it hurt? Is there really a light at the end of the tunnel?"

Cautiously, I grasped his hand. "Nobody can answer those questions for you."

"The thought of just suddenly not being there anymore…gone…just gone…" His lips trembled, and he squeezed my hand tightly. "It's scary. Just gone, extinguished. Disappeared…"

I thought back to the poem he'd written me. "Nobody is just gone, Danny. Part of them always remains. Call it their soul, call it what you want. Something stays. In people's hearts, in their memories. In nature around us, in the light, in the wind. You wrote that yourself."

"I hope I can watch over you from wherever I end up." He smiled weakly. "I mean, someone's got to."

"I'll be okay," I lied. I would never be okay without him. "I'll always have you with me."

"What happens afterward?" His gaze shifted out into nothing again. "Do angels come and pick me up? Or is that just the end? Blackness for all eternity?"

"It keeps going somehow. There'll be life after death in some form."

He bit his lower lip. "Will I see Tina again?"

I pray you will, Danny. I pray you will! "I'm sure of it!"

"Will I see you again someday?"

I bit my lip, too, to keep myself from breaking down. What would it be like if we met up again in heaven? Would I be old and he be the way he was now? He'd turned twenty-three the week before. We both knew he wouldn't live to see twenty-four. Probably not even to see my twenty-first birthday this summer.

"Stop saying goodbye again. We still have enough time." *Enough time. We could never possibly have enough time...*

Abruptly, he stood and rummaged in the bottom drawer of the dresser. I knew what he was looking for. With trembling hands, he pulled out the plastic bag, along with a fresh syringe. "I won't be able to sleep otherwise," he murmured. "And I'm scared," he added, as though that was the excuse for his behavior. And it was.

Danny took the cord out of the bag and wrapped it around his right arm, using his left hand and his teeth to pull it tight. I watched him sadly. His sweaty hair stuck out in every direction, and his wet T-shirt clung to his body. He'd gotten skinny, I realized—without all that muscle mass, he'd lost quite a bit of weight.

Images from the past three years flickered through my mind. The way he'd forced me to give him my phone number at the festival, with an unheard-of amount of self-confidence. Him leaning against the limousine, looking like he'd stepped off the pages of a glossy magazine. His desperate attempts to keep me away from him. Our first kiss, which had given him such a guilty conscience. How helpful he'd been to Christina and everyone else around him. I saw him in the ring, winning one kickboxing match after another. Him effortlessly taking on five guys at once in order to protect me, and beating up that pathetic loser, Angelo, for ramming a knife into Ricky's side. I recalled every detail of the night he'd told me the truth about himself and his life. The way he'd learned to trust me and give himself over to me, bit by bit. And then there were the painful memories—of

Christina's death, him breaking his hand in a rage, his endless screaming into the nights that followed.

Now he was sitting on the floor, dissolving the heroin. His downward spiral had been like something out of a movie. Nothing would come of his big modeling career, and he would never again be a world champion kickboxer, because he'd been sentenced to death.

Christina's death had been what triggered it. I had no doubt of that. Danny had identified with her too strongly to be able to handle losing her, which was why his body had broken down so suddenly. If Christina hadn't lost her life in that tragic way, Danny probably would have been able to stay healthy for years to come. Probably even long enough for the medical world to find a way to stop the disease from progressing.

Christina's killer had two deaths on his conscience.

For the thousandth time, I wondered what Danny's life would have been like if his goddamn father hadn't destroyed everything. But now, for the first time, I also asked myself whether my life wouldn't have been different without him as well. The worst part was, it wasn't like I hadn't been warned. I'd slid into the catastrophe fully aware and with my eyes open. But what I'd told Danny before had been the truth: if someone had turned back time and I ended up back at the moment that defined my entire life, I'd have picked Danny again. Even if I'd known from the beginning how it would all turn out, and how it would influence my life. Maybe even because of that.

I thought back to what he said to me at the paddock about having never had a chance at a normal life. The words were so true, they hurt my soul. Fate really was a cruel mistress. She even sent him a guardian angel on the exact day he'd rather not have had one. When I'd first seen his demolished car, I was shocked at myself for thinking it, but I still knew it was the truth: it would have been more humane for him if he'd just died behind the wheel that morning. But fate hadn't even granted him that.

Danny's fingers were trembling so violently that he missed the vein for the fourth time. Sighing, I got up and went over to sit beside him on the floor. "Give it here." I held out my hand.

He gave me a skeptical look but then hesitantly put the syringe in my palm. I placed his arm on my knee and got the vein on the first try, pressing the liquid out of the syringe in one quick motion and then pulling the needle out again. I held my thumb over the injection site for a moment to keep it from bleeding and then undid the cord and put everything back into the bag. I wrapped the used syringe up in foil and disposed of it in a closed trash container. Finally, I joined Danny on the bed as though it was all the most natural thing in the world.

"I love you," Danny said. "More than my entire worthless life."

"How long you live isn't what decides whether your life is worth something or not. You've probably lived more intensely than thousands of people who've died of old age." I took his hand. "Your life has been more than valuable. You've left a mark on the world!"

He smiled weakly. "Nothing is really dead," he said quietly. "It just changes, takes on another form. Don't forget that later."

"You'll live on inside me," I promised. "I love you more than my life, too."

Danny sank down onto his pillow and rolled onto his side. I snuggled up against his back and put my hand on his stomach. He took my hand in his, pushed it up underneath his T-shirt, and placed it on his chest. After all this time, even though that position had become almost a ritual for us, the gesture still touched me.

I felt his heartbeat slow when he finally fell asleep. A storm was howling outside; dawn was already approaching. In the light of the streetlamps, I could see tree branches bending in the icy wind tearing at the window shutters. It was blowing from the north, I could have sworn it.

Slowly, I stood up and went to the window. I spent a long time just standing there, staring into the dark night sky, searching for that place Danny had shown me from the roof.

The north wind, I thought. I remembered a poem I'd once read:

I feel the north wind again, the promise of the horizon. How many possibilities has he who knows the north wind?

I go with the north wind, I need not know the way.

Epilogue

Summer 2015

Danny died at the end of April 2003, almost exactly a year after Christina. In the early morning hours, he jumped from the 820-foot-tall One Atlantic Center in Atlanta. Danny had told me he wanted to go home…

The amount of heroin in his blood would probably have been enough to kill him if he'd waited long enough.

The report said he "had not survived the jump," which made me burst out into hysterical laughter. That would have been even better!

He left me this letter:

Ducky,

You're probably already suspecting this: I'm not coming back. I'm so unbearably sorry that I'm going like this, but it wouldn't have been possible any other way—you know that as well as I do. And it has to happen, because I'm scared to wait any longer. Scared of what will come next, and that I won't be able to do it anymore! You know! If you can't forgive me for going this way, that's okay. I just hope you can understand someday.

If you're reading this, I'm already in the airplane, so don't drive off looking for me!!!

We've already talked about everything. Take care of Maya, watch out for my dad, and for God's sake, sell that damn car, don't keep it for sentimental reasons— I wouldn't get anything out of that!

Stay in our apartment for as long as you want, and take whatever you like with you. If you ever feel lonely, you know where you can go to feel close to me—and where you can't!

You're going to be happy—husband, house, children. You'll see.

REMEMBER ME!
And I hope I find my freedom, for eternity!
Love you!
Danny

Ducky,

du ahnst es mittlerweile bestimmt schon: Ich komme nicht zurück. Es tut mir so unendlich Leid, daß ich auf diese Art gegangen bin. Aber anders wäre es nie möglich gewesen – das weißt du sogar wie ich. Und es muss jetzt sein, ich habe Angst noch länger zu warten. Angst, vor dem was kommt und daß ich es dann nicht mehr kann. You know!

Wenn du mir das nicht verzeihen kannst, daß ich so gegangen bin, dann ist das okay. Ich hoffe nur du kannst es eines Tages verstehen!

Wenn du das liest, bin ich längst im Flugzeug, also fahre mir nicht nach!!!

Wir haben alles besprochen! Paß auf Maya auf, behalte meinen Alten im Auge und verkaufe um Himmels Willen das verdammte Auto! Behalte es nicht aus sentimentalen Gründen – ich habe nichts davon!

Bleib in unserer Wohnung solange du willst und nimm mit was du magst.

Wenn du dich einsam fühlst – du weißt wo du mir Nahe sein kannst – und wo nicht!

Du wirst glücklich werden – Mann, Haus, Kinder – wirst schon sehen.

REMEMBER ME!

Love you!
Danny

And I hope I find my freedom –
for eternity!

After saying goodbye to me again and again, he'd finally left without saying another word. One morning, he was just gone. I knew why: he didn't want me to follow him.

Danny had put it off for as long as he felt like he could. At the beginning of March, he'd started having major episodes of paralysis. His left arm was practically numb, he'd lost control over various limbs on several occasions, and the tremors had gotten worse all the time. Around mid-April, he'd finally told me he couldn't wait much longer, for fear that he'd lose the physical ability to put his plan into action.

Theoretically, there should have been huge amounts of heroin left over, but I never found it. I suspect Danny flushed it down the toilet to prevent me from getting my hands on it.

Apart from the PML, Danny never developed any other AIDS-related symptoms. His T-cell counts remained solid all the way until his death—his immune system was essentially intact the whole time, he never progressed to full-blown AIDS.

Though HIV is still incurable, medicine has progressed to the point that it can prevent AIDS from breaking out. With proper treatment, HIV is no longer fatal; people with HIV have a near-normal life expectancy and can live nearly normal lives. Thanks to additional breakthroughs, people with HIV can also have healthy children.

PML still results in death within three to twenty months. Eighty to ninety percent of those who develop it have severely compromised immune systems. Researchers have since discovered that PML is caused by a specific virus that only certain people have in their bodies. Those people acquire the virus in childhood. It is still unclear where it comes from.

I spent many sleepless nights wrecking my head wondering whether Danny got *that* virus from his father as well.

Danny's panic attacks became much more frequent during the last eight weeks of his life. He was convinced they were from the PML. I think he was just scared— after all, he'd had a tendency toward those kinds of attacks since he was young. Even so, they only made him even more terrified that the PML would change his personality. Nothing of the kind happened, though. Danny remained his old, clearheaded self, right up until his death. He never changed outwardly, either. Anyone who didn't know him would never have suspected that he was deathly ill.

Ultimately, his death didn't attract any attention. There wasn't even a report in the newspaper. As far as the police were concerned, he'd been just another suicidal junkie, an addict with no story of his own. Danny would have preferred to fly under the radar anyway.

Jörg, Marina, and Ricky flew to the United States to help his aunt organize the funeral. Danny had even left his aunt the money to pay for it and expressly requested to be cremated. His wish was granted.

I didn't join them. We had an agreement.

Three days after his disappearance, before I'd even been officially notified of his death, Danny's car was picked up. The new BMW he'd taken such good care of for me was hooked carelessly to a tow truck and hauled away. His father had arranged it from prison. The title and registration were in the car, as we'd planned. I never saw the car again. I'd have liked a chance to get in there and take some of my things out of it, but they never gave me a chance.

I also never saw a penny of the money Danny had so desperately wanted me and Christina to have. He'd only been saving it so that we would have a place to go after he was gone, somewhere we would be able to feel at home without him. Just after they took his car, I ran to the bank, only to find that his account was already frozen. Even though Danny had put my name on everything, his father had somehow manage to grab it all right from under my nose.

Danny had never made a will. I don't think he forgot—he never forgot anything. More likely, he was completely sure that the preparations he'd made would be enough. Who could have known that Danny's father would get word of his death and his estate so quickly? He couldn't have known anything about the car, nor about the money in the account. Despite his father's repeated attempts to change the situation, the two of them hadn't been in contact for years.

I'd thought the same thing that Danny had: surely a dying man wouldn't care about all those material possessions. Someone like Danny would have found the very idea ridiculous. What good was it going to do his father? Whatever his motivations, he wanted it all to himself.

Jörg tried to sue for Danny's estate on my behalf, arguing that he had been Danny's legal guardian for years. He brought up Danny's past, even putting forward the theory that his father had deliberately infected him, as Danny had always feared.

There was no way of proving it, though. At the time Danny was infected, the fact that his father was HIV-positive hadn't been medically documented anywhere. Of course, there was no telling whether Danny's father had suspected it, or could have suspected it. There was no way of proving that, either.

Jörg lost the trial. According to the judge, standard German inheritance law applied, so his entire estate legally belonged to his parents. Marina was no longer legally competent, so it all went to his father. I was just glad Danny wasn't there to see it, that he was at least spared that circus and died believing everything would turn out the way he'd planned.

After I got word of Danny's death, I left his apartment, fully believing I would be able to return once more. I wanted to pick up some of his things and donate some of them—along with Christina's, which we'd never touched—to charity. But I never got the chance: practically the minute I was gone, the locks were changed and everything inside was auctioned off. I couldn't take anything with me, couldn't even say goodbye.

Danny's father even claimed Maya, Danny's ancient, half-lame pony, and snatched her away from the children's home, selling her for the slaughter price. Jörg and I moved heaven and earth to find the buyer, and finally drove up to Northern Germany to meet him. I rang the doorbell, told them my story, and begged them to give me Maya back. They let me take the pony but told me that it would break their mentally handicapped daughter Amelie's heart—they'd bought the pony for her.

So there I was, the person who thought she knew Danny better than anyone else in the world, with no idea what to do. In the end, I left the pony with the family, sparing her hours of travel in a horse trailer. Maya had a place right by the house, in the company of an old jumper horse, and she had Amelie to love and care for her. I think that was what Danny would have wanted. He was always okay with what I decided.

Maya lived another four years. I visited her six times, and the family consulted me on any major decisions about her.

Three years later, Ricky moved to Berlin, where he got married and had two daughters. I lost contact with Simon. Vanessa and I are still friends. Jörg and I stayed in touch for almost seven years after Danny's death. Alexander is married with a son now, too. We were best friends for years, and I still bring my car to him for repairs.

About two years after Danny's death, his father died in prison of complications from HIV-related jaundice. I think he just squandered most of his son's money, at least to the extent that he was able. Everything else, he secretly sent to his wife, allowing her to start a new life: after her husband's death, Marina reverted to her maiden name and moved back to America. Even today, I still wonder why she hadn't done that sooner. Danny would have gladly paid her way, and he'd have jumped at the chance to go with her. He'd have been happy to be back home.

Leika died on November 12, 2009, about five weeks before Danny would have turned thirty. Had he made it to thirty, like he'd hoped, he would also have succeeded at outliving my dog, like he'd hoped. If Christina hadn't died, he would have made it.

I'm sure of it.

I met a new man in 2010. In 2011, we got married and built a little house with a backyard. Out in the country, of course. We have two dogs.

Our son was born in 2014.

When I look at him, I'm infinitely grateful to Danny, because his promise came true. I'm glad I'm still alive, and that's thanks only to him. And I have my son thanks to him, as well. It's gratitude I can't express in words, so I'm not even going to try.

In all those years, I never told my husband a thing about Danny, but then I slipped up. He spotted the gap in what he knew about my past, and he asked about it. What was supposed to be a short explanation turned into a week-long report. I showed him photos of Danny, ads he'd modeled for, Danny's letters and poems. I'd burned most of them as Danny had recommended, but I'd stored a few things away in a box in the basement.

I never forgot him.

Even today, though, it still hurts to think about him.

Sensing that I hadn't worked through a lot of what happened back then, my husband suggested I write the story out. So I did. For weeks, I ran around with a pencil and a notebook and a distant look on my face, completely caught up in a different time. It was like I was experiencing everything all over again. Night after night, I wrote, grinning and laughing at times, but mostly crying bitter tears. Finally, when I'd put it all down on paper, my husband read our story and encouraged me to type it out on a computer. So I did.

I'd always wanted to donate part of Danny's money to charity, but since I'd never gotten any of it, it hadn't happened. So I decided to turn the story into a book and do some good by publishing it. I'm going to donate part of the proceeds from this book to the AIDS hospice in the Black Forest, to a children's home, and to an organization helping traumatized children.

My long-term goal is to start a foundation in Danny's name someday, to prevent his fears of being forgotten and "vanishing" from coming true. By doing this, I hope I can keep him as alive in others' minds as he is in mine, because Danny is still part of my life even today. Shortly after I met him, I started doing tae bo, a fitness trend combining kickboxing, taekwondo, aerobics, and dance. I hoped it would help me keep up with him. I never managed that, of course, but I still do tae bo today.

I also watch a lot of jumpstyle, a form of dance Danny loved. We often traveled as far as Austria with his dance partner so that they could be part of duo-jump battles. Back then, jumpstyle was new and not very popular, but Danny had always prophesied that it would catch on. Its big break came in 2007 with Scooter's "Jumping All Over The World." Today, there are even jumpstyle world championships. Danny would have been happy about that. Who knows, he might have even taken part...

I think about his eating habits a lot, too. He could never bring himself to throw away food, so he'd eat leftovers in the most ridiculous combinations: cheese tortellini with raspberry jam, for example, or jelly doughnuts with potato salad...

I've stuck to the decision I made thanks to him and Christina—I wouldn't even think of eating dead animals anymore. I've been substituting oat milk for cow's milk for years, too, and the only eggs I eat are from the free-range farm around the corner. My husband went along with it, so now we're both vegetarian. His initial worries that not eating meat would keep him from doing sports turned out to be unfounded, obviously. He and I run a half-marathon together every year. Danny was the best example of the fact that top athletes don't need meat.

I still have the bike he gave me. Years later, long after the red lacquer had peeled away, I repainted it. Royal blue, of course.

I'm incredibly glad and grateful to have met Danny. He kept me from sinking into the uniform sludge of the masses. I'll always be different, I'll always go through life with my eyes open, free of prejudice and rigid expectations, able to swim against the current. I'll never be content with seeing the obvious anymore—I'll always try to look behind the façade.

My time with Danny shaped me forever. I wouldn't trade a second of it for anything. I don't know if it's a coincidence that our house is on a hill. When I get up in the morning, I start by opening the blinds and looking out over the vineyards into the sky. Sometimes I go out onto the balcony to gaze out across the valley below me, and then out to the horizon. That's when I know I'm home!

In loving memory of
Tina and Danny!

***

One Small Request ...

We hope you enjoyed this novel!

The easiest way of sharing your views on this book with other readers out there is to post a review to an online retailer. Your feedback not only helps other readers discover new things, but also helps the author understand what readers liked and didn't like, allowing her to offer you and other readers even better stories in the future.

Apart from that, your impressions and insights are a wonderful token of appreciation for the many dedicated hours that went into this book.

So thanks in advance for taking two or three minutes of your time and writing a short review.

Thanks

I would like to thank my German proofreader, **Andreas Nolden,** my husband **Marvin,** and my friend **Vanessa**. Thanks as well to my mother, who showed a great deal of understanding when reading this book.

Many, many thanks to my German editor, **Sandra Schindler**, for her excellent work with me!

Thanks very much to **Nicole Weiche**, the best and most attentive beta reader in the world.

I'd also like to thank **Marianne Reiß (Mareis)** for allowing me to quote her poem.

Very special thanks go to **Robin Kosan** and **Sam White**, who actually managed to turn what were often excessively long original poems and song lyrics into beautiful, short poems while keeping the content the same. ***Thank you!***

For more information on the author, visit
www.facebook.com/SoNearTheHorizon or www.so-near-the-horizon.com

Be sure to subscribe to our newsletter, so that you can be the first to hear about our **new releases, author news,** and exclusive **giveaways**:
www.so-near-the-horizon.com

Bonus: So Near the Abyss & So Near the Ocean

So Near the Abyss (The Danny Trilogy, Book 2)

by Jessica Koch

Danny is just ten years old when his life goes completely off the rails.

Fate deals his family a terrible blow, prompting them to leave the United States and move to Germany. As if that weren't enough, his father begins drowning his sorrows in alcohol and slips back into behavioral patterns he'd thought he'd finally left behind for good before getting married. Danny is helpless, at his father's mercy - but he doesn't give up.

One year at summer camp, Danny meets a French girl named Dominique. He helps her escape a life-threatening situation, and her love helps him free himself from his family - and thus from the unimaginable forces of destruction threatening his own young life.

A relentless fight begins, a battle for recognition, freedom, justice - and love.

*** *Coming out soon* ***
Visit www.so-near-the-horizon.com to get <u>a free reading sample</u> of
"So Near the Abyss"

So Near the Ocean (The Danny Trilogy, Book 3)

by Jessica Koch

They share the same fate, yet they are completely different: Danny is successful and has achieved hard-won independence after a childhood that was no childhood at all. Tina, on the other hand, has spent the last few years on the streets. The world has been cruel to both of them, but when they meet, the intimacy that develops between them is like nothing they've ever known. Desperately, Danny tries to show Tina that there are beautiful sides to life as well.

Will their friendship help them throw off the shadows of their respective pasts for good? And where exactly is the boundary between friendship and love....?

Coming 2018...

For a complete list of our German publications, see
www.FeuerWerkeVerlag.de

Manufactured by Amazon.ca
Bolton, ON

34720666R00206